THE ATOMIC SEA:

Volume One

THE ATOMIC SEA:
Volume One

Jack Conner

For HPL.

Chapter 1

Whale songs groaned through the hull of the ship as Dr. Avery and the sailors played cards. The cabin reverberated to the sounds—long, tapering peals that stood hairs on end—and alchemical lanterns threw drunken green shadows against the walls. Sailors glanced around uneasily.

Avery tossed his cards facedown and said, "Well, then, lads, if no one will match me, I believe that pot is mine."

The seamen muttered as he raked in his winnings. Some were big men, whalers, hairy and covered in tattoos. The Navy men and women tended to be slimmer, neater. The room smelled of oil, leather and cigar smoke, some of which curled up from Avery's own cigar clamped between his teeth. He was not a large man, but somehow that made him stand out all the more. His smoke drifted around his balding head with its black comb-over and joined the cloud that stirred against the ceiling.

"That's your fourth haul tonight," said Janx, one of the whalers, tall and rawboned. His nose had been torn off in a whaling catastrophe years ago, and a piece of leather covered the hole where it had been, held in place by straps that went round his head. "And three without showin' your cards."

"Feel free to match my bet next time," Avery said. "It has been an unusually good night, I must admit."

It was Janx's turn to deal, and the cards fluttered with surprising grace through his rough, scarred hands. Scars and tattoos seemed to mark every inch of his body. His shaven head gleamed in the light.

"Your luck'll turn, Doc," he said. "See if it don't."

Avery raised his eyebrows. After a look at his cards, he said, "I think not."

"You're bluff—"

The door burst open. Lt. Hinis stormed in, dressed in her environment suit, huge and bulky with its bronze helmet and grilled visor. "Doctor, come quick, we need your help. There's been a killing."

"Another one?" Janx said. "Damn."

"Has the killer been caught?" Avery asked.

"No," Hinis said. "But the patrols are out. The murder happened outside."

Avery crossed to the wall, where with Hinis's assistance he donned an environment suit of his own. Like hers, it resembled a diving suit of antiquity, all treated canvas, brass joinings and big brass helm. There were no true diving suits anymore, of course; no one was insane enough to use one, not for a thousand years. In the background, the whale songs bellowed louder—closer—and whalers glanced at each other soberly.

As Avery reached the door, Janx grunted, and the doctor looked back to see that Janx had flipped over Avery's cards. A two of jades nestled against a three of fates.

Janx shook his head. "Never saw a worse hand." He hesitated, then said, "Y'know, Doc, the killer could still be out there. Might be I should come with you."

Avery waited while Janx shrugged on an environment suit, and they followed Hinis out into the night.

Avery braced himself against the wind. *Shouldn't have had that second bourbon*, he thought as the wind battered him, dragging at his legs, tugging at his arms. It gusted up from the south, whipping mist off the waves that pitched and flung the ship like a cork. Huge and metal-hulled, a fully-armed warship in a time of war, the *GS Maul* plowed the dark waters, and the ocean responded with fury.

As Avery inched his way toward the stern behind Lt. Hinis, their lifelines connecting them to the gunwale, he gazed out over the sea—the eerie sea, the infamous sea. The Atomic Sea. Ever since research had begun into atomic energy some twenty years ago, people had slapped that label on it, accurate or not. Finally, more than a thousand years after the sea's transformation, people had a name for it that wasn't mired in superstition. And the ocean did emit radiation, at least in certain quarters. But that wasn't why people had named it what they had. One glance explained it.

Lightning blasted from wave-top to wave-top, some bolts arcing high into the night, lancing the very clouds overhead. The whole sea roiled and bubbled, as if someone had turned up a giant stove burner on the sea floor. Occasionally a bubble as big as a boat would burst from the depths. The gas alone was enough to kill, but sometimes a stab of lightning would hit a pocket and the whole thing would go up like an Uracuth candle. It was a frothing, mad, electric sea, and the things that plied its waters were strange and dangerous.

"Look at that," Janx said, pointing to something in the distance.

Far off, the geyser-like plumes of whales expelling water caught the star-light—beautiful, strange, and too close for Avery's liking.

"Gorgeous, ain't they?" said Janx. "You'd never guess what terrors they are."

"I can imagine."

"I remember one time years ago when one big bastard smashed me ship—killed everyone aboard, but me. I was thrown up on a strange beach, and, oh, it was a sight. Glittering black rocks far as you could see, great big mountains stretching off into the distance."

"An island?" Avery almost smiled. Half of Janx's stories began with him being washed up on some island.

"Aye," Janx said. "Well, right off a band of fish-folk seizes me and drags me to their village. Dead in the center of it—"

"Almost there," Hinis interrupted.

"Another time," Avery promised Janx. To Hinis, he said, "Has the Captain been notified?"

Hinis nodded. "She or the X.O.'ll likely be taking a look, same as you."

"This will be the second murder in two weeks," Avery said. "You're sure it wasn't accidental?"

"Take a look for yourself."

They rounded the last of the three great chimney stacks, and Hinis raised her lantern as she staggered up the ladder onto the poop deck. Avery's feet slipped on the wet surface as he followed, and he looked down to see that he'd stepped on a starfish-like encrustation growing over the side of the ship. Around his foot something spurted—moved. Though it had the texture of a starfish, it was shapeless and ingrown into the deck. He didn't pause—he was used to the various things that came up from the sea—but yanked his foot free and forced himself to go slower, reeling out the line behind him.

As they crossed toward the rearmost section of gunwale, Hinis's lantern threw back the shadows to reveal a body lying twisted on the deck.

Avery crouched over it, having to balance himself carefully in the environment suit. The body laid on its side, back arched, blood weeping through holes in the suit and thinning in the water that pooled all around.

Avery rolled the body over and looked at the face-plate for signs of breathing, just to be sure. Nothing. Then his own breath caught in his throat.

"*Paul*," he said.

The dead man stared back at him: broad-featured, clean-shaven, and familiar.

"Shit," Hinis said. "Should have told you. I forgot you two were friends."

"Sorry, Doc," said Janx.

Avery tried to cover the sudden swell of grief that rose in him. He blinked his eyes rapidly. *Damn it, Paul.*

Taking refuge in his profession, Avery studied the holes in the suit to either side and beneath Sgt. Paul Bercka's canister of compressed air.

"Stabbed," he said. "Something double-sided, maybe an inch-and-a-half wide. A ... A modified fleshing knife, perhaps. Looks like the killer cut the air line first, probably to disorient him. He locked him about the neck with one arm and stabbed him with the other." Avery sucked down a deep breath, smelling metal, canvas and stale sweat—what Paul's final gulp of air would've smelled like. *I'm so sorry, my friend. You deserved better than this.* "The murderer must be a strong man to have overpowered him," Avery added. "I wouldn't be surprised if the knife thrusts severed the spine. I expect that's what I'll find when I perform the autopsy."

"You'll perform an autopsy?"

Avery turned. The speaker was not Hinis or Janx but the Executive Officer, Commander Lucas Hambry, tall and strange in his suit; some sort of barnacle-like growth clung to the side of his helmet. Captain Sheridan must have sent him in her stead.

"Of course," Avery said. "Protocol demands it."

"You didn't perform an autopsy on the first body," Hambry said.

"Actually, I tried, but there wasn't enough left of Lt. Nyers to determine much." *The sea will do that, X.O.* With a sigh, Avery rose to his feet. "This time I'm afraid the cause of death is obvious."

Commander Hambry stared down at Paul's remains. "So it's murder."

"As was the case with Nyers, I'm sure of it."

"Why?"

"Her lifeline was unhooked, not severed by strain. Someone *unclipped* it." Something pounded behind Avery's right temple. He needed a drink.

Janx moved to the gunwale and examined the torn lifeline. "A clean cut," he said. "I've seen my share of torn lines, and this one was slashed by a blade. No fraying."

"Perhaps the killer meant to make this one more realistic," Avery said, "but was disturbed before he could finish."

"It was Privates Barris and Wathin, Doctor, who found the body," said Hinis. "They were on patrol. The sergeant had come out to check on 'em and make the rounds. He'd already spoken with them and moved on. Wasn't till they finished their tour of the starboard boats—some drift-jellies had been nesting in 'em again, you know how it is;

sometimes their poisons can eat through the metal—that they headed back to stern and found ..."

She gestured to Paul.

"Did they see any sign of the killer?"

"No, Doctor. I was there when they gave their report."

Suddenly, bells tolled throughout the ship. Avery's head snapped up. His first horrified thought was that Octunggen submarines had found them.

The ship's intercom blared: "ALL MEN TO YOUR STATIONS. THE WHALE MEET IS BREAKING UP. REPEAT, THE WHALE MEET IS BREAKING UP. WHALERS PREPARE. GREATEST LEVIATHAN BEARING PORT. TURNING BROADSIDE TO PORT. BOATS AWAY IN THREE MINUTES. REPEAT: BOATS AWAY IN THREE MINUTES."

"I better get goin'," said Janx, and lumbered off.

"Be careful," Avery called after him.

Hinis flashed a smile. "Finally! We bag one of these bastards and we can go home."

"If there's any home left," Commander Hambry said. "The Octunggen were advancing through the Pass last we heard, remember."

"There's still a home," she insisted.

"I'm sure there is," Avery said. "And if we can bring back a whale, it'll be there for a little while longer. Lieutenant, I need you to move Sgt. Bercka to the medical bay. I'll perform the autopsy as soon as I can, but at present I need to be on hand in case of injury."

"Of course, Doctor."

Avery set off toward amidships, Commander Hambry at his side.

"About damned time, don't you think?" Hambry said. "I thought that whale meet would never end. How long can they sing their stupid songs to each other, anyway?"

In his mind's eye, Avery still saw the broad face and friendly eyes of Paul Bercka. The eyes stared, glassy and still. He shook himself.

"Too long," he said.

The *Maul* and its sister ships had been following the gathering of whales for weeks, waiting for them to disband so as to make hunting one or more easier. Normally the whales that plied the Atomic Sea were vicious and mad, driven by pain and fury, too irascible even to tolerate members of their own species. But, every now and then, they would congregate. They would sing, they would mate, and the bulls would fight each other for the females, sometimes to the death. Avery knew Captain Sheridan had been hoping to pick up just such a casualty in the meet's wake, but the whales had not been accommodating. The rest of the whaling fleet had followed along, too, vultures after carrion. Part of Avery still found it strange that the Navy would devote so much time and so many resources to whale hunting when Ghenisa was on the verge of being overrun by Octung, but Octung's advance was precisely why harvesting a whale—and its precious energy-filled lard—was so important.

Hustling whalers beset Avery and Hambry as they reached amidships, the whalers crossing to the harpoon racks to retrieve their instruments. Janx, tall and broad even among the other whalers, selected his own personal harpoon, the notorious Nancy, which boasted what looked like but could not possibly be a bronze head. Its shaft had been shattered and replaced countless times, but that head had slain dozens of whales; their bones had chipped and pitted every bit of it. *Dead by Nancy* was such a common phrase in the Navy that in recent months it had extended to every walk of a sailor's life, not just on the *Maul* but the fleet as a whole. Whether grievously tired, sore or hung-over, a sailor might say "I'm dead by Nancy" or "Nancy take me".

Avery saw Janx touch the spear to his helmet and hold it there for a moment, as if communing, before moving off with the others.

The sailors readied the boats and affixed the whalers' lifelines. Despite himself, Avery felt a smile creep across his face as the boats, laden with cursing whalers, lowered to the toxic black waters. Lightning arced from wave-top to wave-top, one bolt striking a boat—sparks flew high over the sea—but the specially-wrought craft splashed down unharmed. A hiss of steam coiled up from its hull. The sailors gave a hurrah.

Avery hurrahed, too. For a moment, he wished he were down there, adrenaline coursing through his veins, seaspray splashing his face-plate, right in the middle of all that excitement and importance. The lard from a single good-sized whale could stave off the army of Octung for a day or more.

The whalers manned the oars, and the little boats bobbed up and over the heaving waves, headed away from the *Maul*. Ship-to-whale projectiles could be used in an emergency, but only then, as a whale would be drawn to any vessel that fired on it. In the distance, the animals' occasional plumes of mist shot high up into the night, geysers of steam and poisons, the plumes growing further apart as the whales separated. The pilot had aimed the *Maul* at the largest animal and then turned sideways to it.

It was very close.

The whale barreled straight toward the boats. Avery's desire to be down there vanished in an instant, and he uttered a prayer under his breath for the men's safety.

The whale slipped beneath the surface. The boats slowed, and the whalers stood and coiled their arms, ready to hurl their harpoons. Where had the animal gone? The whalers remained steady, but Avery could imagine their sweat, their fear, their rapid breaths fogging their face-plates.

The whale erupted right under one of the central boats. It flung the craft high into the air and the men inside it flew in all directions, lifelines moored now only to splinters. The men struck the water and sank. Their heavy suits dragged them down. Only two managed to fling their lifelines to nearby boats in time to save them.

Before the whale submerged, Avery saw it, and he felt the blood drain from his face.

The whale had blossomed from the sea like a dark god, a mountain, mist spraying everywhere, its great jaws open, sharp teeth gleaming. Several whalers vanished between those jaws along with what was left of the boat. As the spray spread away from it, the light of the two visible moons shown down on the whale, revealing a horror covered in boils and stalks, milky blind eyes staring out from its sides. Its fins sprouted many and jagged, at odd places from its body, some ending in things that might be teeth. Sharp protrusions jutted from its flanks along with curling, groping tendril-like appendages. Some actually grew through the milky eyes. The whale's real, functional eyes glared madly, rimmed in pustules and scars and barnacles.

Then, with a huge splash that rocked the nearby boats, the leviathan vanished from sight—but not before three or four harpoons sailed through the night and embedded in its sides and underbelly.

For several breathless minutes the boats bobbed up and down on the waves. The men that had been flung from their destroyed craft reeled themselves in and with help from their mates scrambled aboard the boats. Avery hoped their suits hadn't ruptured.

The whale returned. It opened its huge, tooth-lined maw and shot toward another boat—the one Janx occupied. Avery felt suddenly cold. Janx had become something of a mascot to the *Maul*, and the crew adored him. Were he to die so would the ship's morale. Not only that, but Avery liked the big whaler.

Visible from far away, Janx stared up at the whale, harpoon cocked and ready. He did not throw, although the men to either side of him hurled theirs right into the whale's oncoming head.

It drove on.

With a thunderous crack, it smashed the boat to splinters, devouring several of the whalers instantly and plunging beneath the waves with such force that one of the nearby boats capsized in the swell. There was no sign of Janx or the other whalers that had been on the destroyed boat.

"Damn," Avery said.

Hambry snorted. "Maybe he'll find his nose in the afterlife."

Mist blew across the sea, and somewhere a few leagues off a burst of lightning must have struck a gas bubble, as a furious ball of orange and white expanded over the water. Expanded, then faded. By its light Avery saw one of the other ships of the line, several leagues to the east, he couldn't tell which one. The night was too dark for him to see any of the other ship's boats, though they must be out there, too, hunting, hunting. The whole fleet would be scrambling.

The whale emerged from the depths.

This time it breached more slowly, and for a moment Avery thought it had grown arrogant, that it would leisurely move to destroy the remaining boats. As if it had heard his thoughts, it swam toward the nearest one, and the men there braced themselves, ready to throw their harpoons.

The whale closed in, mouth agape, but for some reason the men didn't throw. As it neared them, its mouth began to close, and its tail slowed.

Limp, the whale drifted, carried by momentum, until finally it reached an utter stop.

A ragged cheer drifted across the waves.

Only then did Avery see, as one of the moons came out from behind a cloud, that a tall, broad figure stood on the whale's head, leaning on a harpoon—Nancy, it must be Nancy—driven deep into the creature's skull.

Avery laughed and clapped Hambry on the shoulder. "It's Janx!" he said. "He's alive! He's alive! The bloody idiot! He must have ridden it as it went under! Ha!"

The others on the deck—there was quite a crowd—laughed and cheered. Out on the water, the whalers ringed the animal and Janx climbed down its sides to much slapping on the back.

Hooked ropes sliced the air. Sharp steel sunk deep into fatty flesh. The boats began to haul their catch back toward the *Maul*, the boats small and puny against the vast blackness of the whale. They searched for survivors as they went, but there were none. The whale had slain perhaps ten men.

And yet Avery could not help but feel an enormous sense of relief. With the amount of hot lard that would be harvested from the monster, the machines that powered Ghenisa's defenses could be fueled for dozens of hours. Though other substances were used, few were as readily (if not easily) obtainable as the lard of a whale from the Atomic Sea—hot lard. Not radioactive in the traditional sense, but holding powerful concentrations of energy just the same. With the whale slain, the army of Octung might be staved off, at least for a time. Hopefully the other ships of the fleet would make kills, as well.

The whaling boats drew their prize to the *Maul*, and whalers and sailors coordinated tying it to the sides. A celebration broke out. Avery wasn't sure if Captain Sheridan had called for it or not, but she certainly seemed to allow it.

Janx clambered aboard and was instantly surrounded by admirers. With him in their center, men and women retreated inside, removed their suits, and were passed double rations of grog. Avery followed. Somewhere around a corner, he heard Janx toasting the dead. "Tonight they dance in the deep!" Others echoed him.

Before Avery could remove his suit and pour a glass of his finer officer's whiskey, Ensign Tapor ran up to him. Her breath masked her face-plate, and he could just see her wide eyes behind it.

"Doctor, you must come quickly."

Avery had just been in the process of taking off his helm. "Is it necessary?" he said. "I was just about to—"

"It's an emergency."

She sounds odd. "Show me," he said.

He snapped his helmet back on, and the ensign hurried him through the airlock and outside again. Assaulted anew by wind and mist, he grumped. He'd been looking forward to warmth and whiskey, to toasting Paul's memory and Janx's victory.

Overhead a great gas-squid floated against the stars, tentacles squirming, moonlight filtering through its half-translucent flesh, making it seem to glow in places with a ghostly sheen. Celebrating sailors near the bow took potshots at it, laughing.

Ensign Tapor led Avery to the port gunwale amidships. Ropes strained and creaked, and when Avery looked over the side, he saw that they ran from the ship to the whale, which had been tied off snugly—a huge, misshapen, cancerous growth sprouting from the *Maul*, its sides slip-slapping against the ship. Avery had thought all the boats had been raised and secured, but to his surprise he saw that one remained on the water directly below. It bobbed, oddly, in front of the whale's mouth, which sagged open.

Something was being lifted from the boat toward the ship's deck in a canvas sling.

Avery's frown deepened. "I don't ... Did that *thing* come from the whale's mouth?"

He glanced sideways. Ensign Tapor stared downward at the ascending shape, but she turned to look at him, a mix of fear and wonder in her eyes. "Yes, Doctor. She did."

"*She?*" Avery frowned. "A woman?" When Tapor didn't answer, he said, "A crewwoman from one of the other ships of the line?"

"I don't think so, Doctor."

The body reached the gunwale, and Avery rushed over to assist the sailors in setting it down. Only then did he step back, away from it, and see it for the first time.

Impossible.

It was a woman, naked, breathing, with hair too long for her to be Navy, and showing no obvious signs of sickness.

"Amazing," he said. "She should be dead. No one could survive those waters, uninfected, without a suit ..."

Thunder rolled, and lightning lit up the seas. Avery hardly noticed.

Chapter 2

The woman was alive, but injured. She had suffered burns on her legs, buttocks and lower back. For a moment Avery thought she might have been on a ship attacked by an Octunggen sub, that a fire or the explosion of a torpedo had burned her. But then, as he bent to study her, he saw that the burns were acidic. It should have been obvious, but it took him a moment to realize they could only have come from the stomach of the whale. *She had been eaten.* It must have been when the whale opened its throat to swallow one of the whalers that she had dragged herself out of its stomach.

Which of course was ridiculous. The gastric gasses alone should have killed her, not to mention the obvious acids.

And then, the sea ...

"Come," he told two of the crewmen. "Help me bring her to sick bay."

In awe—no one had ever been known to survive the sea without immediate and obvious sickness before—they complied. Avery washed her off in the buffer chamber at the same time they rinsed their suits, using his hands to cup the water and then pouring it over her, a cupful at a time, so as not to aggravate her wounds. Once they were all clean and had hung up their suits, Avery led the men and their charge out of the buffer chamber into the ship proper.

Around them the ship groaned. Great pipes snarled along the ceiling, banging and rattling. The whole place stank of oil and sweat. Avery had never gotten used to it, even though he'd been at sea for three months at the current stretch. Before that, he'd served the Navy on and off since the war began, some four years ago, but life aboard was still foreign to him.

"Don't spread word of this," he instructed the two crewmen in regards to the woman. "The last thing she needs is gawkers, understood?"

"Yes, Doctor."

When they reached the medical bay, he sent for his assistants. They arrived and fussed over the woman, cleaning her of any remaining acids, hooking her up to an IV drip, pumping out the poison from her lungs, while Avery dismissed the sailors who'd carried her, warning them one last time to keep their mouths closed. He knew such a warning to be futile, but it might slow the spread of gossip.

He checked the woman's vitals and made some adjustments, then pondered what to do with her. He briefly considered administering adrenaline to rouse her, if only to be able to question her, but decided that would be more for his benefit than hers. Better to ensure that she was well rested and let her begin to heal. Answers would wait.

His fingers shook, his head pounded, and he knew he needed a drink. *Just a little more*, he thought. *I can go a little longer.*

While his assistants saw to the woman, Avery checked on Paul.

Paul had already been brought to the bay, and he occupied a table behind a thin operating curtain. Avery saw that he was secured and took a moment to catch his breath. Paul V. Bercka, career enlisted man and widower (a circumstance which Avery shared, and something that had helped them bond), did not look peaceful in death. His eyes were now closed, but his face had locked in a terrible grimace, his lips pulled back, his teeth bared and specked with blood. Avery wished there was something he could do to relax his friend's facial muscles, but he was no mortician, and Paul would have to be given to the sea with an animal snarl on his face. *At least you went down defiant.*

After unstrapping him, Avery rolled Paul over with help from one of his assistants, Nurse Reynolds, who'd disrobed and cleaned the sergeant, and studied the wounds on Paul's back: inch-and-a-half gashes angled upward below the tank and at a reduced angle along the sides. As he'd supposed, Avery saw that one of the strikes had cut halfway through the fourth vertebrae. The killer's arm had been strong, the knife thick. The spine severance probably hadn't killed Paul, though. From the frothed blood in his mouth Avery knew that his lungs were filled with fluid; one of the knife strokes had punctured the bottom lining of a lung sac. Paul had drowned in his own blood.

Something heavy settled on Avery.

"Who could have done it?" Nurse Reynolds said. He was a big, good-looking young man with blond hair, a strong jaw but weak green eyes. They made him look soft somehow, though the rest of him was of heroic proportions.

Strong enough to be the killer, Avery thought, hating himself for it. He wondered if he would ever feel comfortable around another large man for the rest of the voyage.

"And why would anyone want to kill Paul?" Avery heard himself add. Bercka had been a good man, respected by those under him, depended on by those above him.

Reynolds had no answer.

"Go," Avery told him. "Check on our new patient."

The nurse studied him quietly for a moment, then nodded and left.

Avery moved to his desk and retrieved a flask of bourbon. He stared at it, unscrewed the cap and knocked back a long swig. Healing waves of warmth coursed down his throat. He downed another. Slowly, the pounding in his head began to fade, and he returned to Paul's side. The purple bruises around the sergeant's throat where the killer had held him showed lividly against his pale flesh. Avery checked Paul's elbows. Sure enough, they were scraped raw. He'd been elbowing his attacker, trying to break free, even as the killer had stabbed him. That meant the killer might have bruises on his chest, belly and arms. If Avery could find the man with those wounds ...

He took a last sip, screwed the cap back on and returned the flask to his desk.

The nurses and junior doctors were gathered around the young woman when he reemerged. One was administering salve to her burns. The rest just stared. The woman had blond hair and was not unattractive, and her body was lean, athletic, well-proportioned ...

"Fetch her some clothes," Avery said, and they leapt to obey. For a moment, there was silence, save the distant sound of revelry in the background. Somewhere someone toasted Janx, and bawdy laughter trickled down the halls.

"Now find something to do or go back to bed," Avery told them, and his assistants hastily occupied themselves, willing to sacrifice sleep for the chance at solving this medical mystery.

Avery assisted in coating salve on the woman's burns, which were extensive. The alchemical agents in the salve would help her heal and reduce her scarring, but they could not erase the scars completely. All Avery could hope for was that the treatments he would administer over the coming days would allow her skin to heal well enough so that she could bend and flex her legs normally, not hampered by tightened skin; she would not be crippled if he could help it.

A throat cleared behind him. Feeling suddenly hot, Avery turned to find Captain Jessryl Sheridan looking at him pointedly.

"Bagged yourself a mermaid, I see," she said, speaking with her upper-class drawl.

He made himself smile. "I'd prefer not to start calling her that."

"Then what is she?"

"I have no idea, but she needs peace and quiet, not the sort of attention from the crew she'd get if we start calling her names."

"Perhaps you prefer to keep her to yourself."

"Far from it," he said. "We need for her to recover fully and quickly. Ideally she can tell us where she came from and how she was able to survive the waters."

Capt. Sheridan approached, rolling her shoulders as she moved. Though not tall, she was solidly muscular and was said to be one of the finest fencers in the Navy. She had steel gray eyes, short auburn hair, and her jaw was slightly squared. Her nose had been broken in some battle years ago, and it still had a small scar right on the bridge. Another scar started over her left eyebrow and cut across her high forehead. Her lips were full and might have been sensuous with lipstick and a smile, but she never wore make-up and her smiles were never sensuous—predatory, more like.

Sheridan grabbed the young woman's chin and turned her head as if inspecting a dog.

"Doesn't look Ghenisan to me," she said. "Nor Octunggen. She's probably from the north, one of the Yorish States perhaps."

"She's not Yori."

"True," Sheridan said. "She has no braids, and her skin's too smooth. She didn't come from a nearby ship—they're all ours—and she couldn't have come from far away, either. The whale she was inside of has been in our sights for the last several weeks."

"And all without a suit."

"I'll have to hand her over to the Navy Science Division when we get back."

"They'll *dissect* her!"

"They'll do what they must," Sheridan said. "If she's immune to the sea, as unlikely as that sounds, perhaps we can use her blood to devise some sort of vaccine ..."

"As chief medical appointment of this ship, she's my charge, and *I* will decide where she goes." Avery tried to lighten his voice. "Besides, she could wake up at any time. *She* can answer our questions."

"We'll see." Sheridan seemed to have lost interest in the topic, though she had acquired an interest in something else. Avery's moment of rebellion had triggered sparks in her eyes. "Why don't we discuss it ... in private?"

Damn her.

"Well?" she said.

Slicking the hair on the side of his head over his bald spot, he said, "Very well. Captain."

Her smile widened, but not with warmth, and she turned smartly on her heel and departed. Avery cast a glance back over his shoulder at Paul, dead on his slab, and at the mystery woman, who might be dissected shortly, and followed in his captain's wake.

"Sergeant Bercka was a friend of mine," he said as they passed down the corridors, their way lit by flickering electric light in spots, but the rest illuminated by candles, both conventional and alchemical, evidence of the struggling generators.

"Let's not talk about it in public," she said. "Keep ship morale high."

She led him down bustling halls, through the officer's quarters and finally into her cabin, shutting the door behind them.

"Now. About Paul," he said, squinting in the darkness. "We have a major problem. It appears we have a serial murderer aboard."

Click. An alchemical light flared. The lantern smelled of smoke and cinnamon, and its red light pulsed on the walls in regular beats. The glowing liquid moved slowly in the thick rounded glass of the lantern, making it seem as if Avery and Sheridan were underwater—red, slowly moving water. She'd had the metal surfaces and ceiling mounted with oaken covers, and the tusk of a sea elephant hung from the port bulkhead. She'd shot the creature herself. Among other things, she was a renowned markswoman.

She stripped off her jacket and threw it on a hanger. Her eyes stayed on Avery. Her stare was flat and gray, but there was something under it, something that smoldered. He thought of a fiery sun masked by smog and clouds.

"Sgt. Bercka's death will be addressed," she assured him. "We'll catch the murderer, serial or not. I'm sorry. I know you were close. But dwelling on it won't help. Let me ... distract you."

"Captain, this is important."

"So is this."

Pushing her would only backfire on him, he realized. Hiding a sigh, he began to unbutton his jacket.

Their lovemaking, if it could be called that, exhausted him as always. Ghenisa was a country whose culture valued athleticism and physical contests greatly, and the captain was Ghenisan to a fault. There was not an ounce of wasted flesh on her body, which could have been sculpted from rock and was nearly as hard. Despite her fitness, however, she was not a good lover. Perhaps she could have been had she wanted to be, perhaps she was with others, but her single goal while she was with Avery was to climax, and after she did she would roll quickly off him, as she did now. She'd never allowed him to finish inside her, and as ever he was forced to finish himself by hand. At least she provided a towel.

Afterward, bruised and sweaty, he flopped back in bed, panting, while Sheridan strode naked to the red-lit bar and poured herself a thick finger of bourbon. She didn't ask him if he wanted any. Avery stared at her rippling, muscular body, gleaming with sweat as she stood at the bar, and marveled that she could look so calm and in control naked.

She eyed him over the rim of her glass. "You've gotten flabby," she said. "You need exercise. Look at you, you can hardly breathe."

"I think that's more ... your fault ... than mine."

"You've gone soft, Doctor."

"Ha."

She was right, though, of course. Back on land he enjoyed taking hikes through the mountains that were so important to his country. Sometimes he would hike for days, pitching tents in the forests, careful to keep to the safe areas. At sea, however, he had little to do but drink and brood, and brood and drink. He admitted to himself that he'd done quite a lot of both.

"I'll start taking walks along the decks," he said.

She rattled the ice in her glass. "Not outside, I hope."

"Oh, no. The inner decks should do fine. I'll take a drink, if you don't mind."

"I think you've had enough of those. And too many while on duty. One's enough to get you hanged."

"Jess, you know I'd never—"

"Don't call me that." She tensed, then softened. "Get it yourself if you must. It'll give you some exercise."

Grumbling, he rose from bed, threw on his pants and approached the bar. She edged away from him. She never liked to be close, except when they were amorously occupied, and even then she would not let him kiss her on the mouth and sternly guarded where he placed his hands.

He poured himself two fingers of bourbon and sipped it neat, savoring the expensive liquor.

She seemed to notice his enjoyment. "If you gave a shit about your life, Doctor, you'd have money to buy your own."

He drank. "My life ended some time ago." He said it more to himself than to her.

"So, what are you now, a ghost?" She glanced away for a moment, and a hint of something that might be sadness flickered in her eyes. In a smaller voice, she said, "We've all had tragedies, Francis."

He started. She rarely called him by his first name.

Washing herself with a wet cloth, she said, "At least you're a decent doctor."

Avery smiled and peered at the bed. "Apparently I have my uses."

"True. You make my other lovers look good."

He felt a small flash of something that could not possibly be jealousy. He wanted little more than to be *out* of this relationship, if that's what it was. It was no surprise to him that she had other lovers. It was well known that she had conquests scattered throughout the fleet.

Buttoning his shirt, he said, "I think I'll go check on my new patient."

"See that she reaches shore alive, Doctor." Sheridan began pulling her uniform back on, piece by piece. "The scientists will want her breathing, at least at first. She could be very valuable."

"To your career, you mean."

She didn't deny it. "I won't be a captain forever. Someday I'll be admiral. Then fleet admiral. Then ... who knows?" She smiled, and it was not a little predatory.

He drained his glass. "Well, if that's all ..."

Her face changed, as if she realized that she'd made a mistake. He didn't give her time to fix it, but made for the door.

"Doctor," she said.

Don't turn. He turned. Sheridan was eyeing him strangely. She sucked in a breath, strode to the nearest bulkhead and removed a painting; it depicted the famous landing of Captain Devorre on the shores of Apolli. A safe gleamed where the painting had been. Sheridan spun the dial and opened it, retrieving a small, lacquered wooden box from the safe's interior.

"Here."

Frowning, Avery stepped forward. "What is it?"

"Look."

She opened the box to reveal the empty casing of a shotgun shell. It sat on black velvet, snug inside a little depression shaped just for it.

He raised his eyebrows.

"Winter of '57," she said. "One of my first wins. The shell that casing belongs to won me more than just a medal." She did not explain what she meant by that but pressed the box into his hands. "Keep it for me."

He didn't know what to say. Skeet shooting contests were an ancient tradition of the Navy and were always practiced on the bow of a ship. He knew that giving him a memento from an early win was a peace offering, maybe something more. Surely it wasn't a gesture of affection. She would consider that a weakness. And yet ...

"I will," Avery said.

He slipped the box into a pocket and ran his fingers over it as he made his way back through the halls. He wondered what it signified, if anything. *Don't read too much into it. This is Sheridan.* He half suspected the only reason she slept with him was because unlike everyone else aboard he had some measure of independence. She liked someone that could stand up to her—to an extent, anyway. As for why he allowed the trysts, he supposed it was mainly to avoid friction. Plus, he admitted to himself, it was nice to have at

least one real human connection left, uncomfortable though
it was.

He returned to the medical bay to find it deserted save
one dozing nurse. He made straight for his new patient, the
mysterious woman from the sea, in her curtained-off
corner.

She blinked up at him.

Her eyes were the blue of mountain rivers, swift and
plunging. They stared at him coolly, and he was struck by
the force of personality in them. The rest of her remained
fevered and sweaty, and even as he approached her eyes
began to close.

"Don't sleep!" he said. "Stay conscious."

He found a syringe, filled it with a stimulant and injected
her. Now that she was awake, he had to keep her from
lapsing into a coma. He massaged the flesh of her upper
arm to help the stimulant pass through, surprised by how
hot her skin was.

She stirred and mumbled something.

"What?" he said. "What is it?"

He leaned forward to hear her better, and she spoke
again.

"Gedden es un ... ?"

Dismay washed over him. He staggered back, nearly
knocking over a tray. *It can't be.*

He forced his eyes to meet hers. *It doesn't matter.* She was
a patient, first and foremost.

Still, he tasted something bitter on his tongue as,
cobbling together the Octunggen he'd learned over the
years, he answered her question. "You're on a Ghenisan
whaling ship. You were found ... believe it or not ... in the
belly of a whale. Can you ..." He heard his voice creak and

cleared his throat. "Please, tell me how you got there, how you were able to survive the waters—the whale?"

Sweat beaded her cheeks and forehead. She said nothing.

"Please," he repeated. "Does Octung have some way to fight the effects of the water?" Octung, he was all too aware, possessed many sophisticated and strange technologies; it would not surprise him.

She seized his arm. Again the warmth of her skin shocked him.

"I ... am not ... *Octunggen*."

"But you speak it."

She trembled, and her eyes rolled up.

"No! No!" He shook her. "Don't go to sleep!" He slapped her face.

Her eyes opened. "Ghenisa ..."

"Yes, this is a Ghenisan ship." He took a breath. "My captain will want to talk to you."

Her face, which had been red from fever, visibly paled. "No ... no ... there are spies. Agents of Octung. All throughout the continent. Ghenisa ... is riddled with them. If you ... tell anyone about me ... I will die."

"What? Why?"

"I ..." She started to shake again. Before she lost lucidity, she said, "I am on a ... mission ... to *stop* them."

"Who?"

Her eyes started to roll up in her head, and he shook her again, almost desperate.

"Stop *what*?"

"Stop ... Octung."

He stared at her, speechless.

The fever took her, and she collapsed into the bed. He tried to rouse her, but without success. She slept on, tossing and turning, sweating and red. He realized that he was trembling.

A noise behind him. "Did I miss something?"

He turned to see the nurse, Jennifer, yawning, her eyes on the patient.

Avery opened his mouth to tell her what had happened, but hesitated. The mystery woman had said Ghenisa was plagued—*riddled*—with spies. He didn't necessarily believe her, of course, and Jennifer surely couldn't be a spy even if there were such creatures about, but if he told Jennifer what had happened, and she told others, and there *were* spies, how long would it be before they moved against the mystery woman? He supposed he owed her claims some thought, if nothing else.

"She came to briefly," he said. "She said nothing and went right back into sleep."

"I thought I heard voices."

"Just me, trying to get her to stay awake."

"I—"

Alarms blared. They were not the long, slow beats that signaled a whale sighting, but fast, urgent, teeth-rattling peals. They could mean only one thing.

"Octunggen," Jennifer breathed.

It was as if her words were a cue. Before Avery could even think the word *torpedo*, a great roar rose up from deep in the ship. Something exploded. Metal squealed. The floor pitched beneath Avery's feet and flung him against a bulkhead. He struck his head and tasted blood on his tongue. Blackness overcame him.

When it parted, he found himself on the floor. Other things joined him, various objects of the bay, a bottle of painkiller, a canister of anesthesia gas, a metal tray, rolling and sliding about. Jennifer was picking herself up, shaking her head. Screams issued from down the hall.

She staggered over to Avery and offered her hand. Shakily, he grasped it and hauled himself to his feet.

"Are you all right, Doctor?"

"We've been hit," he said. He heard the shock in his voice and forced himself to push past it. "We have work to do."

Chapter 3

Blood dripped from Avery's elbows onto his apron. A spray splashed his mask and dotted his glasses. He clamped off his patient's artery and began to sew, as other doctors and nurses hovered over their own patients, bloody and burned. The torpedo had struck one of the furnace rooms, and the results had been catastrophic. Fortunately the sub had only hit them once before Sheridan had sunk it.

"New mask," Avery said, having difficulty breathing through the blood-soaked cotton. After his nurse replaced it and cleaned his glasses, Avery continued sealing up the artery. The sailor's leg had been badly damaged, both by shrapnel and by fire. At first Avery had been convinced that he'd have to amputate, but he'd found a way to save the limb.

"Done," he said at last.

"It looks good, Doctor," the nurse told him.

Exhausted, Avery let a junior doctor sew up the incision while he slumped back and made himself take some deep breaths. The last few hours had passed in a blur. His team of doctors and nurses had rushed to the furnace room and the surrounding chambers, found the injured men and women, some trapped behind flames and debris in the lower levels, helped unearth them, then seen them carried safely to the sickbay, where the doctors had a full range of medical equipment to aid them, as opposed to establishing a triage on-site. After long, weary hours of blood and screams, Avery's eyes had drooped and his arms had sagged. Having no choice, he'd fortified himself with an injection of stimulants.

Now he leaned against a bulkhead, tired and with blood dripping from him. The reek of viscera and antiseptic permeated everything. Around him, men and women were piled up, beds squeezed together in confusion, pipes tapping a beat overhead. The medical bay had only been built large enough to hold twenty patients, but twice that number had been wounded in the attack. The remainder cluttered the floor in the adjoining halls. And those were the lucky ones. The torpedo had killed thirty for certain, and there were still several men and women unaccounted for. There would barely be enough functioning sailors left to crew the *Maul*.

At least they'd had their revenge, and with the submarine downed Captain Sheridan was shoring up the hull breaches and pumping out water. Avery hoped she'd acted quickly enough to prevent infection from spreading among the crew or some creature from the sea getting inside; he wasn't sure which was worse. At least the torpedo that had struck them had been conventional, not one of the acid-explosives or purported time-warps or what-not the Octunggen delighted in using.

Avery's gaze strayed over the dead, the wounded, the weary doctors, exhausted nurses, finally to alight on the woman he had come to think of as Patient X. *My mermaid.* Mostly hidden behind a curtain, she lay still.

He glanced around once more to make sure his attentions weren't needed elsewhere and moved toward her.

She was hot to the touch, and still asleep. Avery withdrew his smelling salts and tried to rouse her. When that failed, he shot her up with adrenaline; whatever risks it held were minor compared to letting the Navy scientists dissect her.

"Come on, wake up, wake up."

Of course, if she did, what would happen to her when the others found out she spoke Octunggen? Neither waking nor sleeping held much hope for her.

The woman slumbered on, her chest rising and falling, and Avery frowned. With a sigh, he checked her dressings. It was then, as he shifted the bandage on her right leg, that he saw it. At first he thought he was hallucinating, but no, there could be no mistake: *the woman was half healed.*

The massive, deep purple scar tissue that had wrapped around her upper left thigh just hours ago was now normal, healthy skin, albeit red and inflamed.

He heard a gasp and turned to see Nurse Reynolds staring at the burn. "I don't believe it."

Avery inspected her other wounds. All showed the same signs of recovery.

"Amazing," he said.

"How is this possible?" Reynolds said.

"I don't know, but this is the woman that survived the Atomic Sea. Hell, she even survived the belly of a whale."

A young enlisted man entered the bay, sweaty and frantic. He approached one group of junior doctors, whispered something to them, and moved on to a pair of patients. Gasps of incredulity and horror followed him. At last he approached Avery.

"Doctor, have you heard the news? Captain Sheridan— she's cutting the whale loose!"

As soon as Avery emerged onto the deck, he swore.

Sheridan strode back and forth before the gunwale while sailors hacked through the stout hemp ropes that bound the whale. A crowd of depressed-looking whalers and sailors, Janx among them, had gathered on deck, and they watched as the ropes sprang free, one by one. In disbelief, Avery pushed his way through the crowd, coming to stand before Captain Sheridan.

"What the hell do you think you're doing?" he said. He realized he'd misspoken as soon as the words were out.

Sheridan stared at him through the brass grill that covered her face-plate. "Watch your tone, Doctor. I'll excuse it this time, but don't address me like that again or I'll keelhaul you."

He blinked. "Captain, please ... I don't understand. Why are you doing this?"

Commander Hambry, who'd been cutting the ropes, approached. With breathing that sounded labored, he said, "It's not your place to question the Captain, Doctor."

Sheridan shoved Hambry back. Raising her voice, she said, "I'll say this one more time, to all of you. *We have no choice*. Octunggen subs are hunting us. A patrol has found us and destroyed three ships of the line already—and crippled the *Maul*. It's all we can do just to keep the engines going and the bilges pumping. We'll be lucky if we can make port. There is *no way* we can haul this carcass back with us."

"But the lard—" Janx started.

Captain Sheridan glared at him. "We have to hope the other ships manage to bring something back."

The last rope was cut.

Dejectedly, Avery made his way to the rail and watched the tortured mass of the whale drift away. Black fins approached it, then tangled the water around it. Avery imagined the unholy feast going on below the waves, the ripping of flesh, the gobbling of lard. His throat felt tight. The men and women of the *Maul* stood around him, staring out at the whale. Small gas-squid, drawn by the stench of rot and now undeterred by the ship, bobbed through the sky and alit on the mound. They slithered over its barnacle-covered hide, ripping at it with their beaks, gripping it with their tentacles. As the ship drew further and further away, they became impossible to see.

"Gods below," Janx said. "It's still got some of my mates rotting in its belly, and she's *let it go*."

If Sheridan heard him, she gave no sign.

"I'm sorry," Avery told him.

Janx kicked the gunwale. In disgust, he turned about and stormed away. Several whalers followed. The Captain ordered the remaining men and women back to their stations, and with lowered heads they slunk off. Avery remained, intending to see the whale off.

Seemingly hesitant, Sheridan approached him. He did not turn to look at her.

"How could you?" It was all he could say.

Sheridan stared out at the sea. Perhaps accidentally, her arm brushed his.

"We all do what we have to," she said. For a long moment, neither said anything. A burst of orange and red on the horizon signaled an exploding gas pocket. At last she said, "Now your patient's more important than ever."

"How is that?"

"As of now, she's our most precious cargo."

"She's not cargo."

"She is what I say she is." Sheridan shot him a warning look. "Take good care of her, Doctor. She could be very significant."

She said she could stop Octung.

The Captain pulled back to confer with Hambry, then returned. "Tend to the Commander. A gas tank blew while he was helping some of our men trapped in the explosion. He was hurt."

Avery led the X.O. inside. Hambry moved in odd jerks, and he favored one side. When Avery got him to the medical bay and out of the suit, he saw why. Shrapnel from the exploding gas tank had caught Hambry on the upper right chest. Some of the pieces must have penetrated deep and were likely close to the lung. Every time he breathed, they cut deeper. He was not coughing blood yet, but he was close.

As Hambry lay half-naked on the surgical table with Avery standing over him, gleaming surgical instruments at hand, the doctor noticed the wounds he had been looking for. With every patient he'd seen to over the last few hours, he had kept an eye out for the bruises Paul's elbows would have left in his last moments.

In addition to the bruising and discoloration around the shrapnel entry points, other bruises showed on Hambry's torso and arms. They were small, and the wounds corresponded precisely to where Paul's elbows would have struck, mostly along the sides and arms, avoiding the middle—and low. Paul had been a shorter man than Hambry, and the bruises were grouped above Hambry's waist, exactly where they should have been if Hambry committed the murder.

At the sight, the pain behind Avery's right eye returned, throbbing in full force. He had to clutch at the bed to steady himself.

"Are you all right, Doctor?"

"I'm ... fine." *But you won't be.*

It took all of Avery's will not to kill Hambry during the surgery to remove the pieces of shrapnel. It would have been so easy. A slice here, a nick there, and Commander Hambry would die of complications to his wounds. Avery himself would perform the autopsy and certify the cause of death. No questions asked. A quick, effortless murder. Even neater and cleaner than Paul's.

Avery knew he could never prove Hambry had done it, not in a court of law. So the Commander had odd bruises, that didn't prove anything.

Avery's fingers itched as he held the scalpel, but he held himself back. He needed proof. He needed to be sure. Also, and just as importantly, he needed to know *why* the

Commander had killed Paul. And if he had killed Paul, Hambry had almost certainly been the one that murdered Lt. Nyers two weeks ago. The killings were just too similar.

Avery's craving for a drink doubled and tripled during the procedure, and afterwards he allowed himself to sneak a few swigs. He did not take care to keep the stitching particularly neat or straight.

Hambry would recover. And when he did, Avery would have his answers.

With all the injured men and women seen to, Avery shrugged off his white coat, said goodbye to Paul and left the bay to return to his private cabin. It was dark, rusty and stank of mold, but it was home. After the stimulant comedown, he felt exhausted, both in mind and body.

"At last," he muttered, taking out a bottle from a cabinet, then a second. He knocked down a shot of bourbon with a chaser of brandy, and sat on his narrow bed. He gulped down deep breaths and tried to let his mind calm.

His gaze wandered where it always did, almost against his will, to a small framed picture mounted to the wall opposite the bed. He felt something twist inside him at the sight. In the picture a smiling woman with long black hair stood before a modest stone house, and a girl with short, equally dark hair and an impish grin held her hand. Moss grew in the house's cracks, and a crowded flowerbed ran along its windows. Muted sunlight shone down on them.

Avery stared at the picture until his eyes burned. He felt suddenly unsteady, as though his sense of equilibrium had been taken away, and the world moved around him.

He knocked back another sip of bourbon, and the world calmed.

Visions of fire, blood and screaming men chased him through his dreams that night, but other, older haunts were there, too. Memories. He dreamed of walking through a dead city, bodies lying scattered all around, some still twitching. He was dressed in a bulky environment suit, hot and cumbersome. A desperate need spurred him on, and he heard himself screaming out two names, again and again. He staggered through the streets, over bodies, around stopped cars, vaguely aware of a bright light flaring from one of the mountains that reared ahead—a red, terrible light. At last he came to a simple cobbled house, the same one from the picture, and time seemed to slow. He screamed, exhausted, tears caking his cheeks, but even though he knew he was running toward the house it never seemed to get any closer. It loomed before him, beautiful and horrible, and he found himself terrified and at the same time desperate to see what waited inside. But the house came no closer, and the red light flared even more brightly from the mountaintop. Fires raged behind him, and somewhere planes droned. The house ... *Mari* ... *Ani* ... *please, let it have spared them. Let it—*

He woke with a gasp. Sweat beaded his brow. Shakily, he dressed and performed his necessary functions. He tried not to let his gaze linger on the picture.

Before he left, he found a cigar in his top cabinet drawer. It was the last one Paul had given him. Together they had often sat in this cabin of an evening, smoking and bullshitting about legends from the L'ohen Empire, or heroes of the Revolution—both men were history buffs—while whale songs groaned outside and lightning lit the portholes. And sometimes, just sometimes, they would talk about their lost families. Only then could Avery speak of his wife and daughter. Of Mari and Ani.

After studying the cigar a moment, he replaced it in the drawer. Perhaps he'd smoke it when Hambry was dead.

With leaden feet, Avery returned to the medical bay. Paul's autopsy held no surprises. He had ultimately died by drowning in his own blood, coupled with severe bodily trauma after being stabbed half a dozen times. Avery had expected it, but he had owed his friend nothing less than a full postmortem.

In a fit of perversion, he placed Commander Hambry in the bed adjoining Paul's corpse—not that Paul would stay there long, of course. The group funeral that was to be held for the slain whalers would include him, too. The dead from the submarine attack had yet to be tallied, and there were some who had yet to be found or identified, so the group funeral for them would be delayed. At today's funeral, only one of the caskets would be occupied. Paul would enter the next life, if there was such a thing, alone.

Subs hunted them.

Along with the other ships of the whaling fleet, the GS *Maul* limped toward safety. Several of the ships had been attacked by Octunggen subs the same night the *Maul* had, and three had gone down. Every few hours a report of a new submarine contact came from one of the ships, and the entire fleet would veer sharply away.

They made for a passing naval convoy, where a fleet of Ghenisan warships shepherded a large number of cargo vessels bound for Hissig, capital of Ghenisa. The cargo was being transferred from Vlakresk, an ally that lay across the Atomic Sea to the east. The Vlakreskin had not yet been drawn into the war waged by Octung and its vassal states, the war which had engulfed the continents of Urslin and Consur, so they still possessed the resources to be philanthropic—not that they had given the cargo away, of course. They'd sold it for a shiny tzan, Avery was sure. But they were bitter foes of Octung and knew that prolonging the war across the sea would delay the arrival of Octung's forces in their own land.

If the *Maul* and her sister ships could reach the convoy, they would be reasonably safe from marauding submarines. Until then they were at the subs' mercy. They could not even radio for assistance, as the Octunggen had triggered some device of theirs, one of their mysterious pieces of technology, which limited the reach of radio signals or blocked them altogether. The ships could communicate with each other if they did not stray beyond a certain range, but the outside world was off-limits. They existed in their own bubble, a limbo between life and death.

It would take a week to reach the convoy.

An Octunggen submarine could come upon them at any time.

The race was on.

"Good as ever," said Lt. Orin, wrinkling her face as she took a bite. They were eating tinned beef and potatoes tonight, and neither tasted particularly fresh, unless one counted the tang of metal.

"At least it's better than what the whalers and enlisted men get," said Lt. Mason, which got a round of groans.

Avery ate without comment. Though he usually dined with the officers in their private mess as was expected of him, he'd never felt a part of their group, always feeling more at home for some reason among the enlisted men and whalers—though he doubted they reciprocated the feeling.

"We're just lucky to be alive," someone said. "After the last few days ... I mean, my gods."

Murmured assent greeted this. The days since the attack had been rough for the whaling fleet, with one ship being attacked after another. Two that had survived the initial assault had broken up, and privately Avery wondered if the *Maul* would be the next to go—and if there would be any ships left to aid them if it did.

"We'll reach the convoy in another two days," Avery said, if only for something to say.

Lt. Orin started to respond, but the blare of the ship's intercom interrupted her. The voice of Captain Sheridan, made metallic by the speaker, rang out:

"ALL HANDS TO YOUR STATIONS. THE *AGARA* HAS JUST BEEN HIT. REPEAT, THE *AGARA* HAS BEEN HIT. WE'RE UNDER WAY TO ASSIST HER. PREPARE YOURSELVES."

Sheridan clicked off.

Instantly Avery and the rest of the diners quit their meals and joined the press of people in the hallways leading outside. Avery went first to the medical bay, which he ordered prepped for immediate use, then rejoined the traffic in the halls. He donned an environment suit and with a group of nervous sailors emerged onto the outer deck. Rain and wind lashed him, and he staggered to clip himself in.

"Bumpy night, ain't it?" said a voice beside him.

Janx.

"What are you doing out here?" Avery asked. Technically the whalers were not part of the Navy but were civilian contractors that lived and worked apart, held in reserve to hunt whales.

"Thought I'd see what's what," Janx said. "Hell, maybe I could pitch in. Gets awful restless down in the Pen."

Around them the sailors readied themselves to board the *Agara* and help shore up the damage, possibly even take on as much of the crew as the *Maul* would hold if it appeared the ship would sink. Avery secured one group's services if he needed them to transport wounded to the medical bay.

Sheridan emerged onto the deck surrounded by officers. From the forward gunwale, she stared out at the night through binoculars, and Avery was close enough to hear her say to her officers, "There it is. Get ready."

Avery strained his eyes and made out the dim bulk of the *Agara*, its thick chimney towers blocking out the stars.

"There's no lights," Janx said.

He was right. The *Agara* was simply a wall of blackness on the sea.

"Perhaps their generators were hit," Avery said.

Janx said nothing.

Sheridan ordered searchlights to illuminate the *Agara*, and the beams played over the other ship's decks at her direction. When Avery saw people there, he smiled.

The smile vanished instantly.

"Dear gods," he muttered. "They're not wearing suits ..."

Though the decks of the *Agara* swarmed with activity, Avery couldn't see a single person wearing an environment suit.

"The idiots," Janx said. "They'll get infected."

"Perhaps a fire forced them outside."

The *Maul* neared the distressed ship, which was riding low in the water, surely due to the torpedo strike, and Avery couldn't help but feel a wave of grief at all the people being infected right in front of him. To see a whole ship-full of people sicken and die ... or change ... As a doctor, it offended him to be so impotent. There was nothing he could do for them.

"Hells," Janx said.

"What?"

Then Avery saw it, too. The people on the decks of the *Agara* acted strangely. As the *Maul* drew closer, Avery saw Agarans crawling over each other, biting and ripping at one another, some even hurling their crewmates overboard. It was as if a madness had possessed them. Every one of them. They were *raving*. Foam gathered at their mouths. Blood dappled their bodies. Some ripped at their chests and faces with their fingernails, as if so eager to cause pain that even their own would do. As the *Maul* approached, the Agarans turned their bloody, shredded faces toward the Maulers, and their eyes gleamed like embers. As one, a terrible howl rose up from the Agarans' throats.

It was almost too late. The *Maul* had pulled alongside the *Agara* and sailors were preparing to throw across ropes and boarding ramps. At a sudden shout from Sheridan, the crew of the *Maul* abandoned the boarding ramps and took up arms instead.

One of the Agarans leapt across the gap that separated the ships and, before the Maulers could stop him, grabbed a sailor and hurled him over the side. As the madman reached for another victim, Captain Sheridan shot the man through the head. He toppled backward over the gunwale.

Other Agarans leapt over, screaming and tearing at the Maulers. One landed near Avery. Janx smashed him over the head and threw him over the side.

While Avery fought for breath, Janx crossed to a rack of harpoons, grabbed one and returned.

"Shove away!" he bellowed to all nearby, and demonstrated by pushing against the hull of the *Agara* with the butt of the harpoon.

Others followed suit, and soon the ships were separating. Meanwhile, Sheridan orchestrated the effort to destroy any Agarans that had made the leap.

Avery helped reel in the sailor who'd been flung overboard; the man's lifeline had saved him. By the time Avery pulled him over, with some assistance from nearby sailors, the *Maul* had pulled away, and the howls of the Agarans were fading into the mist. As he bent over the sailor, Avery noticed blood.

"Damn," he said.

The man's suit had been ruptured. A bloody bite showed under the right nipple.

Avery steeled himself to deliver the bad news. "I'm very sorry, sir. I'm afraid your suit has—"

The man seized Avery. His eyes were bloodshot and the pupils had shrunk to pinpricks. The man's teeth chomped, and spittle sprayed from chewed lips. The man brought Avery in close as if to bite him, but their helms simply knocked against each other. Spittle sprayed the inside of the man's helm.

Sailors grabbed the fellow and pulled him away from Avery. It was quickly determined that whatever contagion had swept through the crew of the *Agara* had been passed onto the Mauler through the bite. Sweating, Avery made his way to Sheridan, who stared at the receding bulk of the *Agara* grimly.

"We have a problem," he told her, and outlined what had happened.

Surprisingly, she said, "I know."

"You *know*?"

"As soon as I saw the *Agara*'s decks, the people there, I knew."

"Knew *what*?"

"The Octunggen must have hit the *Agara* with a plague torpedo. The Agarans were able to shore up the damage, evidently, but they couldn't stop the gas. It contaminated them all. Turned them into ... well, you saw."

Avery stared at the *Agara*, at the still-swarming masses there, just dim shapes in the mist.

"A plague torpedo ..." he said. He'd heard of them, of course, but he hadn't known what they did exactly. He wished he still didn't. "What should we do with the contaminated man?"

She shook her head. "There's only one thing."

She strode up to the raving man and, after some words to Avery and the others to mollify them, shot the man through the head. Along with the other corpses, the man was flung overboard and the deck hosed where he'd lain.

"Scrub the deck well," Sheridan instructed her crew. "Use the strongest cleansers you have."

"I need a drink," Avery said.

Sheridan sighed. "Come with me. We'll drink together." She paused, then said, not without a trace of sadness, "But first I must scuttle the *Agara*. We can't let the contagion spread. I don't know what bothers me more—scuttling it or the fact that we'll have to use one of our last torpedoes to do it."

On the eighth day, the *Grengas*, the only ship of the fleet not crippled, had had enough. It broke off from the others who'd been slowing it down and made a run for the convoy. Just before the *Grengas* passed through the radio silence bubble, its captain sent a frantic communiqué to the ships it had abandoned: "... am turning around now ... full speed ... blockade ... repeat, submarine blockade ahead ... have been spotted and am going full thrott—"

It never returned to the others. A great conflagration was seen just over the horizon to the south, the direction it had vanished in.

News spread throughout the ships. The Octunggen lay in wait, sealing off the convoy from the surviving whaling ships. There was no way around, not with the other subs out hunting them. They were all doomed. Everyone was dead already.

"And how are we doing today?" Avery asked, making his rounds in the medical bay.

Lt. Hinis grimaced and fingered the bandages that wrapped the stump of her right arm, which had been severed just below the elbow. "I'd be doin' fuckin' better, Doc, if you could grow back my arm."

"Well, while I work on that, you should be up and about by tomorrow."

She snorted. "We'll hit the blockade by then."

"I'm sure Captain Sheridan knows what she's doing."

"Yeah? Then why doesn't she go another way? Why's she goin' *into* the blockade?"

"There's no other way. We're low on fuel—the *Grengas* was our remaining fuel storage ship—and we wouldn't be able to make a detour wide enough to avoid the subs."

From his bed across the aisle, Ensign Cashim said, "So we're just going to commit suicide?"

"I believe the hope is that the convoy will draw so close that the Octunggen will break up their blockade and scatter," Avery said.

"Hope Sheridan's right, Doc," Hinis said. "We won't survive another hit."

From the bed nearest her, a man named Myers, who'd been badly burned in the attack, said in his raspy voice, "I just wish I knew what it was all for—the war, I mean."

"World domination, what else?" Hinis said. "Octung's 'Forever Empire'. Fucking idiots."

The man grimaced, his mutilated flesh pulling back to reveal white teeth. "They're doing it for their *gods*. It's a *holy war*."

Cashim adjusted his stump of a leg, looking suddenly uncomfortable. "Don't talk about, well, you know."

For some reason, Avery felt an uncomfortable flutter in his own belly. The gods of Octung ...

"It's bad luck," Cashim added.

"Bullshit," said Hinis, spitting a wad of tobacco juice, but even she didn't look convinced.

"Is it?" rasped Myers. "It's not about world domination, don't you get it? It's about ... *them*." He looked around significantly and added in a low, awful voice, "The Collossum."

Avery tried to wave it away. "The Collossum might be the deities of our enemies, but that doesn't mean we should treat them with any greater respect or fear than any other gods. They're just as—well, not to sound anti-religious, but they're just as insubstantial."

"Maybe, Doctor," said Cashim, and then violated his earlier warning by adding, "But what I heard is, after the Octs conquer a country, they burn all the temples to the local gods and set up new ones to the Collossum. Those that refuse to attend—" He drew a line across his throat. "Of course, they kill enough in their purgings that what do a few more matter?"

"I heard they practice human sacrifice," Myers said.

"Surely not," Avery said. "If nothing else, Octung is a civilized country."

"Civilized!" Hinis said. "They've slaughtered half the continent!"

"Don't worry so much. It's bad for your recovery." He made himself smile. "We'll stop them."

"Yeah. We're doin' a real bang-up job of it so far, Doc. What's that the Ungraessotti say? We've got one foot in the Soul Door already. And by dawn it looks like we'll have the other through."

Avery continued performing his rounds, conscious that he was avoiding a certain patient. Finally, after he had finished checking on everyone else, he realized he couldn't put it off any longer and approached Commander Hambry's bedside.

"How are we feeling today?" Avery asked. *In grievous pain, hopefully.*

Hambry appeared all too healthy. He shrugged and winced. "Tugs."

"Don't move your shoulder. That's why your arm is in a sling."

"When can I get out of here?"

"Soon. Very soon." *As soon as I figure out what to do with you.*

"Soon would be appreciated, Doctor," said a new voice.

Avery swiveled to see Captain Sheridan. "Good day, Captain."

She tipped her head. "Good day, Doctor." Her tone was frosty. She had only requested his personal attentions once in the last week. Avery wasn't sure if it was because she was too busy, too stressed, or if his presence simply embarrassed her now that she was acting fleet admiral. With all the higher-ranking officers dead, she had finally realized her dream, at least temporarily.

"How's the Commander?" she asked.

"As well as can be expected. He nearly punctured a lung."

"But his legs are fine. And he's still got one arm."

"She's right, Doctor," Hambry said. "I should be up and out of here."

"One of your sutures could rupture," Avery said.

"Then give him checkups," Sheridan said. "But get him out of here."

Avery sighed. "One more day, if you would."

Sheridan started to say something, but held it back. "Leave me and the Commander for a moment, would you, Doctor."

Hambry occupied a curtained-off corner of the medical bay, and the two had plenty of privacy. Despite that, Avery heard them speak in whispers as he walked away. What could they need to talk about so confidentially? Without really thinking about it, he tried to listen in, but they spoke too softly and soon he was out of earshot.

He busied himself by checking on Patient X. She continued in her coma—that's what it was, he had come to acknowledge—unmoving, unspeaking. Her fever lingered.

Ensign Cashim went into cardiac arrest at eighteen hundred hours. Avery performed emergency open-heart surgery, but the ship suffered a power failure halfway through, plunging the operating room into darkness. Worse, the machines pumping out the ensign's lungs went still. Cashim died with Avery still massaging his heart. Power resumed, but too late for the ensign.

The generators had been failing more often every day. Avery didn't know if the *Maul* was going to make it much further.

Infuriated, needing a drink, he washed himself of Cashim's blood and marched through the medical bay, searching for Commander Hambry, looking for someone to vent on, though he wasn't sure what he would say when he found Hambry. He tore aside the curtains surrounding the X.O.'s cot and stared at Hambry's bed—at empty sheets and a pillow.

Hambry was gone.

"He can't have gone far," Avery told Dr. Murragne, one of his junior doctors.

"Surely you don't mean to go after him," protested Murragne, as Avery walked toward the door.

"That's precisely what I mean to do."

"But, Doctor—"

Avery patted his shoulder. "See to things while I'm away. I won't be long."

Without another word, he left the medical bay.

Where could the commander have gone? Despite Hambry's putting on appearances in front of Sheridan, Avery knew the man must be in considerable pain. Moving about the ship would be agonizing for him. Hells, he could barely breathe. Avery relished the thought of that, of course, but the reason behind Hambry's disappearance worried him. Hambry had killed Paul and Nyers, Avery was certain of it, and now he was acting suspiciously. Avery needed to know why.

He scoured the halls, from the mess to the bunks to the furnace, questioning sailors as he went. Bangs and rattles passed along the snarls of metal pipes overhead as if the ship were sending signals to distant parts of itself, and Avery wished it would let him in on its secrets. One by one the sailors Avery came across shrugged and said they hadn't seen Hambry, until Avery happened upon Lieutenant Second Class Garun, just coming from the third-deck mess.

"Are you sure?" Avery asked him, after Garun had told him what he'd seen.

Garun nodded, his acne-riddled face tight. "Yes, Doctor. He went through the mid-port lock, I swear. He was coming from the officers' quarters."

"That makes no sense. He wouldn't be going *outside.*"

Garun swallowed. "Could be wrong, Doctor. But I remember him leaning against a bulkhead—had half an environment suit on but didn't seem to have the strength to put the other half on. He ordered me to help him. Then he said something peculiar."

"Yes?"

"He said I'd just done the fleet a great service. That make any sense to you, sir?"

"No. It doesn't."

"Probably out of his mind. The Commander was wounded. Blood was seeping on his chest."

"Yes, it would be ..." Hambry must be quite desperate, Avery thought. But desperate to do what?

"I wanted to get him to the medical bay, but he wouldn't hear it, and he *is* the X.O.," Garun went on.

"Thank you, Lieutenant. I'm sure you did all you could."

Avery struggled with himself, then marched to the nearest airlock and donned an environment suit. The suit was heavy, and he could not imagine a man in Hambry's condition putting one on. Even with Garun's assistance, it would have been difficult, not to mention painful to operate. Nothing about this was making any sense.

A question gnawed at Avery, but he tried to dismiss it. Surely Captain Sheridan could have no part of this.

He gulped down a breath, stepped outside and slammed the metal door behind him. As always, the violence of the Atomic Sea shocked him. Sea spray spattered his face-place and he saw the burst of upward-flinging lightning through prisms of droplets. Thunder boomed across the waves, and the *Maul* pitched beneath his feet. The sea was even stormier than usual, and he had to fight to clip his safety line into place. Once locked in, he looked first one way, then the other, searching for a dark bulk limping into the night. Nothing.

Up above, two figures huddled in the crow's nest jutting from the middle chimney stack, braced under their canopy. Stars and smog-like clouds drifted overhead, and a school of frangelets, violet, phosphorescent anemone-like creatures, floated above the waves to port. There was no one on deck, at least that Avery could see.

Which direction had Hambry gone? Avery remembered Paul. And before that, Lt. Nyers. One had been seen falling from aft of amidships, one had died at the stern. Neither had been found forward. Presuming Hambry was about whatever business he'd been about on those two occasions—if it had been him—he would not have gone forward.

Avery squared his shoulders and lurched off toward the stern.

A great wave smashed the hull and broke over the gunwale. It sent him reeling back. Foam sizzled around him. At the last moment he jerked his lifeline and righted himself. Water sloughed between his feet as he stepped over a fish that flopped along the deck. It snapped its mandibles and electricity coursed along its spines.

Breathing the metallic air inside the helmet, Avery moved on, drawing closer and closer to the stern. *What am I doing? I'm not some private eye in a picture show.*

Paul. He thought of Paul and pressed on.

Avery rounded the stern chimney and saw the poop deck. Right where Sgt. Bercka had been killed—*murdered, choked in his own blood*—stood a figure trudging toward the stern gunwale. From the size of the man, to the way he struggled just to walk, Avery knew it could only be Hambry.

Avery drew back into the shadow of the chimney, with the deck pitching and rolling beneath his feet, and pondered what he should do now.

Hambry limped toward the gunwale, awkwardly unbuttoning a pouch in the utility belt around his waist. The movement forced him to move both arms and stretch his shoulders. Here and there he paused, as if sucking in a sharp breath, then continued on. At last he pulled something from the pouch and held it up.

By the light of the moons and the lightning, Avery saw a plastic tube, perhaps a foot long and five inches in diameter. A device on its tip emitted regular bursts of light, right beside what looked like a radio antenna.

With the tube in one hand, Hambry limped toward the gunwale, while his other hand wrapped securely around his lifeline, reeling him in.

Avery didn't know what the tube was, not exactly, but in that moment he was prepared to guess. It was obviously something that floated, something that was meant to be found in the wake of the *Maul*, something which might contain a message. But a message for whom?

There was only one answer.

Avery's mystery patient had been right. It seemed incredible, but the proof was before his eyes. Hambry was a spy, and he was delivering a message to the Octunggen submarines. That was why Paul had died, and why Nyers had died, because they had caught the X.O. in the act.

Hambry neared the gunwale. He moved slowly, his shoulders rising and falling in rhythm to his labored breaths.

Avery, as if in a dream, stepped forward. Amazed at himself, wondering what the hell he thought he was doing, he clambered up the ladder to the poop deck.

Hambry reached the gunwale and braced against it, taking a moment to recover. Water glistened on his huge brass helmet, on the barnacle-like growths there, making him look for a moment like a monstrous toad, silhouetted against the lightning that flickered up from the water. He clutched the message tube in one fist and the gunwale in the other.

He began to raise the fist. Just a simple flick and the tube would spin into the dark sea below, bearing whatever message it contained.

"NO!" Avery shouted.

In one sudden movement, Hambry spun about. He turned with greater dexterity and speed than Avery would have thought possible given his condition, and once more Avery wondered what he was doing out here. Even in Hambry's weakened state, he was still a match for the doctor. More than a match. But there was no one else. If Avery didn't stop him, no one would.

Hambry stared in his direction. There was still time to back out, to run away.

Avery rushed the commander across the deck.

Hambry braced himself.

Avery struck him at full speed and knocked him back against the gunwale. The message tube spun from the commander's fingers, and for an instant it hung in the air, right over the railing.

It struck the gunwale. Bounced. If it bounced one way, it would soar out over the water. If it bounced the other—

It hit the deck and went rolling.

A powerful fist socked Avery in the stomach. As infirm as he was, Hambry still delivered a blow that doubled Avery over and shot the taste of bile into his mouth. As he hunched over, Hambry's knee came up and smashed his face-plate. The blow flung Avery backward, off his feet and onto his back. His air tank drove into his spine. Breath exploded from his mouth.

Avery's head swam, and something buzzed behind his ears. His abdomen ached, his back flared, and his lungs burned where the air had been driven from them.

A powerful force slammed him in the ribs—once, twice, a third time. Hambry was kicking him. The blows were so powerful that Avery's stomach spasmed and he vomited into the helmet.

Gasping, groaning, breathing in the smell of his own stink, he flopped about on deck not unlike the fish he'd stepped over minutes ago.

In the distance, he heard—perhaps felt—footsteps retreating, and along with them the sound of Hambry cursing.

Through puke-streaked glass, Avery saw Hambry striding back and forth over the deck, searching for the message tube. At last it rolled from its position half-concealed by a lifeline-fastening station. Its lighted tip blinked in the darkness.

Hambry lurched toward it.

Avery forced himself to all fours and climbed to his feet. The world tilted around him.

Hambry bent over to pick up the tube.

Avery stood very close to where Hambry's lifeline passed. Holding his breath, he grabbed it with both hands—and *pulled*.

Hambry made a comical choking sound as he toppled backward. Avery wanted to let out a whoop of victory, but then he saw the tube clutched firmly in Hambry's fist.

The commander rocked back and forth, trying to right himself turtle-fashion. Avery staggered over to him. The deck pitched up suddenly, and Avery wavered but kept his footing.

Hambry found his knees. Started to rise.

With one clean, economic strike, Avery punched Hambry in his upper chest. Right over the surgical incision.

Hambry howled in agony and fell back. He managed to prop himself up with his left hand. Avery stepped forward and punched the spot again. Hambry screamed. Avery grinned, surprised at the bloodlust that welled up in him.

With an animal growl, Hambry launched himself to his feet and barreled into the doctor. By a burst of wave-to-wave lightning, Avery saw a glimpse of his face. Hambry was half-mad with pain and desperation, his veins protruding, his eyes bloodshot and bulged-out, his lips pulled back from large, strong white teeth. In a fury, he drove Avery back and back, slamming him with punches as he went. If Avery had had anything left in his stomach, he would have retched again. Every punch cost Hambry, and by the time they crashed up against the gunwale, he was all but spent.

Avery tried to strike the X.O.'s shoulder again, but Hambry's left hand grabbed his wrist, shoving his right arm up and back.

Hambry hit at Avery with the tube, but Avery grabbed his wrist. Pressed against the gunwale, they struggled against each other. To starboard, lightning flashed up from the sea.

"Why?" Hambry said. "Why won't ... you just ... let me ... *be*?"

"You're a traitor! Murderer!"

"You have ... no idea ... what we're trying to do," Hambry wheezed. It was a small slip, and Avery barely noticed it at the time. "... trying to ... save us all."

Hambry brought his knee up, hard and fast. It slammed right into Avery's crotch. Avery's grip loosened, just enough.

Hambry tore his right hand free. His arm went back, cocked, ready to launch. With one final burst of strength, he shoved Avery aside and—

—threw.

The tube sailed up and out, out over the glimmering waves.

"No!" Avery said. What had Hambry just done? What had that message contained? If it relayed the coordinates of the *Maul*, its bearing, or the strength of the convoy ahead—

Anger filled him.

He wheeled on Hambry, who slouched against the gunwale, breathing in shuddering, pain-filled breaths, and grabbed him by the seat of his suit and by the top of his tank. In a rage, he strained as hard as he could, tipping the Commander over the side. Surprised, Hambry flailed and cursed.

At the last second, as Hambry teetered on the gunwale, Avery wondered how it had come to this, how he, a man who'd devoted his whole life to the aid of others, had come to the brink of murder, and he hesitated.

Then he thought of Paul, of Nyers, of the Octunggen submarines just waiting for Hambry's message, and he shoved.

With grim satisfaction, he shoved, and Hambry fell.

With speed he didn't even know he had, Avery reached out and unclipped the commander's lifeline, and just in time. The line whipped up and away, whirling above Hambry as he plummeted, its clip nearly striking Avery in the faceplate.

Far below, Hambry dwindled against the sea. At last he hit the waves and vanished from sight.

Panting, Avery stared down at the white mark in the dark water where the Commander had gone. He imagined Hambry plunging down, screaming into the helm which dragged him like an anchor, until at last the pressure of the sea burst the faceplate and shattered glass sprayed his eyes. Water would fill his mouth and lungs, and he would drown, just like Paul had drowned. Panic and fear would grip him, then coldness and darkness, and then nothing.

Waves of satisfaction swept through Avery. Then his fingers started to tremble. Next his legs. Soon he found himself shaking all over. He sank to his knees and dry-heaved into his helm.

Some time later, Avery didn't know how long, the hourly patrol found him. As fate would have it, it was Privates Barris and Wathin, the same pair who had found Paul's body, who came upon him.

"Why're you out here, Doctor?" said Barris.

Avery, still sitting propped up against the gunwale, wanted to tell the men the truth, but paused. The fact was that he had killed a man, and there was no evidence Avery knew of to prove that Hambry had been a spy or murderer. The only such evidence, the tube, was lost to the sea.

"I tried to stop him," Avery said. "I tried ..."

"Stop who, sir?"

"Hambry. I went out looking for him after he disappeared. Someone told me he'd come outside, and so ... but I was too late. He fell before I could stop him."

Wathin crouched down next to him. The young man wore a look of perplexity and horror, but not suspicion. "The X.O. ... *fell?*"

Avery couldn't meet his eyes. "Yes," he said. "He leaned out over the gunwale—he didn't have a safety line attached—lost his footing and went over." Everyone knew such a thing was a death sentence. "Gods know what he was doing out here."

"Come on, Doctor," Barris said. "Let's get you indoors. It's a nasty night."

It was only then, as the two privates helped him inside, that Avery remembered the last thing Hambry had said to him. Hambry had used the word *we*. If Avery had understood him correctly, there was another spy aboard the *Maul*.

Chapter 4

The sun shone bright overhead, turning the fog a dazzling white. It gleamed dully off the huge ships that loomed in all directions. Sailors, only half visible in the white-gray roils, stood on their decks staring across at the *Maul* and its sisters, some waving, some calling out. The remains of the whaling fleet had just reached the supply convoy, and jubilation rang from ship to ship.

The convoy cruised east, toward Ghenisa. Sheridan had led the *Maul* and its two surviving sisters through the place where the Octunggen blockade was supposed to have been, but there had been no sign of the enemy. Many speculated that they had broken up due to the proximity of the convoy, frightened off like birds at the approach of a dog, just as Sheridan had said they would.

Avery knew differently.

It had been three days since he'd killed Commander Hambry. He'd thought his sense of guilt would have faded by now, but instead it seemed to increase every day, so much that he hadn't even partaken of the last cigar Paul had given him. He'd thought avenging the sergeant would bring about some sense of closure, but instead he felt worse, plagued by nightmares. He kept seeing the commander, hearing his voice. Sometimes he feared he was going mad. He'd begun drinking even more heavily. He didn't know what else to do. Alcohol seemed to be the only thing keeping his mind dull enough to stay sane, and it was certainly his only recourse to sleep.

If only Hambry hadn't actually done what he'd claimed.

If only he hadn't saved them all.

Staring up at the ships of the convoy, some of which were much larger than the *Maul*, Avery tried for the thousandth time to tell himself it was a coincidence. But for the thousandth time he knew better. Hambry had indeed been a spy, and he had indeed delivered a message to the Octunggen, but, inexplicably, that message had been to spare the *Maul* and the whaling fleet. It was the only explanation for the sudden break-up of the Octunggen blockade. It made no sense, but there it was.

Wind stirred over the deck, unexpectedly strong, and Avery leaned against it. He longed to feel the touch of naked sunlight on his skin, to feel the wind through what remained of his hair, but it would have to wait. He fidgeted with his gloves, tugging at the fingers as he mulled things over.

Who can the other spy be? He eyed the sailors around him. There was Maslyn, the slim, swarthy whaler with the tattoo of a dragon coiling around his neck, invisible under the suit. There was Lt. Bithelhaut, handsome but always ill at ease. Or maybe it was Second Lieutenant Sulley, the plain, freckled young woman with the too-bright eyes.

And then there was Sheridan.

Around Avery the men and women of the *Maul* hallooed the ships of the convoy, who offered them protection and safe passage to Ghenisa. It would take another three weeks to reach home, allowing for the brief stop along the way at Es'hem, an island nation that was said to be beautiful and was one of the last vestiges of the Imperial Republic of L'oh. Avery, a lover of history and in particular of L'oh, pictured Es'hem with magnificent towers and white marble domes. He looked forward to shore leave.

A large hand clapped him on the shoulder. Coughing, he stared up into the face-plate of Janx, and the nose-less whaler grinned down at him.

"You've looked better," Janx said.

"I've felt better. I ... miss fresh air."

Janx inclined his head. "Took me awhile to get used to it, too, years ago. Now if I breathe in and the air don't taste of metal, I get anxious."

It was hard to imagine the big man anxious. The picture amused Avery. "So you wouldn't be looking forward to land, then."

"I'd be happier if we still had a whale."

"Perhaps now that we're safe ..."

Janx shook his head. "The *Maul*'s in no condition to hunt, and this bunch o' ships'd just scare off the levvies. Ain't why I stopped by."

Avery raised an eyebrow. "No?"

"Me and some'a the boys're havin' another game'a cards tonight, now things're lookin' up a bit."

"Is that why there have been no games recently? I'd begun to think I wasn't invited."

Janx barked a laugh. "Games were canceled because everyone thought they were 'bout to fuckin' die, Doc. Bets got kinda hinky. After Bonner bet his peg and then Mare and Hath had to haul his ass around till Strop gave it back ... well, we had to re-think the whole thing."

"But it's back on."

"It's back on."

"I'll see you there," Avery said.

Janx gave a hard grin. "Bring your money, Doc. I'm feelin' lucky tonight, and your bluffs ain't gonna stop me this time." Whistling, Janx turned about and strode off, likely to recruit more suckers for the game.

Strangely, the idea of poker put a jounce in Avery's step, and he was tempted to whistle himself as he continued his walk around the deck. The surface heaved gently, and even the Atomic Sea seemed mellow. Only the occasional burst of lightning flared up from the waves, and some winged clam-things skimmed the sea to port, their wing-flaps sounding wet and meaty and rapid, *wack-wack-wack*. A haze hung over the water through which the many ships drifted like vast ghosts. The calling of the men and the slap of the waves on hulls sounded muted and eerie, lending even this joyous day a repellent quality.

Nevertheless, Avery felt of lighter heart when the *Maul* drew abreast to the flagship of the convoy, the *GS Indomitable*. Boarding ramps were thrown across and Avery watched from afar as Sheridan and half a dozen of her surviving officers, to the blare of distant fanfare, marched onto the *Indomitable* to meet its captain, Admiral Jons. Avery wished their meeting well. As he passed, he could see the lowered heads and shuffling gaits of the Maulers as they gazed upon the shining, intact ships of the convoy. To be aboard the beaten wreck of the *Maul* and the others would be humbling and humiliating to career sailors. Avery felt no such humility, however, only relief. At long last, they were safe.

Tired and sweaty, he retreated indoors. It had seemed like a good idea to take a walk outside and enjoy the sights of the convoy, but wearing the suit had tired him out too soon, and he was hot and stank like metal, canvas, and other men's sweat as he trudged toward the medical bay. He took a quick shower in the patients' washing area, then donned fresh garb and performed a round of check-ups.

Patient X was stable if slightly feverish, but still unconscious. Frustration mounted in Avery. If she were really on a mission to stop Octung, whatever that meant, Avery could not risk it by telling anyone about her—she'd been right about that—yet if she remained asleep she would be cut open by Navy scientists. If Avery couldn't rouse her before they reached the mainland ...

Bootsteps thundered outside the bay. The wheel spun, and the door flew open, framing Captain Sheridan and a crowd of officers.

"Captain, I didn't expect—"

Ignoring Avery, she stepped inside. Behind her followed several of her company. One particularly tall old man boasted a short silver beard and a tanned, leathery face. Hooded eyes stared out of that mask of leather.

"Admiral Jons, meet our chief surgeon, Dr. Francis Avery. Dr. Avery, Fleet Admiral Jons."

Avery straightened. Jons peered at him shortly, but his eyes—which were, as the shadows shifted, revealed as a startling blue—quickly roved to the woman on the table. Her looks seemed to have increased with her health. Blond hair pillowed her head, and her full lips continued to expel deep, even breaths.

With practiced ease, the Admiral grabbed the clipboard at the base of the bed and scanned through it. "Amazing," he said. "It's just as you described, Captain. And you think she could be an asset?"

"Yes, Admiral," Sheridan said. "With her remarkable abilities, frankly she shouldn't exist. She's clearly braindead, or close enough that it doesn't matter. However, I fully expect that when she can be transported to our main lab at Fort Brunt that the doctors there will be able to solve her mysteries."

Jons rubbed his chin. "Yes. If we could achieve immunity from the Sea ..."

Avery cleared his throat. "She's not braindead, Captain, Admiral. I've, ah, witnessed her dream. She will toss and turn. Mutter things in her sleep."

Jons raised his eyebrows. "In what language does she mutter?"

"I don't know. She mumbles too low for me to hear."

"She must be examined," Jons said. "If the doctors at Brunt find it necessary to dissect her, then she will be. Either way we must have whatever abilities she does. The Octunggen wish to drive us into the sea, Doctor. If we were able to *survive the journey* ..." He turned to Sheridan. "You did well bringing this woman to my attention. All and all, you've handled your stint as admiral skillfully. Sacrificing that whale was a big risk, and powering through the blockade took balls."

"Thank you, Admiral."

"I think it may be possible to make your promotion permanent."

He swept from the room, taking his retainers with him. A very pleased Sheridan paused beside Avery.

"Don't chastise me, Doctor. I do what I must."

"But, Captain—"

"Join me tonight. I'm hosting a skeet shoot. The captains of several ships are coming aboard to celebrate—my way of thanking the convoy."

"And you want me there? Why, in case someone's shot?"

She laughed, then followed the Admiral, leaving Avery staring after her. With a sigh, he turned back to the woman from the sea.

"Wake up soon," he said.

"I haven't seen so much loot since my thievin' days," Janx said. Grinning around his cigar, he dragged in his gleaming winnings from the middle of the table. A haze of smoke hung overhead. Sheep-oil candles stuck out from candelabras on the walls, contributing their slightly musky odor to the proceedings. Whitish wax pooled in the brass bases and spilled over, hardening as they did and creating little stalactites. The candlelight threw slow shadows across the walls.

"When were you a thief?" asked Avery.

There was a chorus of groans from the others.

"Don't get him started," said Sydney, who was shuffling the cards with his seven remaining fingers and doing a better job of it than Avery could with his ten.

"He'll be tellin' lies all night if you let him," agreed Salussa, the only female whaler aboard. Nearly as large as Janx, she was big-boned and blunt-featured, but her eyes shone with intelligence. A ragged scar ran from the right corner of her mouth to her ear, and she was so proud of it that she had decorated it with a line of gold piercings that glittered in the candlelight.

Ignoring the others, Janx said, "What, Doc, ya thought I was born a-ship?"

Avery shrugged. Smiled. "More or less."

"Ha! I had a life, shit, maybe a dozen lives, afore I come a-courtin' the sea. I was a sacker, a fighter, a pimp, a bodyguard, a smuggler—"

"I told you," muttered Salussa.

"—and yeah, a thief," finished Janx, shooting her a glare. "An' some other things mixed in. But it was thievin' what brought me to the sea. Oh, I remember it well. I'd just stolen the treasure of Lord Baracus of Helinmnot—"

Salussa sighed.

"—when I met the beautiful Lady Clara. How was I to know she was the Lord's daughter?"

Avery half-smiled as he listened. He figured he could do with some entertainment.

"Well, after scrapin' the walrus for the tenth or eleventh times, I forget, she betrays me, steals back the treasure, and leaves me tied to the bed for her assassins to kill. Well, naturally, I break free, kill them all, and this is me naked and with me bare hands, mind. I actually used one poor bastard's guts as a whip, and—" At Salussa's scowl, Janx cleared his throat. "Well, I escape out the window and steal the lady's suit and yacht—this was at her winter palace, y'know, an island—then sail away into the night, clean as a ten-dollar whore. I saw Clara on the docks, cryin' because I was still alive and cryin' to see me go." He grinned broadly, showing three silver teeth and one gold.

Avery eyed his cards as Sydney passed them around. "There are no lords anymore, Janx. Not for fifty years. Not since the Revolution."

"He's got you, Janx," Salussa laughed.

Janx grunted. "This wasn't Ghenisa. This was in the Ysstrals."

"Bullshit. Since when did you speak Ysstran?"

Janx replied nonchalantly as he anted up. "*A mazen ed cun bizt.*"

Avery, who spoke a smattering of Ysstran, was impressed. And mildly offended.

Salussa's eyes narrowed. "You better be lucky I don't know what that means, you son of a bitch."

"Probably for the best," Avery agreed.

Janx gave a lazy smile, then shifted his gaze to his cards.

"A fivepenny," Millen said, throwing in his bet.

"Match," said Cudreq, throwing his coin in.

"Match," Avery said. "And up another five."

"Anyway, so the Count puts out a bounty on me head," Janx said, tossing out a coin. "Tweren't safe for me in the whole Empire, so I lit out, joined a merchant vessel, hopped ship in the Jade Isles, joined a mercenary fleet and, well, one thing led to another ..."

"Don't give us your pirate crap again," Salussa said.

"What can I say, I was a restless youth." The betting continued, as did Janx. In time, he said, "Anyway, my days as a pirate captain came to an end when Segrul the Gray took over the fleet. He was a mutie, y'know, and he started purgin' the fleet o' true-bloods. Wanted to create a mutant navy, scour the seas. He'd slit men's throats and perform weird rituals at night when only one moon was high. Said there were things in the deep, things what he worshipped. Once I saw him row a boat out, all alone, some distance away, and this weird, white thing, maybe some great albino squid, I dunno, come right under him. They stayed that way fer hours, those white tentacles flailin' around the boat, Segrul with his hand on the kraken's huge head. Well, I figured twas time to look fer a safer gig."

"So you chose whaling," Avery said. "Sensible."

Janx shook his head. "No, that came later. See, for a while I was king of the Othric Islands. Oh, it's a great story. Lissen well ..."

Janx rambled on, and the night grew blacker outside the portholes. The candles burned low, and so did Avery's cash. Janx hadn't been lying. He'd been feeling lucky. Finally Avery stood and said, "That's it for me, lads. I know when to quit. Sadly, I should have quit then."

Some chuckling.

"Ya can't go," said Janx. "I was just gettin' to the good part. After getting bombed out of me castle and havin' to flee the Othrics, the Ysstrals right on my heels, me and Count Baracus, we got swallowed by the same whale, see, a monster he was ..."

Avery grinned tiredly. "I'll have to hear it some other time." Besides, he had an appointment with the captain to keep.

He returned to his suite, donned his official clothes—not that anyone would be able to see them—then ventured to an airlock and pulled on an environment suit. The Atomic Sea roiled and heaved as he stepped outside, and the skeet shoot had already begun. A dozen captains and their retainers had gathered on the bow, and one at a time the captains fired at skeet launched overhead. Avery arrived to find Sheridan flushed and smiling. Perhaps the officers had had a few drinks before the shoot.

"Doctor!" she said. "What took you so long?"

"I had things to do," he said. "I'm a busy man."

That amused her. She turned as a chuckling captain, who shook his head ruefully at his poor marksmanship, marched up to her and held out a shotgun.

"May you have better luck than me," he said.

"We'll see. It's been a windy night."

She stepped to the gunwale, where the captains cleared a space for her. The deck pitched gently underfoot, and lightning flickered up from the sea to the stern. The skeet was launched, and Sheridan's gun cracked once, twice, then she reached for a fresh gun and fired again. Shattered pieces of skeet sailed over the sea, and the captains clapped their hands and whistled. Several patted Sheridan on the back.

"I got lucky," she said, and Avery was surprised at her graciousness.

After handing over the shotgun to the next captain, she stepped back beside Avery and looked at him with unexpected warmth.

"You seem in an awfully good mood," he commented.

"Why shouldn't I be? We're safe and Admiral Jons is talking about promoting me."

He took a breath and asked the question that he'd been dreading: "Any news on the war?" He hadn't heard anything since the beginning of the submarine gauntlet and was starved for news.

She seemed reluctant. "Some. I have it fresh from the Admiral. Are you sure you want to hear?"

"Tell me."

"Octung has taken Heigelmas."

He swore. Heigelmas was a large nation of craggy hills somewhat to the southwest of Ghenisa, once famous for the poet shepherds that roamed its slopes. Now it was an industrial country of brick houses and cobbled streets.

"You've been?" she asked, reading his reaction.

"When I was younger." He waited for the crack of a shotgun before continuing. "Mari and I backpacked through it a few times. Beautiful. Great big slopes, steep and rocky. Lots of sheep, of course. The shepherds were sort of a disappointment. There was this one that liked to dance and play a pipe, and he dressed up in the traditional clothes you see in the picture books and overcharged for photos. For a while Mari and I corresponded with friends we met there." Another shotgun crack, and he pitched his voice to say, "I think she still did, right up until the end. I ... I wonder if any survived the invasion ... the purgings."

"There's more news. You might find this more agreeable. The Black Sect just assassinated another Collossum priest last week, right in Lusterqal."

He smiled at the thought of rebellion in the capital of Octung. "I wonder who they are, the Black Sect."

"You and everyone else."

"Some say they're blasphemers or heretics against the Collossum."

"They're saboteurs, anyway. And apparently assassins."

"Any enemy of Octung is a friend of ours, I suppose, even if they're other Octunggen," he said.

The skeet shoot went on, and Avery allowed himself to enjoy it. He especially enjoyed a more festive Sheridan. He rarely got to see her like this.

In time, they returned to her cabin, and to his surprise she pounced on him as soon as he closed the door. She kissed him frantically on the neck and began tearing off his shirt almost before it shut. Without speaking, she flung him down on the bed and climbed astride him. He'd never seen her so energetic or ... well, *passionate*. She sweated and cursed as she ground her hips against his, and as she whipped her head her short sweaty hair streamed out to catch the light. She was so impassioned that for a moment he entertained the hope that she would let him finish inside her. But no. After she flung herself off him she handed him the customary towel.

Not long after that she dismissed him. Buttoning his torn shirt as he made his way through the officer's quarters, his gaze strayed to a certain locked door. *Hambry's chambers.*

The officer's main room was dark and quiet, but Lt. Hinis threw darts at a board with her one remaining arm, her left, cursing as she did. She was evidently trying to relearn basic coordination.

"Excuse me, Lieutenant, but could you tell me who occupies Commander Hambry's quarters now?" Avery asked.

She threw one more dart and grimaced. "No one's there, Doc," she said. "Cap'n's orders are to leave it be, and what with half the officers dead there's no one needs it anyway."

"And yet she specifically requested it be left alone?"

Hinis nodded, bored. She crossed to the dart board and jerked out her widely-scattered projectiles one by one.

"That seems odd to me," Avery said. "Almost ... sentimental."

Hinis chuckled. "The Captain's about as sentimental as a boot."

"That's what worries me."

Hinis wasn't worried. She offered him half the darts. "Wanna game?"

"Maybe later."

Frowning, Avery departed the officers' quarters. His mind flashed back to that fateful day, remembering how Hambry had only ventured outside after his conversation with the captain. *It can't be*, Avery thought. Sheridan was as loyal as they came. If anything, she was *too* loyal. Hambry had been acting on his own, it must be. It must.

And yet ...

Three days passed, and repair work progressed round-the-clock on the *Maul* and her sisters so that they wouldn't slow the convoy down. On the third day, Sheridan came to Avery, this time while he was taking a walk on deck, surveying the work being done.

"Join me tonight," she said.

"So soon?" He allowed a hint of self-satisfaction to enter his voice.

She only smiled and continued down the deck, leaving him with the sea. Her insatiability puzzled him. She rarely requested two trysts in so short a time. Of course, it did make sense if—

"Damn," he said.

He descended into the whalers' quarters, which stank and were strewn with filthy clothes, beer bottles and various debris.

"Where's Janx?" he asked Corlus.

Corlus, the oldest whaler aboard at fifty-five, was grooming his long silver beard with a crusty whalebone comb. He flicked his head to a certain door. "In 'is cabin. But I wouldn't advise goin' in."

Avery banged on the door. No one answered. He kept banging. At last the door cracked, and a sweaty and red-faced Salussa glared at him.

"Yeah, what?" Sweat dripped from the gold rings that decorated her cheek-scar.

Avery blinked. "I didn't expect to see you here. Hells, I didn't think you even *liked* Janx."

"Who says I do? But he's got the biggest—"

"Who is it, Sal?" barked someone from deeper in the cabin.

"See for yourself." A naked Salussa opened the door wider, affording Avery an all-too-complete view of her. She was solidly packed, with meaty arms and tight pectorals. Her waist was like a tree-trunk, but with more scars. A white scar bisected her right nipple. Tattoos swirled around her navel.

Over her shoulder Avery could see an equally naked Janx lumbering into view. He was even more muscled, scarred and tattooed than Salussa, and he did not look pleased to see Avery.

"What is it, Doc?"

Avery looked from Salussa to Janx, then back. "Madam, I would like to speak with Janx alone."

She opened her mouth. "How dare you—"

"It'll only be for a moment."

"You gonna let him get away with this?" she asked Janx.

Janx shifted his glower from her to Avery. "What the hell ya think you're doin', Doc? We were kinda in the middle of somethin'."

"Again, it will only take a moment." Pushing past Salussa, Avery stepped into the cabin to give his words more weight. "Ship's business, I'm afraid."

Fuming, Salussa gathered her clothes. "Don't ever think of callin' me again, you son of a bitch," she called over her shoulder. She slammed the door behind her with such force that Avery jumped.

He turned to Janx. "I am sorry—"

Janx laughed. "You did me a favor, Doc."

Avery tried not to look at Janx's member as the huge whaler turned about and meandered to his tangled bed. The cabin stank of sweat, filthy laundry, alcohol and illegal chemicals. "How so?" Avery asked, not sure he wanted to know.

Janx found some drawers and pulled them on, for which Avery was grateful. "If I'd-a finished her off, I'd never gotten ridda her."

Avery nodded sagely. "It was all I could do."

Janx's good humor dropped as soon as he turned about. "This had better be good, Doc."

Avery tugged at his mustache absently. For a moment he pondered how to phrase what he needed to say.

Janx collapsed on the bed, located a bottle and commenced drinking. "Go on," he said, punctuating the command with a burp. "Spit it out or get out. If I hurry, I can still flail the whale before it sounds, if'n ya get me meaning."

Avery forced himself to smile. "Yes. Now. Um. Is any of what you said the other night true? Even the littlest bit?"

Janx smiled broadly. "Every word of it, Doc. I'd stake me life on it."

"Be that as it may. Do you actually have any experience ... burgling?"

"What, thievin'? Sure as shit. I stole more loot from more lords than the government."

Avery sighed. "Good. Because I need you to teach me how to pick a lock."

Gasping, Captain Sheridan flopped back on the bed. A lazy smile stretched across her face. "I'm impressed," she said. "All those walks must really be doing you some good."

Avery knew his energy had little to do with exercise. It was fear that drove him. Fear at what he would find in Commander Hambry's cabin. Fear at getting caught.

For once she did not rise for her customary glass of post-coital whiskey, and despite himself Avery felt a flush of pride. A moment of silence passed, and the ship creaked and settled around them. The crimson lights that issued from the fluid of the alchemical lantern swayed slowly, making the cabin seem as though it were plunged underwater in some hellish otherworld.

"You know," Sheridan said, speaking thoughtfully, "if I were made Admiral ... I *could* promote you. You would not be a simple ship's doctor but the medical officer for an entire fleet."

That caught him by surprise. "We would be on the flagship together."

She raised her eyebrows. "Is that not agreeable to you?"

"No. Captain. Certainly, it is. It just caught me off-guard. I did not think you and I ..."

She laughed. "Don't take it the wrong way, Doctor."

"Yes. Of course." The thought of being the captain's pet lover disgusted Avery, or at least part of him. Still, there was another part that was warmed by the intention behind her words, or what he supposed was behind them. Might the captain not be a touch sentimental after all?

She rose from the bed and strode, naked and shining with sweat, to the bar. Unasked, he joined her there, and they shared a drink in silence. The silence became awkward. And yet she didn't draw away from him. He could almost imagine there was some sort of connection between them, a connection beyond the physical.

He knew the second drink was his invitation to leave, but she didn't suggest his withdrawal.

The whiskey still burning his throat, he dressed slowly, and she watched him with an unreadable expression. "You know, Doctor, things will be different when we reach home. As an admiral, I'll be expected to operate with a certain amount of discretion."

"I understand."

"But that doesn't mean I won't see you. Until I'm given a ship, it's possible I could get you assigned to the care of your mermaid, or at least appointed to the committee tasked with studying her."

He had been lacing his shoes. Now he stopped in mid-lace. "I would like that."

"Of course," she went on, fetching a half-smoked cigar and lighting up, "that would mean you need to be open to studying her ... in whatever manner necessary."

His chest felt tight. "Yes," he managed. "I understand."

"Good," she said. "Think about that as you go."

That was his dismissal. Half chagrined, half relieved at the captain's return to form, he finished dressing and left her cabin. He turned one last time before he did. He saw Sheridan lit by lantern-light, naked and gleaming, cigar clenched in her jaws, grab a fencing sword from the wall and slice it experimentally through the air, surely as a prelude to practice. The *swish-swish* of the sword reached his ears, and the door slammed shut.

Feeling strange—about the captain, about everything— Avery moved through the darkness of the officers' quarters blindly, stumbling as he went. Alchemical lanterns lit the gloom, but he had always found that alchemical lamps did not spread light normally. Their sort of light burned brightly but in a contained sphere, as if hoarding the light against the darkness. The lanterns burned in different colors—red, green, blue—creating different pockets of illumination. This late at night, with the rocking of the ship beneath his feet and with no one else about, it felt to Avery that he moved through a different world. A deserted ship, perhaps, or one of Janx's ghost ships.

Bumping his shins and stubbing his toes, he found the door to Hambry's cabin. He removed the two picks Janx had given him—the whaler said he never went anywhere without them—and knelt before the lock.

Janx had told him that this sort of lock, a simple cabin keyhole, was among the easiest in the world to open, and yet Avery fumbled and fumbled with it, scraping the lock so that it squealed, which sent shudders down his spine, dropping a pick, until at last, miraculously, as if delivered by one of the kraken-gods of the deep, the door swung open.

Avery wiped sweat from his brow, took a steadying breath, stood, his knees creaking, and entered the darkness that had been Hambry's living quarters.

He located a lantern and lit it. Purplish light flooded out, lazily probing at the dark corners of the cabin.

Avery didn't know what he was looking for exactly, so he looked through everything. Going as quietly as he could, he tossed the bed, searched the insides of the mattress, tore through the cabinets, checked the bottoms of drawers, hunted for secret compartments to chests.

Nothing.

"Shit." His heart beat fast. He had to hurry. At any moment some officer wandering to the head would see light beneath Hambry's door, and that could only end badly.

He checked behind paintings, checked under the rug, peeled off the labels from the two wine bottles to eye the backs of them. Nothing.

What was he looking for?

Some connection, he reminded himself, some concrete connection between Hambry and Sheridan, something that would prove they were both traitors and spies, something that would prove Sheridan had dispatched Hambry to deliver the floating message-in-a-tube to the black waters of the Atomic Sea, there to be scooped up by Octunggen mariners and deciphered. It was the only explanation. If Hambry was a spy, then Sheridan must be, too. Hambry would not have ventured out onto the raging deck in his condition, not unless he'd been ordered to by a captain whose presence would be too obvious, would be remarked upon. She could not do it herself, so she needed him to. That's why she had come to Hambry in the medical bay, why she had whispered urgently to him in the privacy of their corner. They were traitors. They had to be. Spies for Octung.

And, in the unlikely event that Avery was wrong, something he actually hoped for, there could be evidence linking Hambry with someone besides the captain, exonerating Sheridan and implicating the true traitor. Either way, somewhere in this cabin there must be files, tubes, decryption keys, incriminating evidence of some sort ... *something*.

There was nothing. Avery looked everywhere he could think of, but Hambry, or Sheridan, had been too careful.

Frustrated, Avery made his way to the sink and splashed water on his face. He had to get out of here. He'd been in Hambry's cabin too long. And even if he'd found evidence, who could he tell? Surely Sheridan, or whoever the traitor was, would dispose of it before they reached land ... and dispose of him along with it.

Just as he started to leave, his eyes fell on something, and he let out a startled breath.

A wave of disappointment took him, along with something else. Fingers shaking, he reached through the thick purple light and picked up the small box that rested in its mounting, in plain sight, in a place of honor, on Hambry's sink, where his gaze would fall on it every day and remind him of his place.

Avery blinked sweat out of his eyes and opened the box. And there, lying on black velvet, just as he'd known it would be, was the connection he was looking for, if not the proof, and the explanation why Sheridan had called on him more than usual since Hambry's death.

It was an empty shotgun cartridge, the sort Sheridan kept as mementos of her skeet competitions, and the sort of thing, evidently, that she gifted to lovers.

Avery cursed. It was true. Sheridan was a spy. There was no reason for her and Hambry to keep their affair secret. It was well known that Sheridan had numerous lovers, and nothing was considered amiss about that. No one would have lifted an eyebrow had their affair been known. No, the only reason Avery could think of for the deception was that if people didn't know, they wouldn't associate the two together in any way other than professional. Such secrecy could only mean Sheridan didn't want to draw attention to their affair, and that meant she and Hambry had something to hide.

Damn you, Jessryl. Why? How did they turn you?

Sweating, certain now, he renewed his search. There must be something, Hambry had to have missed something. If Avery didn't find proof, Sheridan would continue—

He found it in Hambry's shoes. The Commander's small shoe rack contained a pair of dress shoes, and Avery, noticing a weight difference between the two, inspected them carefully, then used one of the Commander's knives to pry the soles open, revealing hidden compartments in both.

Tightly-folded letters crammed the spaces, stained by age and time and water that had leaked in through the cracks. Quickly Avery scanned the letters, seeing loose, neat handwriting, snatching a purple phrase here and there—*It has been too long, my dearest*—*Why must we keep this fire between us in the shadows?*—and finally settled on one. Breathless, he read, surprised at Hambry's gushing pen: *My dear Jessryl, I know you said to write nothing down, but I cannot keep this inside me any longer. I must get it out or burst. I pray you will forgive me. Trust that I will make sure it is never discovered. Yet this thing we do, this mission, this holy quest, it fires my mind and body. It is the aether on which I thrive, on which I live, just like your kisses and your hot breaths on my neck. When you told me of my divine blood, how I was pure and must cleave to the old ways, the old gods, I felt struck by lightning, like I had been blind from birth till that one shining day. Now I live only to prove the worthiness of my blood, our blood, and to give glory to the Collossum.*

Avery stared, and his hands shook.

Blinking sweat out of his eyes, he folded the papers and replaced them in the hidden compartments. He felt both elated and crushed. It was true. Captain Jessryl Sheridan was a traitor. He wanted to vomit.

What should he do now? He couldn't risk taking the letters back to his cabin, where someone might find them. And what if they were found by someone loyal to Sheridan? If she had one agent on the *Maul*, she might have others. Also, he couldn't stash them in some obscure location around the ship for the same reason, as well as for the reasons that they might be ruined by weather or nested in by some creature.

With a groan, he realized what he would have to do. He would have to leave the letters here. Of course, if he did that there was the possibility Sheridan would discover and remove them, but he supposed it was a risk he would have to take. Once on land, he would have the authorities here instantly, and Sheridan's charade would be over.

Distant gunfire jerked Avery from bed—loud, forceful and heavy. The guns of warships.

Battle.

Feeling his skin draw tight across his body, Avery slipped on his clothes and picked his way toward the medical bay. Sailors jostled all around him, frantic and pale. He reached the med bay and ordered it prepped for use.

"Situation," he said. "How many are attacking?"

Dr. Fallon looked grim. "You haven't heard? We've reached Es'hem."

Avery blinked. "Es'hem? Then why ... no, don't tell me ..."

"Yes. The Octunggen arrived first."

Avery swore. "Finish prepping. I'm going to see what's happening on deck."

He pressed through the packed halls, found an environment suit and shrugged it on, side by side with dozens of sailors doing the same, helping each other shove helmets down and zip up seams. Their faces were set, their mouths hard, and they moved with speed and efficiency. With them, Avery emerged onto the deck. The night flung rain down from a cloud-covered sky, and great electric tongues licked at each other, some from above, some from below. The sound of heavy gunfire rolled across the water, but it had to compete with the constant thunder, and there were times when Avery couldn't tell which was which.

Short of breath, he latched his lifeline into place, then leaned over the gunwale, straining his eyes to make out the shifting forms in the darkness and rain. The convoy's warships loomed all around him, pitching up and down on the waves. They had formed a perimeter with their starboards facing west. The massive guns pointed into the night, and through the rain and wind and lightning Avery couldn't tell what they fired at. But then he realized that many of the bright flashes he saw in the distance were not caused by lightning or exploding gas but came instead from enemy warships.

The bright flashes seemed to stretch forever, in both directions.

Dear gods. What had to be over a hundred Octunggen warships spat flame and smoke at the Ghenisan convoy. The deck of one of the ships near Avery exploded, the fire startlingly bright and close. Something else exploded belowdecks. Fire mushroomed out, and flaming sailors leapt overboard to thrash amid fiery pools that glimmered on the water. Firefighting teams poured up from the inner decks, hosing down the flames. Other ships, all up and down the line, were similarly bombarded.

The Octunggen did not fight with normal weapons alone, though. A single shell struck a ship to Avery's right—and the ship began to dissolve. It wilted in the middle as though its steel had turned to gel. *An Octunggen acid-bomb.* Avery had never seen one put to use, only heard about them, and the sight made him ill. The ship's middle melted, turning into a gray glue-like substance, which spread and spread, encountering sailors as it went, all of whom screamed in horror as the substance ate through their suits and gnawed away their flesh and bones. They didn't even survive long enough to pitch themselves overboard. The middle of the ship simply bowed down—and down—until finally it sank below the water. By that time the acid had spread to both ends, and they collapsed into the sea, as well.

A blue beam of light fell on a ship to port. It disappeared completely, then reappeared an instant later, but when it rematerialized it appeared to be made of glass and all hands aboard with it. When the next wave smashed against it, the whole thing shattered into a million pieces that glittered like a hailstorm in the light of the fires. Shards of glass blew across the *Maul*'s deck, and Avery hunkered low to avoid them. One chipped his face-plate.

The warships of the convoy fired back at the Octunggen with more conventional weapons, the booms of their guns making Avery's eardrums vibrate even through the helm. For a moment he just stood there, awed. But then he saw something beyond the enemy fleet and came back to himself with a start.

On the far side of the Octunggen warships blazed an inferno. Avery clearly saw flames silhouetting a city on a hill. He saw domes, towers, and magnificent, graceful arches, all limned by fire.

"Es'hem ..."

The last remnant of the L'ohen Empire save one, an empire which had once encompassed all of Urslin and beyond, the island of Es'hem burned brightly. Avery knew that in its palace a L'ohen emperor still reigned, a direct blood descendent of the old lords. Perhaps he stood on some high terrace right now, watching destruction rage all about him. *Paul, it's good you didn't have to see this,* Avery thought. *Hambry spared you that, if nothing else.*

He didn't know how long he stood there, gripping the gunwale so tightly he lost all feeling in his hands, staring at the devastation, but finally he realized the gunfire was growing more infrequent and that the Octunggen ships were diminishing into the distance, as was the funeral pyre of Es'hem. The convoy was, as hard as it was for him to believe, *abandoning* the island.

He stormed forward, pushed past the sentries outside the Control Room, as was his right as chief surgeon, and passed through the airlock onto the bridge.

Captain Sheridan strode back and forth before bleeping screens and grim-faced officers. Her expression barely flickered as Avery approached. "Doctor," she said by way of greeting.

"We're just leaving them! How can you let this happen?"

Her face did not change. "Orders from Admiral Jons. It's the only way, Doctor. The Octunggen number over a hundred and thirty warships, and us forty. They came to conquer Es'hem. We only came to trade with it."

"But—"

"That will be all, Doctor. We're departing, as swiftly as possible. With any luck, the Octs will be so focused on Es'hem that they won't follow us."

"But to let them destroy ..."

She averted her eyes. "Yes. It is regrettable."

She probably loves this. Which other officers had she turned? He glanced around, searching faces. He tasted something bitter on his tongue.

"Our next port of call will be home," she said.

PART TWO:

SECRETS

Chapter 5

Lightning stabbed at the crowded, baroque skyline of Hissig, capital of Ghenisa.

Avery stood at the bow of the *Maul*, staring at the thick spires and squat domes of the metropolis as it crouched like a fat, filthy cat reeling in a ball of yarn. Sickly yellow glows emanated from the tower tips above the fog, illuminating the maze of twisted narrow streets. A cloud of chitterbats swept past the alchemical tower of Gethys, then flew higher, skirling about the peaks of the Parliament Building on its mountain.

Avery frowned. Memories of what had happened here, in this city, had not let him go even far out at sea, and just seeing Hissig made his mouth go dry.

Mari ... Ani ...

Sailors and whalers stood all around him, and they cheered as the convoy entered Illynmarc Harbor, passing between the Bookends, the twin lighthouses on either side built by King Sacran IV (before his assassination by mold poison), then veering to port, far to the port, not toward the endless and tangled docks civilians used but to the somber, more orderly Navy docks that extended from the base of Fort Brunt.

The fortress reared grim and black, huge and primeval. It had been built many centuries ago by the Ysstral Empire. The arrogance and skill of the Ysstral lords showed in every graceful line, in every sinister fold of architecture. The towers with their jagged lines reminded Avery of a child's drawing of pine trees, tall and pointed with downward-facing jags, and yet there was little childlike about them; they were thick, severe and commanding, dripping in moisture from the fog. Thousands, millions of inset gemstones shone from the black stone that composed the fortress, glittering and twinkling. They had always reminded Avery of spiders' eyes, and the spindly, segmented arches of the flying buttresses had always reminded him of spider legs.

If being oppressive and cruel wasn't sufficient reason for breaking away from the Ysstrals, their creepy architecture would have been more than enough. Ghenisa was full of it. Especially Hissig. A stranger might never know Ghenisa had revolted against the Ysstrals four hundred years ago.

The ships of the convoy docked and began to unload. It was a long, wearying process, and Avery occupied himself with moving the injured and various medical equipment.

The mystery woman's coma held. Avery suspected her fever was the reason she hadn't come out of it, and he hoped that when he had her in his main office in Fort Brunt, with the full array of his equipment to aid him, he would be able to wake her. Of course, all of his efforts would be for nothing if Sheridan had her dissected. All the more reason why he wished to be assigned to the team tasked with studying her. If what Patient X had told him was true, even in part, he would do anything to help her. He wished he could confide in someone, but he didn't know whom he could trust. Unless ...

When he finally stepped from the docks onto dry land, he felt the urge to sink to the muddy, rocky ground and kiss it. A lieutenant was monitoring the air with a beeping sensor, and he held everyone's attention. At last he nodded and said, "It's safe, people. You can take off your helms."

Avery did just that. He breathed in a deep lungful of fresh air, relishing the wind that rustled his hair and dried the sweat against his scalp. *It's been too long.* In the background, he heard the whirring of the cleansers, the machines that processed the air and made it breathable this close to the sea. The result tasted slightly like grease and metal, but it was heaven. The cleansers ran partly on the hot lard that the whaling fleets provided and partly on other compounds and derivatives of the sea. Further up the docks, the catch from a more successful hunt—two medium-sized whales, one male and one female—sat like deflated mountains as teams of Navy personnel hovered over them, slicing and cutting, stripping the meat from the bone and the priceless lard from the meat. Carts full of quivering fat were being filled, and they would soon be taken to plants that would convert the lard into fuel for the many instruments Ghenisa used to counter Octung's weapons, as well as the effects of the sea.

Avery noticed large machines, each the size of a bus and covered in a shell of steel, sitting along the shore. They hunched silent and dark, each one over a hundred yards from the other. These were not the air purifiers, he knew, but something new. The Navy had been installing them at the time the *Maul* had set out, and now it seemed as if the installation was complete. They arced around the harbor, waiting for some unseen trigger.

As Captain Sheridan gave a speech to her officers and crew, Avery simply enjoyed the sights of land. The fortress occupied most of his field of vision. High up amid its crags and gargoyles, gray crabs scuttled among the intricate architecture. One bore a pigeon in its claw; the bird hung limp and broken. The crabs vanished into a drainage hole, likely to find their nest. Higher up, a three-foot-long hunter snail slithered up and over a crenellation, on the prowl for food. The great snails would happily eat crab, bird and mouse, and they could grow to immense size. Avery had even heard of drunks falling asleep in alleys only to wake up with a man-sized slug shoving a proboscis at them.

The harbor, docks and sea stretched to the side. The sun lowered over the hazy, noxious horizon to the west, over the clustered towers of Hissig. The stained glass of the Parliament dome glittered orange and red, webbed by inlaid black. Prime Minister Denaris dwelt in her tower there, handsome but stern, warm but reserved. She had been holding the country together almost through sheer force of will lately, it seemed, and her attitude—tough, unwavering, wry—had earned her many admirers. Avery was one.

At last Sheridan wrapped up her speech, and the officers, crew and whalers broke up, said their farewells and followed their various leaders into the fortress. Avery led the medical staff, patients and equipment through a high archway of layered black, triangular projections, and the halls echoed to the sounds of sailors and personnel, but they still seemed cold and still. They gleamed blackly and were decorated with beautiful oil paintings of frowning heroes and austere landscapes. Anything more cheerful would have looked out of place in this building, and Avery wished, not for the first time, that they would just raze the thing and start from scratch.

He marched directly to the medical wing, which occupied a large portion of the ground floor, and continued overseeing the move. Often he itched for a drink, but just as often he held himself back. He needed to be clear. He needed to think. He had a patient who claimed to be able to stop Octung, but unless he could wake her up she would be dissected—and if he *did* wake her up, she would be taken prisoner or simply assassinated by an Octunggen spy.

With a sigh, Avery remembered what he had found two nights ago. He'd returned to Hambry's cabin, just to make sure everything was still in place, so that he could bring the authorities to the evidence as soon as the ship reached shore.

Hambry's letters, of course, had been gone. Even the shotgun shell had vanished.

"So what the hell?"

They hunched in the back of a stinking cab, jostling through the streets. Avery was almost glad it was wintertime, even though he had to huddle in his thick coat, which had been expensive when he bought it but was now patched and, if looked at in broad daylight, somewhat ragged. The cabbage-and-clove stench of the cab nauseated him, though, and it would have been worse in summer.

"You gonna answer me?"

Avery glanced to his side. Janx, huge and scarred, sat draped in the shadows of the cab, with now and then light from a shop striping his nose-less face. Despite the frigid rain, it was a surprisingly busy night, and Hissigites teemed to the sides of the streets, under overhangs and canopies. Taverns emitted music and light, and couples sat under umbrellas in courtyard cafés. Prayers drifted from small, weathered temples. Some of the temples' foundations ran deep, merging with the remains of older, stranger buildings below. Other people poured into and out of the several motion picture theaters, one of which bore a sign boasting a color projector.

"All in good time," Avery assured him.

Janx bunched his jaws. "Godsdamnit, Doc, you better not go mute on me. You told me you'd tell me why the fuck I taught you how to lock-pick once we hit land. Well, shit, it's been a week and—nothin'." His voice lowered, became a growl. "I don't like bein' put off."

"I am not ... putting you off." Avery turned away. The truth was that he hadn't contacted Janx to tell him about the lock-picking, though that was certainly part of it. There were bigger issues involved. Of course, now Avery wasn't even sure Janx had come in response to Avery's summons or for his own reasons. The big man wanted answers, that much was clear. But Janx had bad timing. "I simply have my mind ... somewhere else."

Janx stared at him, then sat back. His expression softened, or at least suggested softening. "I won't leave till I know. When the ship's doctor is spyin' on the officers, I need to fuckin' know what's goin' on. You some kinda spy or somethin'?" His voice hardened at the end, and he tensed in the shadows. Avery could see the stiffening of his limbs. Janx could rip Avery limb from limb if he wanted.

Avery let out a breath. "No. I am not. If I were, I likely would already know how to pick a lock, wouldn't I? But ... someone is."

"*Who?*"

Wheels spun on asphalt, and rain pattered on the roof. Outside, cars honked, the sound muted by the weather. Droplets prismed the colored lights from a passing tavern.

"Who?" Janx demanded again. Avery was aware of the tension beside him as a mouse is aware of a circling owl, by the prickling of his neck.

Avery kept his gaze forward, not deigning to look at the whaler. "I will tell you ... but, for the love of the Three, hold your questions. Let me do this. We'll speak when it's done."

Janx groaned. "But it's a fuckin' lake out there!"

"Nevertheless."

The cab rolled forward, and a sullen silence descended over the passengers. From somewhere outside the national anthem blared from a faltering speaker. Banners depicting

Prime Minister Denaris, with her cleft chin and cool green eyes, flapped in the breeze. Slogans exclaimed *We will prevail!* and *Freedom will not bow!* Other signs mounted on building façades gave instructions in case of bombing and pointed to the nearest bomb shelter.

The cabbie, a dark-haired man who must hail from Nalakith to the northwest, cursed and honked. Avery hadn't even been aware that Octung had begun invading Nalakith, but he wasn't surprised. The Octunggen had been quite active while he'd been away, and Hissig (and Ghenisa as a whole) was even more overburdened with refugees than before. Avery saw them huddled under canvas overhangs in alleys, shivering in groups around barrel fires. Grime-smirched children stood close to the flames, eating what was likely charred rat, or possibly fish. *Please let it be rat.*

He strained his eyes into the dark, searching for certain signs among the refugees under their leaking overhangs, in their grimy alleys. Sure enough, it wasn't long before he saw hunched backs and black scale-like growths on cheeks and hands. He saw what looked like hands fusing together, or noses disappearing, and more, stranger mutations, bulges on cheekbones, the widening of one leg over the other. *We're failing them.* These people had been forced to eat black market seafood, food that had not been processed and so was cheap—and contaminated. Avery knew there was nothing to be done for those who'd eaten it. Neither medicine nor alchemy could help, and the Octunggen technology stolen by spies over the years had not included machines or medicines to heal the infected, if there were such things. No one even knew how Octung had gotten its hands on its strange, otherworldly technologies in the first place.

Avery tried not to think about it as the cab wound throughout the dark, dripping city. Huge, massively encrusted domes hunched between squat towers, leftovers of the Ysstrals, later occupied by Ghenisan royals. The former palaces and mansions of the aristocracy still reared, their gargoyles and serpentine dragons spitting water, the stained-glass windows gleaming, but their stonework showed cracks, their insides signs of fire from the Revolution half a century ago. Many sagged in disrepair or ruin, home to the refugees that now crowded their halls.

Janx seemed to feel it, too. "It's all comin' apart, ain't it, Doc?"

Avery didn't want to own up to his own dismal thoughts and said nothing.

A sort of whistling noise escaped around the leather patch over Janx's nose hole. "Worst part is, things were gettin' better, weren't they? Before the war."

Avery nodded reluctantly, not wanting to dwell on it. As the cab drove on, they passed museums, art galleries, ancient halls of philosophy, the Gethys School of Alchemy, and more. For centuries Hissig had been renowned as a hub for art and music and learning. After the Revolution and the numerous failed governments that had replaced the aristocracy, that had changed, enlightenment taking a backseat to survival, but before Octung had launched its first attacks, Ghenisa had finally been coming into its own again, shedding the bloody history of the Unsettled Times with its executions, coups and paranoia. A new age had come about, spearheaded by Prime Minister Denaris and a stable, respected government—a time of renewal and renaissance, of art and poetry. The New Dawn.

"Perhaps we can get it back," Avery said. "If the war ends."

"The only way it'll end is with Octung's boot on our throat, and you know it. They've conquered near everyone else from sea to sea. We won't be any different."

Avery looked at him. "Then why fight? Why do you risk your life to stop them?"

Janx glanced off. "Why do you?"

The cab wound through the twisting streets, struggled up alternately cobbled and paved roads, ascending to one of the peaks of the foothills, Mount Ibrignon. The houses grew larger and more elaborate the higher they went.

Avery braced himself. They were very close now. He felt his nails digging into the palms of his hands. The thorns of the roses he carried pricked him.

When he finally saw the wrought-iron archway of the cemetery, his heart sped up. Beads of sweat swelled on his forehead. *I shouldn't have put this off*, he thought. It had been too painful, and he'd kept finding things that demanded attention at Fort Brunt. At last, when he'd forced himself to come, not even Janx's arrival could deter him.

"I won't go any further," the cabbie said, drawing the vehicle to a halt before the archway.

Ibrignon Peace and Love, the archway read. Its rusted, pitted surface glistened in the rain, the letters bleak and false to Avery's eyes. A road led into the little cemetery, but evidently the cabbie dared not take it.

"Fine," Avery said. "Wait here." He cracked the door.

Janx touched his arm. "Want some company, Doc?"

Avery forced himself to smile. "No. Thank you, no."

Janx sat back.

Avery stepped out into the night. Rain spattered his face for a moment before the umbrella blossomed, and he enjoyed it. Cold wind whipped at him, billowing his clothes, tearing at the umbrella. He squared his shoulders and marched through the archway. The purring of the cab's engine dwindled behind him.

During daytime and in good weather the little cemetery on the hill afforded a magnificent view of the panorama of Hissig, with temples and domes and former palaces marching to the sea, in between handsome modern spires bristling with gargoyles and ornamentation. One could almost imagine what the city must have looked like in its heyday, before the Revolution, before the spread of that terrible notion of democracy. When a person was down below, in the folds of the city, he could see all the scars, all the defects, but from up here Hissig looked pristine, new, glorious.

Night hid much of the glory. Now all Avery could see was rain and darkness, with two of the pale, ivory moons wrestling to illuminate the city with a ghostly sheen, and even the sheen was mostly hidden in the rain.

Tombs and mausoleums surrounded him. Angels, devils and gargoyles leered down, rain dancing in their eyes, making their mouths seem to move, their fangs to slaver. A giant statue of a many-limbed goddess reared before him, holding in each of her twelve hands a broken urn. On this rocky promontory, most of the dead had not been buried but interred in tombs and mausoleums. Only the wealthy slept here, mainly descendents of the old noble families.

Avery's throat tightened as he wound through the dripping tombs, seeking his family out. The rain blew colder. It soaked into his camel-hair jacket and hemp shirt, and from above he heard a rolling crack.

Avery pushed forward, clutching the flowers to his chest with one hand and holding off the rain with the other. He rounded a tomb whose visitors had left alchemical lanterns burning, impervious to the rain, before the names of their loved ones, along with old, scattered flowers and a figure made of wax, and at last he arrived at the small but beautiful mausoleum where his wife and daughter had been interred. Rain dripped from its sides, shone on the faces of its angels, and glistened on the door which sealed Mari and Ani from the world of the living.

Avery felt pain and looked down to see that his hands had made fists and that his fingernails were driving deep into his palms. He slowly unclenched. His chest hitched, great racking sobs that shook him like a baby's rattle. Suddenly losing all strength, he sank to his knees and wept, hard, and stayed that way for a long time.

When at last he was done, he stood and straightened.

He was ready.

Now for Sheridan.

The Headless Drake, the apartment building Avery lived in, stood on Clower Blvd. near Graeslyn Park. Avery had once enjoyed strolling through the park on his visits to Hissig, city of his childhood. Now refugees from the war filled the park. They huddled under the skeletal branches of trees, their ragged tents pitched along the water. As Avery passed the park, he stared out over the endless rows of shabby tents and took a deep breath. This war had to end soon or Ghenisa would collapse under the strain.

The Headless Drake waited, rain bubbling over its cracks and stains, cascading from its peaked roofs and dribbling from its gables. Once it had been a beautiful building, the palace of a duke, but the duke had been lynched and butchered into thirteen infamous parts during the Revolution. The building's red-brick towers still stood proud and elegant, but their bricks were chipped and stained, many replaced entirely with different colored substitutes or simply not replaced at all. Cracks showed in the windows. Shutters sagged at odd angles.

Avery saw movement high up. A land octopus crawled over the building's façade, rain dripping off the animal's tangled fur, its body bunching and lengthening as its tentacles dragged it along. Luckily Avery saw no open windows for the animal to slip through, there to feast on leftovers, pets, even infants. He hoped some refugee made a meal out of it before the night was over.

The cab jerked to a stop before the Drake's entrance, and Avery paid and disembarked. With a grunt, Janx followed. Rain pelted them as they ran up the steps to the doorway, and with some heaving the great wooden monstrosity swung to. After the Revolution this building had at first been converted to a hotel, and the lobby was a large, high-ceilinged affair of smoky wood with brick only showing here and there. A long counter mounted with ancient, cobwebbed cash registers ran the length of the rear wall. A huge wooden bas-relief of a wingless, serpentine dragon, its head hacked off, was etched into the wall behind it. The dragon had been the symbol of the old royal family and was why people often referred to them as Drakes.

"Nice place," Janx said, staring around at the gloom and cobwebs.

Avery shrugged, droplets of water spraying from his coat to the elaborate carpet. Gold and crimson and purple, it was the carpet of kings, or had been. Now it was frayed and torn, and Avery suspected that if it were moved it would disintegrate entirely.

"Did you know, they say the ghosts of those hanged here still haunt the building?" he said.

"This place don't need ghosts to be haunted."

Off that vague pronouncement, Avery led the way up the wooden staircase, and they wound up into the palace proper. The brick walls were barren of the beautiful oil paintings that had once adorned them, the handsomely-wrought windows were cracked, paint peeling around the edges, and the high arched ceilings were spanned by webs and inhabited with many-eyed scuttling things that set their webs to shuddering with the passage of travelers below.

Avery's apartment was on the fourth floor, and he felt a weight lift off his shoulders when he stepped inside. It was medium-sized, sparsely furnished, and paneled in dark, chipped wood. Sagging bookshelves lined the walls, filled with historical books, romances from the L'ohen Empire, adventures set during the War of the Severance, and all manner of others. Drooping couches and chairs slouched in the living room, grouped around a sad coffee table and a soot-stained fireplace that seemed to radiate cold, not heat. Just as many webs spanned the arched ceilings as the hallways outside.

Avery flipped on the electric lights. A few dim bulbs buzzed. The building's wiring had long since gone south, and the frequent blackouts had only destabilized it further. Thus Avery had a collection of alternate lighting, from tallow candles to alchemical lamps, to the fireplace that could roar with flame but rarely seemed to emit warmth.

He went around the rooms, lighting candle and lantern, throwing strange and different-hued illuminations into the suite. The bubbles of lighting struggled against each other, red with green, white with yellow. Weird shadows reigned.

Janx grunted, running a finger along a dusty surface. He seemed more amused than disgusted, and Avery wondered about the whaler's own quarters. Avery's suite simply seemed lonely. Draped in darkness and need.

Avery crossed the living room to start a fire in the fireplace. While he tended to that, Janx sparked a cigar and leaned against the mantle. Dripping candles crammed most of its surface, and here and there were wedged pictures of Mari and Ani, Avery's own little shrine to his family. Janx frowned as he eyed the pictures, then turned back to Avery, poking logs into place.

"So what happened to 'em, anyway?" Janx asked. When Avery didn't answer immediately, he seemed undeterred. "And that graveyard! What a place! I don't imagine the heavens'll look much posher. How'd you manage to meet such a rich broad?"

"She wasn't a broad." Avery lit a long match and touched it to the kindling beneath the pyramid of logs. Sparks danced up. He stood back, admiring the glow.

"Well, how'd you meet her?" Janx said.

Hearing his own voice as if it came from far away, Avery said, "They were nobles, her family——"

"Shit! I didn't know there were any of 'em left. After the Revolution ..."

"Yes. But some made it into hiding. Mari's parents did, and she was born that way. *Raised* in hiding. Living under false names, pretending to be normal, trying not to flinch whenever a fellow noble was ferreted out and hanged or butchered. Well." Avery waved a hand, putting that to the side. "So her family was in hiding in Benical. I was a young medical student there, unable to afford a school in Hissig. Mari's mother, a low duchess by birthright—though I didn't know this at the time—she fell ill, and they came to the hospital where I studied. I assisted in her mother's care, and Mari visited every day. We ..." He swallowed.

Janx gave him a moment. The big man's eyes went to the picture of Mari standing under the olive tree. "She was pretty."

For a moment, Avery could say nothing. Words were born and died in his throat. "She was beautiful."

He moved to the dilapidated kitchen. His prize stood on the counter, its amber glass gleaming. He poured both he and Janx a glass.

When Janx eyed the label on the bottle, he whistled. "Valyankan! But——" He stared at Avery with new respect.

Avery nodded, smiling a little. "That's why I was willing to pay for it."

"But how? Valyanka's overrun. There's no more of this stuff even being *made* ..."

Avery sipped his glass. The whiskey burned his throat and warmed his belly. The fire spread outward, numbing him, lightening him. Finding a chair overlooking the fireplace, he collapsed into it and sipped some more. "Old stores, I suppose, or else the last batch ever made. Possibly the last batch ever *to* be made. Isn't that a sobering thought? That Valyanka could cease to be? At least, as we know it."

Janx muttered sounds of appreciation as he drank. He lowered himself onto the drooping couch, which drooped even further under his weight. Dust billowed up.

"Best shit I've had in years."

For a moment, they sipped their drinks in silence, and the fire crackled in the background.

At last Janx said, "So, you were sayin', what happened to 'em. Your family?"

"You really want to know?"

Janx shrugged his broad shoulders. "I'd like to know the story, if it ain't too long."

Avery's gaze strayed to the fire. A log popped, and sparks flared up. "When the war came to Ghenisa, before our hot lard processors were complete, there was an Octunggen raiding party in the mountains. One of many, I suppose. They carried the Deathlight."

"Gods below. Yeah, Benical. I remember now."

Avery nodded. "It's against the mountains, you know. The Octunggen made it past the ngvandi, past our sentries, and crept up on us. I don't know how long it took them to set up their equipment, but ... they did. I was at the hospital when I saw that strong red light shining from the mountaintop. I was able to get to an environment suit in time. Mari and Ani weren't so lucky. I remember coming home ... through a city of the dead and dying, that red light shining ... I remember walking up to our cabin ... approaching it, slowly, knowing what I would find inside ... I still dream of it, every night ... and in the dream I'm walking up to the cabin, and I know, I *know*, what's waiting in there, but there's always a little doubt ... maybe *this* time it will be different ..." He closed his eyes. "I found them there, at home, in each other's arms."

"Dead?"

Avery shook his head. Ice rattled in his glass, and he realized his hand was trembling. "But almost. I spent every last penny I had. Nearly every last penny Mari's family had. She was the sole surviving child, and by that time her parents had passed. She was all that was left. She would whisper to me her dreams that, if the war caused the splintering of the Ghenisan government, then people might look toward the old aristocracy. The Drakes. She said maybe she was the highest royal still alive, and she would be the queen, and Ani the princess. The queen and princess for a new age. Well, I protected my little princess, my little Drake-let, and her mother. I used all my skills as a doctor, meager as they are. I prolonged their lives, spent our last resources bringing them to Hissig to seek the best help money could buy ..."

"Musta been hard. Bein' a doctor, not bein' able to heal your kin."

Avery didn't have to answer. "We sought help, but ..."

He drained his glass. He saw that Janx had finished his, too, and rose to refill them both. From the kitchen, he said, "A light that can kill, cause plague—we had nothing that could fight that, not before the processors were complete, maybe not even now. When I think of Hissig, I still remember those days, of tending to Mari and Ani as they faded, day after day ..." He heard his voice grow thick. "I had just enough money left for their alchemical preservation, internment and mausoleum."

"I'm sorry," Janx said.

Avery nodded, unable for the moment to do anything else.

When he could, he rejoined the whaler, and they sipped their whiskeys and watched the fire.

The time had come.

Avery turned to the whaler. "So. You want to know about Captain Sheridan and Commander Hambry. About why I needed to know how to pick a lock. Very well, then. Here is the story. Afterward, I'll need your help to devise some plan of action. It's why I contacted you. We need proof, and I think you're the man to help me get it."

After Avery had told the tale of Sheridan's and Hambry's espionage, he and Janx sat there in silence, logs popping in the background. Eventually Janx said, "That's a hell of a story, Doc."

"I know it's a lot to take in."

Janx's eyes speared Avery. "So how did it feel?"

"How did what feel?"

"You know."

"I'm afraid I don't."

Janx looked at him in exasperation. "Killing Hambry. How'd it feel?"

"Ah." Avery found it interesting that of everything he had told the whaler, Janx would fix on that. "I was sick."

"But how did you *feel?*"

Avery started to answer, then saw Janx lean forward in his seat. As he did, the shadows shifted around him, and his eyes fell into a dark pool. Still, they glittered. He said nothing, but Avery could feel some strain coming off of him. Obviously the question was important. Perhaps some test.

Avery remembered watching Hambry plummet to his death, remembered him falling, falling. He remembered Paul's corpse, his staring eyes.

"It felt ... good," Avery said.

Janx nodded. He drained his glass and stood. To Avery's surprise, the whaler poured a drink for them both. "It was your first?" he asked.

"Well ..." Avery started to say that he had seen many deaths as a doctor, but that wasn't what Janx had meant. "Yes."

Janx passed him the glass, then made a toast. "To your first." He drank.

Avery hesitated. *To your first.* The words sounded ominous. After a moment, he tipped his glass. The drink burned his throat. "Hopefully my last."

"We'll see. If you really want to begin this business, though, I don't think it will be. You prepared for that, Doc?"

Avery studied him. Janx was serious but no longer tense.

"I would prefer not to kill anyone," Avery said.

Janx sat down. "How d'you intend to start it, then? What exactly is it you want done? Sheridan's a traitor, you say. A spy. There may be others. If you're right, and say I believe you, moving against them will be tricky."

"That's exactly why I need your help."

"Can't we just go to Admiral Jons or one of the other higher-ups?"

"And say what? That Sheridan is a traitor? She would just deny it and I would be locked up for spreading lies and accusations in a time of war. At the least I would be fired and Sheridan would be free to continue spying for Octung. At worst Admiral Jons might be a cohort of hers, another agent of Octung, and he would have me executed. We can't trust anyone in power until we've seen the extent of Sheridan's network. We need proof. If we can get that, we can hand the evidence over to the authorities. We would deliver it to multiple people under the theory that at least one of them, hopefully all, would be loyal and untainted by Octung. But it all hinges on gathering that evidence. I was hoping with your connections—if you're as plugged into the underground as you claim—we might arrange for Sheridan to be ... tailed. Those that did it would follow her and gather the proof. We'll need professionals."

Janx grinned, and it was not an entirely reassuring grin. "I know just the people."

Avery thought about it. "I'll want to meet them."

"Fine. Come by tomorrow after my fight and I'll introduce you. After that it's up to you."

Chapter 6

At the appointed time, Avery stood, threw on his jacket and left his apartment, but not before one last sip of Valyankan.

Outside, cold wind shivered through the city streets. It didn't seem to deter Avery's fellow Ghenisans, however, and his blood was warm enough from the drink. The streets thronged with natives and refugees alike. Brightly-colored lamps hung from icy stone walls. Glowing alchemical orbs had been shoved into gargoyles' mouths, and strings of lights hung from the horns of serpentine dragons. People wandered the sidewalks, tramping from tavern to tavern, from vaudeville theater to picture show, some festively costumed over their coats and jackets. They dressed as the Three Sisters themselves, the Sun King, or the innumerable Star-Lords whose stories populated myth and fable.

This was the traditional three-day holiday of Vruthaen, when two of the Sisters eclipsed. Looking up past the clouds, Avery could see all three moons wheeling through the stars between long ribbons of cloud. The eclipse was to be tomorrow, Vruth Eve, when the Mother passed over the Waif. It was supposed to be a symbol of birth and rebirth for those who belonged to the Trinity faith. Massive orgies and drunken revelries during the time of the Drakes had helped popularize the holiday and now it was officially celebrated every eclipse, though these days with less debauchery. That had been one good thing about the Drakes, Avery supposed. They had known how to celebrate.

Huddling in a cab with a broken heater, he watched the gaily-costumed revelers totter through the streets, and he thought their red, laughing faces and ribald calls showed a certain strain. After all, they had been forced to endure rations, blackouts and general declarations of coming doom for months, years. The holiday was a time when they could release their tensions, but it seemed to Avery that it only expressed their fears more nakedly. Their laughter was too shrill, their dancing too frantic, their passion too obsessive.

Still, it was hard not to be moved by all the men singing drunkenly on street corners, children eating candied apples (however old and shrunken), women strutting in slinky, furred costumes, and bright lights blazing everywhere.

The revelry grew even more raucous in the direction Avery went: the Tangle. In the Tangle, heaping tenements stacked up like fungi, some huge, some listing dangerously, many mashed up against each other. Tiny hovels squeezed between monoliths, permanently in shadow. Streets wove nearly at random through the mad buildings: winding, dead-ending, doubling back, merging with tiny tributaries that wove and forked and ended in sinister cul-de-sacs. Factories belched smoke into the sky over the crumbling roofs of tenements, blocking out the stars. It was a seedy labyrinth, known for danger and seduction.

The cabbie dropped him off at the Blazing Tiger. Once the building had been a small factory that made ship parts, and its chimney stacks could still be seen rearing above, but competition with larger companies had closed it down long ago. Now a huge neon sign over the doorway depicted a flaming tiger leaping through the air. The lights flashed in such a way that the tiger, Kaugen, seemed to move, flames crackling off him. Kaugen was an ancient god of war and sex, belonging to a cult from Laisha. Appropriate to the building, naturally.

Avery waited in the short line and paid the bouncer the cover. As he stepped through the huge metal doors, Avery entered a bastion of warmth and noise, and he smiled gratefully. Spice and grease and ale and cigarette smoke and roasting meat filled the air, but they had to compete with the stench of thousands of people and the sweat of the men they watched. Sailors and roustabouts and criminals and factory workers and a myriad of others pressed close against each other, shouting and jostling, placing bets, laughing and cursing. Vendors sold hot dogs and fried, mutton-filled peppers, flatbread and mushrooms, boiled turtle on a stick. And beer. Lots of beer. Everything was drastically overpriced, of course—food was still rationed, and much of this was black market stuff—and the victuals' presence alone seemed opulent in these meager days. But there were evidently plenty here with money to spend, which was encouraging.

Avery, not as flush as he would like, ignored the vendors that besieged him as he shoved his way through the crowd. He wished some of the patrons had washed more thoroughly. Their layered clothing didn't help, especially now that they were indoors. He felt more than one weasely denizen of the Tangle brush up against him and was glad he'd hidden his wallet in an inside pocket of his jacket. The thieves wouldn't have gotten much, but these days even a little was a lot. He walked through a cloud of cigar smoke, then a pocket of spice.

At last he reached the periphery of the ring and stared up in awe at the bare-chested titans battling it out on the boxing platform. The crowd roared, and the huge, awesome form of the taller one smashed his bare-knuckled fist into the face of his opponent, who grunted and staggered back.

Sweating and fighting for breath after delivering the blow, Janx looked like something Kaugen would approve of, covered in scars, tattoos and blood, a great primal creature built of slabs of muscle and steely sinews. Hard eyes, one half closed under a bruise, glared out to either side of the leather patch that covered his nasal cavity, and spittle sprayed from his broken lips.

His opponent, a man nearly as tall as he and possibly even more muscular, with a livid tattoo of a winged serpent coiling across his back and disappearing under his red trunks, recovered from the blow and launched himself at Janx. He ducked Janx's swing and pummeled the whaler in the abdomen, one hit after another, driving him back. Avery could hear the slap of fists on flesh even over the screaming crowd. Janx's opponent forced him up against the ropes. His fists beat against the whaler in a flurry, a meaty slap-slap-slap that reminded Avery of something he might hear in a butcher shop.

At last Janx, almost leisurely, shoved his opponent away with one hand and smashed him under the jaw with the other. The vicious uppercut actually lifted the man off the ground, sweat flying, and flung him to the mat with a thud. The crowd roared. Janx prodded the man's ribs with a foot, but the man didn't move, save to breathe in and out. The referee counted to ten, then raised Janx's arm, with Janx's help. Bells rang. The crowd roared louder. Janx grinned a bloody grin at his worshippers.

While the audience members collected on their bets and ordered more food and beer, Avery pushed his way into the clearing around the ring. Two bouncers moved to stop him, but he flashed his medical ID. "I'm Janx's doctor!" he called. That seemed to confuse them, since Janx's doctor was busy patching up the big man's eye.

Fortunately Janx saw the activity. Avery heard his booming laugh over the murmur of the crowd. "Let 'im through!" Janx demanded, spitting out his mouthpiece, then slumped back in his chair. The doctor swabbed at his bad eye.

Grateful, Avery approached. "That was quite a fight," he said, staring up at the mountain of blood and muscle and ink that was Janx. He supposed it shouldn't surprise him that the whaler would prizefight when he wasn't whaling.

He was a man of action, of violence, and if he did nothing between voyages but drink and whore he would likely go mad. Of course, Avery was sure there was plenty of drinking and whoring, too.

"You ain't seen nothin' yet, Doc," Janx said, wincing as the other doctor taped up his eyebrow.

"Don't tell me you're fighting again."

Janx chuckled. "Fight till ya drop. That's the game. Ya get paid by the round as well as the win."

Avery eyed the whaler's mass of bruises and cuts. Fighting bare-knuckled had obviously taken a lot out of him. "Are you sure that's wise?"

"I don't think that's what it's about, Doc."

"I'd like to talk to you about that other matter. About that ... ah, group of people we're supposed to meet."

"After, Doc."

"But—"

The bells rang.

The attention of the crowd returned to the ring. The announcer, clad in a gaudy tuxedo and flanked by two half-naked women, strode across the stage bellowing: "AND NOW FOR YOUR VIEWING PLEASURE, LADIES AND GENTLEMEN, I BRING YOU OUR NEXT CHALLENGER, ONE OF YOUR FAVORITES AND MINE, THE TITAN OF TERROR, THE FANTASY OF FREAKISHNESS, THE REIGNING SULTAN OF THE UNHOLY, THE UNMATCHABLE HORROR OF ..." Somewhere there was a drum roll "... MU*IR*BLAAG THE *MON*-STERRR!!"

On the other side of the ring the crowd parted and a huge form emerged draped in a shiny black robe. Large bouncers escorted him, but he dwarfed them in comparison. Avery had to stop his jaw from falling open. The next challenger was not simply big but *inhuman*.

Pulling himself up with a half-claw, half-flipper, Muirblaag the Monster climbed into the ring.

He was not poorly named. However, at first Avery wasn't quite sure what he was looking at. There were certainly non-human intelligent life-forms in the world—the amphibians of Talis, the goat-people of Naderhorn, the lizard men of Qerwig—though members of these races tended to stay among their own cultures. Avery had only met a few humans who'd even claimed to have encountered one. Muirblaag didn't seem to fall into any of these racial categories, however. He was, Avery realized belatedly, a mutant human, someone infected from contact with the Atomic Sea. It was the only explanation, unless—

But no. Avery wouldn't think of it. None of *them* would dare descend down *here*.

Still ... most infected victims' deformations were ragged, incomplete, unfinished, like the refugees he'd seen on the way to the cemetery. They did not look like *whole* beings.

Muirblaag looked whole. From universally scaly skin to two fully-formed webbed hands, to the straight crest that adorned his hairless head and ran down his broad back, he looked all of a piece, a complete and perfect specimen of ... well, he was undeniably piscine. His eyes shown completely black, with no whites or visible irises, his lips bulged, he had nearly as little nose as Janx. A glittering silver earring that looked suspiciously like a fish hook dangled from the bony ear hole on the right side of his thick head. His scales glistened blue-gray. The suggestion of gills quivered on his neck immediately below his jaws.

Muirblaag may have been human once—or perhaps not if Avery's suspicion was correct—but in any case he wasn't human now. Poisoned food or possibly even birth (from infected parents, as Avery suspected) had transformed him into a fish-man of monstrous dimensions. His shoulders were broad and powerful, his arms thick and knotted as tree trunks. Scars crisscrossed his body. An alchemical tattoo on his bicep glowed in the shape of a reverse mermaid, with her upper half piscine and her lower half a naked woman. A cigarette jutted from her wide lips and, thanks to the alchemy involved, the smoke seemed to writhe about her head.

Wearing only a pair of gray trunks, Muirblaag strode on webbed feet toward the center of the ring, dripping water as he went. He had either come from a bath, shower or dowsing. Perhaps like a fish he must stay moist.

Janx met him at the center of the ring, and Avery saw to his astonishment that the fish-man stood a full head taller than Janx.

Janx glared up at him, and Muirblaag glared down at Janx. Avery sensed the lingering trace of some old animosity. The announcer shouted more inducements to the crowd to get excited—hardly necessary, for they seemed in a rare state of exultation; this was evidently a famous rivalry—and shouted for the fight to begin.

Bells rang. The two titans flew at each other.

Janx struck first. He punched at Muirblaag's face, but the fish-man wove with surprising speed and sent a scaly fist into Janx's belly. An explosion of air from Janx's lips bathed Muirblaag's face. Janx reeled back, cocked his arm, and sent a mean right hook to the fish-man's ribs with an audible slapping of meat. Muirblaag staggered, growled and leapt at him.

It was a colossal battle. Huge fists flew and slammed into glowering faces. Blood sprayed through the air, some red, some inky blue. The titans roared and smashed at each other, and it seemed the ground shook with every impact. The crowd went mad, shrieking at the fighters, waving cash over their heads for bookies to collect, jostling each other for better spots. Vendors sold roasted peanuts and beer by the armload.

Despite himself, Avery found himself enjoying it all, even though he winced every time Janx took a punch. He decided a beer would help, then two, then, why not, a box of peanuts.

At last the fight ended. With one mighty punch in the sixth round, Muirblaag sprawled Janx across the mat. The whaler fell with a terrific thud; Avery could see the mat jump at the impact, see Janx's cheeks warble.

Bells rang, scantily-clad women strutted, and Muirblaag was declared the winner. After slapping him conscious, Janx's doctor/trainer led him out of the ring.

Still munching peanuts, Avery followed. "I'm with him," Avery told the bouncers, and Janx grunted agreement. Staggering, the big man led the way into the dressing room. There he showered, dried off and dressed while a few fans waited outside. Avery finished his peanuts. The dressing room stank of sweat and mold.

When Janx emerged from the shower, he looked like he'd been through a meat grinder. Cuts and bruises covered every bump and curve of his body.

"You should find a better hobby," Avery said.

Janx grunted and pulled on his pants. "I like this just fine."

"He's a star," growled the doctor/trainer, who had taken out his medical bag and was looking through it. He was a tall man with a flat, broken nose and iron-gray hair. He'd obviously been a fighter in his youth. "Can't you see that?"

Avery could hear a fan arguing with the bouncers outside. "I suppose. Is that what it's about then, the attention?"

Janx grinned slowly. "What do you think it's about, Doc?"

Avery nodded. "Women. I should have known. Well, about those friends of yours you're going to introduce me to—"

Janx shook his head, curtly, just once, obviously warning Avery to silence. Did he not trust his own coach?

"I'll talk to you about it later, then," Avery said.

"Yeah." Janx winced as his trainer dabbed alcohol on a wound. "Later."

The older man smiled a hard, sadistic smile as he applied more alcohol. "This could take a while."

It did. Afterwards, Janx signed a few autographs for children. Apparently he was quite the big man in the Tangle, and the kids looked up to him as a hero. However, just as Janx had indicated, or at least Avery thought he had, there were several shapely women waiting for him as well, and they did not seem to be the boys' mothers. He whispered in each one's ear, and they giggled and left, one at a time.

"What did you tell them?" Avery asked when he, Janx and the trainer were under way, making toward a rear exit.

Janx produced a cigar and began unwrapping it. "I just made plans for the week."

"You scheduled dates with them every day of the *week*?"

Janx grinned. "I wouldn't call 'em dates, Doc."

Avery had to admire the man, at least a little. "Quite."

Janx lit up his cigar, looking smug.

Outside, he and his trainer split up, and Avery walked with Janx through the cold night. There were still plenty of revelers on the streets, but it was well after midnight and the celebration had begun to wind down for the evening. Crushed glass from lights, glitter and streams of ribbon from costumes littered the streets. Avery felt glass crunch beneath his feet as he walked.

"Now," said Avery, "I'd really like—"

"Hold that thought," Janx said. "Wait till we have some privacy."

The whaler led him to a tenement, and then up the wrought-iron fire escape whose ladder had conveniently been left down. The fire escape trembled and squealed under their weight, and Avery felt a swell of nausea.

They reached the roof, and wind howled all around them. Avery felt his jacket flutter and billow, and he had to shove his hat down low on his head. Janx didn't pause but led Avery to the edge of the roof, which butted up against another building. The big man found a doorway and led inside. Janx ushered Avery to the roof of this second building, then over a bridge constructed of bolted-together pipes to the roof of another. From one roof to another Janx led, from time to time singing some obscene ballad under his breath but for the most part silent and thoughtful. They climbed mountains of stone, brick and crumbling mortar, then descended into cold valleys, then back up and around again. They passed through rooftop taverns and secret gardens.

At last they clattered down a certain metal ramp and into a secluded courtyard on top of a building. They were between high walls of buildings on three sides, with a view of the panorama of the city to the fourth. In the distance, the lights on the harbor glittered. It was immediately obvious to Avery that this rooftop courtyard had been in use for some time. Rusty chairs crouched in a ragged circle before the huge, sagging water tower, and faded pennants of favored sports teams streamed from the pigeon coop. The pigeons squawked and ruffled their feathers, but the occupants of the roof paid them no mind.

A disparate band sprawled across the chairs or leaned against the water tower or gazed off at the horizon smoking hashish. There were half a dozen of them, and they looked rough and hard, scarred by lives of crime and marginalization. A crest of red hair stood up on one man's head, a chittering monkey scampered up a woman's arm, a small man in a black leather jacket sharpened a knife, a fat black man ate mutton wrapped in flatbread.

And, in the center of them all, hunched in his chair and counting a thick wad of cash, waited Muirblaag.

Avery started upon seeing the fish-man, and at first he thought this must be an ambush, that Janx's enemies had lain in wait for him. Then Muirblaag glanced up, saw Janx and laughed. Janx, chuckling, stepped forward and the two embraced, wincing as they did. Each was still sore.

"Glad to see you made it," said Muirblaag.

"Wouldn't miss the fucker, would I?" said Janx. "This is my party."

"Ours."

The others crowded around, clamoring at Janx and Muirblaag, ignoring Avery entirely. He was beginning to get used to it.

"You're late," said the woman with the monkey, glaring at Janx. She wore a top hat and ratty formal jacket. The monkey hopped up and down on her shoulder. A silver hook gleamed where her left hand should be.

Janx shrugged. "Had to satisfy the mob, now, didn't I?"

Muirblaag thrust a wad of money at him. "That's your cut."

Janx thumbed through it. With a raised eyebrow, he told Avery, "*This* is what it's about."

"Wait," Avery said. "You mean to tell me it was all a set-up? That fight was a *sham*?"

"Fight was real enough," Janx said. "At least, till the end it was. Mu and I'd figured when I needed to take the dive beforehand. Just had to make sure each other lasted till then."

Muirblaag rubbed his bandaged jaw. "Almost didn't."

"Let's drink," said the scurvy little man with the knife.

Avery hadn't noticed, but there was a barrel wedged beneath the water tower, and as he watched each of the ruffians put a crusty glass under the tap and filled up a mug with beer, one by one. Janx gestured for Avery to do likewise.

"No thanks," Avery said.

He frowned as the others talked loudly, drinking, cursing, occasionally engaging in some ribald song as they waved mugs at the moons, only two of which were visible. Folk music drifted over the rooftops from an apartment, and some of the ruffians danced. The small man put away his knife and produced a violin. He played and jigged, and the others danced around him. It was quite a merry scene, or would have been if Avery had been in a better mood. Besides, it was obvious to him that this was a close-knit group. He was an outsider here. He didn't even know the words to their ridiculous songs.

At last he took Janx aside and said, "Damn it, man. We have *business* to discuss."

Janx burped. "Then speak up."

The crew glanced up expectantly. The monkey chattered, and the woman in the top hat fed it a date.

Janx waved a hand at the group. "These are your spies, Doc. Who d'ya think'll be followin' our fair wee admiral around, eh?"

Avery had been afraid of this. "But ... I thought you were going to use professionals. I'm paying good money for professionals ..." He'd pledged all that was left of his new bonus to do it, too, and that had just been a down payment.

"We *are* professionals," Muirblaag said, sounding mildly offended.

The black man said, "We've been hired on jobs too numerous and varied to relate. And we couldn't anyway, because they're confidential."

Avery forced himself to silence for a moment, then said, "So you're thieves?"

"Entrepreneurs, more like," said Muirblaag.

"With some thievin' thrown in," said the woman with the monkey.

"Who do you think placed the bets tonight?" Janx said. "Mu and I couldn't do it, now, could we? Not without lookin' queer. See, we've worked many jobs together, the lot o' us. You said you wanted the best. Ya came to the right place."

Avery passed a hand over his face. *This is all wrong.* "How can I trust you? You're criminals! Do you know what's at stake here? It could be ... well, it could be everything."

Muirblaag lifted his hairless eyebrows. "Everything?"

Briefly, and to Avery's horror, Janx related what Avery had told him of the situation, with a quick aside to Avery: "They're riskin' their lives. They need to know."

Afterwards, there was some swearing and shaking of heads.

"This is *big*," said the woman with the monkey. "Fuck me."

"Exactly," said Avery. "What we're doing is not only important, it may determine whether Ghenisa stands or falls. And even whether Octung is stopped or not."

The little man spat. "Damn."

Concerned, Avery drew Janx to the side once more. "I don't think they're up to the job," he said. "And I still can't believe you told them the truth."

"They're up for it," Janx said, sounding very sober. "But since you're payin' for this, I can see why you'd want to be sure."

"It's not about the money, although I have precious little of it. It's—"

Janx broke off and conferred with his group in low tones. Several cursed. The woman with the monkey shrugged. Muirblaag said, "We ain't gettin' paid enough."

"It ain't always about money," Janx said. "'sides, I think we got that part covered." He tapped his bulging pocket.

Muirblaag frowned. "I'm in if you are. We've already started the damned job, anyway. Why not see it through?"

"Binding, you mean?" said the black man.

"I think that should cost more," said the woman with the monkey.

"Fine," Avery said. "I'll double your fee." This was a bald-faced lie, of course, since he had nothing more to give. He could pay in installments forever and not pay what he would owe. But if whatever this *binding* was made them take the assignment more seriously, it was well worth the lie. "Payable after it's done."

"All right, then," said the woman. "I'm in." She considered. "Shit, I don't need double. Tell you what, bones, I'll do it for just twenty percent more. I mean, if it's that all-fired important, if we can really throw a wrench into Octung's plans."

"Thank you," Avery said, and meant it.

"You're a sweetheart, Hildra," Janx said. "Alright, twenty percent more. Now, if that's settled, I'll be right back."

"Where's he going?" Avery asked, as the whaler disappeared up a fire escape. "What did I just pay for?"

"He went to get some things," Muirblaag said.

"What things?"

"It's just somethin' we do from time to time, like when some richer hires us to do a job, steal somethin' or whatnot, but doesn't trust us. Well, we started this little thing you're about to see. It keeps us true, like it or not—and it's helped us get many a job."

Shortly Janx returned, a sack slung over his back. He extracted some wood, built a small pile on the rooftop, then squirted it with lighter fluid. The strike of a match, and fire blazed loudly, throwing sparks high into the night.

The others grumbled but meandered over. They seemed willing to follow whatever lead Janx and Muirblaag provided, if halfheartedly. All grouped around the fire.

Janx produced a heavy, aged volume and read a passage in what sounded like ancient L'ohen—Avery was shocked—and the criminals recited the passage, then another. At first they spoke listlessly, but their enthusiasm gained substance as they went on. During one particular passage, Janx tossed something that looked like dust into the fire. The fire blazed up, brighter than before, and turned, to Avery's surprise, green.

The criminals grew quiet, and the eerie green light bathed their faces. Muirblaag, assisting Janx, took out a hunting knife from the sack. He closed his eyes, muttered something in L'ohen, and slit his palm over the fire. Inky blood fell into flames. He wiped the knife blade clean, using alcohol, then passed it to Janx, who said something himself, it sounded like some sort of private prayer, used the knife himself and passed it on. So it went, from criminal to criminal, each swearing some oath and bleeding into the fire. At last Janx looked up and said, "Your turn, Doc."

"Me?"

Janx inclined his head. All the others turned to watch Avery.

Swallowing, he stepped forward. "I don't normally pray," he said.

"That's fine," Muirblaag said. "Just call to whatever gods you believe in, bind our oaths to you."

"And what are they?"

"Whattaya think?" Janx said. "To follow your orders. To finish the job."

"But don't get fuckity," said the small man. "You can only bind us to what we've already agreed to."

"Do you know what you're doing?" Avery said. "What you might be swearing yourselves into? What you've *already* sworn yourselves to?"

"Do you?" said Janx.

Avery hesitated, then joined the circle around the fire. Someone passed him the knife. Without a second thought, he raised his hand over the fire and prepared to cut. He paused for a moment, then, only because he had no gods to pray to. Generally when he prayed it was to the fates, or to whatever god might be listening. Then he thought of Mari and Ani, and he slit his palm. As his blood fell into the crackling green flames, he said, "I swear to the Three Sisters to lead these men and this woman against Sheridan, to collect evidence that she's a spy, to stop her at whatever cost, to protect my patient and to help her save Ghenisa."

Wind howled around him as he passed the knife back, and the burning in his palm hardly bothered him. Someone passed him a flask, and he drank from it gladly.

"So," Janx said, "you trust us now?"

Avery peered around at them, somehow feeling closer to them. *This could work*, he told himself. *It has to.* "Yes," he said. "I believe I do."

"Good."

Avery regarded them all. "Tail Sheridan. Find who she's meeting—the other spies, of course, but most important is her handler. The spymaster. If we can find him, or her, we can bring down the whole network." If they could do that, he thought, his mermaid would be safe.

Janx rubbed his forehead. "She may not go to her handler much, if at all, Doc, from what I know about spies. How're we gonna make sure she sees him?"

"Leave that to me."

Chapter 7

"You see yourself the improvement in her," said Doctor Wasnair, stabbing at the woman's medical chart. He, Avery and three of the other committee members stood over Patient X's bed. She looked quite well today, attractive and healthy, yet she slumbered on, unaware of their discussion.

"Her fever's lower," Avery allowed. "But how can she ever get better in this place?" He gestured around them.

The subbasement the lab was located in was dank and dark. Composed like the rest of Fort Brunt of huge stone blocks, the room stank of mold and strange chemicals, and Avery constantly feared that some nasty infection would creep into his patient. Yet the committee would not move her. This was one of the Navy's secret labs, and it was covered in work benches, instruments, crammed with cold storage units, festooned with weird things in jars and huddling under dangerous substances in innumerable vials. Avery hated just to step foot in here, and yet the committee would see no change despite his repeated attempts.

"Nonsense," Wasnair said. "*This place* is having no ill effect on her. Quite the reverse, I think—and that is what you want, isn't it? Hasn't it been you that's led the charge in bringing her back, as opposed to studying her anatomy?"

Avery nodded as tolerantly as he could. "Yes, but it is in spite of this place that she's improved. I say her recovery would accelerate if she were moved, perhaps to a place with fresh air, a view of the sun."

Dr. Wasnair sniffed. He was a tall, skinny man, with spotted skin, a thin nose, and a worse comb-over than

Avery's. "The sun! The sun will not cure her. Only our treatments will, and we cannot house her in the main hospital."

Avery sighed. He knew he could not win this battle. Best to let it go for now so as not to endanger his standing with the others, who did not appreciate his obstinacy on the matter. The men and women of the committee were secretive and mysterious, used to conducting strange and likely unethical experiments far away from prying eyes. In theory their studies were intended to help win the war or at least stave off defeat for a while longer. Rumors spoke of dark, desperate research being conducted on lower sublevels, resurrection projects, alchemical plagues, but Avery's clearance wasn't high enough for him to venture down there.

"Very well," he said. "She stays. Now—if we can move on to discussing the change in the antibody solution. I think increasing the levels is a mis—"

Alarms blared throughout the lab. Sharp, heavy blades of sound.

The doctors and scientists stopped what they were doing and stared up at the ceiling, as if trying to see through the heavy stone. It wouldn't surprise Avery if a few of them could. Gods alone knew what they had done to themselves. Some barely looked human, with translucent skin and colorless eyes, some with veins that glowed slightly, sometimes red, sometimes purple. Rumors maintained that some of them were over a century old, that they had even performed research for the Drakes themselves.

"An attack," hissed Dr. Evra Sayd, a squat woman with thick lips and bulging eyes. Too-visible veins ran beneath her grayish, papery skin. Hair like a mop haloed her large head.

"Damn it all," said Dr. Wasnair. "I'd hoped conquering Es'hem would have delayed them more."

"It doesn't matter," Dr. Ragund said. "Battle's not our place. Let the grunts handle it."

"It matters if we lose," Dr. Sayd snapped, looking suddenly afraid.

"We should send a member up to be our eyes," Dr. Sayd said. "If the battle goes ill for us, we need to prepare."

"A *junior* member," added Sharra Winegold, swiveling her bespectacled gaze to Avery.

All eyes turned to him.

"Very well," Avery said. "I'll go. Just don't make any decisions regarding our patient while I'm away."

Dr. Wasnair smiled thinly. "We wouldn't think of it, Doctor. Now go. I want a full report when you return."

Alarms blared overhead as Avery made his way through the reinforced subbasement tunnels and up through the bowels of the fortress, and he felt a flutter in his belly with every strident peal. Periodically he passed through checkpoints and had to sign out. He rose up through four levels before finally reaching the ground floor, where he found himself surrounded by soldiers tugging on jackets and helmets, following shouting commanders toward the main entrances. The soldiers looked especially grim, and Avery didn't wonder why. If Octung had decided to launch its navy against the Hissig-based fleet at last, then the end was finally upon them. Avery tasted bile in the back of his throat and hoped he didn't embarrass himself by throwing up.

Following a phalanx of soldiers, he emerged from the fortress into the night. The wind off the sea braced him, and as he breathed in the acrid, electric taste he felt his eyes water. Lightning blasted across the dark waves, and foaming crests broke against the black rocks of the beach. Hundreds of military ships heaved up and down on the swells. Some swarmed with sailors readying for battle.

Avery stood on the broad stoop of the fortress, staring out over the sea, shoulders hunched, hands shoved into jacket pockets. He saw no sign of the enemy. No warships, no shells exploding. He could not even hear gunfire. When the next phalanx of soldiers jogged past, he called out, "Where's the enemy?"

The soldiers did not reply. Numerous units mustered in formations on the shore as if awaiting an enemy landing party. They loaded guns and mounted machine gun emplacements, took positions behind barricades built long ago, and dropped into trenches that had been cut into the hard rock of the beach for just such a day. And still there was no sign of an enemy.

The knots in Avery's belly began to unwind. It was a relief to be out of the labs. *If only it weren't so damned cold.* Shivering, feeling his sinuses begin to run, he waited.

A familiar shape hurried by, then paused when it noticed him. "Look at you, out of the labs. I thought you'd turned into a mole like the rest."

Avery smiled, or tried to. "Not yet," he said.

"Well, stay safe," Lt. Hinis said. She had adjusted well to life on land, Avery thought. In times of peace she would have been allowed to retire from military life after her injury, but at the moment a well-trained woman with one good arm was better than nothing.

"Can I ask where the enemy is?" he asked, before she could rush off.

"They're comin' from the water."

"Submarines? The harbor's too shallow."

"Shit, I wish it was subs. I wish it were anything but what we're getting."

"I don't—"

"Gotta go. 'luck, Doc."

She hurried up the beach and dropped into a trench swarming with activity, and he frowned, staring out over the water, waiting. His legs began to ache. He was just about to retreat indoors for a cup of coffee when, without warning, it happened. The whole world seemed to stop. All his attention riveted on that one insane thing.

Water burst on the beach directly before a certain phalanx of soldiers, not far from Lt. Hinis's trench. Spray glittered under the moonlight, and some awesome, monstrous form exploded from the surf. Time may have slowed for Avery, but the soldiers were prepared for it. Commanders screamed orders, and gunfire sounded. Tracer rounds flickered through the dark and punched into the shape that had materialized from the harbor.

Undeterred, it clambered up the beach toward the soldiers, claws snapping with cracks like thunder. At the sight, Avery felt the strength sap from his limbs.

At first he was not sure what he was seeing. It was simply some nightmare given substance, all claws and weird insectile limbs sticking out at odd angles, mandibles snapping, sparks flashing. But then, when the water sloughed away from its scaled armor, and the lights along the beach picked it out a little bit more, he realized what it was, and a part of him wanted to laugh.

It was, quite simply, a lobster. Or rather its distant ancestors had been lobsters. This abomination had been spawned by the far-flung descendants of the first lobsters to survive the encroaching foulness that had gripped the ocean a millennium ago. Over twenty feet tall, perhaps a hundred long, the creature was not a thing of the sane world. Mutated and made strange by the sea, it was a horror, with too many claws, eyes sticking out at odd places, some with antennae growing through them. Slabs of armor overgrew each other, creating odd mounds. Lightning arced from claw to claw, from claw to antennae, from twisted legs to gnashing mouthparts. It was a mad thing, an electric thing, a true scion of the Atomic Sea.

It clambered up the beach, pincers clacking, and gunfire slammed into it from half a dozen positions. Lightning flashed from one of its strange claws into a group of soldiers. White fire exploded, and screaming men and women flew through the air. The atomic lobster clacked its claws again, and another burst of electricity skewered the man operating the machine gun. The gun and its heavy shells erupted, spraying fire and shrapnel into the soldiers behind the barricade. Those in the trench, some on fire, scrambled out, howling in agony. One was Lt. Hinis.

In a rage, half a dozen troops ran at the decapod, guns spitting. To his shock, Avery realized that one of them was Hinis, slapping at the flames on her right stump with a hand that held an automatic rifle. Her one-armed silhouette was easily recognizable.

When she and the others in her group drew within ten yards of the decapod, it opened its mandibles and did the strangest thing of all.

It *screamed.*

It was a high, weird wail, one that reminded Avery of nails across a chalkboard, but amplified immeasurably. The wall of horrible, teeth-rattling sound hit Hinis and the others, and it had an effect Avery never would have believed had he not seen it firsthand. The lobster screamed—*and the soldiers melted.*

Like candles with a flame set too high, Hinis and the others wilted under the blast of sound and melted from the tops of their heads to their feet. The flesh and bones, brain and muscle, it all dissolved into fluid, and like heated wax the soldiers' bodies puddled at their feet, which liquefied as well.

"No!" Avery shouted, but of course there was nothing he could do, nothing anyone could do.

The crustacean scuttled over the melted figures toward the men and women in the trenches and behind the barricades. Already it was weakening under the hail of bullets, but it still struggled up the beach relentlessly.

Before it reached the barricades, more bursts of foam and water erupted from the shore behind it, and more decapods scuttled up out of the water, claws snapping, lightning arcing. Half a dozen at first, then a dozen, then two dozen of the crustaceans picked their way across the beach toward the soldiers. The men and women fought back, firing with everything they had. The decapods' shells absorbed all but the largest-caliber weapons, and their lightning blasts destroyed the machine gunners and their guns. Commanders shouted for heavy artillery to be brought to bear, but the huge pieces took time to maneuver, and the battle could be over by then.

Breathless, shivering, fearing that the end had come at last and wondering how it had happened, how the Octunggen had manipulated these nightmares, perhaps even bred them in the cauldron of the sea, Avery took stock. He had no guns, no weapons of any sort, and they were all but useless against the creatures anyway.

The lobsters swarmed up the beach, snapping men in two with their claws, spearing them with bolts of electricity, and, when they deemed it prudent, melting them with unearthly screams.

The crustaceans overran the troops' positions. Men and women fell back, and back. Melted flesh ran across the stones.

Several of the soldiers had been injured, and they lay on the ground bleeding—from shrapnel wounds mainly, caused by exploding machine gun mounts. The doctor in Avery could not sit by. Summoning what was left of his courage, he rushed down the beach. Other medics, embedded in the phalanxes, crouched over the injured, giving what aid they could, but there were too few of them.

Just as Avery approached the nearest injured soldier, three decapods broke through directly before him.

Claws snapping, they rushed in. He could smell their mineral reek, see the barnacles hugging their armored sides, hear the rasp as sections of their carapaces scraped against others. Lightning crackled from claw and mandible. The lead crustacean drew near and towered over him, stalks waving above its head, mouthparts gnashing.

Avery jumped back. The crustacean drove on. Avery retreated, knowing as long as he drew the creature's attention it wouldn't attack the soldier he'd been coming to help. The other two crustaceans found other targets.

The decapod followed Avery. The doctor backed toward Fort Brunt, but he slipped in blood and fell.

The decapod opened its mouthparts to scream.

SNAP.

Avery heard the tremendous, metallic sound, then another, and another, and all at once a strange *hum.* The hum grew into a great wall of noise that washed over him and the beach, filling him with pain. He clapped his hands over his ears. On the beach soldiers covered their ears, too.

The lobster over Avery paused, its antennae twitching.

Vaguely Avery realized what must be happening. He had noted the strange blocky, bus-sized machines that stood along the beach when he'd first arrived, and over the last few weeks he had inquired about them and been told that they were defensive weapons powered by the same hot lard the other machines and processors that protected Ghenisa from the unworldly weapons of the Octunggen were.

Now he found out what they did.

At first the machines simply clicked on. The click was like a giant mousetrap snapping. Each one clicked in turn, from the ones near the fortress all the way up the beach to the civilian marina to the north, a domino chain of monstrous mousetraps. Next the machines began to hum. The hum grew louder and louder until at last it drowned out the sound of gunfire, burnings and decapod screams. The sound grew so loud it wedged into Avery's skull like a hot shovel through his brain. He saw others all up and down the beach drop their weapons and clutch at their heads. Some fell to the ground and rolled about, driven mad by the noise.

The great crustacean that had been advancing on him had stopped. The stalks on its head stood still.

Three of the lobsters had fallen under the barrage of gunfire, and their dying bodies floundered horrifically on the beach. The rest that had been sweeping the men's positions halted, seeming to hesitate. The sound bothered them, possibly, or else the noise was simply a by-product of the machines' true purpose. Either way, the lobsters ceased their advance.

Then, gradually, as the humming grew in intensity, one of the crustaceans turned back. It clacked across the beach and slipped beneath the surface of the sea. Moments later four others followed. Then more. And more. At last, the lobster towering over Avery turned about and retreated. Avery trembled in relief.

Encouraged, some of the men and women that could still bring themselves to function trained their weapons on the remaining decapods, who were evidently unsure what to do, and opened fire. That broke the creatures' indecision. Hailed by heavy gunfire, they turned around and slipped beneath the waves.

The soldiers hurrahed. Even Avery hurrahed, screaming into the buzzing hum of the machines, though he could barely hear his own voice.

The machines continued sounding for some time after the retreat of the crustaceans, then began to taper off, finally ceasing altogether, though Avery's head still rang. He realized he'd been holding his breath and took a deep one. All up and down the beach soldiers were looking at each other strangely, relief mixed with confusion and fear. Many spontaneously embraced and clapped each other on the back. Others fingered their ears and shook their heads. Many retched. Avery almost did. A few who had received their earplugs in time to use them—this had not been so unexpected, after all—merely removed the plugs and looked around, dazed but sensible.

Yawning to pop his ears, Avery stared at the giant crustacean carcasses, one of which still clutched dead men and women in its claws. Bodies littered the beach around them. Avery wondered if what was left of Lt. Hinis's body could be identified. If so, at least her ashes could be returned to her family.

He heard a laugh and turned to see none other than Jessryl Sheridan.

"Impressive, aren't they?" she said. "The machines, I mean. When I heard the sonar readings, I had to see them in action."

"Captain—I mean, Admiral—"

"Come to me in an hour." From the tone of her voice, she did not have to say for what. It was the first time she'd requested his attentions since they'd reached Hissig. Evidently battle got her blood going.

Not waiting for a reply, she walked down the steps toward the recovering soldiers, leaving Avery popping his ears and staring after her. His heart still beat rapidly, and his limbs still trembled. How could she possibly be in the mood after what had just happened? Then he realized it.

This is it, he thought. *This is my chance.*

He dusted himself off and made his way down the beach to help the injured.

"That was quite something," Avery said, pouring himself a glass of brandy. He'd recovered (somewhat) from the shock of battle, though he was certain he'd be dreaming of giant crustaceans for some time to come. He and Sheridan stood on a high terrace of Fort Brunt, staring out over the sea. The terrace jutted from Sheridan's apartment, which was wide and luxurious compared to the simple quarters occupied by most soldiers. All admirals based out of Hissig lived at Fort Brunt, and Avery understood that Sheridan's quarters were nothing compared to the high admirals who lived on the top level. Still, they were impressive. As was the view.

The dark waters of the harbor frothed below, and electricity flared up from the waves. No sign of another attack.

"You mean, the repellers?" Sheridan stretched herself out on a chair. She wore only a towel wrapped around her middle, and her skin still glowed from sex and shower. "Yes, they worked sensationally."

"Is that what they're called? Repellers?"

She lit one of her thin black cigars. "Developed among other things to break Octunggen hold of their pet monsters. They breed them on the Vursulan coast, near the seat of their navy." Octung was a landlocked country, Avery knew, but it had essentially purchased the government of the poor, corrupt Vursul decades ago—Vursul being a relatively large country occupying an entire peninsula unto itself—and Octung's navy had grown into a mighty armada. "Our agents reported that the Octunggen were finally prepared to use them, so we made provisions to defend ourselves. Sadly, the repellers drain our stores of lard quite rapidly."

"And we had to let the one whale go ..."

"You still hold that against me?"

Avery leaned against the wrought-iron railing and stared out over the harbor. "We need the lard. We can't have much left in our stores."

Her cigar crackled. "No. And Octung knows it. It doesn't have to succeed in its attacks, merely drain our stores until we're vulnerable enough, then deliver the killing blow."

Which you're helping it deliver. "Surely there's something we can do."

"It's not for us to decide." Ice clinked in her glass. "Yet."

"You still plan on climbing the ladder, then?"

"And why not? War makes for rapid promotion. And, I think, with the war headed the way it is, people will grow tired of the Prime Minister's handling of things."

That caught him by surprise. "You can't mean ..."

She chuckled. "Surely you're not that loyal to Denaris. You, whose own wife had to live on the run for so many years, whose family was hounded by the government."

"That was different. What you're talking about ... a military coup ..."

"Obviously I wasn't talking about a coup. That would be idiotic. I just think the people will tire of Denaris's bungling."

"Some say she's all that's holding the country together."

"No, *that* would be the military, and *that* is run by our own Admiral Haggarty."

Avery raised his eyebrows. He knew there was a very public rift between the Grand Admiral and the Prime Minister. The Grand Admiral supported sealing off the borders, admitting no refugees, ousting those already here, and declaring neutrality in the war.

Sheridan seemed to see his understanding. "The people will soon see that the war cannot be won," she said. "Not by us. They'll gravitate toward Haggarty, I'm sure of it. And here I am in the perfect position to achieve influence."

Ah. It began to make sense, her plan. She wanted Ghenisa to back out of the war, to make it easier on Octung. When Octung had defeated the surrounding countries, it could come back and subdue Ghenisa at its leisure. *Clever.* But he didn't have to make it easy on her.

"To what end?" he said. "Neutrality will only delay the inevitable, and it'll mean we stop aiding our allies. Then *they'll* fall, and we'll be picked off all the sooner."

"So what do you advocate?"

It was time for it, he supposed. He made his voice uncertain. "We must fight. It's just that ..."

"Yes?"

"What can we *do* against them? We're nearly out of hot lard, our navy's broken, our army's outmatched, our allies are falling one by one, and the only thing saving us from total destruction is the fact that the mountains block the Octunggen off on two sides, and Cumnal blocks them to the south. But they're coming through the Pass soon, and Cumnal can't last forever ..." He made a noise of frustration, then gestured toward the right, to the dark shore beyond. "We're teeming with refugees we can't feed. Soon we won't even be able to supply them with pollution pills, and what then? The very air will kill or change them. And meanwhile they're succumbing to the temptations of the black market, diseased food and the like. I've heard some are even selling themselves into slavery overseas, giving their families the money and letting criminals take them away, to who knows where?"

She nodded, eyeing him with interest. "I don't think I've ever seen you so animated, Doctor. I think this battle's brought you out of your shell. If you'll forgive my choice of words."

He leaned against the railing. "It all just seems so ... pointless."

Something passed across her face. "And yet you would defend the government that's led you here?"

He glanced up at her, careful to keep his expression impartial, curious. This is what he'd wanted, for her to reveal herself to him, to try to seduce him into her games.

"Do you know of an alternative?"

She stared at him for a long moment, weighing, judging. At last she looked away and inhaled on her cigar.

"I'll think on it," she said.

He let out a breath. Nodded. It wouldn't do to appear overeager. "I think it's time for me to go." It was three in the morning, and he needed to get what sleep he could.

"It's a long trip back to the Drake," she commented, seemingly off-hand.

"Are you ... are you offering me a *bed* for the night?"

He couldn't read the expression in her eyes as she said, "Captain Marsh just died today, melted by one of the crustaceans. His room's on the next level down. Just say the word and ... it's yours."

He rubbed his head. Her offer was tempting, certainly, and it revealed something in her that almost smacked of tenderness. On the other hand, he did not want to be her pet lover, living just a beck and call away, under her constant supervision and sufferance.

"Thank you. But no. I need the comforts of home to get to sleep these days, now that I'm back on land. Suppose I'm getting old."

She shrugged, but—and he might be imagining this—he thought he saw something sad rise behind her eyes, then quickly be dragged away.

"Very well," she said.

He dressed in the living room. Clothes were strewn everywhere, draped over plush couches, sprawled at the roots of antique chairs. Candlelight glimmered on the brass fixtures of the marble fireplace.

Sheridan's bagrith chittered at him, and Avery tried to hide his shudder. He'd always hated batkin. He couldn't understand why anyone would want one as a pet, though he knew it had pained Sheridan to leave the thing behind while at sea.

Criggred was the size of a dog, but he still possessed the nightmarish form and face of a bat. His front claws, trailing their vestigial wings, scraped at the ground.

The vile thing hissed at him, then, wanting to gain some height, climbed one of the ornate pillars monkey-like and lifted its lips at him, affording Avery a good glimpse of needle teeth. He had heard there were batkin that lived in the Borghese that had grown to the size of men and drank blood, but he suspected these were just rumors.

He buttoned the last button on his shirt, snapped his pants up, and left Sheridan's apartment. She remained on the balcony, smoking and staring out into the night. He wondered if he could really convince her to trust him, to take him into her confidence and engage him in her espionage. Part of him still hoped he might be wrong about her, that Hambry's letters had been the ravings of a lunatic. *If only she would just smile,* he thought. *A real, human smile.*

He descended the many levels of the fortress, eschewing the sometimes-functioning lifts that had been installed some thirty years ago. He wanted to walk. He wanted to sweat. Making whatever he had been making with Sheridan had not been enough. His knees protested after a few levels, his heart pounded, and before long he was sweaty and laboring for breath—his body reminding him of his age. The pleasant buzz the brandy had given him began to recede.

Down a hallway, he heard the crackle and hiss of a radio. Some announcer rattled off a series of casualty figures, detailing the costs of a recent battle. Octung was advancing through the mountains. Nothing surprising there. One interesting item caught Avery's ears, though, and he paused in the hallway to listen: "... and our agents report conflict in Lusterqal tonight. That's right, violence erupts in the capital of Octung. What is the cause? We can't know for sure, but sources tell us that the mysterious Black Sect have struck again, this time against the priests of the Collossum. The backlash has locked the city down. What the Black Sect is still remains a mystery, but at this juncture ..."

Avery moved on. A few dead priests weren't going to help anything. Still, it was reassuring to know there were saboteurs working the other side.

When he reached the ground level, he hesitated. Sheridan had been right. It was too far to the Headless Drake and there were only a few hours before he was due to report in for the morning shift at any rate.

He descended into the subbasements. Night guards scanned his ID as he passed through the various checkpoints.

"Late night, Doc?" one asked.

He nodded tiredly. "Or an early day."

In Laboratory Eleven he found to his mild surprise the gargantuan corpse of one of the lobsters. It towered in the center of the room, rust-colored, barnacle-encrusted, massive claws draped across the floor. It still stank of the sea, accented with the strange mineral odor he had noticed before and a lingering trace of ozone.

Dr. Wasnair and a team of scientists stood near its head, just beyond its thick, bump-covered stalks. A clutch of black, unblinking eyes stared at them, glassy in the artificial lights that flickered overhead. The men and women poked and prodded at it, occasionally snapping pictures or writing things down in notebooks.

Dr. Wasnair smiled in delight as he saw Avery approach. "Doctor, you simply *must* come here. Isn't it fabulous?"

Avery reached them and stared at the huge blunt head, the inhuman eyes, the complicated mouthparts.

"Beautiful," he said.

Wasnair laughed, clapping his hands in glee. "Yes, isn't it? The Octunggen produce them, you know, but I can't help but wonder if they grow naturally or if the Octunggen have found ways to manipulate their maturation, or some combination of the two. In any case, they're lovely."

"They'd make great pets."

"Just think of the possibilities. This amazing creature can melt people with a *sound*. What if we could discover the apparatus that *allows* that? What if we could *amplify* it, melt entire Octunggen *legions* with a device modeled after it? Wouldn't that be amazing?"

Avery nodded guardedly. "Yes." It sounded very much like an Octunggen weapon, he thought—very much, in fact, like the one that had killed his wife and child, even if the effects were different. "But what if you happen upon its electrical organs instead and end up frying yourself?" He laughed. "I'd let the junior doctors handle it."

Wasnair relaxed a bit and chuckled. "But then who would get the glory?" He seemed to really notice Avery for the first time. "What are you doing here at this hour, anyway?"

Avery didn't want to say he'd come to find a corner to curl up in. "I wanted to check on Patient X before retiring."

Wasnair nodded doubtfully, obviously curious about where Avery had been for the last two hours. "You never did report back to us after the battle."

Avery kicked at a huge, barnacle-encrusted claw. "It seems you found out what you needed to."

He turned away, and Wasnair and the others returned their attention to the lobster. For the sake of appearances, Avery strode toward the curtained-off quarter of the room where the mystery woman slumbered. He grabbed a chart and pretended to review it as he slipped behind the curtain. The curtains were only drawn at night, as during the daytime when the investigative committee was on duty she had to be viewable.

Yawning, Avery sat the notebook down and collapsed in the hard metal chair near the woman's bed. Now, finally, he could get some rest. Wasnair and the others would be so consumed with their new find that they wouldn't even notice his absence.

Before he closed his eyes, his gaze drifted toward the mystery patient, as it had a thousand times before.

She stared back at him.

Chapter 8

Once again, Avery was struck by how blue her eyes were, like the sea after a storm. Slowly, tiredly, they blinked. She shifted and stirred, turning her gaze from him to the drapes, the ceiling, taking it all in. She didn't seem surprised by her surroundings. Perhaps she had been awake for some time, or at least in the process of waking.

He sat there, riveted. His breath came fast and shallow, and he felt all traces of sleep evaporate.

"Damn," he whispered, unable to help himself.

The woman's eyes returned to him. She was more beautiful than he had remembered. Then again, he had only once before seen her with her eyes open. The difference it made was incalculable. She was lovely.

"Gedden es unkul rae?"

The Octunggen chilled his blood, as it had the first time. "You are in a hospital," he replied in the same language, though not with the same fluidity. "How long have you been awake?"

"Some time. I did not like the look of the others. I hoped you would come."

"You did? Why?"

"You did not betray me last time." Her words came out slightly slurred. She was still weak.

"How do you know?"

"I still live." She let him process that, then said, "I should not have confided in you then, but I was weak. I needed someone. This ... it does not look like ... a hospital." Her eyes dared him to lie.

He nodded slowly. "It's a military hospital."

"You are ... a soldier?"

He tried on a smile. It felt false. "I'm a doctor, as you know. You ... you've been sick. For a long time."

Suddenly she looked uneasy. "For how long?"

"Months. You've been in a coma. We found you ..." He sucked in a breath. Now, finally, he would get the answers he had waited so long for. Sudden anticipation made him sit up straighter, made him lick his lips and straighten his jacket. "We found you at sea. In the belly ... in the belly of a great whale." He could hardly contain himself. "Could you please tell me how you arrived there, if you know? How you survived the sea in the first place? You were naked, without protection."

The woman stared at him. Pain filled her eyes. She wrenched her head away, whispered something in bitter tones that he did not catch and wiped at a tear in the corner of her eye. "Months ..."

"Yes. Not to harp on this, but how did you wind up in the whale?" He heard the desperation in his voice but couldn't help it. He *had* to know.

She continued to stare upward. "*Hizven!*" she said, an Octunggen curse word. Her hands balled into fists, and her fists shook at her sides. In the background Avery heard the laughter of the scientists and the whine of a bone saw. He need not fear being overheard.

He leaned forward. The movement earned him the woman's attention, but her eyes narrowed as they fell on him, and suddenly he felt cold. Whoever she was, she possessed a powerful personality. He could feel the weight of it whenever she looked at him, and the absence of it when she didn't.

"And you healed," he heard himself say. "You healed unnaturally fast. I ... I've never seen anything like it, in all my medical career. Or *heard* of anything like it. It's almost ... inhuman."

She hardly seemed to be paying attention. Suddenly she started to sit up, apparently impatient to be on her way, but even her amazing body had experienced muscle atrophy over the two months of her coma. She groaned in pain and collapsed to the bed, gasping. Sweat beaded her brow.

He patted her forearm. She wrenched her arm away.

Clearing his throat in embarrassment, he said, "It'll take some time before you regain your strength. Of course, with your regenerative abilities, this might be accelerated now that you can exercise, but ... it will still be some time." He indicated the intravenous tubes that connected to her arms, pumping her full of medical and alchemical substances. "I think eating proper food again will help. We've been feeding you through the tubes, but I must confess I wouldn't want to eat what comes through there." He had to struggle with the words, and he knew he must sound like a fool to a native Octunggen.

Perhaps he was right, as she glared at him haughtily. Then, slowly, she softened, and her body sort of sagged. She breathed out a long breath. He supposed she must be realizing that she needed him for the moment, that for now she was helpless.

"I must leave here," she said. "It's urgent."

"I'm sorry, but that's impossible." He imagined what would happen if Dr. Wasnair and the others discovered that the woman was Octunggen. People like them had invented most of the torture techniques used during the time of the Drakes, and the ancient torture chambers were said to be conveniently located the next level down, home now to secret research—the resurrection projects and the like—but easily cleared for special guests, Avery was sure.

Yet what *could* he do with her? He'd pondered the matter for months and hadn't come up with anything satisfactory.

His silence and evident brooding seemed to intrigue or disturb the woman. She went from sulking and staring at the ceiling to reluctantly looking at him. He could see her out of the corner of his eyes grudgingly begin to view him as an actual person, a person with an agenda of his own.

"What ails you, Doctor?" she said. Still he said nothing. It seemed to worry her. "You are enemies of the Lightning Crown."

Still not looking at her, this time deliberately, he said, "Of Octung, yes. Rather *it* is the enemy, if it is not too theatrical to say, of the world."

No longer were her eyes haughty. They were blue and mysterious, and they gazed at him beseechingly, latching into him like hooks. "You *must* help me, Doctor. I can't tell you all, but I am on a mission."

"Yes, you said before."

"I don't remember."

"You said you were on a mission to stop Octung. It's the only reason why I haven't spoken of you to anyone. Please, tell me more."

"Get me out of here and I'll tell you everything."

"Again, that's impossible. The others consider you property of the Navy. I'm afraid they'll never let you go, especially if they learn you're Octunggen. Not everyone is as gullible as I am."

Her face was tight. "You are not gullible. I'm telling the truth. And I'm not Octunggen. Fine, if they won't let me go, then *you* must, Doctor."

"Tell me how you plan to stop Octung."

"No. I ... cannot. Just know I will, that I will end the war."

He studied her. There was nothing deceitful in her manner, only earnestness and urgency. Could she possibly be telling the truth? It was absurd. And yet ...

"It's not that easy," he said.

Her voice became leaden. "Then Ghenisa will burn. Octung will raze it and set up shrines to the Collossum in its ashes."

"Who *are* you?"

"I am ... have you heard of the Black Sect?"

"Yes. Yes, of course. Heretics and saboteurs."

"We're a lot more than that. We're enemies of the Collossum."

"But they're just gods. Myth ... superstition ..."

She sank back, looking tired. "You would not believe."

"Why don't you let me decide what I'd believe?"

She didn't answer.

"Fine," he said. "If you're part of the Black Sect, you should be an ally of Ghenisa. I could bring in the others."

"No! Spies would find out. Assassins. They would kill me as soon as anyone knew who I was. You can say nothing, Doctor. *To anyone.* If you do, it will mean my death."

She was right, of course. If she could truly harm Octung, Sheridan would kill her or have someone do it for her.

"Can you speak anything other than Octunggen?" he asked.

Slowly, haltingly, she said in Ghenisan but with a strong Octunggen accent, "Speak me small volume languages many."

He winced. "You must pretend, in front of the other doctors, to still be asleep."

Her eyes widened. "I must leave. I will never—"

The bone saw escalated in the background as it drilled through a particularly thick section of carapace, and Avery imagined what other uses Wasnair might find for it.

"You must," he said. At last he looked her in the eyes again, but this time firmly, asserting the power of his own personality. "If you don't, you will die."

Her chin jutted out, but she did not argue.

Reluctantly, he stood. She had no more answers to give, not yet, and now that she was awake he couldn't afford to draw attention to her by staying here. Sooner or later, Dr. Wasnair would surely draw him aside to admire some anatomical feature of the crustacean before letting him go back to sleep.

"Say you'll pretend to still be comatose," he said.

Frustration showed in her face, and she made a growling sound. "But I must grow strong again! How can I become well enough to finish my mission if I'm bedridden?"

"I'm your doctor. I'll help you get well. However, I still haven't decided what to do with you once you *are* well."

She started to say something, but she was obviously exhausted from talking so long. "I can stop ... Octung ..."

"Close your eyes. Get some sleep."

With obvious reluctance, she obeyed. Within moments her breathing became regular, and her eyes rolled under her eyelids.

Wondering at himself, he reached out and tucked her in. He said not one word to Dr. Wasnair and the others as he left the lab to find a quiet spot to sleep in.

Avery visited her the next night, and the night after that. Every night he helped her exercise. He fed her real food, for which she seemed grateful. He worked throughout the days, running blood tests and developing cultures, keeping up his pretense of trying to find out what and who she was. Privately he'd given up on such experiments. He'd found a better, easier way to get his answers. Yet she refused to give away her secrets, only hinted at vast agendas. He still wasn't sure he believed her, but he'd decided to win her trust and go from there. If nothing else, she was a good actress during the days, playing her part as coma patient well.

Between his work during the day and his labors during the night, he found little time for sleep, and it also meant that he had less time for the commute to his apartment. He hadn't been this exhausted since his days as an intern in Benical. Reluctantly, he took Admiral Sheridan up on her offer and bunked in the late Captain Marsh's quarters on the floor below hers. This naturally led to more frequent trysts with the admiral herself, which further spent him. He honestly didn't know how long he could keep this up. At forty-two, he was not a young man.

Added to this pressure were the reports that flooded in daily regarding the war. Octung had finally subjugated Asrakad and was bringing its full powers to bear on Cumnal, which was immediately to the south of Ghenisa and a close ally. To get to Cumnal, the Octunggen first must plow through the highlands of Ungraessot, land of the God-Emperor, home of the Soul Door, but with its might freed from the mire of Asrakad this was less problematic, and Ungraessot was half crushed beneath the boot heel of Octung already. At the same time, Octung also waged war on a host of other nations—the Confederation of Sorwed to the south, Hygaerd with its famous and wealth-producing inland sea, the Illith, and, trampling over the ruins of Asrakad and its brother countries Nalakath and Mureen, drove into the eastern regions of the Ysstral Empire to the north, just across the Borghese Mountains from Ghenisa. And everywhere they went the Octunggen set up their temples to the Collossum and purged the populations of ethnicities and religions disagreeable to them. Rumors spread of strange and horrific experiments being conducted on the prisoners, and on facilities to which prisoners were brought healthy but left either dead or ... inhuman.

Ghenisa, even though sheltered by the Borghese, was not safe. Octung had already tried to strike through the Korwen Pass, through which Ghenisa had historically traded with Ungraessot, but Ghenisa had collapsed two mountains into it, stymieing the Octunggen advance. Not to be put off, Octunggen engineers worked day and night at removing and destroying the debris, aided by their strange technologies, while aerial, dirigible-mounted patrols sought for ways around the pass.

No one knew where Octung had acquired such technology, nor could any other country even build similar machines on their own. Some scientists claimed that the devices used what they called *extradimensional* capabilities. In any event, the only way to counter the otherworldly weapons was by stealing information related to them (and sometimes parts) to produce similar weapons. Thus it was a war of spies and counter-spies, and Avery knew he must stop Sheridan before she disclosed something vital to Octung, if it was not too late already.

He didn't push her. He didn't want her becoming suspicious of him. Still, he was eager for her to take him into her confidence. She didn't follow up on their discussion the night of the crustacean attack, not immediately, but sometimes he would catch her staring at him, eyeing him as a man might eye a dog that he wanted for his own yet was afraid might bite.

Meanwhile, Dr. Wasnair and his cabal continued their research into the crustacean, and in a magnanimous display he bade Avery to assist. This was Avery's invitation to join a wider world of scientific pursuit and a possible step on the ladder of promotion.

On the morning of the eighth day after the attack, Dr. Sharra Winegold and three assistants—or at least their remains—were found as puddles of rotting flesh on the floor beside the great decapod. Winegold's distinct puddle was identified by her horn-rimmed spectacles, whose frames had remained mostly solid.

Instead of being saddened or intimidated, Dr. Wasnair rejoiced, exclaiming that the gland that caused melting could not only be located but was still operable. Sadly Dr. Winegold's notes were ruined by her own dissolved flesh and so much of the carapace had been cut open that it was impossible to determine what anatomical feature she and her assistants had been studying at the time of their accident.

Piles of carapace were stacked in the corner, carefully photographed and analyzed. One by one they were sent to the incinerator. So went the remains of Dr. Winegold and her assistants once they had been scraped off the floor.

Avery, when his time came to investigate the crustacean, limited his researches to familiar-looking organs.

From all this, he gained an idea.

"Dr. Wasnair thinks he's hit upon something," he said. He and Sheridan lay in bed together.

Sheridan, lighting a cigar, seemed only half-interested. "Yes?"

Strictly speaking, Avery was not supposed to divulge any information related to his research to anyone not in the scientific strata of the Navy. In fact, he was only supposed to report to the investigative committee and its immediate supervisors. Just by saying anything, he was technically committing treason. He hoped Sheridan appreciated this.

"The crustaceans' ability to melt enemies," he said. "He thinks he's discovered the apparatus responsible." This was nonsense, of course. Even if Wasnair ever located the organ, Avery knew it would be years before he could use it to create weapons. And Ghenisa did not have years.

Smoke drifted up from Sheridan's thin black cigar. She turned her gaze toward him. "Oh?"

"He plans to develop a device to amplify the ability. Destroy entire Octunggen legions at once with just a sound."

Flame crackled on the tip of her cigar. "Why are you telling me this?"

He interlocked his fingers behind his head. "No reason. It's just interesting, that's all."

She said nothing, but he could feel her gaze on him. At last she said, "Is this machine ... in development?"

How far should he go? "Not yet," he said. He could almost feel her breathe easier. "But soon." She tensed. "Certain engineering principles must be worked out. This technology is all quite alien, you know. It reminds me very much of the weapons Octung has been using against us, in fact."

With an unladylike grunt, she leapt up from the bed and strode to the bar. The muscles of her shoulder blades and buttocks flexed and rolled as she walked. Criggred, her hideous bagrith, chittered and approached her. As she poured herself a drink, she tossed him a cube of ice. Criggred caught it and crushed the cube between his rear teeth with a snap like breaking bone. Avery winced.

Sheridan sipped her drink at the bar with one hand, smoked with the other, and a thoughtful look came over her. For some reason, Avery felt his skin tighten, his hairs prickle. Had he gone too far—pressed her too obviously?

Her bedroom was large and opulent. Made of oak, her sturdy bed hunkered beneath white fur blankets, and sealskin carpets draped the stone floors. The barnacled head of a whale calf jutted from one wall, fangs curling out, and a pair of crossed fencing blades hung from the other. Two tall tallow lamps burned with warm light, making the five eyes of the whale calf seem to move.

Sheridan, in a sudden series of motions, sat down her drink, jammed her cigar between her jaws, crossed to the fencing blades, ripped one loose—

—and sprang tiger-like onto the bed.

The mattress bounced under Avery. Shocked, he stared up at Sheridan, gleaming with sweat, standing-straddling him, the point of her blade pressed lightly into his neck, but not so lightly that he didn't feel it prick. A thin trickle of blood welled out.

"Um, Admiral, I don't think ..."

She kicked the furs away. He was utterly naked, and his scrotum contracted. Her voice came, as sharp and hard as her blade: "Commander Hambry's cabin was searched."

Shit. "That's interesting, but—"

"Silence!" She pressed the blade deeper. He gasped. He felt the warmth as more blood trickled down his throat. "I know it was you. You were seen in the officers' quarters late that night, after we reached the convoy. Lt. Ambrum was on the way to the head and recognized you. She said you looked nervous." Sheridan grinned hard around the cigar. "I bet you look more nervous now."

Avery licked his lips. For a moment, he thought of lying. However, Sheridan knew enough that a lie, at least the wrong lie, could get him killed. Hearing the stammer in his voice, he said, "Y-yes. I ... I admit it. I searched his cabin."

"Ha! I knew it." She lifted one foot and shoved it down on his chest, pushing him into the mattress, making it hard for him to breathe. At least it had the effect of lessening the blade's pressure on his neck. Her eyes narrowed, and her lips turned into a thin line. "Why?"

He swallowed. "Because—"

"No lies!"

"I suspected you two were seeing each other. I wanted proof."

One side of her lips curled up. "You expect me to believe that? You, a jilted, jealous lover?"

His mouth was very dry. "I know it's true. I found the shotgun shell. You can't deny it."

Her foot eased on his chest. He swallowed a deep breath. "You're full of shit, Doctor. Fortunately for you, it's a brand I find amusing."

"I don't know what you're talking about."

She stared down at him for a long moment. "You can't be working with anyone," she said. "You must be independent."

She eased the blade away from his neck and stepped back. Leaping down from the bed, she paced back and forth, reminding him of a jungle cat. She seemed to be thinking. Perhaps picking up on her feelings, Criggred arched his back and hissed at Avery.

Sheridan spun to the doctor. The suddenness of it startled him. "What exactly do you want?" she said. "Why did you tell me of Dr. Wasnair's plans?"

Carefully, Avery sat up. The movement caused Criggred to hiss louder. He tried to ignore it. Slowly, staring Sheridan in the eyes, he said, "I only want to help."

"How?"

Her body tensed, and her breathing stopped. She fixed him with a look that he knew to be lethal. If he answered wrong, that was it. He would never be seen again. Perhaps she would say Criggred had gone mad and ripped him apart. Perhaps he would have taken a suicidal plunge off the terrace. Or perhaps she had other, subtler ways of disposing of enemies.

Sweat popped out on his forehead. "I want the war to end, as soon as possible," he said. "Should this sound weapon be developed, it will only delay the inevitable. I think ... in the end, if the war is prolonged ... even more will die."

"And if certain information were passed on to Octung, and Octung was able to build a defense against the weapon? Or if the efforts here were simply sabotaged?"

He shrugged, as if the answer was obvious. "Octung would prevail that much quicker, and peace would be restored to the world. I may hate Octung, but I hate the war more."

"But the purgings ... You're against them."

"The purgings are inevitable. Octung will win, that much is certain. The only thing that remains in doubt is how many die between now and then. I mean to see that as many survive the war as possible. I want peace, no matter what."

"And the man that helped Octung achieve that peace would be rewarded, I suppose. And spared from any purgings."

"Or woman."

"Hmph."

"And yes, that is an interesting point," he said. "But that should not be a primary motivator. And I am, of course, simply thinking out loud here. I don't mean anything by it."

"Of course," she said. "Neither do I."

A long silence passed. She stared at him, then her sword. At last she let out a breath, and he could see the tension leaving her.

They exchanged a look. For a moment she almost appraised him with warmth. And Janx said he couldn't bluff!

She flicked the blood off the end of her blade, placed the sword back on the wall, and said, "I'll think on it. Meanwhile, would you like a drink?"

He laughed. "After you, of course."

She smiled grimly and poured. "Wise man."

Two days later he found Janx's message. It had become Avery's habit to return to the Headless Drake every few days for fresh clothes, supplies, and to make sure no squatters had moved in. Just as importantly, he felt it necessary to tend to his expensive bottle of Valyankan bourbon.

But there was another reason.

He and Janx had arranged a drop-spot behind a loose brick near his door, and he checked it every visit. Generally either Janx or one of his cronies would leave a crumpled slip of paper, usually saying that there was nothing to report. Avery had just been on the cusp of thinking the whaler wasn't taking this as seriously as he should; Janx had agreed to have Sheridan tailed, yes, but so far neither he nor any of his agents had turned up anything.

This time was different. The note ran: *Intercepted message from S to handlers. Read and replaced. S requests meeting tomorrow. Will try n eavesdrop.*

Elation filled Avery. Finally! Sheridan had left a message at her own drop-spot, and either Janx or his people had found it. Now Sheridan was going to meet with her handler, surely to relate the information Avery had let slip regarding Dr. Wasnair's theoretical device. He grinned.

"I'll make a spy of you yet," he told himself.

He tossed the note in the fireplace and helped himself to an extra finger of bourbon. Now all he had to do was sit back and wait.

Thunder boomed outside his windows two days later, when Janx came to visit him. The whaler's nefarious friends had indeed followed Sheridan, and one had even managed to get close enough to overhear her meeting with her handler. The meeting had happened at the restaurant known as Claver's, and the man she'd been meeting was called Gaescruhd.

"Gaescruhd?" Avery had heard the name, but for the moment it eluded him. "Isn't he some underworld figure?"

"*Some*? They don't come much bigger than him. Hails from Ungraessot. Sells drugs, sex, even slaves."

"In Ghenisa? You must be mistaken."

Janx shook his head. "They're around. Because of bastards like him. Lately he's made a mint off a bunch of ships he bought. Some old fishing company, I think, goin' belly up because of the war, couldn't afford hot lard anymore for their processors. Well, ol' Gaescruhd comes along, buys the ships, an' now he's runnin' a refugee racket. Pity the poor fuckers that take refuge on one of *his* ships. Slavery's just the start of it."

Avery felt something twist in his gut. "And he's Sheridan's contact?"

"He's got no scruples. Why not let himself be hired out by Octung? Probably why his ships never go missing at sea. Wouldn't surprise me if he took money from refugees, put them on a ship, then delivered them straight to the Octs."

"That's terrible." Avery collected his thoughts. "You said there was a transcript?"

"That's right. Hildra scribbled down their conversation for you, at least as much as she could hear. You remember her?"

"I do. She's the one with the monkey."

Janx passed over a notebook with some tight, irregular writing, along with a photograph. Hildra or one of the others had actually managed to take a picture. In it, Sheridan lounged across the table from a fat man with curling dark hair and an unbuttoned shirt.

Janx moved to a window and peered outside, giving Avery space. While the big man surveyed the outdoors, Avery read the conversation between Sheridan and Gaescruhd that Hildra had recorded.

Sheridan: ... not bad, better than last time ...

Gaescruhd: I told you 1340 was a poor year for the Versaigne, couplet. Haven't heard much from you in a while.

Sheridan: Been busy with paperwork. The wheels are in motion for me to take land duties.

Gaescruhd: Interesting.

S: There's no ships left for me to commandeer. We're trying to buy some used ones from Looris, but till then, well. And since the invasion's coming through the Pass any time now, all units are being rearranged. Haggarty's pushing for the Navy to take the lead. It's the biggest military structure in the country, it's the one that's expanding. Denaris is fighting it, but she won't win. And with what I'm doing for Haggarty, soon no one will be able to stand against him.

G: Oh, I'm painfully aware. He's not cheap, is he?

S: Anyway, it works out for our purposes. The more land-based I am, the more influence I'll be able to wield.

G: True. And that is the point, I suppose.

S: Well, one point. By the way, thanks for the heads up about the crustaceans.

G: It was not my decision, couplet. You know that. They are cute little things, though, aren't they?

S: Whatever idiots decided to send them should be shot. They've got the lab monkeys trying to reverse-engineer them.

G (setting wine glass down): I'm listening.

S: I have a source that says Ghenisan scientists are trying to find a way to use your pets' anatomy to build some infernal device that could slaughter legions of our troops at a time.

Finally, Avery thought. It was the first time Sheridan had admitted openly that she considered Octung her side. Avery wished Hildra had possessed some sort of recording device, so that they could take a record of this conversation to the authorities, but of course such a thing would be too heavy and cumbersome to use. Avery returned to the manuscript.

Gaescruhd: That is upsetting. I'll have to get someone to look into it.

Sheridan: Please do. (Pause) I have an inside man that might help us, the one who gave me this information. He—ah, here's the waiter.

(pause to give order to the waiter. G ends with "and the lobster bisque, if you would.")

Sheridan: That's not as amusing as you think (To the waiter) I'll have steak—the most expensive you have. My friend is paying.

Gaescruhd: Haven't lost your spark, I see.

(waiter leaves)

S: You haven't lost your disgusting appetites. Why should anything change?

G: Oh, I believe in gaining more disgusting appetites over time, not shedding them. I support acquisition, not loss. On that subject, something has come to my attention—something I think you'll find most interesting. (Pause) We think some of the Black Sect might still be on the run.

S: You're kidding. I thought the Council had suppressed them all.

G: Oh, those at home are in hiding or dead, certainly, but I'm talking abroad.

S: Still? I was told they'd been destroyed. You mean ...

G: Yes. He, she or they could be here in Ghenisa. We're not sure how many of them are still alive. Possibly just one. The Collossum have detected an extradimensional signature—maybe signatures—but cannot pinpoint a location, though they're thought to be in this general region.

Avery frowned. They were talking about his patient, he was certain, as she was of the Black Sect. But why would a saboteur emit an extradimensional signature? As far as he knew, such phenomena were related only to the Atomic Sea and Octunggen weaponry. He read closely.

S: Interesting. What would he, she or they look like?

G: I thought you had been to temple.

S: Once or twice. But never one with a Collossum in residence.

G: They look like what they are—gods! As close to gods as a human can look and not stand out, anyway. Tall, beautiful, often blond. They've been living in Octung for many years, of course, so they will either only speak Octunggen or else with an Octunggen accent.

Avery had to force himself to put his wineglass down without spilling it.

"What is it?" Janx said from the window.

He gaped, unable to speak. Finally, he managed, "I don't know. She's one of the Black Sect, I knew that, but ... a *god?* One of the *Collossum?*" He shook his head. "Let me read."

S stares at G.

G: Something on your mind, couplet?

Shit, Avery thought. *She's put it together, too, only she knows what it means.*

Sheridan: If this missing Black Secter were found, what would be the orders?

Gaescruhd: "Don't tell me. Can it be? (laughs) Brilliant! There could be a big bonus in this for us—for you, I mean.

S: Don't get too excited. I can't say for sure. (Pause) It never occurred to me that one might just fall into my lap like this. I thought she must be some mutant, some infected woman, but ... yes, maybe, just maybe ...

G: Where is this godlike personage?

S: She's a specimen of the scientists. In one of the sublevels.

G: Can you get to her?

S: I ... perhaps. There is a man, the one I mentioned, a doctor. I can turn him.

G: Not a ringing endorsement, couplet. That last one didn't work out so well. What was his name, Hambry, Hampsted? Went overboard while delivering a message? I do hope your other recruits have better footing.

S: I can turn this doctor. He can get to her.

Avery swallowed.

S: And if he doesn't, someone else will.

There are others. Avery remembered what she had said earlier. Even Grand Admiral Haggarty was somehow corrupted. Avery realized he could trust no one in the Navy.

Gaescruhd, suddenly very sober: I must ... speak with someone. There is someone here in Hissig that I report to. He will know what to do about your little runaway. I have a feeling he will want your doctor friend to take out his scalpel, but I can't give the order myself. Not regarding one of them. Wait a few days. I will be in contact.

That was it, the end of the conversation.

Avery stared at the words, feeling numb. Then, blinking, he reread the conversation once, then again. At last, his fingers shaking, he took a long sip of his drink.

"You've read this, I take it?" Avery asked Janx.

"Yep." Janx looked grave.

"What ... do you think?"

"Could that patient of yours really be ... a Collossum?"

My mermaid, Avery thought.

With a creeping dread, he reached a decision. He strained a smile. "I'm going to do something very stupid," he said. "And I'm going to need your help to do it."

"What?"

"My patient is an enemy of Octung, it seems. I still don't know what she is, not really, but she claims to want to end the war."

"Welcome to the club, sweetheart."

"She claims to be able to do it. What's more, the Octunggen fear her. Why? The only thing that makes sense is because she can hurt them."

"You dodged the question about her being a Collossum."

Avery hesitated. "I think Gaescruhd was mistaken," he hedged, unsure if he spoke the truth. "At most I think she's some sort of saboteur. At any rate, if my patient can hurt Octung, we should help her." Avery looked to the shrine of his family, lit by candlelight and mounted in solidified wax.

"That may be too big for just us, Doc."

"Maybe, maybe not." Avery refilled his glass and downed a sip. For some reason, now that he had finally reached this decision, he felt oddly relaxed. His hands only shook a little now. "She *can* hurt them, Janx. She's one of the Black Sect. And the Sect, it's more than we thought."

"Yeah? What is it?"

"I'm still not sure exactly. According to what Sheridan and her handler said, they're powerful. Not Collossum, that's crazy, but maybe she can actually do what she claims. But right now she's at the mercy of the Navy, and that's run by Haggarty, who's been corrupted by Sheridan." Avery grimaced ruefully. "I *know* Sheridan's a traitor, but there's no way I can prove it, and those I proved it to might be traitors, too. Don't you see, Janx? It goes all the way to the top. Now, unless I do something about it, Sheridan's going to kill the one person that may be able to stop Octung. The only thing that's prevented Sheridan from killing her so far is that she thinks *I'm* the one that's going to do it."

"Are you saying what I think you are?"

Avery sucked down a deep breath. *Once I start this, there's no going back.*

"We have to help her escape," he said.

Chapter 9

Heart pounding, Avery sawed off a section of the giant lobster carapace. It stank of decay, salt and nameless minerals. The whine of the saw filled his ears, and fine dust from the sawing bathed his face. Fortunately he wore a mask and goggles, but even so the air stank of pulverized lobster shell and rot. Avery had walked along beaches where he'd come across the putrid bodies of conventional crustaceans and jellyfish, and their stink was nauseating enough, but this was exponentially worse.

He finished sawing off the carapace section and, with the help of his junior doctors, carted the shell over to the mound of similar sections. Some were quite massive, ten feet long or more. Dr. Wasnair and his crew had wanted whole pieces so that they could study the carapace from the inside out, the better to understand the lightning phenomenon. All the pieces were tagged and photographed.

Wiping sweat and shell dust from his forehead, Avery turned back to the gargantuan mound of rotting crustacean and said, "We're free to probe the area now. Who wants the honors?"

The junior scientists gazed at each other nervously.

One raised a reluctant hand. "I drew the short straw."

With a lowered head, the young man approached the monstrosity, and the others backed away. He took out his instruments and set to work, eyes wide, forehead bathed in sweat. Very gingerly, he carved into the flesh, while the others held their breath. When he didn't dissolve instantly into a steaming puddle, they exhaled, but didn't relax. The young man said a prayer under his breath and continued working.

Over the next hour, each young scientist went at it, none of them willing to spend more than fifteen minutes at a stretch.

Several more researchers had died grisly, nightmarish deaths following the melting of Dr. Winegold and her assistants. Three had pierced something that looked like a spleen that had emitted a black gas that ate their lungs like acid; they had died vomiting blood. Four more had been poisoned by some substance that squirted at them from a piece of anatomy. Their eyes had boiled in their sockets and their brains had run out their ears. The current death tally hovered somewhere around fourteen. Hence the reason Avery had insisted on sawing into the shell. After that wearying task, he could claim he'd done his duty for the moment and needed time to recover. Of course, his assistants had quickly caught on, and at the beginning of every shift they gambled for who got to saw. Avery, who had learned a few tricks over the years, almost always won.

Counting the minutes till the end of the shift, the young scientists worked, sweating buckets as they did. They examined the backside of the lobster today, the safer side, but did not seem relieved. The pitiful monster itself looked shabby and naked, half its shell torn away and its salmon-colored flesh (not white like a normal lobster) revealed for all to see. Much of its meat had also been sawn away to give the researchers better access to its organs. The problem now seemed to be that organs were too accessible, which is why Avery's assistants had pleaded to work on the backside.

Even this, apparently, was still too dangerous. Half an hour before the shift was over, one of his assistants came up to him sweaty and pale. "Dr. Avery, come, see this."

Putting down his paperwork, Avery approached. Carved flesh gaped on the lobster's back.

"There," said one of the assistants. "Do you see it?"

They pointed, and with a start Avery noticed a glistening black thing poking through folds of flesh.

"It's the spleen," he marveled. Of course, only the gods knew what the organ actually was, but the researchers had taken to calling it the spleen because it vaguely resembled the human version of the organ. After killing Dr. Nayed and his assistants, it seemed to have migrated, vanishing entirely from the area of study.

"You've found it," Avery said.

They looked wan and nervous, but excited. As much as they wanted to avoid danger, they also wanted the recognition and possible advancement that studying the organ might achieve. "What shall we do, Doctor?"

"Clamp off any connecting veins, arteries or tissues and remove it."

Their eyes widened.

"*Remove* it?"

"That sounds ... dangerous," another added.

"Wrap it in plastic," Avery said. "Make it airtight. Then remove it. Place it on Table 3. Go. Now. We don't have all night."

Sweating, they turned back to the specimen and did as instructed. With the plastic sheeting in place, they appeared somewhat relieved, and they managed to remove the organ without any fatalities. Avery was quite pleased. Now he had an excuse to dismiss them early. When it was ten minutes till shift's end, he said, "Well done, doctors. For your efforts, I'll let you knock off for the night."

They breathed deeply and wiped sweaty foreheads. The young woman currently investigating the spleen hastily quit, stepping back gratefully.

"Are you sure, Doctor?" one asked. "There's still a few loads bound for the incinerator."

"That's fine. Just place it on the cart for me. Start with that big piece, there, no to the right, yes that's the one. Just put it on the cart—yes, like that. Careful now. And a few hunks of flesh, too. It does stink an awful lot, doesn't it? All right there, that will be fine. Have a good evening."

"You too, Doctor."

They gathered their things and fled, filing out without a look back. They stood straighter and easier with every step they took. Then they were gone.

Avery, very slowly, turned to his mystery patient.

"And now you."

He had to be fast. The next shift would come on duty in just a few minutes. It was late, though, well after midnight, and often the later shifts straggled in to work. With any luck they would be tardy. *And if they're early? What then?*

He yanked back the curtains.

The woman looked mostly the same as she always did, blond and attractive, though there was an extra flush in her cheeks now, and she looked healthier overall due to a week of fresh food and exercise. Dr. Wasnair and the others had noticed it, too, and exclaimed that she must be healing; Avery let them believe what they wanted.

"Come on," he whispered in Octunggen. "It's time."

Warily, she opened her eyes. When she saw that he was the only one around, she said, "At last."

Groggily, she sat up, and he helped her.

"Let's just get these," he said, reaching for the needles in her arms. In a few quick movements, he had removed them and slapped bandages over the wounds.

She rubbed them and grit her teeth. "Itches."

"You've had them in for a long time. It will itch."

She started to get up from the bed, but he placed a restraining hand on her shoulder. Curious, she stared up at him.

"What?"

"Before I do this, before I go through with it, I need to hear it. What's your plan? We'll be risking our lives because of you. I'm leaving *everything*. My home, my position, my life. I'll be a hunted fugitive for the rest of my days for this."

"We don't have time for this, Doctor." She started to rise again.

He shoved her down. "You *will* answer me."

She stared up at him but stubbornly said nothing.

He studied her for a long moment, seeking truth, seeking answers. It was painful to realize that though he had been growing more attached to her all this time, his whole life revolving around her in a sense, she had been unconscious, unaware and uncaring of his efforts.

She still said nothing, and at last he surrendered. For the moment, he would have to trust her.

"Very well," he said. "Come."

He took her arm as she climbed gingerly out of bed and hobbled across the floor. She was still weak and unused to activity.

"One more thing," he said. "I need something to call you."

He saw her hesitate, unsure how much of herself she should give away.

"Very well," she said. "In Octung I am called Layanna. Layanna of the House of Uul."

He pushed his glasses further up his nose, taking that in. "It's good to meet you, Layanna. I'm Dr. Francis Avery. Of the House of Avery."

They reached the long low metal cart. A huge section of the lobster carapace arched atop it. Beneath and around heaped rotting chunks of flesh.

"Your chariot," he said.

Layanna did not look as disgusted as he would have thought. "It will do. Oh, yes."

Frowning, Avery helped her fold back a sheet of flesh and crawl underneath the great ribbed length of carapace. When she was in place, he threw a tarp over the cart and with some effort wheeled it out of the laboratory. Tires squealed, and the cart listed to the right. The massed flesh and armor was heavy, which is why he typically sent his assistants in pairs to dispose of the waste. Grunting and straining, he shoved it down one dark, metallic hall after another. The halls stank of mold and cleanser.

At an intersection stood one of the checkpoints, attended by four guards. One stepped forward as Avery approached.

"Another load, eh?" said the guard. "You've got the forms, Doctor?"

Avery handed over the paperwork, and the man scanned it. Avery tried not to sweat, tried to get his heartbeat under control.

"Looks in order," the guard said.

"I saw something move in the cart," a female guard said. "Under the tarp."

"The rotting flesh," Avery said. "It's settling."

The female eyed him. "Just get rid of it. It stinks."

Avery forced a smile. "Will do."

"Night, Doctor," said the first guard.

Avery grunted and shoved the cart forward. He rode the lift upwards to the groan of chains and bang of metal. On the level just below the ground floor, he stopped and shoved the cart down another hallway, enduring one more checkpoint before reaching the large metal doors of the incinerator room. Located conveniently to both the sublevels and the hospital in the wing of the fortress above, it should be unoccupied at this time of night.

Sure enough, Avery found the large, dark room empty save for the roaring flames of the furnace. The room stank of metal and smoke. Shadows clung to great pipes and bulbous machinery.

He maneuvered the cart forward, toward the metal bed that was used to place objects over the fire, and threw back the tarp.

"Come now," he whispered. "Quickly."

He dug through mounds of flesh, wincing as the bloody stuff enveloped his hands. It was probably his imagination, but he thought he could feel it gnawing away at him like acid.

He hauled out the last chunk with a groan. There, in the darkness under the carapace, Layanna lay in wait. At the sight of her, Avery sucked in a breath.

"Dear gods, what do you think you're *doing*?"

Like a wild animal, she crouched in the rancid shadows, gnawing on a hunk of crustacean flesh as if she had been starved for weeks. Blood coated her mouth and chin, her hands, and it pasted her hospital gown to her breasts. She looked up at him, almost growling.

"You've gone mad," he said.

She ripped another strip of flesh free with her teeth, chewed it and then—with obvious reluctance—set her meal down. Like an insolent little girl, she wiped the blood off her mouth with the back of her hand. She burped.

"That was good," she said.

"How can you ... ? Never mind. Just hurry up, for love of the Three."

To Avery's relief, she climbed out from under the carapace, and he backed away as she unfolded. She seemed stronger now. Her eyes blazed. Her skin was flushed even more than before. Firelight from the furnace shone on the gobs of flesh and blood that clung to her cheeks, her dress and hair.

"I don't understand it," Avery said. "That flesh is contaminated."

"To you, yes. To me it contains extradimensional elements that are compatible with my own." She smiled, and it was a ghastly smile, so much white in all that redness. "It is *tasty*."

"But I've fed you ..."

"Only food that nourishes this." She touched her belly, indicating her body. "But there's more to me than this."

He shook his head. "Explain later. The next shift will discover your absence any minute, and then we can expect a full lockdown. There, in that corner, you'll find a new set of clothes, a doctor's uniform. Yes, that's it. Use that bucket and sponge. I'd expected you to be dirty from the cart. Not *that* dirty, but ... yes ... ah—"

Without paying him any attention, she tore off her gown and bathed herself. He caught a brief glimpse of firm breasts and buttocks, and then he hastily turned away. He felt his face grow hot, and tried to think of his escape plans.

"I'm ready," she said shortly, and he turned.

She looked as professionally dressed as him, although her hair was a little wet, her clothes a little wrinkled. He had hidden them in a dark, dusty corner, and they had suffered accordingly. Still, to look at her one would never know that she had been a feral beast just moments before. Her cheeks were a bit pink, but that was all.

"Let's go," he said.

Walking quickly, they left the incinerator room and made for a stairwell. They needn't worry about the checkpoint, which was set up to monitor comings and goings from the sublevels. He had already passed it and was considered in the upper portion of the building.

"Don't say anything to anyone," Avery warned her in a whisper. "Even in Ghenisan. Your accent will give you away."

They rose to ground level and entered the medical wing of Fort Brunt. The sleepy bustle of a nighttime military hospital surrounded them. Nurses checked up on patients injured during the lobster attack or some battle at sea. Wounded soldiers called for more morphine or made weary banter with each other. Most slept. The air smelled the familiar odor of rot and antiseptic and offal from bedpans. Layanna eyed the patients with an inscrutable expression. If she had spent as much time in Octung as Avery thought she had, it must be quite a shock to see the results of Octung's war. Then again, she was trying to stop it, so the results had obviously distressed her before.

They exited the building and cold wind gusted around them, bringing with it the salty, electric scent of the Atomic Sea. A few patrols prowled the grounds, and gnarled trees swayed to the wind. Even at night, bright lights blazed from the exterior of the fortress, illuminating the compound. Avery and Layanna wound through ornamental hedges and statues of Navy heroes, bound for the street that trickled past the fort, bordering its west-facing wall. The walls of the fort's compound rose high and thick, and to Avery at that moment they appeared impassable.

"Don't worry," he whispered. "The walls are designed to keep people out, not in. This isn't a prison."

They passed the parking lot that facilitated people like Avery who worked at the fort but did not live there, and he wished at that moment that he owned a car. A taxi would be waiting for them, though. He had everything arranged.

The guards at the entry checkpoint knew him by sight and waved him through. He wasn't worried that they would ask for Layanna's ID. They only checked ID on the way in. Of course, that might change after today.

Avery held his breath as they passed through the heavy archway, under the thick wall. Leering gargoyles laughed down at them. Avery knew in medieval times those gargoyles' mouths had gushed with burning oil or boiling water during invasions. How many people had died right where he was walking? At any moment he expected the blare of alarms to sound behind him, for the metal gates to slam closed ahead. He had to grit his teeth to keep them from rattling.

Then, miraculously, they were out. He hadn't noticed the wind's absence till it reappeared, busily gusting through his thin hair, billowing his coat out behind him. Even Layanna seemed to relax.

The taxi idled just where he had instructed it to, sulking along the curb on Hangman's Blvd. just beyond Brunt's walls. Smoke from the exhaust roiled up into the night, and the cab's engine made a chugging, purring noise. Somehow it reminded Avery of a great cat.

"Almost there," he said, hearing the tightness of his voice.

He reached the cab, opened the rear door and gestured for Layanna to get in—

Alarms blared behind them. Avery spun to see activity at the gate. The guard captain reached for a ringing telephone. The peals of the alarm made hairs prickle along Avery's spine.

"Get in!" he said.

Layanna swung inside the cab, but before Avery could follow the panicked cab-driver screamed, "Get out! Get out!"

"Grab him," Avery told Layanna.

He didn't pause to see if she complied—although the cabbie's screams hinted that she had—but hurried around to the driver's door and jerked it open; Layanna's distraction had prevented the cabbie from locking it. Avery seized the man by the jacket front, physically hauled him out of the vehicle and deposited him on the city street. Without hesitation, Avery slid behind the wheel and locked the door.

"You! Stop!" shouted the guards at the entry checkpoint. Avery saw them take out their guns and run toward the cab. Their captain barked something. One of them fired.

The bullet punched a hole in the rear window of the auto. Glass exploded. Shrapnel hit Avery's ear.

He stomped on the gas. The car jerked forward, its owner beating on the window, then falling away. At the next street, Avery swung the wheel hard left and careened around a corner. Cars honked at him, and one bumped his rear. He shot forward, teeth set, back hunched.

Just before he passed out of sight of the fortress, black vans barreled out from another gateway, lights flashing from their roofs.

"This could get rough," Avery said.

Layanna said nothing, merely fastened her seatbelt. Then: "Go faster."

He obeyed. He swerved down a broad street, smashed against another taxi, and scraped forward. Sirens screamed behind him. He cut hard, swinging into the next side street. Lights flashed on shop windows in his rearview mirror. He mashed the gas pedal.

He wound down one street, then another. He took alleys, back roads, main roads when he had to. Always he avoided the flashing lights that reflected off buildings behind him. When he saw them, he veered away.

Finally he bundled up an alley and jerked the car to a stop. Shattered glass tinkled in the back.

"The police will be on the lookout for this car by now, and the Navy certainly knows it," Avery said. "We need another."

He climbed out and looked around. Crumbling tenements reared over them, and the car crouched in shadow. At any time a gang of criminals or desperate refugees could happen upon them.

Joining him, Layanna said, "I'm sorry for all this, Doctor."

"I knew what I was getting in for." *But Janx's crew doesn't.*

He grabbed her hand and led her down a grimy alley. He wasn't even sure what part of town they were in. The Rickles, he thought, but wasn't sure. He'd been driving too recklessly, randomly.

Noises ahead. Shouting, laughs, singing, young boys playing, people haggling over prices. Music.

Avery and Layanna emerged from the alley into a crowded courtyard. To his surprise, he found himself in the midst of a bazaar. Lights like creeping vines overgrew the stalls, and children in tattered jackets danced around fireworks that snapped in the intersections. Avery could not help but stare even as he hurried along.

Refugees filled the bazaar, people from all over the continent. Exotic clothes swished and jangled. A tall man with thick eyebrows wore a crown-like circlet made of brass coins. A gaggle of women walked by sporting colorful dresses—red, green, turquoise-and-gold—that had seen better days. A little person leant against a post, wearing a proud scarlet tallhat. Priests from Myzkrai begged and prayed in their purple silk robes; square jade buttons flashing on their fronts. Prostitutes from Getsyr shivered in thin jackets yet allowed their long legs to protrude from dresses slit to the hip. Strutting violinists from Ungraessot bore tattoos of the God-Emperor's crest and symbols of the Tunnels of Ard.

And there were mutants. Many, many mutants. Avery was shocked to see them all. He had never seen so many in one place.

Sirens wailed in the distance, and he picked up his pace.

"We have to find a car," he said, and Layanna nodded, but her eyes were on their surroundings. So were Avery's.

A fish-faced man hawked spices. A woman with tentacles where her breasts should be sold doubtful-looking flour to a young boy with the arm of a crab. An old man with shark-like teeth and all-black eyes stood behind him. An otherwise beautiful woman had the mouth of a fish, and she occupied a small stage singing to a rapt crowd some strange and fishy song. Avery and Layanna passed a stall lined with glowing squids in strange glass jars. He saw monkeys chained to posts, dogs being roasted over spits, belly dancers from Icai working the crowd. Greedy merchants offered positions of indentured servitude to desperate refugees.

Mounds and mounds of diseased-looking fish heaped in stalls and were being sold by the pound to willing customers. A man with scales all over his body and secreting a viscous fluid forked over a handful of cash and shambled away with a bag of runny flashfish. A hunched woman with the carapace of a stone crab and the tongue of a sea anemone bought an octopus with a riot of misshapen and misplaced limbs, some of which had eyes growing where the suckers should be.

"I don't understand," Avery said. "They're knowingly eating diseased food. Why would they do this to themselves?"

Layanna didn't seem bothered by it. "They don't think it can get any worse. So why starve? They've already survived the disease, after all, so they're not worried about that."

"But the risk of further mutations ..."

It took him a moment to realize she'd spoken Octunggen. Fortunately the bazaar was too noisy for anyone to have overheard, and amid the many accents and languages he doubted anyone would care. There were other countries besides Octung that spoke dialects of Octunggen. Nevertheless, he warned her to watch what she said.

To his surprise, she seemed relaxed, at ease. To his questioning look, she said, "These are my people. People of the sea. Oh, there! I must."

She was staring at a fishmonger who sold long, diseased eelfish that bristled with catfish-like tendrils jutting from irregular points along their bodies. Avery knew the creatures emitted bursts of electricity along those tendrils to scare away predators. Of course, in a healthy fish the tendrils would be more evenly spaced and they would not still be moving about, however sluggishly, after death.

Layanna scampered over to the stall, giddy as a girl of eight. Looking all about him, hating this waste of time but not knowing how to stop her, Avery followed. They had better make this quick.

The fishmonger, a stout man whose flesh had the look and texture of a seahorse's, smiled at Layanna and said, "And what may I help you with, young lady?" His eyes lit up as he studied her.

"I take two," she said, pointing at the eelfish.

The fishmonger did not raise an eyebrow at her Octunggen accent. "Best ones in Hissig. And I should know. I hail from Wirzal, home of the best fishing in the Axid Isles. All overrun now, of course."

"I didn't know," she said. "I'm sorry." She sounded sincere. "You pay," she told Avery, as she accepted the sacked eelfish. Reluctantly, he did, and she beamed like a happy child. To his disgust, she grabbed a wooden fork, impaled one of the eelfish, and began eating it raw.

People around them stared at her, horrified. Even the most heavily diseased of them would clean and cook the things first, and she showed no signs of infection.

"Come on," Avery growled, taking her arm. "We don't have time for this—and you're attracting attention."

Eel slime smeared her lips and chin as they emerged from the market. To Avery's great relief, he saw that a fleet of taxis idled on the main road, waiting for custom. He and Layanna climbed in the first one, Avery told the driver their destination, and they shot off into the night. Layanna continued eating her foul meal there in the back of the cab, and Avery felt his gorge rise. The eelfish stank like a mixture of seaweed and tainted mustard.

The cabdriver stared at her in his rear-view mirror. "Hells, mister, you sure she should be eating that?"

"No."

Layanna lowered the eelfish. Belched. "I grow strong. Too long without."

Avery saw the driver's face frown at her accent, but he did not try to excuse it. The less said the better. Let the driver invent his own reasons.

The cab swung into an artery and suddenly hit a nest of stalled cars, each honking its horn loudly.

"Shit," said the driver. "What's this?" Angrily he honked his own horn.

The lines of stopped cars did not move.

"I might know what it is," Avery muttered, feeling his stomach clench. He grabbed Layanna's hand, opened the door and hauled her out. The eelfish dropped to the seats, slicking it with mucus. The tendrils still writhed.

"Hey!" the driver said.

"Sorry about the mess. We can't wait." Avery threw a couple of dollars at him, turned and set off, tugging Layanna along behind him. Sure enough, when Avery looked up the street he saw that police cars had blocked off the intersection. Cops strolled up the lines of stopped cars, flashing lights into the interiors and showing the occupants pictures.

"They didn't waste any time," Avery said. Sheridan must be using her admiralship to orchestrate the manhunt. *Well, she can't have shut the city down entirely. Gods, I hope they don't summon the rays.*

Layanna no longer looked so childish. Indeed, the abrupt change to adultness was startling. "What next?" she said.

He scratched his cheek. "There's an L line a few blocks away. Come on."

Avoiding the main roads, he took her to the elevated train station, which was more or less where he'd thought it would be. That was one piece of luck, at least. In silence they rode the rattling L over the city, and Avery tried not to meet the eyes of his fellow passengers. As they disembarked and made their way through the endpoint station, he heard a loud radio blare through the high, graffiti-covered halls:

"... and if you've seen this man and woman, you are to report immediately to the police. Again, their descriptions are as follows. The woman is blond and slim, with blue eyes and ..."

Avery's blood ran cold. He lowered his head as he walked. Layanna's hand tightened on his. After what seemed like an eternity, they stepped out into the night.

"Too close," he breathed.

She had taken a break between her first eelfish and her second, but now she removed the second half of her feast from its sack and began tearing into it. Watching her, he felt sickened all over again.

"You know where going?" she said between chews.

"We're in the Tangle now. Almost there. Just a little more and we can rest."

"No need rest. Am strong now."

He nodded, sweat beading his brow, his breath coming in labored gasps. "You may not need it, but you're not the only one here."

He led the way down narrow streets and alleys, wishing he had some weapon, any weapon. He hadn't wanted to take a chance on sneaking a gun past Brunt security. Now he was defenseless. And there was another worry, too. *What will Janx and the others say when they realize how important*

Layanna is? Avery had not told them what he believed her to be. He couldn't afford for them to balk. But there was no hiding it now, not with the city shut down. What would they do?

The alleys stank of rot and refuse, and though there were buildings to all sides somehow the chill wind found the channels between and howled down them, driving against Avery and tugging him backward. Composed and flushed, Layanna finished her grisly meal and tossed the eelfish remains in a metal trashcan. Feral cats and batkin hissed at each other for the scraps.

Finally they reached the rear entrance to Janx's tenement. Inside the wind couldn't get at them, and Avery breathed easier. When he did he tasted onions and cabbage heavy on the air, along with mold and mildew. They made their way through leaning, sagging corridors with paint peeling in strips off the walls, past heavily bolted doors, or doors that were open and dark and sinister, past apartments thumping with music or the screech of fighting families. Behind a too-thin door, a couple rutted noisily. Roaches crawled across chipped cement floors, and bare electric bulbs flickered when they weren't out altogether.

Janx's rooms waited on the eleventh floor. When Avery at last knocked on the door, which was more massive, metal, and heavily fortified than any of the others he'd seen, he was breathless and drenched in sweat, his clothes sticking to him. Why couldn't this building have a functioning lift? Layanna, by contrast, appeared perfectly at ease, only mildly winded. Perhaps he should try diseased eelfish.

Locks scraped and shot. Janx's door swung open with a metal creak.

"Finally," a voice said. "We were beginning to worry about you."

Muirblaag, newly moistened and glimmering, ushered them into Janx's room. He wore only boxing trunks and shoes.

Layanna eyed him with interest, his crested head, fishy skin, whitish mouth, symmetrical design.

Muirblaag returned her look, but it was not idle curiosity in his eyes. "Well, hello there."

"Hello."

He closed the door behind them and bolted some of its many bolts, somehow contriving not to take his eyes off her for a moment.

Avery didn't care. "I need a drink."

Janx's large quarters sprawled in every direction, both dismal and regal. Shabby walls with mortared-up cracks were hung with priceless pictures, some oils, some abstracts, many originals by prominent artists, none of them matching. Plush, expensive chairs perched beside rotting, sagging ones. Massive urns squatted against idols and statues inset with gems and diamonds. One particularly vulgar statue depicted two nymphs cavorting with a satyr; the water issued from a very lewd place. Against the wall, an antique cabinet bar hunched under a thousand cheap and gaudy knickknacks collected from countless ports. Janx displayed some of the best taste and absolute worst taste that Avery had ever seen, all side by side. How much of the loot had been stolen, how much bought with stolen or conned money, and how much with Janx's considerable semi-legitimate earnings through whaling and prizefighting Avery couldn't guess. Judging by the excess, he was quite sure Janx could have afforded a penthouse somewhere, but he knew just as certainly that Janx would never be comfortable or happy there. Here in the Tangle he was a hero, a champion, and though he lived in a bleak, murky warren, it was a bleak, murky warren adorned with the treasure of kings.

Movement in a shadowy region that Avery thought must be the kitchen, redolent of spices and garlic.

Janx himself stepped out, smiling boldly. Light from a dozen expensive lanterns lit his thousand tattoos, bald head, and scarred, nose-less face. "You made it!" To Avery's shock, the big man embraced him in a crushing hug.

"I—well—thanks—"

The hug may have been a ruse, however, to allow Janx to grip Layanna in an even more clinging embrace. She accepted it, raising her eyebrows at Avery.

"We need to leave ..." Avery began.

Janx wasn't paying attention. Still laughing, he guided them to dusty but expensive chairs and supplied them with fluids. It was beer, not whisky, but it was an excellent porter, thick and black, and Avery sipped his gratefully.

The rest of Janx's crew of criminals and spies was present, too, as Avery had expected. He needed the help of all of them. Hildra, the young woman with the hook instead of a left hand, paced, smoking, her monkey jumping up and down in shared agitation. Byron, the little violinist, leaned against the wall, arms folded. Holdren, the large black man, shot balls in a desultory fashion at the billiards table.

All shifted their attention to the red-headed Jaimesyn when he stood up from the radio. Screwdriver in hand, he said, "There, that should ..."

A burst of static filled the room, then a voice.

All leaned tensely forward, listening:

"... and the manhunt will continue through the night until these fugitives are caught. New details are just now emerging. A high official in the Navy has declared that an Octunggen spy embedded in the naval science community has broken loose an Octunggen prisoner. The woman is actually a secret Octunggen project recovered by our intelligence operatives. She has been contaminated by poisons that could, if released, wipe out the city. 'If they are not found and returned to the Navy posthaste, Octung will have a new source of mass violence to wage against us,' says Minister Sorqin, head of the Navy Expenditures Subcommittee."

"One of Sheridan's agents, no doubt," Avery said. "She's obviously colored information, or perhaps—"

Holdren shushed him.

"The Navy is hard on the hunt," crackled the voice on the radio. "Rays are being called into service even now. When found, the fugitives shall be dealt with severely. To aid the hunt, here are their descriptions once again ..."

Avery rose and turned the radio off. "I think we get the idea."

For a long moment there was silence. Avery could almost feel the tension radiating off those in the room, and he knew it was his fault. *Now it comes*, he thought. *I should have been honest with them from the beginning.* But what if they'd refused to help?

From outside screeched a siren. It rose in volume, and those in the apartment tensed further. The siren faded, but they did not relax.

"We're in deep shit, Doctor," said Hildra. "You said you'd pay us for our trouble, but this ain't worth what you're payin'. Nothing would be."

"I didn't sign on for this," Byron agreed. "No one did."

Janx stepped forward, frowning, severe. "This isn't how it was supposed to go, Doc. You said we were only supposed to hide out a saboteur—"

"I never actually said she was only a—" Avery said.

"The shitting *Navy*'s after us!" said Byron. "Admiral Haggarty! Rays! Fuck, *rays!*"

"This is bullshit," said Jaimesyn. "We were just supposed to hide out some fugitive, not bring down the wrath of the whole fucking country."

"Should we even be in the same room with her?" Byron edged backward, away from Layanna. "I mean, if she's some kinda poison bomb, we shouldn't even be breathing the same *air*."

Avery raised his hands, placating. "That was just a cover story. They obviously don't want to say that she was *their* secret project, not Octung's. She is *not* a poison bomb."

"Then what is she?" Janx bunched his jaws. His hard eyes swung to Layanna. "It's time."

"No. It's not," Avery said. "In fact, we—"

"Quiet," Janx said, shooting him a stern look. The whaler returned his attention to Layanna, and so did everyone else, staring at her expectantly. Beads of sweat clung to their brows. Their faces drew tight. Byron looked on the verge of snapping.

Layanna gazed back at them mildly, impossible to read.

"Tell us who you are, woman," Janx said, in a voice that could have leveled mountains. "I mean *now*."

"Come on," said Muirblaag gently. "We're all friends here."

"I ain't friends with nobody who brings the Navy down on my head," Janx said. "Don't you realize what this means? It means if they connect the Doc to us, our lives are *over*." In a rage, he kicked a kingly lamp, and it smashed into glittering fragments. Electric sparks flared, then died. Seething, Janx balled his fists at his sides and looked as if he were trying to find something else to smash. His eyes settled on Layanna. *Who are you?*

"Yeah," said Hildra.

"Fuckin' aye," said Holdren, setting the pool cue down and slapping a fist into the palm of his hand. A revolver showed in a holster under his armpit.

"We don't have time ..."Avery started.

The others exclaimed loudly, drowning him out, demanding explanations, demanding to know what they had gotten into.

Silently, Layanna met each gaze in turn. At first she didn't seem inclined to speak, but then she gathered herself and said, in garbled Ghenisan, "Dr. Avery you should to listen. We now go. I cannot tell whole story. Later."

"Godsdamn you, you better start talking," growled Janx.

She knitted her brow. Taking a deep breath, she said, "You know what is extradimensional, yes? Ultra-planar?"

They exchanged looks.

"Why?" Byron said.

"I am ... you will believe this not, is why I would say nothing ... but I am extradimensional being."

"What?" said Jaimesyn.

"There are ... others. My friends. We are hunted. We can stop war."

Janx scowled deeply, throwing his face into shadow. He threw a glance at Avery, who nodded.

"How?" Janx said.

"No time," Layanna said. "But can it we do. With help."

"Now this is some major shit," said Holdren.

"See?" Muirblaag drawled, coming to stand beside her. "I knew there was a good explanation."

"Fuck the explanation," Byron said, pushing himself off from the wall. "Fuck the war. Our lives are *ruined*."

"They will be ruined worse if we don't get a move on," Avery said quietly. "While we've been arguing, the Navy will have been tracking us. We encountered many people on the way here. Some have doubtlessly heard our descriptions and called in. I suggest we leave as soon as possible. Now. *Right* now."

Janx glared from him to Layanna. "I—"

The door exploded inwards, and a phalanx of armored troops burst in.

Chapter 10

Avery wheeled to see the troopers enter, shields carried before them, a moving wall of barricades and weapons. They were Navy shock troops.

It all happened very fast.

Byron scampered for the window, presumably to crawl out to a fire escape. A gun roared, blood sprayed from his thigh, and he collapsed screaming.

Both Jaimesyn and Holdren carried guns, and apparently on instinct they drew them, ducked behind furniture—Jaimesyn behind the couch, Holdren behind the billiards table—and fired. Sparks flashed on police shields and whined off helmets. Troopers leveled automatic weapons at couch and table—and fired. And fired. Bullets drilled through furniture and riddled Jaimesyn and Holdren, flinging them back like rag dolls, broken and ravaged and spraying blood. They fell amidst red pools and twitched mindlessly, dead or dying.

"Don't move!" the unit captain shouted to the others. "Raise your hands and *don't fucking move!*"

The troops swarmed into the apartment and surrounded them.

Despite the warnings, Janx grabbed a lantern and tried to smash it over a trooper's head, but half a dozen others slammed electric prods into his ribs and rifle butts into his skull. Screaming insults, he fell under their blows. Muirblaag succeeded in smashing two of the troopers' heads together and rendering them unconscious before he was driven to the floor.

Avery raised his hands and kept quiet. So did Hildra and Layanna. Hildra's monkey screeched in fear and huddled tightly against her back, shaking.

Police surrounded them, shoving guns in their faces. Someone secured Byron.

"Nice goin', Doc," Hildra said.

Avery couldn't meet her eyes. He tried to contain the beating of his heart, the swelling and shrinking of his lungs. Then he heard a familiar voice and glanced up to see the tides of troops parting like a black sea, light glinting on shields and helmets. And, there between the parting waves, Admiral Sheridan strolled toward him, polished and gleaming in her official uniform, peaked beret slanted rakishly.

"Thought you could escape, did you, you traitor?" she said.

He found his voice, but it was thin and tight. "*I'm* not the traitor."

"Do tell."

He started to say more, but knew it would make no difference. Sheridan would just have him silenced, and painfully.

She marched lion-like back and forth, eyeing her prisoners as they were dragged into line before her, even bleeding and mewling Byron. Janx and Muirblaag were hauled up, as well. They prodded at their swollen faces and bruised ribs. Janx spat out a silver tooth.

At last Sheridan's eyes settled on Layanna. "I very much look forward to speaking with *you* later."

Surprisingly, Layanna did not look intimidated. "I do not think so, you bitch," she said in Octunggen.

Sheridan's eyes widened slightly, and she started to respond, but then thought better of it. Likely she didn't want to reveal how fluent she was in the enemy language.

"Why don't we continue the conversation at Fort Brunt?" she said. Her eyes lingered on Avery's, looking almost apologetic. "This was ... unnecessary, Doctor."

"You don't have to do this," he said.

"I wish that were so." Her voice sounded genuinely sad. "The only solace I can offer is that you won't suffer long."

Because you fear what I might say. Good. Then there were still decent people in the Navy. They hadn't all been corrupted. And at least it meant he'd die quickly. But Layanna ... Avery had no doubt Sheridan would get her own men to interrogate Layanna. If Layanna had any secrets, Sheridan would get them.

"Take them," Sheridan told the troop captain. He nodded and barked orders to his people, who took out handcuffs and electric prods and closed in.

This is where it ends, Avery thought. He and the others would be dragged into black pits beneath Fort Brunt, tortured and put to ignominious death. But he had not reckoned on one thing, which was the entire reason for the whole affair in the first place.

Layanna was not a normal woman.

And, as soldiers laid their hands on her, she revealed exactly how.

She tried to be nice about it.

Her eyes narrowed, her voice hardened, and she said, in Ghenisan so that the troops could understand her, *"Get. Hands. Off."*

They laughed. Handcuffs caught the light.

"Touch. And. *Die*," she growled.

They forced her hands behind her back and tried to shove her to her knees. Her face screwed up in anger and effort. It turned red, and sweat popped out on her cheeks and brow. The very air around her seemed to change, to ripple, and, kneeling nearby, Avery felt an electric charge. His hair lifted.

Sheridan, frowning, stepped back. Her hand reached for the pistol at her hip.

"Don't do it," she said, jerking her gun free. It was longer than it should have been, strange and bulbous. Avery, long accustomed to Navy sidearms, knew this was no normal service piece. "I'm prepared."

Layanna did not give her the chance to use the weapon, whatever it was, for, just then, the air around Layanna blossomed with strange colors, scents and sounds, ammonia and purple and the flash of sunlight on alien waters. Suddenly, the strangeness exploded outward with an oceanic roar, and as if a great wind had struck them everyone standing around Layanna flew backward and hit the floor sliding.

Sheridan, too, struck the floor, and when she did her gun leapt from her hand and spun across the cement.

Avery, gasping, found a chair and struggled to pull himself to his feet. As he did, he turned back to Layanna to see that she was only getting started. With the air around her rippling in strange colors, lavender, purple, white, she ceased to be the woman he thought he knew. Her shape remained the same, but overlapping it, superimposing the image of her standing there—arms flung out, face uplifted—spread the shape of some *thing* very much like an amoeba. Shapeless and horrible, yet beautiful at the same time, it oozed out from her, with her in the center, bathed in jellyfish-white. Toward the edges the form superimposing her turned purplish and lavender. Its thrusting pseudopods ended in starfish-like tips, and from these tips writhed fringes of beautiful tentacles and flagella, slightly white, slightly pink. As the pseudopods spread out, sometimes brushing up against walls, toppling furniture, sometimes passing *through* material objects altogether, the fringing tentacles coiled and grasped with great dexterity.

One lassoed about Avery's chest and picked him up. The reek of ammonia and ozone filled his nose, making him dizzy. Other tentacles gathered up Byron and Hildra. Janx and Muirblaag grabbed up lamps or broken chair legs and leapt back, away from it. Layanna's amoeba form swelled ... and swelled ... filling up the room.

Sheridan scrabbled toward her gun, which lay in a corner. She had to scramble around her troops, who had been flung back, and over toppled furniture.

The troops picked themselves up, turned to the monstrous amoeba spreading outward from Layanna and enveloping the room—and fired. Guns roared, and troopers cursed, sweated and ducked behind furniture. Bullets punched into the amoeba-form but seemed to have no impact. More and more bullets hit it with the same lack of result.

Avery, struggling and gasping in the grip of the lacy, pinkish tentacle, stared at Layanna, who now floated in the midst of the beautiful, horrible being as if it buoyed her up, her eyes closed, her face serene, otherworldly light bathing her and streaming her hair out behind her. Organelles bobbed amid the amoeba, green and purple and turquoise. Avery knew this was the result of the crustacean's meat, and the meat of the eelfish; Layanna had told him such food nurtured parts of herself—extradimensional parts, evidently—that he couldn't see. *Now I can.*

Tentacles whipped toward Sheridan, but she dodged and ducked, eerily adroit. The attacks only delayed her in her progress toward the gun.

Other tentacles wrapped around armored troops and hauled them screaming off the floor. Some passed electric current into the men so that they jerked and spasmed. Some tore the men and women open in geysers of blood, ripping them violently in half and flinging their pieces across the room. Some stung them with what might be jellyfish-like venom, or brought them, kicking and cursing, through the purplish wall of the amoeba's sac and into the thing itself. There the substance of the being ate them like acid, dissolving their flesh and bones slowly and creating majestic swirls of blood that trickled throughout the being's body, running through amoebic veins and tingeing organelles.

"No!" Avery yelled at Layanna. "Don't kill them. They're just following orders."

She slew one soldier after another.

Avery told himself that it was necessary, that despite being good men and women the soldiers would have followed orders to have him and the others tortured and killed, that they would have prevented the good Layanna might be capable of, that simply by following orders they would only hasten the collapse of Ghenisa and the deaths of countless millions. Yet, as they screamed and were torn apart, their blood spattering the walls, Avery thought, *I'm helping a monster.*

Sheridan reached her gun. With a victorious shout, she wrapped her hands about it and turned toward Layanna.

A pinkish tentacle wrapped around the admiral's foot. She screamed. It hauled her up into the air, dangling her upside down. Some excruciating poison must have passed into her, as she threw back her head and screeched in agony. Veins stood out on her forehead. Her body writhed and jerked.

She almost—almost—let go of the pistol.

But then, even through her misery, she seemed to gain control over herself. Avery saw her jaw clamp shut, her eyes narrow, and her gun arm rise toward Layanna.

"Watch out!" Avery said.

Too late. Even as Layanna stretched out another pseudopod toward Sheridan, Sheridan pointed her strange gun directly at Layanna and fired.

The shot distorted the air immediately around the gun, and for a moment Avery thought he saw odd colors and lights.

The bullet punched through the phantasmagoric substance of the amoeba form, barreled straight toward Layanna, through swirling clouds of blood and fantastic organelles, and struck Layanna in the abdomen.

Immediately, Layanna's eyes opened, and her expression of serenity became one of pain. Just as immediately, the amoeba form shrank, dwindling and dwindling, seeming to be drawn directly into Layanna's body, and Avery heard a vast, wet sucking noise. A weird reek lingered on the air, a smell of sulfur and ammonia, seaweed and rot.

The weird lights and smells vanished, as did the amoeba form. Layanna collapsed to the ground.

Sheridan, suddenly not dangled upside-down by the tentacle, dropped to the floor and groaned.

Avery, also no longer supported, fell on the ruins of an old couch. He rolled off, hitting his head on the floor.

Bodies and parts lay everywhere, strewn about the room along with wrecked furniture, priceless antiques that were now rubbish, a dozen shattered lanterns, broken sculptures, and assorted expensive debris. Blood rolled down oil paintings on the wall that would have fetched a fortune at an art auction.

When he recovered, Avery found himself next to the upper half of a soldier's body. The man stared glassily. Blood drooled from his mouth.

Out of the corner of his eye Avery saw Sheridan reach the door and slip outside. Avery grabbed up the soldier's sidearm, climbed to his feet and, a bit unsteadily, pointed his weapon at the door, but it was too late. Sheridan was gone.

"What the fuck just happened?" Janx roared.

"I-I can't believe it," stuttered Byron, clutching his bleeding leg and staring about at the wreckage. All the troops were dead—in pieces, poisoned, dissolved.

Avery's gaze settled on Layanna.

He dropped his gun and ran toward where she lay, bleeding and unconscious, on the floor. The air still rippled vaguely about her and smelled of ammonia, but as the seconds passed this faded too. He checked her pulse and examined her wound, a red hole in her side just below her ribs.

He spun to Janx. "You've got a first aid kit, don't you? For sparring?"

Janx nodded and vanished down the hall, saying over his shoulder, "We don't have time for this." Moments later he returned with a far more advanced kit than Avery had hoped for. He remembered the big man's criminal operations and the need to avoid certified doctors that might be duty-bound to report certain wounds, and thought he understood.

"We need to go," Hildra said. Her monkey hunkered low and subdued on her shoulder, eyes darting all around.

"She's right," Janx said. "That bitch'll have armored transports on the street, with more men, and they'll be up here soon."

Avery nodded. "Very well. Come then."

And, very carefully, he gathered Layanna in his arms and followed the others out the window to the fire escape.

Wind howled around them, and Layanna seemed to grow heavier against Avery as they ascended, the fire escape rattling and scraping against the brick sides of the tenement. Soon they reached the roof. With Janx in the lead, they found a makeshift bridge composed of wooden planks nailed together with rusting iron that spanned the gap to the next roof. They crossed over, found a bridge to the adjacent building, then the next.

They climbed mountains and descended valleys of brick and stucco and concrete and wood, and at times Avery heard shouting in the distance and twice the crack of guns. Desperate, they ran, and ran, sometimes disappearing inside buildings, sometimes plunging down into basements and taking tunnels that connected to basements in other buildings, then ascending to the rooftops once more. This was the Tangle, and Janx's band knew it inside and out, surely better than their pursuers. Byron cursed and complained with every step, and not without reason; blood pumped through the gauze Avery had hastily tied around his thigh, and he must be in considerable pain. Still, he showed remarkable fortitude in forcing himself on. Avery had to shift the burden of Layanna to Janx eventually, who carried her for a ways, then transferred her to Muirblaag, who seemed to enjoy it a bit too much.

Avery tried not to think about what he had seen in Janx's apartment. Tried not to think about *her*.

At last, close to dawn, they paused for a breather atop a certain rooftop garden, and Avery checked on Layanna's wounds.

"I think we lost them," Hildra said, gasping for air. Her monkey Hildebrand climbed down, investigated a patch of vegetables, then the water tank.

"Yeah," said Byron. "'less they really do send out rays."

They looked at each other uneasily.

"Depends on Sheridan," Avery said, wiping his patient's bullet wound with alcohol. The pain didn't rouse her. "Whether she can convince the higher-ups that Layanna's that important. Of course, she's already convinced them to lie to the populace, to conduct roadblocks, raids and what-have-you. From what I understand, she's controlling

Haggarty himself. According to the radio, they were already summoning rays."

"That her name?" Muirblaag asked, staring down at the unconscious woman. "Layanna?" At Avery's nod, Muirblaag's wide, fishy mouth turned downward at the corners. "What *is* she?"

Avery sighed. "I don't know."

"I have to get to my stash," Janx said.

"Come again?"

"I've got bolt-holes all over. Stashes of cash and gear in case I have to light out. We'll need money, and one of my stashes is near. I'll go to it while you play doctor."

Janx disappeared over the next roof as Avery prepared for surgery. Hildra helped during the procedure, handing him necessary tools and restraining Layanna when a spasm seized her. The operation proceeded slowly, handicapped by instruments, conditions and even Layanna herself, who jerked in pain. At last Avery removed the bullet and carefully sewed Layanna back up.

"She should be healing better," Avery said when it was done. "Now that she's fed."

They had all been quiet about what had happened in Janx's apartment. Stunned by their friends' deaths and the manner of Layanna's transformation, if it was a transformation, everyone seemed afraid to bring it up. Nobody wanted to poke it for fear of waking it. But the dam had to break at some point.

"What the fuck did she *do*, anyway?" Byron said.

As soon as he spoke, the others erupted in questions. Avery looked at them warily. Janx was just returning, a money belt slung over his shoulders, a revolver strapped under his arm, and he heard the chorus of questions, too.

"Come on, Doc," he said, throwing down the belt with a grunt and leaning against a wall that contained a riot of winter greenery. "It's past time we knew what we've gotten ourselves into. Tell us. What by Thog's cancerous cock happened down there?"

Avery leaned back and looked up at the stars and moons. "She told me that this ... her physical body ... was only part of her. She's an extradimensional being, as you heard her say, and part of her, perhaps most of her, exists *outside*." He let that sink in. "I think we saw a glimpse of what the rest of her looks like. She brought it over to save us. But it cost her."

"The bullet, you mean?" asked Muirblaag.

"That too. She has extraordinary healing abilities. I've seen them in action. I saw her heal herself from terrible burns inflicted on her by the gastric juices of a whale, and from the sea itself. I think she could heal now if she hadn't spent so *much* of herself bridging the dimensional gulf, bringing the amoeba-facet over." He saw them staring at him in awe, as if he knew what he was talking about. "Of course, I don't really know. I'm just guessing, putting what I do know together. But I think if we brought her some unprocessed seafood she would be able to regain her strength, maybe recover."

They exchanged secret glances amongst each other, and he let them. They were a closed group, a wounded group, with two of their members down. They needed to maintain their exclusionary status to maintain any status at all. If they opened to him, they might just dissolve.

Finally Muirblaag stood. "I'll go. I know all the finest rotgrub in the city."

The others agreed wordlessly. While he was gone, Avery tended to Byron, who had drunk himself into such a stupor from his flask that he almost didn't seem to mind. The bullet had passed clean through the meat of his thigh, but it had nicked an artery, just barely, and done considerable damage to the muscle. He was lucky to be alive, and it was possible he would be crippled for life. Avery patched him up as best he could, but he knew it was not his best work. He had neither the proper instruments nor resources.

The pain seemed to provoke Byron enough that he regained a semblance of sobriety by the time Avery finished. "Thanks for the patch," he muttered, grimacing. He tipped his flask to take another sip, but only a drop came out. A sly look entered his eyes. "Hey, Doc. Got any painkillers?"

"Any painkillers I gave you would render you incapable of flight." Avery held Byron's gaze to make sure he understood. "Do you want me to give you one, or would you rather live?"

Byron sulked a bit, and Avery knew the pain must be extreme and felt a bit bad about his tone. It worked, though.

"Alright," Byron said. "But I want double later."

"We'll see."

When Muirblaag returned, he carried an assortment of dodgy seafood, from mutant squid to clams with teeth to iridescent, faintly glowing spinefish. Layanna, still unconscious, had to be hand-fed. Avery twisted the clam, wringing its juices into her mouth. He gutted the spinefish and let its liquids fall past her lips. He placed a small, rubbery piece of squid onto her tongue, helped her chew and coaxed her to swallow. It worked. She seemed to stir, and her temperature decreased.

Her eyes opened.

Avery couldn't help but laugh. He hadn't realized how nervous he'd been, not just for her sake but for his and the others. It would have been farcical if they had destroyed their lives to aid a dead woman. For him it almost would have been worse if she'd remained unconscious, if he had to tend her through another coma.

When he saw her eyes open, however, something ran through him, and he knew there was something more to it than that. Perhaps tending to her for so long reminded him of caring for Mari. He didn't know. But there was a tightness in his chest that lifted when he saw her wake.

"Can you hear me?" he said.

She nodded, and the others crowded around, murmuring.

Janx crouched next to Avery and stared down at her. "You sure got us into a heap of shit, darlin'. Two of my friends died 'cause of you."

Pain creased her brow. "Many more will die, I'm afraid," she said in Octunggen, and Avery translated. She could understand Ghenisan better than she could speak it.

"You mean the war?" Hildra said.

Layanna nodded again. She tried to rise, but her face screwed up and she collapsed, trembling. "The war will sweep the world," she said, then continued in a smaller voice: "All who don't bow before the Lightning Crown will die. It's why we gifted our technologies to them, so that none could stand against them. Octung will dominate the world, and through it the Collossum will exercise their will. And that will be the beginning of the end of all you know."

Wind hissed around them, blowing soot and soil and splinters of cement. It grew colder.

"What makes you the authority?" Byron said.

"You have seen it," Layanna said. "You saw that I am not ... like you."

The small man eyed her, both in disgust and fear. "You're not *human*."

Avery started to speak, then hesitated. But these people had risked their lives. Their friends had died for this. They deserved to know whatever he did.

"She's part of the Black Sect, the Octunggen saboteurs," he said. "And there's more. I think ... from what Sheridan said, it sounded like Layanna may be one of the Collossum. I'm sorry, Janx. I lied to you."

As one, they stiffened. Some backed away. All stared at Layanna as though they'd received a bucket of ice water in the face.

"Is this true?" Janx said. "You some kinda Octunggen god, darlin'?"

She studied them for a long moment. At last she said, "I am one of the Collossum."

Shocked silence greeted this. Wind hissed and howled.

"Well, shit," Hildra said, visibly trembling.

"And the others," Janx said. "The other Collossum. Are they all like you? Can they all do ... what you did back there?"

"I did not *do* anything. It's what I *am*. And some of them, some of the other Collossum, are much more powerful than I am. Much older, stronger, steeped in the energies of the Outer Lords. And now they're hunting me."

"Holy fucking shit," Byron said.

"I can stop it," she said. "The war. At least ... I think I can." She opened her mouth to say something, then grimaced and stopped. Her eyes were dimming. She didn't have much strength left.

"Tell us quickly," Avery said.

She gripped his hand. Her voice shook as she lifted her head and stared into his eyes.

"The Black Sect has broken from the Collossum. We have ... gone against them. We wish to preserve humanity, not destroy it."

"How?"

"I need to reach the others. The surviving members of the Sect that set out with me. Most are in Lusterqal, but some ... we set out on a mission ..."

"Where ... ? Where did you go?" Avery knew that Lusterqal was the capital of Octung, where the Great Temple of the Collossum was located.

Breath shuddered from her lips. "Just know—those that went with me on the mission, there may still be some living. We were attacked, but ... there is a presence, in the mountains. If there are any still alive, that is where they would be. Take me there and I will ask no more of you."

"Why? What will you do there?"

"Once I rejoin the others, together my friends and I will have strength enough ... to venture to ... Lusterqal."

"Why would you want to go *there?*" Hildra said, when Avery had translated. "Last place I would wanna go!"

"To give the Black Sect the plans. For the machine. The machine that can end the war."

The group glanced at each other once Avery had translated, then back to Layanna.

"Whoa," Byron said. He licked his lips. "Okay, before we even start on this machine business, I've gotta say one thing—*fuck* going to Lusterqal. The capital of Octung? You're crazy to want to go there, of all places, and you're even crazier if you think we're taking you."

"*You* do not have to go," Layanna said. "Only my comrades in the Sect and I must go. But even that ... may not be necessary," Layanna said. "We may be able to find ... an altar."

"Like, to a god?" Hildra said, when Avery had related Layanna's words.

"To the Collossum," Layanna replied.

"You won't find one of those outside Octung, blondie," Hildra said. "Or places they've taken over, anyway."

"No. There are some. Scattered groups outside Octung worship the Collossum, too, but where ... I don't know. If we find one, my friends and I can use the altar to transmit information to the Black Sect hiding in Lusterqal. If I can send them the plans ... the design I made, based on what we learned on our mission ... I can stop the war."

"What plans?" Avery asked.

"A device ... *the* Device, as we call it; the machine is that important ... they'll build it from my plans. The reason we made our journey was to research how to design it. It's why so many died. Why *I* almost died." Her voice caught, then went on. "The Device will disrupt the extradimensional frequencies of Octung's weaponry. It will render them useless."

When Avery had translated this, Janx and the others blinked, and some of them looked at each other in shock— and appreciation.

"Like, disrupt their weapons *forever*?" Hildra asked.

"For long enough," Layanna said. "If the Black Sect can build and activate the Device, the Octunggen will no longer be able to use Collossum technology in the war."

"But without those weapons, we could beat the fuckers," Hildra said. She sounded surprised.

"The Octs are spread thin," Janx agreed. "Only thing keeping 'em on the warpath is their damned weird gadgets, like whatever controlled those lobsters the other day. Without those, we could drive 'em back. Crush 'em."

Layanna looked like she needed rest, and soon. "Take me to the presence in the mountains, and I will be able to make my way from there with my friends, either to Lusterqal or an altar, where we can transmit the plans— send them to the Black Sect in Octung. If we can, they'll build it. The Device. And save us the trip."

"Can't you just pick up a phone?" Hildra said.

"Can you transmit the plans for a skyscraper over the phone? And the Device is infinitely more complicated than any skyscraper. I need to either return to Lusterqal, where I can give over the plans directly, or find a functioning altar. Only from such a one ... can I communicate with the Black Sect on extra-planar levels."

"Tell us what we need to do," Avery said, seeing that she was fading.

The others leaned forward, eager to hear what she had to say.

Layanna spoke in Ghenisan, in a soft, ragged whisper. "Take me," she said, "into the Borghese. Now need some ... rest." She closed her eyes.

The water tank rattled as someone took a shower down below. Hildebrand scampered away from it, screeching.

No one said anything. Then:

"Fuck." This came from Byron. He said it in such a way that it sounded profound, expressing the opinion of them all. "The mountains ..."

The members of the band appeared pained, perhaps ready to quit. No sane person wanted to venture very far into the Borghese Mountains.

Avery made his voice stern. "You swore an oath."

"I swore to fight that bitch Sheridan," Byron said.

"You swore to stop her," Avery reminded him. "And her goal is to kill Layanna. Thus the only way to stop Sheridan is to save Layanna—and make sure she accomplishes her mission."

Byron looked as though he had swallowed something bitter.

"Actually," Hildra said, sounding crafty, "I think we really only swore to help the doc on *his* mission of stopping Sheridan ..."

Byron's eyes lit up. "That's right! Doc! You've gotta quit this fucking ride. Don't do what that bitch wants. Take us into the Borghese? She's mad! Just say no, Doc. Maybe we can end all this right here. Turn her in, the cops'll let us go. Hells, there may even be a reward."

Avery stared at him as coldly as he could, and at last Byron dropped his gaze. "I'm going on," Avery said. "If you can break your oaths with your gods, that's between you and them. But as for me, I'm holding you to them. I'm going to help end this war if I can—and to hell with anyone that doesn't follow."

Thunder rolled in the distance.

Hildra looked up. Sudden worry lined her face. "We've got more pressing problems, boys," she said. "It's a fucking ray."

Chapter 11

Startled, Avery turned. His breath caught in his throat. Sure enough, a ray arced across the sky—huge, magnificent, and terrible.

The band rushed to the roof wall and stared out at it, transfixed. Only Avery stayed, unwilling to leave Layanna. His eyes moved across the thing, spellbound and horrified. He'd heard of them, of course. They had originally been bred by the Octunggen on some island, but the Ghenisan Navy had captured the island in the early days of the war—a rare victory—and put the creatures to use. Mostly they patrolled the sea. But not today.

It was a living thing, an animal, and in aspect it resembled something like a manta ray, if a manta ray could stretch a mile wide, a mile long. A huge delta shape, black and gray by the dawn light creeping over the haze of the horizon, it boasted a great, broad, flat head, with an obscene mouth gaping, seemingly unable to close, fringed at each corner by a tendril. The massive, broad wings trailed away to either side, of one piece with the rest of the creature. And the tail—the long, spiny, razor sharp tail—trailed out behind it for what seemed like miles.

No normal physics could hold such thing aloft. It defied all logic, at least on this plane. But these creatures were not bound by normal physics, or any reality of this world. Like the lobsters, they were scions of the Atomic Sea, bred and created with the aid of tools from other dimensions entirely, and it was to those planes that they were fused, even more so than with this one. They existed across multiple realities, but they were certainly deadly enough in this one.

"Gods below," breathed Janx. "There's *three* of 'em. I didn't even know there *were* three of 'em near Hissig."

Indeed, sweeping in from the south, two more rays slowly glided out over the city, their shadows devouring entire blocks. They were things that should not exist, much less fly, and yet there they were, their bodies spanning dimensions (so it was said) as they arced across the sky and blurred the air around them.

It was not thunder Avery had heard, but the sound of their wings, slowly fanning up, then down. As he watched, the sound came again, battering the air around him, shaking the leaves of the plants in the garden. Upon each ray's broad back would be an assortment of crack troops, as well as snipers, commanders, and, most deadly of all, the psychics who controlled the creatures. The psychics could use the rays to amplify their abilities, like a man shouting through a bullhorn, and they could wield those magnified abilities to sow terror into the hearts of an enemy host, to confuse and disorient them and make it easier for Ghenisan soldiers to prevail. But if used against an individual ... if *three* were used against an individual ...

Avery frowned. He peered down at Layanna.

"We have to go," he said, raising his voice over the sound of false thunder.

Reluctantly, still transfixed by the rays, the others gave him their attention.

He patted Layanna's hand. "Our charge here will give off a powerful extradimensional signature. Gaescruhd said as much at Claver's. The psychics should be able to detect her easily when they get close enough. That's probably what they're trying to do."

"We'd better set off, then," Janx agreed. "I've got the cash, Doc's got the girl. Anybody got a plan?"

"We need to get out of the city," Avery said. "As soon as possible."

The monkey chittered. Hildra bent down and it clambered onto her shoulder. "We really gonna take her into the mountains?" she said.

"You wanna crap out, that's your business," Janx said. "But I don't think any of us can afford to stay here. The mountains are our best bet out."

"He's right," Avery said. "They won't expect us to go there."

"There's a reason for that," Hildra said.

"It's where Layanna needs to go."

They descended from the heights, quickly and quietly. Janx and Muirblaag left to fetch some basic supplies while Hildra stole a vehicle for them. It was a rusty pickup, mustard yellow paint flaking off it. When Janx and Muirblaag returned, the band piled in, Avery and Layanna and Muirblaag in back. The morning sun caressed their skins and coaxed little beads of sweat from them.

As they lurched off into the streets, Janx driving, Avery remembered to take his daily pollution pill. He'd thought to bring enough for himself and the others, but he only had a supply for another few days. By then he hoped to be far enough away from the sea that it wouldn't matter.

"Wow," said Muirblaag.

They'd reached a high place, and he was facing back, toward the city, which was now unobstructed by buildings or smaller peaks. Avery, who'd been drowsing, opened his eyes and felt a touch of awe.

Silently, in sync with each other, the three massive rays glided through the sky over Hissig, morning sun beating down on their charcoal flesh, on their huge broad wings, on their long, trailing, barb-tipped tails. They swept over towers and domes, parks and apartments, searching, searching. The air crackled and shifted around them. Avery's eyes hurt, but it was hard to look away.

"They think we've gone to ground somewhere in the city," Avery said. "That should buy us some time."

Muirblaag regarded him levelly. "We're really going into the Borghese?"

"It's what she wants." Avery nodded to Layanna, who slept fitfully, at times stirring or rolling her eyes. Hopefully that meant she would wake soon. "Is that a problem for you?"

The fish-man looked wary. "You know what I am. You've guessed."

Avery nodded. When he'd first seen Muirblaag, he'd noticed the mutant's unusual degree of symmetry and wholeness. Most mutants were either cobbled together variations, or ostensibly human with deformities. Muirblaag looked like a complete specimen of some unknown species.

"You're *ngvandi*," Avery said. The word meant *feral* in L'ohen. It was also translated in Ghenisan as *monster* or *barbarian*.

Muirblaag turned his head to stare at the looming peaks. "The Borghese are my home." Bleakly, he added, "I left them for a reason."

Avery understood. Long ago when the Atomic Sea had widened to encompass the coasts of Urslin, it had spread infection among the countries there, among peoples who had not been prepared for it. Millions had died or been mutated. The rest fled the coasts, and for the three hundred years of the Withdrawal they stayed away, abandoning the cities along the shore to the infected. At last scientists and alchemists devised means of counteracting the poisons, and people returned—the Resettling—only to find mutants occupying the cities.

The infected had thrived there, in a bloody and savage chaos, worshipping strange gods of the sea and practicing human sacrifice. They refused to relinquish control to the new settlers, and a series of wars began—street to street, house to house—until eventually the mutants that did not surrender were killed or driven off. In Ghenisa, the mutants found sanctuary in the vast and rugged Borghese Mountains, where they lived to this day, the stuff of myth and nightmare, known as the ngvandi.

"It's the last place I want to go," Muirblaag said.

"Are you full-blooded?"

"No. They got my mother in a raid on a goat ranch, but most ngvandi half-breeds take after their fishy side. Shit, I can't believe I'm actually going back."

"It won't be for long," Avery promised. "We'll just deliver Layanna to her friends and be on our way. We'll have to relocate afterwards, of course, find new identities, but in the chaos of the war, and with your sort of contacts, it should be achievable."

"You really think it'll be that simple?"

Avery's gaze wandered to Layanna. *Please be the right thing to do.* He knew that without his leadership and commitment to making them keep their vows, the others would likely quit.

"Sure," he said. "Why wouldn't I?"

"And you think she can really do what she says—end the war?"

"If she can truly build this Device of hers and disrupt Octung's weapons, then yes. We just need to bring her to her friends and they can go on from there by themselves."

"But why would her friends be in the Borghese? Trust me, I'm from there, and there's nothin' good that way."

"It will work," Avery assured him.

Carried on the wind, the thunder of the rays' wings reached Avery's ears, and he felt hounded and out of his depth.

"I need a drink," he said, half under his breath.

Muirblaag surprised him. "You mean, like this?" He revealed a flask he'd been hiding, twisted the cap off, and offered it.

Avery hesitated. Long years of conditioning had instilled in him a fear of contact with infected people. Science, however, had taught him that the disease could only live outside of the body for a few moments.

He wiped the lip, counted to ten, and knocked back a sip.

He whistled.

Muirblaag laughed. "Strong shit, ain't it?"

"I'll say." Coughing, Avery took another. The liquid burned his throat, but it was divine fire. He handed the flask back. "By the way, I've been meaning to ask. 'Muirblaag'— is that your real name? It sounds ..."

"Bullshit?" Muirblaag laughed. "Yeah, it's a stage name." The fish-man swigged deeply of the flask, grimacing. "Naw, the bastards that raised me called me Czan. When I broke out and took Mom back to Hissig—she was old and diseased by then and wanted to die at home—I asked her what she'd wanted to name me. She said Frank. I guess that's my name. But shit, Doc, I've been Mu now too long to be anything else. It fits. It's a self-invented name for a self-invented man. Muirblaag the Monster." He raised his flask to the sun, a toast. "World, watch out." And he drank.

The roads ended. Mountainous frontier beckoned.

"From here on out it gets rocky," Janx said as they left the truck behind. "'least our leg muscles'll get a working."

"Great," said Byron. Avery had found some alchemical pills in a first aid kit and administered a couple to Byron; they would aid his recovery given time, but for now he was uncertain on his feet. With Avery and Hildra taking turns helping him, the group set out. Janx and Muirblaag had procured some rudimentary camping and climbing supplies along with the rest, but they weren't much, and no one besides Avery had any experience hiking anyway.

It was late afternoon the day after they'd stolen the truck. They'd wound through mountain roads that grew increasingly primitive, and fortified frontier settlements perched among the rocks and pines periodically. The people that lived up here had to hold out against ngvandi, and they tended to be strange, stand-offish and insular.

The air was colder here, and thin; Avery felt winded quickly. He scanned the forest around him, alert for ngvandi, and it almost amused him that he was more worried about mutant savages than Octunggen. Octunggen soldiers would be here, too, navigating through the peaks, the ngvandi and the frontier families. They would be in small, dirigible-mounted raiding parties but no less dangerous for that. Octung itself was not overly large and yet it had subdued two entire continents and was not done yet.

The band passed ruined fortresses overgrown with trees, vines and vegetation. Stone walls piled in moss-covered heaps. Arches sagged and ruptured. Leafy canopies of live oaks and pines thrust through the spaces where ceilings of great halls had given way. Other trees grew from rearing bulwarks of stone, their roots penetrating soil-filled cracks. Avery saw a batkin of unusual size crouching on a broken tower, gnawing something with noisy rips and tears.

"Amazing," he muttered. "We're passing through history."

"Fuck history," Byron said.

"You should show more interest. I'm something of a student of the past—L'ohen's, especially, and our own. Ghenisa was forged right here, you know. How many men and women died to win our freedom from the Ysstrals? The War of the Severance lasted for centuries."

"They didn't die for freedom," Janx said. "The revvies died for that fifty years ago."

"So what did they die for?"

"Independence."

Avery nodded judiciously. "So they did."

"Whatever," said Byron. "What does it matter what a bunch of old dead people died for? They're not even bones anymore."

Hildra glanced up at the trees, at the light shining down, and she wore a strange smile. Even her monkey seemed subdued and respectful. "I think it's romantic," she said. "All those princes, all those counts and dukes, building hundreds of fortresses, warring against each other over great canyons and high peaks, princesses getting kidnapped, princes becoming heroes. My favorite tale is the one about Prince Cort and Princess Syra."

Avery smiled. "I was just reading one account of their adventures before I left. Sadly, I was forced to abandon my books."

"It's a great story."

"One of my wife's favorites, too. Of course, there are so many different versions of the tale, it's hard to know what really happened. Some scholars don't even think Prince Cort and Princess Syra existed at all."

"Oh, they did." Hildra sounded certain. "I know it. They say the war never would have ended without them."

"That is the legend," Avery agreed.

"Well, I don't like the legends," Muirblaag said. In his arms he held the sleeping Layanna. "They all make my folk out to be savages. Mindless killers."

Hildra looked at him apologetically, and they lapsed into silence.

They walked throughout the day and into the night, shining flashlights before them when needed. Janx had bought several. At last Avery prevailed upon them to quit using the lights for fear of alerting enemies to their presence, and they found the ruin of what looked like an old mill that moldered beside a trickling stream, lichen and moss covering its sides. Huge batkin roosted within and had to be forcefully evicted. As Avery and the band settled in, the batkin wheeled through the sky overhead, chittering angrily.

"Won't they ever shut up?" Byron said as he shook out a blanket. The air stank of bat offal and musk.

"They'll move on," Janx said. "Best post a watch. Don't want anyone sneakin' up on us."

"I'll take first watch," Avery said. Staring up at the huge bat-like creatures that swarmed against the stars, he added, "I doubt I'll sleep anyway."

They didn't retire immediately, though. For a long time the band sat together over a fire that Avery tried to convince them not to light, telling stories of their lost mates, Jaimesyn and Holdren. Then, to Avery's considerable surprise, and after generous amounts of the cheap liquor they had brought along, Muirblaag revealed some inking equipment. The others seemed to have expected it, and at their request he tattooed stylized versions of Jaimesyn's and Holdren's names into their arms, backs or chests. With blood still weeping down his arm, Janx returned the favor for Muirblaag, who grimaced and drank.

Studying their tattoos, Avery noticed other names mixed in among the pictures of dragons, hellspawn and sea nymphs. In those names he saw a reflection of a shadowy network of friends, allies and accomplices, some dead, some possibly still living, some likely in prison, stretching across years and geography, their friendships forged in blood and danger and lawlessness. For a moment, despite himself, Avery felt jealous. He could only sit and watch as they grieved, as they bonded. Layanna, still unconscious, lay in her blankets.

Avery wrestled with himself. At last he cleared his throat. When the others looked to him, he rolled up his left sleeve.

"They died because of me," he said. "I would be honored to bear their names."

The others glanced at each other, apparently uncomfortable. Maybe by being marked with their friends' names he would become one of them, and they did not want to open their group up—not to him, not tonight, even if he was the person they had sworn to follow. *Come on*, he thought. He needed this. It frightened him how much he needed this. Mari and Ani were long gone. Sheridan was a traitor. He had no one, not one person in this world. He didn't even have a home, or a bed to curl up in.

Finally Janx nodded his huge head and came to sit beside him. Lifting his needle, he said, "You ever had a tat before?"

"No," Avery admitted.

"This'll hurt."

"I'm ready."

Hildra and Muirblaag came forward. Hildebrand chattered loudly.

"It'll hurt less with this," Hildra said, and shoved a bottle into Avery's hands. He drank. Muirblaag clapped him on the back, and he coughed.

"You ready?" Janx said.

Avery sucked in a breath and nodded.

Janx hadn't lied. It hurt like hell.

His arm itching, Avery traipsed through the forest the next day, right behind Muirblaag. Between them they carried Layanna on a makeshift stretcher. Avery's arm burned, but he held on tight. Sometimes Layanna slept, sometimes not. Avery would catch her staring up at him, or the sky overhead, and he felt oddly self-conscious. He felt closer to the others than he had before, and it may have been his imagination, but he thought they acted more openly around him, too.

Toward afternoon, Layanna climbed out of the stretcher and walked a ways by herself, limping along with the help of a wooden stick Muirblaag carved for her. She could only walk for a short period before she needed the stretcher again, but in another hour she was once more afoot. The periods of walking grew longer and the periods of resting shorter. Avery was amazed again at her recuperative abilities. He reflected that nothing about her should shock him after seeing her turn into an amoeba monster. He still remembered the screams of the soldiers dying in her stinging tentacles or engulfed in her otherworldly acids.

That night the band came across the ruins of a small village that crept up a mountainside. Stone houses jutted like crumbling teeth through undergrowth, and large spiders wove webs between half-collapsed walls. After burning out the spiders, the band made camp for the evening. The mountain winds blew very chill that night, and Avery only protested a little as Janx and Hildra made a fire in the shelter of a wall. Layanna was placed near it and fed with the meager foodstuffs they possessed. She tore into the jerky and gulped water like a fish.

Avery smiled. "You have a healthy appetite."

Smacking her lips, Layanna glanced up at them. "What I need now is something from the sea." She'd spoken in Octunggen and Avery had to translate for the others.

Hildra smirked. "The only thing fishy we have is Mu." She slapped him on the shoulder. "Eat him with my blessing."

Layanna's gaze moved to Muirblaag as if sizing him up, and the fish-man shifted uncomfortably.

"Hildra was joking," he said.

"Good for you," Layanna said in her thickly-accented Ghenisan.

The others chuckled nervously.

"Why don't we get some shut-eye?" Janx suggested. "We've gotta go down into the valley tomorrow, or find a way across to the next mountain. We need our sleep."

"Fuck that," said Byron. He was staring at Layanna. "It's been long enough. She's awake now and I want answers. For starters, what the hell *is* a Collossum, honey?"

"I don't think that now is the time," Avery said.

"Not human," said Layanna, surprising him.

The others leaned forward. "Where are you from, sunshine?" Hildra asked.

"Not here."

"Did the Octunggen make you in some lab?"

"No," Layanna said. "I say further nothing about that."

She doesn't trust us with the truth, Avery realized. The thought that she couldn't even tell them what she was, after all they'd been through already, disturbed him more than he wanted to admit.

She yawned, and Avery said, "I think that's it for tonight. Let her rest."

"No," Byron pressed. "One more thing. She hasn't even told us where we're *going*. Some presence, she said. Well, what presence?"

The others murmured agreement, and Layanna returned their gazes quietly. She seemed about to say something, then hesitated. At last she yawned again and said, "I am tired much."

She closed her eyes and stretched out, and the others stared at each other. Avery shivered in a sudden mountain wind.

"She won't even tell us where we're *going*," Byron said. "Not what she is, not where we're going. Gods *damn*, but I don't like this."

They began seeing rays.

At first it was simply one, far off, a black wedge against the sky drifting over the mountains. A few days later, they spotted a second. They were far apart, miles and miles to either side of the band. After a week, three rays cut the sky. They circled closer, then closer.

Pressing on, the group crossed the shoulder of one mountain to another. They ascended through a pass, then picked their way down into a tangled, dark valley, littered with recent bones and ruins. The smell of rot was thick on the air. The trek up the next mountain was arduous, and as they climbed toward its summit cold winds howled around them, sometimes pocked with snow. Winter began to set in with a vengeance, worse with the elevation. Snow-covered fortresses hunkered from cliff sides, austere and beautiful. Avery huddled in his coat.

He showed the others how to camp and find trails. They were city-bred, unused to nature, but his father had taken him camping often growing up. Avery remembered the long nights of listening to the creatures of the forest outside his tent as his father told him a story. Avery's memories stirred as they went deeper into the mountains.

He tended to Layanna often. Her wound had become infected, and he cleaned and dressed it with care. She would have been at risk for severe fever, even death, but after feeding her extra-planar facets in Hissig her uncanny recuperative abilities were able to help her, along with Avery's attentions. His small medical supply dwindled, and he tried to use it sparingly. As they pushed even deeper into the mountains, and Layanna grew better, she guided them; she said she could sense where to go. On previous hikes, Avery had stuck to the foothills, to the relatively safe frontier, the areas where ngvandi typically did not go, but now he might as well have been on a different planet. He could no longer see Hissig save the lights of the city reflected off clouds to the east, and that only at night.

They pressed deeper, and deeper. Mountains piled up around them.

The rays followed.

Chapter 12

A ray glided to the west.

Avery sat in the ruined tower of some ancient fortress smoking one of the last cigarettes side by side with Hildra, also smoking. In companionable silence, they shared a flask containing the last whiskey and stared at the sky, where to the west floated the great shape of the ray, visible mainly as a blackness against the low-lying clouds. To the north floated another.

"Think they can sense her?" Hildra asked. "Your mermaid?" Her monkey Hildebrand perched low and apprehensive on her shoulder, staring in the direction of the nearest ray. He had a nut halfway to his mouth but was too distracted to eat it.

Avery sipped from the flask and grimaced. "They must. She's drawing them closer and closer. It's only a matter of time before they come on us."

She accepted the flask back, took a swig. "Then what? We're screwed?"

He took a drag on his cigarette. He didn't smoke often and found it harsher than he would have cared for. Nevertheless he enjoyed the pleasant lift it brought to his mind. "Layanna says she thinks she can counter whatever psychic blasts the rays might hurl at her. But even without the psychics, the soldiers on the rays have weapons that can hurt her, even kill her, like Sheridan did."

"I'm more worried about us."

"They can kill us, too, of course."

Hildra rolled her eyes.

"You wouldn't like to see the war ended?" he asked.

She expelled a column of smoke at the sky. "Sure. Why not? I'm in. But if it comes down to it, a choice between us or her, no offense, bones, but I'm sidin' with the humans. She won't even tell us what she is or where we're going." She took a long pull on the flask, made a face. "How can we trust someone like that?"

"She's told us she's one of the Collossum, and she did save our lives."

"She needs us, that's all. And don't forget about Jay and Hold."

"I won't." He touched his arm gingerly, though it had healed.

She nodded, accepting this. "I know, bones. But ... shit, I saw Jay's brains explode out the back of his fucking *head*." She blinked as if to get the memory out of her mind.

"For what it's worth, I think Layanna feels badly about their deaths."

"How can you tell? She's so ... cold."

Avery had noticed that, too. "She needs to be. She can't afford to get attached to us. She can't allow herself to hesitate if it comes time to sacrifice one of us. Not unlike what you were just saying about her, I might add."

Hildra sighed and slumped against the wall. "I don't like this, Doc. This is out of my normal line, if y'know what I mean. I guess I've helped out a few fugitives, but ... fucking *rays*? You've gotta be kidding me." Her eyes flicked to the horizon, where a ray was just sweeping before a snow-capped mountain peak. The creature's wings flapped once, slowly, with a crack of rolling thunder, and its spiny tail dipped up and down. That was all. Except for those small movements, it might as well have been a statue, vast and black and merciless.

"We'll make it," Avery said with more assurance than he felt.

"Pardon me for sayin', bones, but you're full of shit."

"You're not the first person to say so." Taking the flask back, he sipped, then sucked a drag off his cigarette. He let the smoke play in his mouth, mix with the taste of cheap alcohol. "We'll make it."

He glanced at the ruined fortress around them. It was huge and sprawling, with a dozen great towers lancing the heavens, all capped white with snow. Most were broken, their tops missing, even snapped off halfway through, and their remains lay at the towers' bases, huge mounds of snow-covered rubble. From time to time a cloud of batkin would shiver from the inside of one of the towers and sweep off into the night, or return to their roost gorged and full and dripping.

Down below in one of the frost-covered courtyards Janx strolled, unlit cigar clenched in his jaws. Layanna was resting in the ruins of the keep, where presumably Muirblaag and Byron rested, too. Over the past few days, Avery had learned that Byron was an accomplished singer, and when the band judged the night to be safe, he would entertain them with songs of adventure, gilded cities and tragic romance. For someone who despised history so much, he certainly could make it exciting.

Hildra touched Avery's arm suddenly and pointed out at the night.

A ray drifted closer, its huge broad head aimed in their direction.

Perhaps afraid, Hildra pressed against his side, and he could smell her, a mix of spice and musk, whisky and cigarettes. He was grateful for the contact, and the warmth, for he felt suddenly cold.

"Maybe we should get goin'," she said.

"Leave Maar Keep?"

It was a private joke between the two of them. They had decided amongst themselves that this must be the infamous fortress of Count Hyssmyr, who had held Prince Cort prisoner for years and finally walled him up in the catacombs only for the prince to escape, rescue Princess Syra and flee into the mountains, there to engage in the epic adventures which had made them immortal and, if legend held true, had ended the War of the Severance.

Hildra did not smile. "I mean it, bones. That fucker's comin' straight at us."

Avery frowned, studying the ray. It was not actually coming directly at them, he saw, but at a slight angle. Its psychic pilot must sense Layanna's general direction. If he came close enough ...

"You may be right," Avery said. Snow settled on his hair and mustache and began to melt. He drew his jacket tighter about him.

"It's coming from the east," she said. "If we leave here and bear north I bet we miss—"

A scream rang out. A long, terrified scream.

Then another, and another.

Avery and Hildra stared at each other. As one, they ran down the stairs.

Hildebrand chittered in fright as they reached the courtyard and bounded across it.

Janx was already moving, rushing around a blasted statue toward the mass of the keep that reared above them, its roofs and gables crusted with age and snow. Fierce gargoyles with bloodstone eyes glared down at them, some with horns or tongues missing, some with lichenous growths jutting obscenely from them, making them look eerie and monstrous.

Janx reached the great archway, where hundreds of years ago a thick metal-banded wooden door would have hung but was long gone, and vanished inside.

Heart pounding, Avery followed.

It was cold but dry inside, and the wind blew weakly. Ice-slicked stone pressed down on him, inset torch sconces a mockery of warmth and light from a distant age. A small light flickered ahead, around a bend in the tunnel. A candle hunched at the base of a set of winding, age-bowed stairs. Janx leapt up them, two at a time. Avery came after, not as adroitly, breathing fast and shallow. Screams echoed off the walls.

They passed down another hall, with the roof missing above and snow fluttering down, then another, this one with roof intact. Lights flickered from a room ahead, making shadows dance across the corridor walls.

Avery, hard on Janx's heels, burst into the chamber, what must have been some concubine's bedchamber at some point long ago, or even a holding cell. Legend held that Princess Syra had been locked away in the highest tower, but who really knew? She might have been locked in this very room, if she had ever existed at all.

Layanna, Muirblaag and Byron had laid out sleeping blankets on the cold stone, but they weren't asleep at the moment. Muirblaag and Byron struggled under netting that had been thrown over them, while Layanna occupied the center of the room, arms flung back, head uplifted, floating amidst the substances of her otherworldly amoeba-self. Pink-tinged tentacles and flagella wriggled from bulging pseudopods, and strange lights shone from the amoeba's interior.

Gripped in these tentacles were half a dozen ngvandi. It was the ngvandi who screamed so hideously. They writhed and twisted in the grip of the stinging, electric tendrils, convulsing and shuddering. As Avery watched, Layanna drew one of the creatures inside the amoebic wall, causing the surface of the material to ripple as the ngvandi was engulfed. Her organelles bunched aside, and the otherworldly acids began eating at it. Skin peeled from muscle, muscle dissolved against bone. The ngvandi screamed soundlessly as its eyes boiled away and streamers of flesh floated about its head.

The other ngvandi howled and twisted, but soon enough they went limp in Layanna's embrace, and she laid them almost tenderly on the floor. Smoke trailed up from two of the corpses, while others appeared chemically burned.

"Shit," Janx said, sounding stunned. He shook his head and crossed to Muirblaag and Byron, helping them out of the nets. "What happened?"

Muirblaag struggled from the netting, winded and out of breath. "Fuckin' bastards ... just pounced on us."

Avery studied one smoking body. It could have been a brother to Muirblaag, though it was not quite so tall and muscular. Another of the corpses had yellow-and-red fish scales, and another green.

Layanna still floated, encased in her amoeba sac. The fluids of the ngvandi she'd drawn into herself swirled around organelles and ... into them. *She's feeding*, Avery realized. Gooseflesh crept up his arms. Of course, it made sense. The ngvandi would have the same extradimensional elements as anything from the Atomic Sea.

"I think we'd better go," Avery said.

"Fuckin' aye," Byron said, dusting himself off. "I've had it here."

"Hildra and I saw a ray coming this way."

"We don't need any rays," Janx agreed. "And fuck knows if the mutes'll be back."

Muirblaag looked bleak. "They will. This is what they do when they find travelers in the mountains. They send in a stealth party to steal the women to breed with, then the real attack comes."

"I'm not so sure about that," Avery said. "They made no move against Hildra." He turned to her.

Or where she should have been. She had been right on his heels.

There was no one there.

"I ..." He felt weak all of a sudden. The ngvandi had taken her, quietly and with ease, right from under his nose, and he hadn't noticed a thing.

"Damn." This was Byron. He blinked and began to pack his things.

Janx turned hard eyes on Muirblaag. "What'll they do with her?"

"What do you think?"

"Gods *damn*!" Janx's eyes bulged in rage. "We have to get her back."

"Agreed," Muirblaag said.

Byron wiped a hand down his pale, sweaty face. "Shit, guys, you really wanna ... ? I mean ..." They stared at him mercilessly, and he sagged. "Shit."

Avery heard a sound in the distance, faint but audible. "I don't think so," he said.

"Hells with that," Janx said. "We're goin' after her."

"I meant I don't think we'll get the chance. They take the women first, then massacre the men. By now they will have figured out one of their kidnapping parties hasn't returned, and—"

Avery heard more distinctly what he'd detected a minute before. There came the scuffings of feet on stone, of powerful bodies propelling themselves down cold halls. Something hooted. Something shrieked.

They were very close.

Avery reached down and wrestled a metal trident out of the hands of one of the smoking ngvandi. The weapon was cold and heavy and charred. He stared at it in wonder. *Am I really doing this?*

"Shit," said Janx, drawing his pistol.

Muirblaag claimed another trident. "Guess I always knew it would come down to this."

Byron looked as if he wanted to weep. Then his eyes settled on Layanna. "*She'll* save us."

Layanna remained entranced in her ethereal substances. As Avery watched, she seemed to float higher off the ground, and her amoeba sac swelled. Strange lights filled the gelatinous substances inside. There was little left of the victimized ngvandi now, just bones. Even those were dissolving. Avery knew it hadn't been the creature's flesh that she had truly craved, however, but the energies within it, or fused with it on some other plane.

"They may not kill us," Muirblaag offered. "They may just make us *wish* they had."

"Sell it dearly." This was Janx's advice.

The hooting and gibbering drew closer, and the scuff of feet and claws on stone.

Sweat beaded Avery's brow. *Cornered*, he thought. *Mari, Ani, I'll be with you soon.* Squaring his shoulders, he backed away from the doorway that had no door and joined the others as they formed a semi-circle facing the entrance. Layanna occupied the center, swollen, majestic and terrible.

Visibly shaking, Byron drew out his knife. "Fuck me."

Something hooted in the hallway beyond. The ngvandi had found the right floor.

Avery raised his trident. It was a fitting room to die in, he thought. The room that Princess Syra herself may have been a captive in.

The ngvandi came closer.

He blinked.

A howl sent shivers down his spine.

No, of course not. Foolish ...

The ngvandi screamed in bloodlust. They had almost reached the room.

But maybe ...

Shuffling, scraping. Very near.

Maybe ...

Holding his breath, Avery swiveled his head. His eyes scanned the room. *It can't be,* he thought. *Surely.*

A horrible screech shook the room.

He quit the line of defenders and marched toward the far wall. All the stories agreed that it had been through the wall opposite the doorway that Prince Cort had come. It was always important because he'd been within sight of the door. Even as he'd spirited Princess Syra through the secret entrance, someone had opened the main door, spotted them and raised the alarm. The breathless escape that followed, including the masquerade, was one of the highlights of the tale, no matter which version.

Avery probed the wall.

"What the hell you doin'?" Janx said. "Get your ass back here!"

Avery threw down his trident and studied the wall.

The ngvandi burst into the room. The stink of fish and rot filled the chamber. Their howls chilled Avery's blood. He turned once, to see the piscine or brachial, or both, figures fall on the line of defenders. Janx fired his pistol point-blank into one's face. Brain matter mushroomed out the back of its head. Byron ducked one creature's claws, stabbed it in the gut, then slashed the throat of another. Muirblaag rammed his trident into the ribcage of an attacker, and it reeled back, knocking into another.

Layanna's amoeba form swelled still more. She lifted higher off the ground, her sac glowing brighter. Her limbs shot out.

The ngvandi screamed as her tentacles and flagella wrapped around them, crushed them, stung them, shoved them inside her sac wall. Others fell back and dropped to their knees, seeming to pray.

Avery returned his attention to the wall. His fingers felt, probed, explored. There! A sconce. Perhaps *the* sconce. Some versions held that it was twisting the torch which opened the door. The torch was long gone, but Avery played with the niche, his fingers probing. Nothing happened. Others held that a stone near the floor beneath the sconce did the trick. Avery tried it.

Byron screamed behind him. Janx cursed.

Shit. Avery shouldn't be wasting time with this. He should be helping the others.

Still, he had to try out one more version. This one held that by depressing a stone to either side of the sconce ...

Nothing.

Muirblaag hollered behind him.

Avery started to turn back. *No*, he thought. *Just* one *more.* Some versions held that it wasn't the stone immediately to the left and right but top and bottom—

He shoved. Something ... *gave.* He pressed the stones even harder. The mechanism was ancient, rusty and reluctant. With all his strength, he shoved, one hand on one panel, one on the other.

Shouts and echoes behind him.

With a groan, a panel in the wall swung open. Avery stared at it, astonished. The opening was smaller than he would have imagined, no more than four feet by four, and it was dusty and cold, spanned by spider webs, but—

"Come on!" he shouted over the sounds of battle. "This way!"

One by one, the others noticed what he was gesturing them to do. Shocked, Janx, who had fired his last shot, smashed one more ngvandi over the head with his pistol and loped toward Avery. Muirblaag and Byron followed.

Avery scooped up a lantern and motioned for them to enter the opening. Byron went first, Muirblaag second, then Janx. Both had to stoop and squeeze to fit. Layanna, swollen and monstrous, held off the advancing ngvandi.

Avery paused at the door. "Layanna!" he shouted. "Come on!"

She remained where she was. She was not even engaged in combat with the ngvandi anymore. Instead, they ringed her, chanting and prostrate. They bowed toward her, lifted themselves up, and bowed again. Something cold slithered through Avery's guts.

"Come on!" he shouted. "Hurry, while they're distracted!"

Still she floated there, serene, basking in her worshippers.

A handful of ngvandi slipped around the edges of the room, making for Avery and his tunnel. He had time for one last try.

"Please!" he shouted. "All this will have been for nothing without you!"

She turned, just once, and made eye contact with him. "Go." He heard the word even through the sac. Perhaps she had sent it directly to his mind. Then she returned to her worshippers.

Avery just managed to slam the door in the faces of the oncoming ngvandi. Holding the lantern, gasping, he turned to Janx, Byron and Muirblaag. They huddled on a tight set of stairs. Ngvandi fingernails scratched the stone on the other side of the wall. Avery heard muffled, horrible howls.

Byron speared a huge spider with his knife and shook it off. Avery's lantern illuminated more spider webs beyond.

Janx and Muirblaag stared at Avery.

"She's not comin'?" Janx said.

Avery ran a hand over his face. "No. She's not."

Fists pounded the door on the other side. More nails scratched.

"Let's move," Byron said.

The little man led the way, and Avery tried not to think about Layanna as they filed down the tight staircase, found a connecting tunnel, another set of stairs, and kept going. The secret ways wound and forked, narrowed and widened. A whole system of hidden passageways lurked between the chambers of the fortress. Avery did not really believe that this was Maar Keep, it couldn't be, surely, the world didn't work that way, and the chamber he had found the passageway in surely couldn't be the old cell of Princess Syra, but either way this was a quite a complex system of secret halls. Some ancient lord had been quite paranoid, or perhaps he had simply liked to spy on the chambermaids.

In any event, in their bumbling, cursing fashion, the four eventually found an opening to the outside on the ground level. Cold air gusted in, bringing with it snow and the scent of pines. Avery wrapped his coat about himself and marched outside behind the others. Beyond was snow and mountain.

And a horde of ngvandi.

Layanna stood in their center. She was not encased in her amoeba-form anymore but looked normal, healthy, and strangely sad. The ngvandi grouped around her worshipfully. Hildra, bound and gagged, struggled against her captors some yards away.

Layanna stepped forward, toward the four, who now huddled by the opening, wary and tense. "I'm sorry, but the ngvandi have known of the secret passages for years," she said in Octunggen. "They're small and cramped and impractical for their use. Please, tell the others to drop their weapons."

Avery translated, but Janx and Muirblaag made no move to disarm.

"Tell them not to worry," Layanna said. "I've informed the ngvandi that I'm a god, and I've instructed them not to harm you."

"Tell 'em to release Hildra," Janx said.

Layanna spoke to the ngvandi in their own language, and in moments Hildra, freed of the ropes that had tied her wrists, hurried toward Janx and the others, cursing and rubbing her flesh where the ropes had dug in. Janx, surprising Avery, kissed her on the forehead, then passed her a knife. Muirblaag patted her on the back.

"You were right to run," Layanna told Avery. "They would've killed you. But no more. They're going to take me to their leaders, the Mnuthra—and hopefully to my friends in the Black Sect. My former Sect-mates and I agreed to meet at the place where the Mnuthra dwell if we ever got separated."

"What about *us*?" Avery said.

The sadness in her face deepened. "I'm safe now, Doctor. You don't need to go any further if you don't want to."

"Excuse me?"

"The ngvandi will take me to the Mnuthra and my friends, if any still live. The Mnuthra will tell me the location of an altar and together my friends and I will be able to make our way there and transmit the plans for the Device. The Mnuthra are the presence I came here to find. The ngvandi will help me, but I fear they'll be hostile to you, and the powers I go to meet ... they will be even more dangerous."

"And you think I'd send you to them *alone*?"

She stepped forward still more and squeezed his hands. "It must be your choice. I've gotten two of your company killed already, and I would not want to be responsible for more."

Avery thought of risking Janx and the others further when he didn't have to. Even if he chose to continue on, he could release them from their vows. *And then I could protect her against the* ngvandi *with what—my wits?*

"I'm going with you," he told Layanna. "To the bitter end." He did not have to add that he wouldn't be going alone.

"Very well. But do not say I didn't warn you."

Chapter 13

"Wow," Hildra said.

The view was impressive, Avery agreed. The ngvandi had marched them through a narrow pass and out the other side, and now jagged peaks piled higher and higher on the horizon, an infinite series of snow-capped walls and fangs that marched all the way to Ungraessot, clouds like a layer of sea foam drifting between them. The sight stole Avery's breath.

Directly before them yawned a mist-filled gorge.

"We're almost there," Layanna said, raising her voice from the front.

"Thank the gods," Byron said.

The ngvandi had led them on a march for days, rarely stopping, over one mountain, along a shoulder to another, then another. Avery's feet had bled, and his soles had grown thick and hard. Constantly he'd kept on the lookout for rays, especially the one that had been sweeping in their direction the day of the attack, but if any were present, trees and bulwarks of stone kept them from view.

Wind blew up from the gorge, carrying with it chips of ice and snow. The ngvandi led the party toward it, and Avery saw that a rope-and-wood bridge spanned the space between this mountain and the next, a span that seemed enormous, maybe a mile across. Through the mist Avery couldn't tell what waited on the other side. The bridge simply disappeared into a white wall.

"Don't tell me we have to cross *that*," whined Byron.

They did. The ngvandi and their guests filed across, only a few permitted on the bridge at a time. When Layanna crossed, no others went with her, such was their deference, and the group had to wait for what seemed like half an hour or more before horns sounded from the other side, signaling that Layanna had arrived safely. Then, with shouts and threatening gestures the ngvandi encouraged Avery and the others over the abyss, all at once. The bridge creaked and swayed beneath Avery's feet, and he wanted to mash his eyes shut but didn't dare. The drop below sucked at him, pulled him, almost hungrily.

As he approached the other side, the mist thinned, and he saw a great mountain face dotted with ruins. All three moons shone down, bathing the scene in ghostly splendor. The great fortress of some long-dead lord reared above the cluster of buildings, its towers limned in moon-lit snow, purple light flooding from its tall, stained-glass windows, many broken. Keeps and smaller dwellings thrust out from the cliffs beneath it, as well as slopes and flat areas covered in buildings. It was a sizeable town, perhaps a city. Likely it had been taken and re-taken by both sides more than once during the Severance. When Avery saw the dark cave-like openings in the mountainside, he understood. *Mines.* The mountain must be riddled with mines, and as such would be quite valuable.

The ngvandi herded him and the others over the bridge and into the city. Cobbled streets wound and forked, snaking up the mountain and down, a city built on tiers. The buildings leaned and crumbled. It was clear the ngvandi had made attempts to brace and repair them, as Avery saw hastily-applied patches of mortar and stones of various colors set in scars along building façades and sides, but the place was still a ruin. Despite the night's comparative brightness, Avery stumbled often on the uneven roads, and he made himself go slowly, or as slowly as the ngvandi would let him.

The corpses of men hung from parapets and walls, some mutilated and rotting, some mere bones, and Avery was glad for the curtain of night. Crows and batkin pecked at them and wheeled away. Grisly monoliths stood in the city squares, towers of obsidian with shadowy heaps at their bases; indiscernible at this distance, but from the shape and smell Avery could tell they were composed of corpses and body parts, surely human. Sacrifices? The ngvandi bowed to the monoliths and moved on.

Ngvandi clans huddled behind icy, moss-covered walls, nesting in hay and mud. Some stripped flesh from bone; the bones looked human. Others sang eerie songs in high towers.

"What is this damned place?" Janx asked Muirblaag.

"I've never been here," Muirblaag said, "but I've heard about it. If this is the place I think it is, I've sometimes heard it called the Mnuthra-con, the city of the gods."

Bare-backed men and women were whipped and beaten as they applied repairs to buildings, cleaned gutters, or were driven in and out of the dark mines, which seemed to be in use. The slaves, probably captured Ghenisan and Octunggen soldiers, dragged blocks of black stone from the tunnels. Many looked infected. Avery noticed a fish-like ridge growing along the spine of one woman, a skull transforming into a dark, mottled carapace on a man. Others simply looked sickly and pale. *Intentionally infected*, Avery realized. It must be. *But why?* To infect the prisoners the ngvandi would have to force-feed them diseased seafood, and the sea was far enough away to make transporting food from it a burden. It made no sense. And the black stones—what were they used for?

Several ngvandi elders emerged from a large building and conferred with those who'd brought Layanna, and when she made the air shimmer around her (some demonstration of her power? Avery thought so) they fell to their knees in worship. When she bid them rise, they gladly led the way toward the fortress above.

"Runners have come before us and prepared the way," Layanna told Avery. "The ceremony is already begun."

"Ceremony?"

"We go before the Mnuthra."

After Avery translated, Muirblaag swore and appeared unnerved. Byron noticed and grew even more agitated. "What?" the little man said. "What is it?"

"We're going before the ngvandi's gods," Muirblaag said.

"You mean, like a statue or something?"

"No. I mean their *gods*."

The ngvandi led through various courtyards and up a winding cobbled road, toward the great fortress that hunched above the town. Purple light blazed from the stained-glass windows, and as Avery neared the building the chanting he'd heard grew louder. Layanna and the ngvandi leaders—priests, judging from the respect the others showed them, as well as their robes—led through the fortress's ornate entrance, and Avery followed, grateful to be out of the chill mountain winds. He saw a great fireplace, but unfortunately no one had lit it. Didn't they get cold? He was tempted to offer to do the honors himself. Numerous depictions of the Crowned Phoenix, the symbol of the Ysstral noble house at the time, looked out from the walls, but the images had been defaced and vandalized over the years; it was impossible to tell by whom, or if the Crowned Phoenix might be replacing some older Ghenisan symbol.

The strange chanting reverberated down the high stone halls, magnified and staggered with echoes, making the sounds even more monstrous and eerie.

Elder ngvandi, perhaps more priests, joined the group, and they pressed on, into the heart of the fortress. Avery was struck by how ragged even the priests looked. While they wore more clothes than the more savage creatures of the city—their subjects, he thought, or at least their flock—the clothes they did wear, long robes and cowls, showed many patches and stains, and then stains on top of *those* stains. Caked in layers of filth, almost saturated in it, the robes were ancient and falling apart, soiled to the point where they stank (perhaps they had never been cured properly), and made of some sort of leather or hide Avery wasn't familiar with.

Some sort of *hide* ...

... and they worked their slaves mercilessly, didn't they?—even pushing them on through the night. How many must die from their labors?

How many then became clothes?

It was an awful thought, but in that moment Avery knew it to be true. The taste of bile shot into the back of his throat. The chants grew louder and louder, coming from somewhere ahead, and he shivered, suddenly miserable and more frightened than he could ever remember being. The stinking fish-priests in their rotting human-hide robes, their grimy, unwashed scales glimmering only vaguely where they could be seen at all, showed the way.

"Just what sort of ceremony are we in for?" Avery asked Muirblaag (Layanna was up ahead), trying to keep the quaver out of his voice, but he could not help but think of the shadow-draped mounds at the monoliths' bases.

"I don't know, but ... the legends I was brought up with ... We worshipped the great gods of the sea when we inhabited the coast, and some of them were said to come with us into the mountains when we were driven out ... Their priests have strange powers, and we were terrified of them in the village I grew up in. But I never really believed ..."

Avery was shocked to see the big fellow almost trembling. Even Janx was looking at him in worry.

"They think she's a god," Muirblaag added. "To them, it's a meeting of gods."

Perhaps I should have accepted Layanna's offer, Avery thought suddenly. *This is a mistake. It's all a mistake. These things are brainwashed monsters who kill and enslave human beings, and what's worse—THEY MIGHT BE RIGHT. They worship some awful god or gods, but if Layanna believes in them they must be real—and we're going to meet them. This is insane.*

He swallowed the hysteria down, or tried to, but he was aware that his fingers had begun to shake, and his breath could not come fast enough.

The group passed out of the fortress proper and into the mountain, where it grew warmer but ranker, and the sound of chanting increased. The hall wound, forked, twisted and encountered numerous side-tunnels, giving Avery the impression of a honeycomb, or perhaps an ant nest, then finally widened to become a large cave, a natural feature of the mountain, and to Avery's surprise a creek or river bubbled down its center, disappearing out of sight in both directions. Ngvandi lined the river's banks, but they bowed to something forward, hidden.

Bowing to their gods.

The group followed the creek, which at last emptied into a vast chamber.

"This is it," Layanna said. "The chamber of the Mnuthra."

Before them stretched a huge grotto in what must be the very heart of the mountain. The lake—an actual, full-sized *lake*—in its center frothed and bubbled, and odd mists whirled above it, seeming to move of their own accord. Ngvandi bowed along its shores, chanting and swaying. As Avery drew near, he saw that the lake was deep, deeper than he would have thought, almost as if this mountain had been a volcano at some point whose caldera had somehow been flooded—except that the water stank undeniably of *salt*. This was water from the *sea*, gushing and boiling and charged with otherworldly energies. Avery, without even thinking about it, dry-swallowed a pollution pill, then passed them out to the others.

The ngvandi's chants rose up to the high, shadowy ceiling. Avery could just make out stalactites plunging down through the darkness above him—stalactites circled by bats that could only be seen due to their numbers, swaying and shifting currents of shadow—limned by the purplish light of the torches. The same otherworldly light glittered on the waters, but only the edges, as the lake was so broad darkness hid its center. With the mists, the currents of down-sweeping bats, and the frothing waters, the darkness seemed to move, smoky and ethereal.

Ngvandi bowed to the lake, raising their heads and arms, then lowering them, chanting all the while. Whatever they worshipped, it was in the water. Avery stared at the bubbling surface, fascinated and horrified. The hysteria rose in him again, worse than before, and he only just barely kept it in check. He sensed more than saw movement under the surface, far below, but, perhaps mercifully, he could not see what caused it. The lake was deep, perhaps infinitely so, if it truly did connect to lava tubes and fissures.

A ngvandi that must have been a high priest to judge by the relative cleanliness of his human-hide robe, which was somewhat less stained and filthy than the others, stood on a projection out over the water, a little peninsula, chanting and reading from a heavily-bound book. He stood over a man lying on a black, dripping block of stone. The prisoner was mutated, dying, and he appeared drugged, because he didn't resist as a second priest carved into him, slicing his flesh and organs.

"I don't believe this," said Hildra.

The voices of the ngvandi pitched higher, for some reason making Avery feel unsteady, as if he'd had a few too many drinks. The chants came faster, and his head swam. He started to list to the side a bit, unable to balance himself for a moment, before he made himself straighten.

The chants came even faster, and Avery wanted to cry out, wanted to scream and tear his hair. *This is more than wrong. Don't you feel it? I've walked into a dream, a nightmare. This is utterly—*

Something exploded from the water. The huge, dark, amorphous shape that emerged from the lake curled over the tip of the peninsula, almost leisurely, and when the man who would be sacrificed fell under its shadow his drugged state fell away, and he screamed.

The shape, which seemed to be the limb of some giant being in the water, slammed down with brutal force. Blood sprayed and bones cracked. Strangely, however, the sacrifice was not completely pulverized. His body *passed into* the limb, which was nearly opaque, but not quite, and Avery realized he could see into it. Though dark and smoky, it was gelatinous, and through its folds and ripples he saw the body of the prisoner—just a dim shape, but showing the unmistakable beginnings of acidic destruction. Flesh blistered away, and the slave, still alive, arched his back and screamed, though Avery heard no sound. The man thrashed as the juices ate away at him, and particles of his flesh swirled around him. *Just like Layanna*, Avery thought, remembering the ngvandi she'd fed on.

Then, just as suddenly as it had appeared, the great limb slipped back beneath the roiling waters and was gone, taking the remains of the slave with it. Waves lapped the shore.

"Gods below," Janx muttered.

Layanna did not look at him as she said, in Ghenisan, "Quite."

The ngvandi seemed to notice her. Led by their high priest, they wrapped up the ceremony and filed out of the great chamber, many bowing to her on their way. The high priest actually kissed her feet. She remained serene, upright, eyes on the water, and soon the members of her group were alone with the ones that had brought them, who must also be high-ranking priests, as well as a few junior ngvandi that might be guards, as they were all armed. Several held rifles and pistols, likely taken from prisoners over the years, and Avery wondered if they were to guard the members of Layanna's group, or *against* them.

With Layanna between them, two priests bearing tridents strode out onto the projection of rock and into the semicircle created by the half dozen altars at the projection's edge. All looked slick with blood. Avery's group had just come upon the last sacrifice, it seemed, not the only one. The ngvandi raised their tridents and shouted unfamiliar words to the beings in the water, and the roiling of the lake increased. The air shook, seeming to flex and snap and stretch, like a rubber band pulled apart by large hands, then twisted and wadded up, then pulled again in a different direction, then again, until the air buzzed with the strain and Avery felt a prickling on his skin, his hairs standing on end. He received the impression that all this was the byproduct of some communication he could not quite sense.

At last the ngvandi fell silent and bowed their heads, and the tension in the air faded, but did not go away.

Layanna seemed very alone out on the projection, very vulnerable, with priests to either side of her and gods-knew-what in the water before her. Summoning his courage, Avery stepped forward to join her, but the armed ngvandi blocked his way.

"I don't think so," said Janx.

He and Muirblaag moved beside Avery, and the guards, perhaps afraid to cause a scene during this most propitious moment, or perhaps thinking that friends of a goddess should be allowed to do what they would, stepped back.

Feeling adrenaline course through him, strangling the hysteria that once more reared its head, Avery walked onto the projection, and Janx and Muirblaag followed. With water on both sides, Avery felt more unnerved than ever, and he knew that any moment some amorphous limb could reach out and drag him under. As he approached the half-ring of altars, he saw littered bones and dripping blood. The stink of split intestines intensified. How many sacrifices did it take to commemorate a meeting of gods?

The filthy trident-bearing priests turned to Layanna and said something. She nodded, then spoke in Octunggen to the ones in the water. Avery wondered if she was only speaking so he could understand her. If so, he appreciated it. Likely she communicated on some other level to the beings themselves.

"Lords of the High Waters, I greet you," she called, inclining her head. The waters frothed, and the air shook and snapped and bulged. "I've heard rumor of your existence here for long enough. Dark times have come to the world, and I'd hoped your time of isolation might come to an end. That is why I've sought you out."

The waters roiled, bubbled, and the air trembled violently. A piercing whine filled Avery's skull. He gasped and fell to his knees, pain overcoming him. Janx, Hildra, Muirblaag and Byron collapsed as well, shoving their hands over their ears.

The ngvandi bowed and drew back to the neck of the peninsula, as did Layanna. *Making room for something*, Avery realized. Hastily, he picked himself up and followed suit.

The water erupted.

Some dark Thing emerged. Gelatinous and huge, a mountain, it oozed out of the waters with a great stench of ammonia and sulfur and seaweed. Avery had to crane his neck to take it all in, and some part of his brain shut off. Another part, one that still thought rationally, recognized it as something distantly akin to Layanna's amoeba form—only this one stretched ten times larger and higher, and was hideous to look upon. Massive ungainly limbs flailed all around, slowly, undulating, unconstrained by gravity, as if the being were underwater still. Avery gazed up at its black bulk and shuddered. His skin prickled, his scrotum contracted, and his mouth went dry. The thing rolled over the altar on which the slave had been sacrificed, then beyond. The air blurred around it, and strange lights could be seen glimmering through its folds and jellies, but they were no lights of this world, and they did not illuminate it.

Layanna gazed up at the great being and bowed. "Thank you for meeting me," she said. "I've come to ask for your help. Octung hunts me. Our own kind hunts me. I need allies. During an attack by the Elders, my friends and I were scattered and separated. I seek news of them. I'd hoped, if any were in the region, that I might find them here. Please, my friend, tell me ... have you word?"

The air rippled. The great abomination quivered, then subsided.

Pain showed in Layanna's face. "No ..." She sighed, blinked tears away, and seemed to forcibly gain control of herself. "*All* of them, are you sure?" A pause. "Very well. I ... had feared as much." A long moment passed. When she had herself together, she said, "This complicates things. I need to reach a functioning altar. Your own altars are probably not plugged into the nexus, but we could activate them, unless you fear reprisal. If so, you could direct me to another. Please, help me. You've been cut off for ages. Isolated. Made pariahs. Surely you've no loyalty to the Elders. I beg you ... join me. Join my attempt to end this war."

Avery stared. She wanted to join forces with that *thing*? With the god-creature whose followers enslaved, killed and *wore* human beings?

The Mnuthra stayed silent for a long moment. The water boiled below, hinting at the movement of other similar entities.

When it moved, it moved almost too fast for Avery to see.

One moment the Mnuthra loomed amidst the blood-spattered altars, staring down at its visitors with unseen eyes. Then, in one sudden surge of movement, it shot forward. Dim, dripping limbs smashed down at Layanna, clearly meaning to crush her.

Before the limbs could reach her, she *shifted*. Her amoeba form grew from within her, superimposed over her, then blossomed outward, pink and white and fringed with flagella. Compared to the great, ugly bulk of the Mnuthra, she was beautiful.

She grew to a size Avery had not seen before, but she was still tiny against the vast squirming mass of the Mnuthra. The air shook and thundered as the limbs and pseudopods of the titans collided with each other. The ground quaked. A piercing shriek cleaved Avery's mind. He cried out and fell to the ground again, clawing at his ears.

Even the ngvandi priests seemed pained and awestruck. They dropped to their knees and crept aside, to the edges of the promontory, giving the gods room.

Purplish limbs strove against murky black ones. Dark tentacles tore and ripped at soft pink-white flesh. Phantasmagoric blood filled the air, floating and majestic and flaming, purple and pink and red and black and yellow.

Layanna was strong. The Mnuthra, however, was of great size and power and age. It had surely gorged itself on sacrifices for hundreds of years. *That* was why the ngvandi deliberately mutated their slaves, Avery realized. They turned people into food for their gods. They only wore the ones that didn't make it that far.

The Mnuthra's huge bulk glommed forward, toward Layanna's main mass.

"Don't you touch her!"

This came, surprisingly, from Muirblaag. In some strange fit of chivalry, or perhaps in rebellion against the gods he had fled as a youth, he rushed forward. The ngvandi priests tried to stop him, but they were unprepared and he barreled them aside. Only when he neared the Mnuthra did the being seem to notice him, and then it was only to fling out a pseudopod and dash him to the ground.

Janx leapt toward him, but the two priests had picked themselves up. They blocked his path, stabbing their tridents at him. He cursed and jumped back. One sprang at him, and he dodged aside, clubbed it to the ground with a fist. The other leapt, its trident raking his ribs.

Avery, still overcome by the psychic cry of the Mnuthra, forced himself to his feet, meaning to help Janx if he could.

He saw that Byron and Hildra were fighting the guards on the mainland, slicing at them with knife and hook. Four had guns, though, and Hildra was using one of their brethren as a shield. Byron made a leap for one and wrestled the gun away. A shot rang out, and he stiffened. Just before he collapsed, he threw the gun to Hildra.

Avery turned his attention back to the Mnuthra. On the other side of Janx and the priests, the being began to surround Layanna, to engulf her. Avery felt a twist of fear as its dark mass enveloped her, its murky substance blocking her from sight. He could only see her dimly, here and there, through huge squirming limbs and bulwarks.

... see *her* ...

... her human body ...

A sudden thought chased the fear from him. Riding a wave of strength, he staggered over to one of the priests, the one that lay on the ground, felled by Janx's blow. The ngvandi glanced up at him distractedly, even as it shook its head and tried to climb to its feet.

Avery kicked it in the face. The ngvandi screamed and pitched backward, into the bubbling waters. Before it disappeared, Avery grabbed the trident and wrenched it from its hands.

While Janx and the surviving priest circled each other, Avery slipped around them, toward Layanna and the Mnuthra. He knew Janx could take care of himself, and he had something to do that couldn't wait.

His breath coming short and fast, unable to believe he was really doing this, he stepped forward, toward the titanic battle. The great mass of the Mnuthra loomed over him. It had all but eclipsed Layanna now. However, as Avery had imagined, it had left itself vulnerable in the doing. For, like Layanna, it had a human component.

It was a man, Avery saw—naked and wasting, a forgotten relic of itself. Likely it had existed for countless years in its other form. It hadn't completely forgotten its human self, though. Even as it attacked Layanna, it had shifted its otherworldly bulk toward her, leaving its human part toward its rear, as far away from her striving tentacles and pseudopods as it could get. As Avery rounded its rear bulk, falling under the shadow of its glistening, rippling self, engulfed in its briny, ammonia-like reek, having to move around its immensity lest he slip into the waters—*What am I DOING?*—he saw that the human inside the Mnuthra was very close to the wall of otherworldly flesh that composed the being's rear.

The man floated off the ground, head bowed, eyes closed, drifting.

"Got you," Avery said. He raised the trident.

The man opened one eye. It fell on Avery.

A bulge in the being's side stretched out toward him—

Avery plunged his trident deep into the Mnuthra, pushing it through the strange flesh and stabbing the man through the ribcage. With all his strength, Avery shoved— deep, deeper, feeling the crack and scrape of bone, then feeling the bone give—

The man's face twisted in pain, and the bulge in the Mnuthra's side faded.

The old man grabbed the shaft of the trident. Avery tried to push it deeper into him but the man was too strong. By then the acids had eaten away at the weapon enough to dissolve the portion of it inside the sac wall, and Avery staggered back and threw away the handle. Its truncated end smoked.

The entire substance of the Mnuthra boiled and shook. The air vibrated. The Mnuthra shrieked, both physically and psychically. The cry lanced Avery's skull, driving him back. Hands pressed to his ears, he stumbled, hit one of the altars and nearly went over the other side. Blood and other bodily matter that adorned the altar pasted his shirt to the small of his back. *Still warm.*

The Mnuthra quivered and raged. Its flesh boiled. Droplets of it ripped free and drifted through the air, oily and dark, disappearing into nothingness. Some flamed. The whole massive bulk of the thing churned, and as it boiled away it grew smaller and smaller.

At last Layanna emerged from its tar-like substance. Still encased in her amoeba-form, she dragged herself loose. Her sac was ripped and torn to shreds, eaten by other-dimensional acids, reduced to a thin shell of protection around her. As she squirmed free and the last bulks of her enemy continued to dissolve, she released her other-self and fell gasping, panting, to the floor.

Meanwhile, Hildra, enraged and standing over the body of Bryon, who was clearly dead, a bullet hole through his upper left chest, fired into the ngvandi that remained—

several were already down—using the gun Byron had sacrificed his life for. One ngvandi pitched to the floor. Blood exploded out of another's back. The rest of the ngvandi, disoriented and lost under the psychic backlash of the Mnuthra, fled from the chamber.

Avery swayed to his feet and made his way to Layanna, edging around the shrunken Mnuthra. He knew they didn't have long. Hopefully the trident thrust would kill the being, but then again the Mnuthra might recover at any moment and launch itself at them. And there were still, apparently, other Mnuthra in the lake to contend with.

Covered in sweat and blood, Layanna retched onto the floor. Avery helped her up.

"Thanks," she wheezed. "You ... saved my life."

He half-supported her to the cavern wall, where she was able to prop herself up, but barely. She looked pale and shaky, and he wanted to stay with her, but he crouched over Byron and examined him just to be sure.

"I'm sorry," Avery told Hildra. "He's gone."

She swore viciously, and to Avery's surprise tears glistened in her eyes. Gasping made Avery glance over his shoulder.

Muirblaag was picking himself up off the floor. Janx staggered away from the priest he'd been fighting—the priest was down—his fists bloody, his chest heaving, and bent to help Muirblaag to his feet. The fish-man sucked in great breaths, clearly in pain.

"You okay?" Janx asked.

"Yeah," Muirblaag said, his voice ragged. "Better than ever."

They saw Byron and stopped.

"Damn," said Muirblaag.

Janx, leaving Muirblaag to catch his breath, bent over the fallen man, sighed heavily, and closed Byron's eyes.

"You went out like a champ," Janx said, his voice as gentle as Avery had ever heard it.

Behind Muirblaag, the Mnuthra stirred.

"We have to—" Avery started

He had time to see the exhausted, pained look on Muirblaag's face, had time to note the burns on his abdomen where the Mnuthra's limb had struck him, before—with horrible suddenness—a tendril wrapped around the fish-man's waist and wrenched him off the ground. Muirblaag lifted his head and screamed so loudly Avery feared his lungs would burst.

Janx bolted forward, but huge, gelatinous limbs erupted from the water—the other Mnuthra—and strove toward him. Avery grabbed him and reeled him back. Great, glistening limbs, bulwarks of phantasmagorical flesh, oozed from the lake.

"Mu!" Janx shouted, his face locked in horror. Avery could still hear Muirblaag screaming, though he was now out of sight.

The first Mnuthra swelled—Avery's strike did not seem to have killed it, after all—and rushed toward them. The ground shook beneath it.

They had no choice but to run.

With Avery and Janx supporting Layanna, and Hildra firing backward, the band fled the grotto. They passed up the main hall and turned a bend. The floor rippled beneath them. A great psychic scream struck Avery, and he wanted to collapse, to vomit. It was all he could do to stay on his feet. The walls around him vibrated, and dust drifted down from the ceiling. The ground shook violently.

The Mnuthra were coming. All of them.

The shaking continued behind the group, louder and louder, and the floor bucked wildly. The reek of ammonia and sulfur filled Avery's nostrils, stung his eyes, and made his head woozy. The Mnuthra were closing in.

From behind issued a great, inhuman roar, almost like the song of a whale, but even more awful and terrifying.

The band passed into the larger tunnels. Ngvandi crouched beside the bubbling streams and rivers. Their eyes rolled and foam beaded their lips. Some bashed their heads against the walls. Others flailed helplessly. It was clear the psychic backlash of the Mnuthra's rage had undone them. A few made halfhearted efforts to clutch at Avery's legs, but he kicked them away. He stole a staff from one, Hildra another gun.

The roar grew louder behind them. The caverns shook. A stalactite broke off and crushed a praying ngvandi.

The group hurried up the mining tunnels. Dust and rock rained down from the ceiling. The rotten timbers that buttressed the tunnel looked ready to split. Janx eyed them and grunted. As he passed a particular one, he stopped and said, "Wait."

He hefted up his trident and began bashing the supports. A great anger had seized him. Hildra and Avery, seeing what he meant to do, pitched in, digging at the rock, smashing staff and gun butt against the timbers and stones. At last, with a sinister groan, the buttress cracked.

"Run!" Janx said.

As the tunnels collapsed behind them, they ran as hard as they could. The halls caved in with a great whoosh of sound and air. A storm of dust chased them down the halls and enfolded them, and Avery wheezed for breath.

He could almost feel the rage of the Mnuthra as the beings reached the blockage. A great, primeval roar shook in his head and staggered him. He knew it would not take them long to break through. How far could they go? They were creatures of the water. Avery imagined them swimming along chutes and tubes deep underground, threading their way into vast black lakes and rivers, forging their way to the sea, to chambers in other mountains. But land? He did not think they would go too far. He did not think they could maintain their otherworldly selves for long outside of the water. It had cost Layanna a great deal to do so. And they had allowed their human selves to grow too weak and frail to support them on their own.

Nevertheless, he ran. With all his strength, he ran. His lungs burned, and sweat stuck his shirt to his back, his pants to his knees. His legs cramped and flamed.

The group passed out of the caves and into the fortress, where the ngvandi rolled about on the floor much as they had in the grottoes, clutching dumbly at the air. They offered no resistance.

Outside, night smothered the land. A light snow drifted over the city, and screams and shouts echoed up from the shadowed streets. The ngvandi that occupied the city had not been as deeply affected by the psychic screams of the Mnuthra as those in the fortress, perhaps because of distance, perhaps because they were not as high in the echelons of the faith and thus not as connected to their gods. Even as Avery and the others threaded their way through buildings and roads, they saw the ngvandi prowl the streets in groups, dragging screaming slaves out from hovels and tearing into them indiscriminately with bare hands and claws. Slaves ran panting down the streets, terrified, some bleeding. Avery's group ducked into an alley after seeing one slave gutted in a town square.

"Why're the ngvandi attacking their own damned slaves?" Hildra said.

"I don't know," Avery panted. "But I think—they don't know what's going on—just some attack—from non-ngvandi—"

Layanna said in Octunggen, "They'll know soon."

"Over the bridge," Avery said. "It's the—only way."

"We can cut it behind us," Janx agreed.

"Wait!" said Hildra, when the others had started to move. They turned to her. "Where can we go once we get over? Bridge or no, they'll be after us. There are other towns."

"She's right," Layanna said.

Suddenly Avery remembered the Octunggen slaves. "I have an idea."

Slaves ran down the streets, fleeing from the enraged ngvandi. It wasn't long before Avery picked out one of the Octunggen and with Janx's help wrestled the man into an alley. The fellow fought against them, but Janx was too strong. Avery saw that the Octunggen already showed signs of infection, black growths along one cheekbone, and one eye bulging out, fish-like, its pupil transformed.

"Release me!" the man cried in his native tongue. "They're on my heels!"

Avery thought of what the Octunggen had done to Mari and Ani, and he felt no pity. "Tell me where your dirigibles are, and we'll let you go," he said.

The man stared, shocked.

"Tell me!" Avery demanded. He knew the Octunggen raiding parties, like those that had attacked Benical and killed his wife and daughter, used dirigibles to hop from mountain to mountain. They were the ideal vehicle for such purposes—small and light and silent.

The howls of the ngvandi drew closer.

The Octunggen sweated, and nodded. "Fine. They're no use to me anymore. It's not as if I'm in any condition to escape. We came here to attack them, but—"

"Just tell us," Avery said.

The man scowled. "My mate Sunctanis was just sacrificed to the fish-gods yesterday. If you really did kill one, mister, you have my blessing to take as many ships as you want. Here's how you'll find them ..."

Chapter 14

Wind rustled through Avery's hair as he slumped against the dirigible gunwale, exhausted. Below ngvandi hordes howled and raged. Some flung spears. Hildra laughed at them and made obscene gestures, while Janx piloted. It had been a tense day since their escape from the Mnuthra-con, and the mutants had hounded their steps every inch of the way, having been summoned from other cities or towns. The dirigibles had been right where the Octunggen had said they would be, under tarps on the top of a certain summit. Avery and the others had taken one just as a ngvandi patrol had come across them.

The dirigible rose higher—higher. Avery clutched the gunwale and gulped down deep breaths; he felt as though he'd been running forever. A stitch flared in his side. The mountain peak grew small below, as well as the howling mob. The creaking and swaying of the dirigible was strangely reassuring, and Avery almost smiled as he caught his breath and lifted his head to behold the panorama of the mountains, whose snow-capped summits stretched in every direction for as far as the eye could see.

Layanna's ragged gasps drew him. She'd said little since the events in the cavern. For most of the journey, she'd been unconscious, pale and shaky, and it was clear she was terribly wounded, if not on this plane, then in another. Several times she'd vomited, and her veins showed, too visible, beneath her skin. Whatever had happened to her in that other dimension, if that was the proper way to think about it, was affecting her here. Avery wasn't sure if she would survive.

Janx continued to pilot, his face a mask of misery. Avery wanted to reassure him but knew it would be at best useless and at worst resented. Janx and Muirblaag had been close friends, almost brothers, and the pain of losing him clearly cut deep. Janx needed to mourn. He would grieve about losing Byron, too, of course, and the others who had died in Hissig, but their deaths would not have affected him like Muirblaag's. Avery would just have to give him time, and space.

Hildra paced back and forth, smoking and staring at Layanna. The Octunggen had left stores of food, whiskey and cigarettes, as well as first-aid supplies. They had probably also brought their strange weapons with them, but these they must have unloaded to use against the ngvandi. Now that the thrill of escape had worn off, Hildra looked like she was working herself into a fit. Hildebrand chattered in shared agitation as he climbed the rigging.

"Alright," Hildra snapped at Layanna. "I've had enough. First Jay and Hold, now Mu and By. I don't want any more of us to die for this bullshit. Saving the world! Who do you think you are, lady?"

It's my fault, not Layanna's, Avery wanted to say. *Layanna gave me the option to go back, to prevent what happened, but I chose to go on, and to bring you all with me. If you want to beat up on someone, Hildra, beat up on me.* He thought about saying this, then saw the set of Hildra's face and said nothing.

"I am sorry for your losses," Layanna said, apparently willing to take the blame. Silently, Avery thanked her.

"Lot of good that does us," Hildra said. "You want us to—"

Janx interrupted her with an upraised hand. To Layanna, he said, "Just tell me this: was it worth it? Did Mu and By ... did they die for nothing?" There was a raw edge to his voice, a strain, and something crazy gleamed in his eyes. It was a fierce anger, Avery realized, a bottled force that was ready to explode—and would, Avery sensed, if Janx got the wrong answer.

For a moment, the world took a breath and waited to see which way the fates would blow, and then, to Avery's intense relief, Layanna said, "No." He translated as she added, "I got what I needed. When I was ... engaged with the Mnuthra—and he was a powerful one, one I had heard of long before, known as Uthua—I was able to touch his thoughts. I learned what I came to find: the situation regarding the nearest functioning altar."

"And?" asked Avery.

A dark look crossed her face. "They've all been compromised. The Collossum watches them. Monitors them. There is no safe way to transmit the plans to my comrades in the Black Sect."

"Shit," said Hildra, looking crestfallen. "So it *was* all in vain?"

"Not at all. Now the path forward is very clear, or at least its destination. And it is just as clear whom my traveling companions must be."

Avery felt hollow. "Lusterqal," he said dully. "You mean Lusterqal. The capital of Octung."

"And you want us to take you there," Janx said.

"Through a warzone," Hildra added. "Into the heart of the Crimson Hell itself."

"I am sorry," Layanna said. "When I was engaged with Uthua, once I learned of where I must go ... where we must go, if you would come with me ... I tried to find out the best, the safest, route to getting there."

"Did you find anything?" Avery said.

"Nothing I understood. But I saw a waypoint. A place known as Cuithril. So, you see, it was worth it. Your friends' sacrifices *were* worth it."

Hildra swore.

Furrows wrinkled Janx's face. "But ... but that's not even a real place!"

"He's right," Hildra said. "Isn't Cuithril the afterlife of the Ungraessotti?"

"Yeah," said Janx. "A city in the Underworld. Where you go when you die, right through the Soul Door. If you worship the God-Emperor, anyway."

"It's a real place," Layanna assured them. "The Ungraessotti attach mythical connotations to it, but it's real enough—a great subterranean city in the northeast of Ungraessot, near Maqarl, the capital. It's only accessible through the system of caverns that runs beneath the country. Actually, they run beneath many, even stretching most of the way to Octung. I believe the Ungraessotti call them the Hallowed Halls, or the Tunnels of Ard."

"Ungraessot," Avery mused. It was one of Ghenisa's nearest neighbors, and it lay just over the Borghese to the east. He had always wanted to visit the country for its L'ohen history. Slowly, he nodded. "If we could travel underground most of the way to Octung, that would indeed be the safest way. It's why you must have found that location, Layanna. Uthua knows this area. He knows the quickest and the best route from here to the Great Temple."

"I believe so, yes."

"Then that's where we're going. To find access to the Hallowed Halls."

"You're insane," Hildra said. "We can't go *there*. Ungraessot's under invasion by Octung. It's liable to fall any day if it hasn't already."

"It's the safest way," Layanna said.

Hildra groaned. "Let me get this straight. You want us to find some mythical underground tunnels on the other side of a godsdamned *warzone*?"

"You took an oath," Avery reminded her.

"*Fuck* my oath. This is batshit!"

Janx rubbed her shoulder, but she shook him off and retreated into a corner, where she sulked and smoked in private. Janx nodded his head at Avery.

"I'm in," Janx said. The crazy gleam in his eyes had vanished, but the anger was still there, lurking just below the surface, ready to erupt—only now its target would not be Layanna but anyone that stood between him and the Hallowed Halls. "No way I'm letting Mu or any of them die for nothing. And don't worry about Hildy. She'll come round." He paused. "Mind, she's right. This thing we're doin' ... well, it's a suicide run, you realize that?"

"We'll find a way," Avery said.

Janx gave him a doubtful look. "I'm in, but if we're really gonna survive this ... you'd best start thinkin' of a plan." He moved off to comfort Hildra, and Avery gripped the wheel.

Layanna seemed pensive. When Avery asked what was wrong, she said in Octunggen, "There is one problem."

"What?"

"You cannot tell the others this. I don't want them to despair."

"Go on."

"It's Uthua. The Mnuthra."

"Could he ... have survived?"

"Uthua is quite old, and powerful. He'd let his human self wither, but yes, he survived. What's more, I sense that he's ... stronger now than before. How I don't know."

She gnawed at her bottom lip.

"There's more, isn't there?" Avery said.

"When our minds touched, there is a chance, however small, that Uthua was able to read my thoughts, as I was able to read his. It's possible he knows our destination."

"You're not telling me ..."

"Yes, Doctor. He could try to intercept us on our way to Lusterqal. And he knows our route will take us through the Hallowed Halls, if only we can access them. I wasn't able to defeat him last time, and I certainly won't be able to next time."

"If you can't stop him, and if being stabbed through the chest can't do it, what can?" When she didn't answer, he asked, "Will he alert the other Collossum?"

"Certainly. But he's much closer to us than they are and can reach us faster."

Avery felt a momentary flutter in his belly, but he was able to push the fear aside, at least for now. It would come back later, he knew. Oh yes, it would come back.

"Then the race is on," he said.

Avery piloted for a while. He was far from an expert dirigible pilot, but he slowly began to get the hang of it. Gears and levers jutted up on either side of the console, and pedals stuck out below. The rear propellers could move them faster or reverse to slow them down, even stop them. They could also be positioned to angle the ship up or down. And the balloon, the stiff, ovoid envelope, could be filled with hotter or cooler gases, or combination of gases, that would make them rise or fall. He experimented— unsuccessfully at first, to the curses of Janx and Hildra—but slowly improved. It was not surgery, but it was not child's play, either ... although, after a time, he couldn't help but feel a sort of thrill, despite everything. He was *flying*.

I wish you could see me now, Mari. I wish you could be here with me. You and Ani both.

All the while, Hildra shot dark glances at Layanna, and Avery could tell something was building in her again. Finally, Hildra stormed up to her and said, "If we're really gonna do this, blondie, really gonna go to—to *Cuithril*, of all places—I want you to do one thing for me. Just *one fucking thing*."

Layanna waited.

"I want you to be honest," Hildra said.

"I have not lied to you," Layanna said, and even Avery could tell that there was something evasive in her tone.

"But you haven't told us the truth, either, have you?" Hildra leaned forward, her face deadly serious. "If you want my help, that's my price."

"What *truth* do you require?"

Hildra's eyes glittered. "Just what are you, sunshine? And don't give me that line you used before. You're kin to that ... that *thing* that killed Mu. Just saying you're an extra-whatsit, that's not gonna cut it. I want to know *exactly*. What the fuck *is* a Collossum? Byron asked you, but you wouldn't tell him, and now he'll never know."

Layanna glanced to Avery as if for shelter, and he hid a twinge of discomfort. Even now, she didn't want to give up her secrets.

Keeping his voice gentle, he said, "It's time, Layanna. We need to know. Please. We've earned that much." When she hesitated, he made himself smile. She regarded him warily. "It will be all right," he said. "If it helps, I can guess some of it. You're ... when you said you weren't from *here*, you didn't mean Urslin, did you?"

Layanna appeared surprised. "No. I did not."

"What gives?" said Hildra, her gazing flicking from Layanna to Avery, as if they shared a secret.

To Hildra, Avery said, "Remember the salamander people that used to live near your hometown? The Suulm?"

"Yeah ..."

"It was said that they hailed from another world. You believed it."

She nodded, slowly. "Yeah. I guess." Her gaze moved back from Avery to Layanna. "You sayin' that's where she's from? *Up there?*"

"It was true with the Suulm," Avery reminded her.

Layanna, with a visible effort, made herself look Hildra in the eye. It was clear that, finally, she was ready to come forward with the truth, and in spite of everything, Avery couldn't resist a surge of anticipation. Now, at last, he might get the answers he'd been seeking since he helped pull her out of the water long months ago. She began to speak in low, clear tones, and he translated as best he could. The others listened raptly.

"The universe is stranger than you think, Hildra," Layanna began. "The fabric of space strains, twists, rips. There are folds, hidden abysses, vast labyrinths and honeycombs where voids emerge from voids, where dimensions shift and merge and tear. Where I come from, reality is different. Our race, the R'loth, was vast and strong, advanced beyond your ability to understand. I'm sorry if that sounds patronizing, but ..." She sighed. "We delved too deeply into ... well, you might think of it as arcane lore. We plumbed the secrets of ancient mysteries. You cannot imagine our creations, our cities, our worlds, our gods. A vast empire, with cities and inhabitants spanning a myriad of worlds, dimensions, our machines and our very natures capable of twisting planes and spheres, of existing across them. But we delved too far, explored too recklessly.

"We investigated the depths of distant abysses, seeking answers to mysteries hinted at in our scriptures. We dredged them, the great gulfs in the fabric of the voids, and brought forth things ... beings. Some thought them gods. We thought they could be our allies. Gods or not, they worshipped the same over-deities as we. But they turned on us. A great war consumed Luz'hai, the Forever Empire, and we developed more and more devastating weapons to combat the Muug, the H'ss'rul, the beings we had summoned. At last we sundered that which we sought to save, and the Muug, greater and more awful beings than we, at home amidst the splintered and twisted fabric that had become of Luz'hai, inherited the ruins.

"We, the few survivors, fled from our quarter, our universe, our planes. We fled through the twisting labyrinths of the voids, and at last passed into your quarter. We found your world, a world with a great sea, which we required, and something else, which we desired. The latter proved impossible, but the former, viable. So we came here. We inhabited your depths, built anew our cities. Much of our civilization is irrevocably lost, of course, but it is a beginning. We've had to transform your world into one that could sustain us. Our natures are different from yours. Thus ... we changed the sea."

Hildra gasped, and Avery blinked rapidly.

"Gods damn," Janx said.

"It ... it was *you*," Hildra said, her eyes riveted on Layanna. "*You* made the Atomic Sea!"

"We changed it into what it is, yes," Layanna said. "And with it the world. Now the planet can begin to sustain us, be a reflection, however pale, of the worlds we left behind."

"Amazing," said Avery.

"But we needed more," Layanna continued. "To rebuild our civilization, we needed to conquer the stars, to spread throughout the galaxy, then beyond. But to do this swiftly we needed to strip this world, to denude its resources. We knew we would leave behind only a burning, naked rock, and that your kind would resist us—unless they were under our power. Thus, in time we selected a nation, a mighty nation, Octung. It would be our herald on the surface world. It would subdue the surface people, bring about order so that we could rule, so that we could have our slaves carve up the planet for our needs. We gave the Octunggen leadership, technology—religion.

"In order to do all this, we needed to deal with humans directly. And in order for them to treat with us, we had to make ourselves into forms that they would find appealing, desirable, worthy of respect, not flee from in terror. Thus a small segment of our race was ... changed. Changed so that our material representation in this plane appeared human. This ..." she pinched the skin of her forearm "... this is not how most of my kind look. I am human, at least on this plane. I have been fundamentally altered. I still require the sea, or things from the sea, but as long as I do not bring my other facets through very often I can exist on dry land.

"Those of us that were altered became the ambassadors of our kind. The Octunggen hailed us as gods, as we had intended. We became the Collossum and dwelt in a great temple in Lusterqal. There we were revered and worshipped for many years. Then, finally, after ages of planning, we engineered the war. Octung would subdue the world for us."

"But something changed," Hildra said. "You didn't go through with it. Well, a few of you didn't."

"Some of us, a small segment, began to see the war as evil. Millions were dying because of our labors, and though that might not have mattered to us in the beginning, that was the price we paid for being human—we'd come to appreciate humanity. This awakening came at a very inconvenient time, of course—the war was already launched, and Octung was winning handily—but it was too late; we'd already sided with humanity. So we decided to stop it. The war.

"We broke away from the Collossum. They called us blasphemers, heretics, denounced us as the Black Sect while they were the True. Debate and intrigue gripped the temple, and at last most of us were forced from it. We worked against them when we could, sabotaging their efforts, whittling away at their priesthood, but it was not enough. The human powers in Octung began to stir. Fearful, knowing we must act quickly, a group of us ventured to the sea, returned to our greatest city in the depths. Xicor'onga. There we petitioned our Elders to end the war. In secret, however, knowing they would refuse, we used the petition as a ruse while some of us scoured the city for certain information. Information to build a machine, a wonderful, powerful machine. I was one of those so tasked, and I have that knowledge in my head.

"The Elders refused our request, as we knew they would. But then they did something that we had *not* planned. They found out about our investigations ... and moved to destroy us. Having no choice, we fled through the sea, and they gave chase. They crushed our ship and killed most of us. Some were scattered. I was wounded, and I drifted, dying, in the depths. A whale devoured me, began to digest me, and I was too weak to heal or even wake. I would've died. And yet, and here is the strange part—the war that I tried so hard to stop saved my life. Whalers after the hot lard of the whale, a tool for war, killed the whale, and you know the rest."

She lapsed into silence, and the only sound to be heard was wind hissing over the dirigible.

Janx rubbed his stubbled head. "That's quite a story, darlin'." He looked at Avery. "What do you say, Doc?"

Avery frowned. "I ... think she's telling the truth, incredible as it is. However, the question I'm wondering is this—if you *are* telling the truth, Layanna, what was the Mnuthra? Why did you think it would help?"

Layanna bowed her head. "Yes, the Mnuthra are not as I thought."

"What are they?" asked Hildra.

"Fellow Collossum," Layanna said. "Or they were. The Mnuthra went rogue centuries ago and disappeared from Lusterqal. Or at least we *thought* they'd gone rogue. When I was engaged with Uthua, as I said, I touched its mind. I discovered it and the others weren't acting independently. The Elders had *dispatched* them. And there are others, throughout the mountains, the caves, the forests of the world. They gather the mutants, the ngvandi and their like. It's the mission the Elders have sent them on. It's why they departed Lusterqal in secret so long ago."

"What for?" asked Janx.

Layanna leaned her head back against the dirigible wall. She looked spent. "Apparently my kind intend to nurture the mutants, make them our people, our instruments. They're superior to humans in that they are creatures of the sea. As such they can be used as sacrifices."

"Sorry I missed out on that," Hildra said.

"This is what I discovered when I touched Uthua's mind. If certain programs are not far enough along, my people intend to betray the Octunggen once the war is done. They will use the Octunggen to weaken, divide and depopulate humanity, and then they will allow the technologies gifted to Octung to stop functioning. The Octunggen, now rulers of the surface world, will be defenseless when the ngvandi rise up—when the ngvandi destroy and devour and rape and burn them. That is what the Mnuthra are doing, organizing the ngvandi to serve the Elders and one day rise up against the Octunggen—to destroy humanity once and for all."

Janx, Hildra and Avery shot glances at each other.

"What happened to the other Black Secters that survived the destruction of your ship?" Avery said. "The ones we came to the Borghese to find?"

"My friends and I'd planned to regroup where the Mnuthra lived if we were ever separated. We thought they, as rogues who had abandoned our kind, could be our allies, aid us against the Collossum. But it was a trap. The Mnuthra were not independent as we'd thought; they were still part of the Collossum—high members, even, on an important assignment. As I touched Uthua's mind, I felt what he had done. Uthua had ... he had killed them all. All of my friends. *Eaten* them."

"I'm sorry," Avery said, meaning it.

"Yeah," said Hildra.

Layanna took in a deep breath and let it out. "Now I'm the only one left who knows how to build the Device."

"So how do we do it?" Janx said. "What's our next step, darlin'?"

"The only resources available that can assemble the Device are in the hands of the Collossum—and the Black Sect. The members that did not accompany me to the city in the sea are in hiding in Lusterqal, striking at the Collossum when they can. With my knowledge and their resources, we can build the Device. We can end the war. If we don't reach Lusterqal, if we fail, all of humankind will be washed away, and my people will go on to rule the stars."

Hildra visibly shuddered. "And you don't want that, honey? For your people to win? I don't get you, sister."

"We brought the Cataclysm on ourselves," Layanna said. "We may do it again. I think ... I think perhaps the only thing that can save us is *not* to overreach ourselves this time. To stay small. And I believe your people are worthy— worthy of life, at least, and freedom. You have potential, and I would not take it from you."

"This is some messed-up shit," Hildra said.

"There's more," Layanna said.

"What?"

When Layanna spoke, her voice held a grimness Avery had not heard before. "The Octunggen cannot be allowed to capture me alive."

Avery shifted uncomfortably. "Why not?"

"Two reasons. Both important. The rest of the Black Sect, those being hunted and in hiding in Lusterqal—only I know how to find them. If the Octunggen capture me, not only will I be unable to build the Device, but I also might be forced to betray the others. Then all hope of resistance against the Elders will die."

"What's the other reason?"

Her voice hardened. "The research I did that enabled me to design the Device, it *could* be used for ... other purposes. I've designed the Device to null the abilities of the Octunggen's extradimensional technologies. But the plans *could* be used to ... amplify them."

"You mean ...?"

"Yes. Octung would be able to win the war that much sooner. If they catch me alive, *nothing* can stop them."

"Hell," said Janx.

To Avery, she said, "You'll do what must be done?"

He knew what she was asking. *How can I kill her, though? She's our only hope.*

He nodded.

"Thank you," she said.

"Shit," Janx said suddenly. Pointing, he said, "We've got company."

Avery looked, and instantly wished he hadn't.

Chapter 15

Three rays swept toward them over mountain jags to the south. They must have been among those that had pursued Avery and the others. Now, huge, indomitable, the creatures glided over the snowy peaks toward the dirigible. Red light fell across great, broad delta-shaped backs, each a mile wide, across the innumerable troops that clustered there, glinting on armor and helmets, rows and rows, and on the weapons, some of them unconventional, bulky and strange. Bathed in crimson light, the three great rays aimed directly at the small dirigible and increased speed.

"Shit," said Hildra.

Avery didn't waste time agreeing. Though he suddenly began sweating, and his fingers trembled, he gripped the wheel tightly. He pressed a button. Mashed a pedal. The dirigible lurched to port, then shuddered upward. Janx was flung against the gunwale. Hildra slammed into Avery, nearly knocking him over.

"What the fuck do you think you're doing?" she said, pushing herself off.

"Sorry." Sweat stung his eyes. He tried again. This time he angled the ship down, toward the nearest mountain peak.

"You're gonna crash us," Janx warned.

"Maybe. But I'm not going to let us get caught."

The rays were miles behind them, ten or fifteen at least, but they were moving faster than the ship, and sooner or later they would overtake it.

Avery shoved the dirigible down. Breath caught in his chest. The mountain peak loomed ahead, its tip glittering white with snow. The glare stung his eyes.

"I hope you know what you're doing," said Hildra, hanging onto the ropes that wound along the gunwale. Hildebrand clung nearby, shrieking.

Avery swung the dirigible toward the mountain tip. Clustered further down from its pinnacle, the ruins of some castle huddled, its broken battlements encrusted with snow, its sides stained with time. The mountain approached, blotting out all else. Carefully Avery edged the dirigible to the side, pumping pedals and jerking gears. The craft swung clumsily and edged around the great bulk. Jagged towers of the castle heaped below, scratching at the gondola as it passed. Avery was so close he could see the piles of bones in the centers of rooms whose ceilings had collapsed and the stir of giant batkin roosting along the edges, hanging upside down and still dripping blood.

Avery risked a glance over his shoulder. The rays sped forward. Metal winked from the lead ray's back—some weapon, surely pirated from Octung.

An eerie green light fell over the gondola. Immediately, as if the light contained heat, Avery felt his skin blister. Pain suffused him. He cried out and nearly sank to the deck. Only his grip on the wheel kept him up.

Beside him, Janx and Hildra screamed. They crumpled, still clutching at the gunwale. Blisters bubbled under Janx's skin. One popped on his arm, spurting blood. Avery felt similar blisters sprouting on his own flesh. Hildra clawed at her arms and screamed in confusion. Hildebrand hopped around like a mad thing, but he showed no signs of the blisters.

The dirigible listed toward the mountain, ramparts of stone rearing ahead, ready to smash the ship to splinters. With a grunt, Avery jerked the wheel, swinging the dirigible away. The ramparts receded.

The green glare intensified.

Burning pain filled Avery, nearly crippling him. Only dimly did he notice the green light had no effect on the wood and rope and canvas of the dirigible. It targeted human flesh alone.

Gasping, he flew the ship back toward the mountain, this time in a controlled veer. The dirigible, with painstaking slowness, slipped around the back of the mountain, finally blocking out sight of the rays and their weapons. As soon as it had arrived, the green light faded, and with it the pain.

Avery panted and slumped against the wheel. The blisters on his arms and hands began to grow less livid but did not disappear. He felt like steam should be rising from him.

Janx stared at his arms, horrified and amazed. Sweat drenched the whaler's face. "Fuckers aren't playin' nice, now are they?"

Avery noticed Layanna's skin was slightly flushed, but that was it.

"They're using stolen Octunggen weapons against us," he said. "We can't allow them to catch us in the open again." He aimed the dirigible at the next closest peak, maybe ten miles away.

"I wonder if Sheridan's on one of those rays," Hildra said.

"I'm sure she is," Avery said. "As an admiral now, she's probably leading them. Remember what we overheard at Claver's. She controls Haggarty. That means she controls the Navy, and those rays are the Navy's prize pets."

He neared the next mountain peak and began a pass around it. Craning his neck, he saw that the rays were just beginning to appear around the bulk of the first peak. Acting quickly, he pulled the levers that controlled the propellers. Accidently, he reduced their speed the first time, then corrected himself and whipped them to full throttle.

To Layanna, he said, "Is there any way you can help us?"

"I can hold off the psychics, I think, but that's all. I need food to heal. Food from the sea."

"The sea's the other way, sweetcheeks," said Hildra.

"I think she's aware of that." Avery banked the dirigible around an outcropping of rock. He had to stay low, hugging the mountain, keeping its walls between him and the rays. Between him and Sheridan. Would the woman never leave him alone?

He passed to the backside of the mountain, put it between the dirigible and the rays, and aimed for the next one. The sun had vanished to the west, but a hint of crimson still gleamed on the horizon. Before long he would not be able to see the mountains well enough to risk getting close to them. He hoped that meant the rays would have difficulty seeing the dirigible, but he didn't count on it.

The sun's light finally vanished, and the wind gusted colder and more frigid. For the next few hours, Avery guided the dirigible to and around the dim bulks of the Borghese, aiming toward Ungraessot, land of the God-Emperor, which lay just over the mountains to the east. By starlight and moonlight, Avery could not see the peaks around him clearly and kept his distance, but not too distant. He had always to keep the mountains between the dirigible and the rays. After several hours, he grew exhausted and Janx relieved him. He awoke to find that Hildra had relieved Janx, and Janx slept fitfully under a blanket to the rear of the ship, with Layanna in the bow looking forlorn.

"How long was I out?" Avery said, stretching. The horizon seemed lighter. Had he slept the whole night through?

Hildra shrugged. She gripped the wheel with hook and hand, eyes on the next peak. The sky behind them gave no sign of the rays. "Dunno. A long time, I guess. Janx piloted forever. An' I've been at it a good while." She yawned widely and blinked her eyes with exhaustion. Hildebrand lay curled on her shoulder, his little chest rising in and out.

"I'll spell you," Avery said.

"Not yet. I wanna see the sun before I sleep."

He helped himself to the dried foodstuffs of the Octunggen soldiers. Munching on a stale oat bar, he wondered at a race that could possess such fantastic technologies yet eat the same indifferent dried food the Ghenisan soldiers did, or close to it. He supposed Layanna's people hadn't felt obliged to improve on military cuisine. To wash it down, he helped himself generously to water stored in a canteen. It was stale.

At last his attention returned to Layanna. Slowly, oddly reluctant, he made his way forward, toward the jutting prow where she lay. A pale face peeked out from the black blanket she'd wrapped herself in, and blond hair spilled over it. She cracked her eyes as he crouched over her. They were very blue.

"I just wanted to check on you," he said.

She said nothing as he took her pulse and temperature. She was pale and feverish. Her veins showed like blue eels beneath her skin. Her breaths came fast and harsh, irregular.

"Am I going to make it?" Her voice was forced and light.

"I don't know anything about your kind. Your body on this plane seems human, and that part, at least, is well."

She nodded, as if this explanation helped, though it could not possibly, and stared up at the dark sky. With a sigh, he sat down beside her and put his back to the gunwale. They shared a windy, companionable silence.

In a low voice, she said, "I'm truly sorry I brought all this on you and your friends."

"It's not your fault."

That seemed to catch her off-guard. "But it is."

"No. You only did what you thought right. Remember, I'm the one that made the decision to come with you. I still don't understand something, though."

She turned to look at him. "What, Doctor? What don't you understand?"

He gave a strained smile. "Francis. You can call me Francis."

She paused. "Francis." She tried out the word. "*Fran*-cis. What don't you understand, Francis?"

"You, for a start."

She let out a long breath, looked away, up into the fading night. "What do you want to know? I've lived in Lusterqal for hundreds of years, orchestrating things, the integration of our mythology into Octung's culture, the development of technologies that they could use. Weapons. We studied the Octunggen, learned from them. Learned about being human."

"You did nothing but work, in all those years?"

"Oh, in secret I would abscond from the Temple. I would go out into the streets, pretending to be one of the people, and I would have adventures, as I thought of them. Over time I even made contacts. Friends." A sad smile touched her face. "I had lovers. They grew old, but I stayed young. In the end, it would pain them to see me, but they could not let me go." In a sad, soft voice she added, "I know all the graveyards in Lusterqal."

He opened his mouth to speak, but no words came.

She patted his hand. "It's all right. There's nothing to say. I learned to love humanity. I wasn't the only one." Clouds like palls of smoke drifted across the sky, obscuring the moons, the stars, then revealing them in bursts of glory. Wind stirred her hair. Her eyes misted. Suddenly she turned to him. "Why are *you* here ... Francis?"

He hadn't expected the question, and a hitch developed in his throat.

"I fight for this." He reached into an inner pocket of his jacket and pulled out the item which he kept over his heart.

The picture of Mari and Ani was bent and smudged, corners ripped away, holes torn through it. But Mari and Ani were still visible, still recognizable, their smiles still white and clean. They stared out at him from the picture, the one he had taken so long ago, the one that had looked out at him from his cabin bulkhead on the *Maul*, giving him comfort and strength.

Gently, Layanna reached over and took the photograph. She stared at it for a long, quiet moment.

"Your family?"

He nodded. His eyes stung, and it surprised him to feel tears trying to force themselves out. He didn't let them come.

"Mari and Ani were killed in an Octunggen attack," he said. "Some sort of plague caused by a light."

Her brow creased, as if something troubled her. "*Uls Arctulis*. The Deathlight." She handed the picture back. "Yes. I am ... familiar ... with the weapon. I am sorry." She seemed to gather her strength and said, "My family, too, have died."

"How?"

"Once I revealed myself to be a traitor, my whole line would have been ... purged. Exterminated."

"That's awful."

"Like yourself, there can be no going back for me. I can never return to my people, my home. All is denied me. The lights of Xai'nala, the shimmering gardens of Sere ... Oh, my race is wondrous, Francis. Brutal and terrible, yes, but wondrous. Beautiful. Our cities straddle dimensions, times, and so do we. Passing down a city street, we may pass through a hundred dimensions at once, a thousand, each one different second by second. Dimensions are born and die like flowers, blooming and fading all around us, through us. Our old civilization spanned the galaxy, Francis, and the galaxies or their analogues of innumerable other planes. The Luz'hai. The Forever Empire." She hesitated. "Somewhere out there it still exists—warped, twisted, malevolent."

She wrapped her arms across her chest and rocked back and forth. She almost looked ready to cry.

Avery had never seen her so open, so vulnerable. Surprising himself, he lifted an arm and, in seeming slow motion, wrapped it around her shoulders.

She appeared equally stunned. She stiffened.

Then, miraculously, hideously, she softened. She leaned against him. She was very warm, and, though he found the contact awkward, part of him relished it. Together they sat like that, huddled under the freezing mountain winds, while the dirigible flew on, and after a time, despite himself, he felt his eyes start to close, his mind start to drift ...

Sounds of wonder woke him.

Janx and Hildra had gathered on the port gunwale, staring out into the night. Avery rose, blinking the sleep from his eyes.

"Holy fuck," Hildra said.

Before them, giant squids drifted through the sky, rows and rows of them. Air bladders inflated, the great beings floated over the mountains, heading north. The sky was still dark, *and the squids glowed.* In a thousand fantastic colors that shifted moment by moment, the squids' phosphorescent bodies shown brilliantly against the pale stars and black sky. In shades of purple and pink and violent crimson, in electric green and throbbing fuchsia, in aquamarine and ruby and cyan, the squids glowed, and their hues bathed the peaks below, a shifting kaleidoscope of color.

There were hundreds of squids, each a hundred feet long or more, and they bobbed effortlessly through the air, like phantoms, like gods. Colors would strobe down tentacles like flashing lights, then blink off, then the torpedo-like head of one massive giant would burn with vermillion, and then a dozen more would follow it. Whole forests of color blinked, flushed, flickered out, then burst into new glory.

"It's beautiful," Layanna said.

"They migrate north every winter," Avery said. "No one knows why. In Hissig we have a great celebration on their return."

"Squid Day," said Janx, then grunted. Casting a sideways glance at Layanna, he said, "And *you* did this, darlin'?"

"We changed the oceans, yes."

Wind hissed and fluttered, and somewhere came the eerie hoot of a giant squid, then another. Hildra laughed, almost girlish.

For a long time the four just stood there, staring out at the great, glowing squids as they bobbed through the skies. Thousands of tentacles swished lazily, and streamers of light glowed and flashed, coursing along surreal bodies. Avery and Layanna stood very close to each other. At last the column of squids vanished over the peaks to the north and disappeared from sight. Avery felt as if the air had gone from his lungs. He and the others still stared at the place where the squids had gone, as if hoping for one last look, until the sun rose over the mountains to the east.

It was then that Hildra swore.

"Octunggen!" she shouted. "Octunggen to the west!"

Chapter 16

Avery scrambled to the opposite gunwale, the others with him, and strained his gaze toward the west, where dim black peaks were just visible. The newly-risen sun threw crimson across the horizon, and by its glow he saw the faint glimmer of dirigibles—several, perhaps as many as ten or more. A complete raiding party. The red light coated their rounded backs, hinting at the gondolas below. It was too far away, but he knew if he were closer he would recognize the Lightning Crest on their envelopes.

"They'll think we're one of them," Avery said. "We have the same emblem and colors."

"Until they look through a spyglass," Janx said.

"That ain't the worst of it," Hildra called.

She indicated the trail behind them. The bloody light of dawn fell across the shapes of rays sweeping in from the east. The great dark wedges cut the sky, trailing their long barbed tails. They had drawn very close to the dirigible over the course of the night and now were no more than six miles behind. They had ascended the skies, presumably to have a better view of their quarry—and to make it more difficult for the dirigible to put mountains between them. Even then the dirigible was nearing another snow-dusted peak, but Avery wasn't sure it would be enough.

And there were not just three rays. Miles behind and to either side of the main trio came another three. Sheridan must have roused the whole fleet against them. *Between the iron and the fire*, Avery thought.

The lead rays seemed to have noticed the dirigible at the same time the occupants of the dirigible noticed them.

A green light flashed from the central ray.

Shit. It was all Avery had time to think before a green glow fell over them. Avery felt his flesh grow warm, and then a lance of agony shot through him. Blisters bubbled under his flesh.

Hildra shoved gears angrily. The dirigible jerked to the side.

The green light faded. Avery's boils subsided, and he inhaled a deep, shuddering breath ... but then the light fell on him again. He screamed. Janx bellowed from the stern.

Hildra was not to be deterred. Even as a boil popped on her throat, spurting the wheel with pus and blood, she twisted it and grappled with the levers. The dirigible jerked to the side, throwing Avery against the forward gunwale. Layanna pitched up against him.

Avery started to turn back and snap at Hildra, but then he saw what she was doing. She was aiming the dirigible at the Octunggen raiding party.

"You're mad!" he said. "They'll ..."

"They'll what?" Hildra said. "*Kill us worse than the rays?*"

She drove the dirigible at the Octunggen, but indirectly, threading between mountains to screen them from the rays and their green glare. As she flew around the broad midsection of one mountain, a press of hoary, hairy goats stared at them blankly. The animals were so close Avery could smell them. Relieved to be out of the green light, he sagged against the gunwale and absently brushed the blood of a burst boil on the back of his hand against the netting.

Layanna was breathing heavily, and her skin was reddened, but she showed no signs of the boils that had deviled Avery and the others.

"You're immune," he said.

"We didn't give the Octunggen weapons that could be used against us—at least, not easily. Obviously they've found ways." She touched her side where Sheridan's bullet had found her. "Although I believe *that* gun was designed by my kind ... to kill me."

The craft lurched again, and Hildra said, "Hang on."

She had rounded the last mountain in her path and flew the dirigible right at the Octunggen raiding party, which appeared to have just left one mountain behind and were drifting toward another.

"This'll be interesting," said Janx, the cords of his neck bunching.

The Octunggen noticed them, and their ships fanned out, creating a half circle in the sky that pointed toward the approaching dirigible. Surely they would also notice the Lightning Crest on its balloon, Avery thought. *But what if they look through a spyglass?*

Suddenly lights glittered among the Octunggen ships, and the half-circle realigned, pointing toward something else. Avery glanced back. The rays had reentered his line-of-sight. *Here it comes.* He braced himself, expecting another blast of the green light. Instead, the three rays, who had formed their own triangle formation, now pointed straight at the Octunggen. *They* had to be dealt with first.

The lone dirigible shot toward the raiding party, and Avery's group drew so close he could at last make out individual Octunggen soldiers in their crisp black uniforms, moving along the gondolas amongst bulky machines, some cranking gears, others stabbing buttons. Unwieldy lenses swung toward the approaching rays. Strange, bulbous barrels bristled.

The Octunggen gave a cry of welcome as the dirigible entered their circle. Then, almost immediately, they stopped what they were doing and stared at the occupants of the vessel. Avery had the distinct pleasure of seeing looks of shock, anger and utter bafflement cross their faces. Then the little dirigible passed through their ranks and out the other side. Its occupants flew on, away from the Octunggen, toward the west.

Avery half-expected the Octunggen to break up and fly after them, not simply to pursue them but to escape the advancing rays.

"They've got to run," he said, staring at them and the massive wedges of the rays approaching from the east. "They have to." The rays could simply hold more weapons than the dirigibles could, and half the weapons would be those stolen or pirated from Octung. Not to mention the psychics ...

"They won't run." There was a note of pride in Layanna's voice. "Not while there's hope of victory. They are Octunggen."

With shocking suddenness, battle commenced between the in-sweeping rays and the half-circle of dirigibles. The air between the parties blurred. Lights flashed. A weird roar of some machine thundering reached Avery's ears and staggered him backward against the gunwale. One of the dirigibles erupted in blue fire. Breaking into pieces, it plummeted from the sky, soldiers and odd weapons spilling out of it like corn kernels from a split sack. The balloon exploded. Other dirigibles flamed, too, scattering the mountains below with fiery debris, some of it human. A few of the dirigibles simply drifted off, their crews disoriented by a psychic blast.

The Octunggen were not to be outdone. A great ripple of air blurred into existence before the lead dirigible, then the others. The blurring intensified and shimmered, as if the dirigibles were combining their energies. At last the blur rolled outward, gaining speed, straight toward the ray that took up the right rear point of the triangle.

When the blur reached the ray, it was as though a huge cleaver sliced the creature cleanly down the middle. The vast being, the thing that stretched a mile or more and trailed its tail out for miles behind it, divided in two. Dark ichor and unidentifiable fluids spurted from the wound even as the two halves fell from the sky, spilling its host of soldiers and equipment as it did. Avery saw them from afar, hundreds of men like tiny dots plummeting to their deaths. The massive sections of the ray fell with them, and Avery felt unsteady at the sight. The gargantuan halves of the animal struck the mountaintop, and ichor and snow exploded upward. Rockslides thundered down the slopes, and Avery saw the ruins of an old keep obliterated by the avalanche.

Sheridan, he thought. *I wonder if Sheridan was aboard that ray.*

For some perplexing reason, he hoped not.

The dirigibles and rays continued their battle, and Avery could only stare in awe. One dirigible seemed to flicker, blink out of existence, then flicker back on, again and again, faster and faster, before it finally winked out entirely. Another dirigible seemed to pass half into another dimension, then return utterly leeched of color, black and white, and so brittle that it disintegrated like charred wood, her men with her, in the next gust of wind. The Octunggen struck back, and it was a fantastic, awful battle. Thunderous cracks blasted, and the air shivered horribly.

Janx laughed and clapped Hildra on the back. "You did it!" he said. "Pitted the bull against the bear. Beautiful!"

"And don't you forget it," she said. She lit an Octunggen cigarette, and Janx helped her cup the flame against the wind. Smoking, she guided the ship behind a mountain, and the battle vanished from view. Avery hadn't realized he'd been holding his breath until he gasped in a great lungful. He leaned back against the gunwale. His fingers trembled, and sweat beaded his brow.

For hours the dirigible drifted over the mountains, heading west. The battle between the Octunggen and the rays was far behind them, if it still continued, which Avery doubted. The Octunggen force had been only a light raiding and scouting party, after all. The rays would be plowing ahead, over the ruins of the smoking dirigibles, their masters hunting Layanna and the other fugitives with the same indomitable will they had displayed so far. At least the Octunggen had bought Avery and the others some time, and he would shed no tears for a party the likes of which had killed Mari and Ani.

He began to see scattered settlements clustered among the mountains, simple stone buildings with goats roaming the fields. To his horror, vultures wheeled over the towns and bodies rotted in the grassy roads. He and the others clustered at the bow, staring down at the carnage in shock.

"Octunggen," Hildra said.

Janx ground his teeth. "Couldn't even let the bloody *mountain* folk alone. What bastards."

Layanna's voice was hard. "The mountain people supply meat and produce to the cities. Without food, the cities cannot fight. It's an old tactic."

Once Avery had translated, Janx grunted. "Well, me stickin' my boot up Octunggen ass is an old tactic, and I mean to do it soon as boots and asses allow."

Avery noticed that the dirigible was drifting slightly off course, and he returned to the wheel. He'd replaced Hildra, who curled up at the stern, an Octunggen blanket thrown over her. A white, stylized bolt of lightning marked it.

Avery steered west, taking them over more and more villages. They were entering Ungraessot, dark scion of L'oh, currently under massive invasion by Octung. He passed over scenes of destruction that churned his stomach, bodies heaped in village courtyards and burned, nailed up on posts, severed heads mounted on fences and poles. Crows picked at the carcasses. In the more recent massacres, batkin feasted on corpses' half-clotted blood. It was needless destruction, designed to instill fear in Octung's enemies. Nevertheless, it was obvious that the Octunggen had reveled in the slaughter.

Soon villages became larger, and Avery saw cities sprawling across mountainsides. Some cities spanned more than one mountaintop, as the valleys were too narrow and rocky to support a population; great, sturdy bridges arched over the misty gaps. Many were broken or heaped with the dead, and mounds of burned corpses piled higher than the squat churches in the city squares. Factories had been shelled, mansions sacked, great cathedrals collapsed.

Eventually Avery saw active campaigns, dirigible packs sweeping over mountains, smoking cities on the horizon. Great airplanes split the skies, bombers, rumbling as loud as thunder. A great formation of them returned from some bombing raid. Small fighters grouped around them, protecting them. Many displayed the scars of battle, black scorch marks and pocks like bullet holes. Smoke fumed from several engines.

"The Ungraessotti are fighting back," Avery noted.

"Not for long," Layanna said. "They're nearly beaten. You were asleep last night, but I saw fires on the mountainsides and valleys. Campfires. The Ungraessotti are fleeing the cities. I don't imagine Ungraessot can hold out for long—a couple of months, maybe, if that."

He began to see huge zeppelins gliding through the air in the distance. Sunlight glared off massive silver balloons emblazoned with the sigil of the Lightning Crown. They moved through the sky like monstrous torpedoes, straight and sure, but slow, dignified. Avery presumed Octunggen commanders rode the zeppelins, overseeing the war from just behind the battle lines. Others would be leading from the front, in constant communication with these superiors.

Below streamed supply columns, transports, great smoking tanks. They crunched through the ruins of burnt towns, trundled over corpse-heaped bridges, smashing aside burnt-out vehicles and rolling over the dead. Some of the larger, more palatial buildings had been preserved and taken over by the Octunggen. Avery imagined sweaty barracks, soldiers toasting their victory over bottles of stolen champagne, women from towns that had been plundered being raped. Ungraessot was an ancient country, and it had a complex and layered culture stretching since back before L'oh had conquered it and transformed it more than three thousand years ago. The Ungraessotti were renowned architects, stonemasons, engineers and artisans. There would be much loot to steal, and much invaluable treasure inadvertently destroyed. History was being wiped away.

Toward noon Avery noted blinking lights on the steering console. He swore.

Janx looked up. He and Hildra had been playing cards amidships. The cards were Octunggen and featured unfamiliar characters, but, not to be put off, the two had invented a game that loosely resembled Jury-and-Tackle.

"What's up?" Janx said.

Avery tapped the blinking lights. "I think we're running low on fuel, or maybe gas for the balloon." He shrugged. "It's unlabeled."

"Crap."

Avery scanned the gauges. "I think we still have time."

"For what?" said Hildra.

That was a good question. Avery knew they couldn't simply stop and ask the Octunggen to refuel them.

"Perhaps we can steal some fuel," he said.

Janx rubbed his stubbled scalp, big fingers digging into scarred flesh, molding it, wrinkling it up. "We don't even know what fuel to steal. Or gas. Shit, the fuel depots'll be guarded anyways."

"What do you suggest?"

"Maybe steal another ship."

Hildra rolled her eyes. "You think those'll be *less* guarded?"

Layanna, who had been dozing fitfully, glanced up from her pile of blankets. "Keep going," she said. "Maybe we can outfly the warzone, set down behind Ungraessotti lines and go from there."

Avery translated, then added, "It sounds like our most reasonable course of action."

Janx and Hildra reluctantly concurred, and they flew on. Clusters of dirigibles, giant zeppelins and in-sweeping bombers grew tighter and tighter. Airships of all kinds surrounded the commandeered dirigible, some passing very close. Avery feared at any moment the alarm would go up and the ships would converge on them. The group was passing right through the front lines of the enemy. Their colors had saved them so far, but surely, eventually, someone would stop them.

At last, toward dusk, just as Avery was about to ask Janx to relieve him at the wheel, the concentration of aircraft grew very dense indeed. The ships buzzed and zoomed and drifted to the northwest, and Avery stared at the confusion of activity, trying to make it out. There was something there, something large, something at the heart of all that commotion, something ...

He gasped.

That drew the others' attention, and he pointed. Their eyes roved toward the activity, and, as one, they cursed and made sounds of surprise.

All except for Layanna.

"So," she said, in musing tones. "They've done it."

"Done *what?*" said Janx.

Avery's eyes roved over the clustered zeppelins, roped together, bound together, hundreds of them. They supported great platforms, runways, airstrips, mooring docks for vessels of all kinds. But there was more. Buildings, huge buildings, rose from the highest, most central platforms. The structures loomed—large, monolithic—thick spires and heavy domes. A *city*, he realized, with dawning dismay. The Octunggen had built a city in the sky. It was unwieldy and bulky. It looked like something that should not possibly exist, that could not sustain itself, support itself, and yet ...

"Done what?" Janx repeated. "What the fuck *is* that?"

Layanna rose from her blankets and leaned against the gunwale. "The Over-City. For years, ever since the war started, the generals have complained of the scattered fronts, the need to centralize command, a mobile command that could be on one front a certain day, a different front the next. They built small ones at first, floating stations for the officers. But the high authorities demanded to be involved, to be active in the day-to-day running of the campaigns. So ... they expanded. They've been working on it for a long time. They must have deployed it while I was away."

"I've never seen anything like it," Hildra said, her voice low and filled with wonder.

Crimson light bathed the city in the sky, outlining its buildings and courtyards in red. The buildings were square-hewn and gave the impression of great solidity. Typical Octunggen architecture. But around the city buzzed constant air traffic, fighters racing off runways in large convoys, zeppelins docking and much more. Some of the zeppelins carried large objects dangling below their gondolas. Avery saw cranes, building materials and supplies being unloaded and moved. The city was still being built, even as it flew.

"Amazing," he said. Unconsciously he had aimed the dirigible toward the Over-City—to get a better look or out of simple gravity he wasn't sure, but he recovered and veered away. The last thing he wanted to do was get too close.

Layanna frowned and stepped away from the bow, toward him, though not by intent. It was almost as if she were stepping away from the city, drawing back from it. *Recoiling.* Curious, he glanced at her, and what he saw surprised him. There was *fear* in her face. Not wonderment, not consternation. Fear.

She reached him and gripped the steering column absently, as if fumbling to keep herself from falling.

"What?" Avery demanded. "What is it?" But inside he already knew.

Layanna turned and stared at him, her face full of horror. *"He can feel me too."*

Instantly, the ships in the immediate vicinity of the Over-City stirred. It was as if a great confusion gripped them. No. A great urgency. They scrambled about in the air, reversing positions, changing formations.

Then, as one, they aimed for Avery's dirigible.

Janx began cursing in the manner only a veteran sailor could.

Chapter 17

Fear filled Avery as the great mass of the Over-City moved toward him. Inexorably, the huge aerial construct, a flying city in truth, drew toward the small dirigible in which he and the members of his ragged band hunkered. Worse, the Over-City's vast fleets shot out from it, directly toward them.

"Fuck a duck," said Hildra.

Avery no longer cared about preserving the dirigible's fuel reserves. He punched buttons and stomped pedals wildly, throttling the rear propellers up to full speed. The dirigible shot forward. He aimed it toward a city smoking on a nearby mountain, the same city he had seen the bombers returning from. He didn't know what he hoped to find there, but if nothing else there was resistance to Octung behind its walls.

He heard a roar of planes behind him. He wrenched his head around to see a wedge of fighters zip past the dirigible, their aluminum skins glinting in the sunlight. The grind of their engines rattled his ears, and the wind from their passing knocked the dirigible off-course and whipped what was left of his hair. He tasted their greasy smoke on his tongue and spat it out.

"Damn," he said, jerking the wheel back, returning the ship to its trajectory.

"They don't want to destroy us," Layanna said. "Not yet."

"They want you alive."

"Remember what you promised."

He looked behind them. *Dear gods*. Ships, hundreds of them, maybe thousands, raced toward him. Some bore huge guns, some small. Any of them could take the dirigible out. But, if Layanna was right, he needn't fear the fighters which now flooded the air around him, shouting through loudspeakers for him to draw the vessel to a stop and prepare for boarding. No, what he feared more were the dirigibles, filled with their strange Octunggen weapons, which could, among other things, paralyze him with pain and force him to stop flying.

A hundred dirigibles and a score of giant, glittering zeppelins—likely capable of carrying even larger, more powerful weapons—struck out from the floating city, their red-lit prows aimed directly at him. Even as he watched, he saw soldiers wrestling with bulky machines in the gondolas. Strange lights began to blink on the vague bulks.

"Shit shit shit," said Hildra, while Janx stared daggers at the Octunggen in their airships.

Ahead, the smoking city drew closer. Individual buildings began to materialize, huge and shattered, burst like rotten fruit by Octunggen bombs. Streets snarled along winding, angled mountain slopes. Portions of the city sat higher while the rest hunched lower along the mountainside. There seemed to be several different wide areas where slopes had been hewn out and made level, and upon these stood the primary buildings of the city, old and proud. Others had been hewn out of the mountain itself. Avery saw a familiar landmark, and his heart sank.

The Amber Ziggurat of Azzara, a wonder from another age that sat on the top tier of the city, was composed of huge amber blocks, each one with a prehistoric insect trapped inside; some alchemy in the blocks' construction gave the insects the illusion of life, and supposedly when one walked through the amber halls it seemed as if the bugs buzzed all around. The Ziggurat lay smoking and sundered, and shapes that must be corpses littered its now-pocked tiers. Once, long ago, it had been the capitol building of

Ungraessot before L'ohen conquerors had relocated the capital to Maqarl, where they had been able to send out armies through the Tunnels of Ard.

Avery expelled hot gasses from the dirigible's balloon and lowered it from the sky. He pointed the ship straight at the Ziggurat.

Behind him bullhorns called from fighter planes and dirigibles. They shouted in a myriad of languages, trying to make themselves understood, but they all said the same thing: "DRAW YOUR VESSEL TO A HALT NOW OR BE FIRED UPON. PREPARE TO BE BOARDED. REPEAT, DRAW YOUR VESSEL TO A HALT!"

Avery plowed on. Janx, Hildra and Layanna huddled around the steering column, around him, as if seeking protection from the group. The monkey Hildebrand clung tightly to Hildra's arm, his eyes huge and darting all around.

Avery guided the dirigible over the first walls and buildings of Azzara. Ahead he saw a stir of activity. Men swarmed around what he at first thought to be a factory but then recognized as a processing plant, designed to filter the air from Octunggen plagues and defend Azzara from otherworldly weapons. That gave Avery a flicker of hope.

Ungraessotti soldiers on the rooftops wheeled large anti-aircraft weapons around to face him.

As the first ones fired, Avery jerked the dirigible aside. Something exploded to his right. Shrapnel filled the air. He heard it punching into the gunwales, heard the sharp rasp of fabric tearing. Another shell exploded, then another. Black smoke swirled around him, acrid and sooty. He coughed it out of his lungs, blinked it from his eyes. Over the sound of explosions he heard the hiss of air.

The dirigible was sinking.

"We're hit!" Hildra said, needlessly. She and the others hunkered low against the gunwales, protecting themselves from shrapnel. Avery stood alone.

Buildings thrust up at him. He steered wildly, swung the dirigible around one building, passed down a street. Tanks and soldiers fired at him. A building to the side erupted in stone and glass. Something chipped his arm, his back. Grunting, he steered on. He guided the dirigible away from the soldiers, down a side street, swinging the wheel and shoving gears wildly. His stomach dropped at the sudden turn, and Janx cursed. The dirigible scraped along a building, the dirigible vibrating at the contact; Avery's stomach lurched. Glass shattered.

Avery swung the vessel back. More soldiers and tanks down this road. His muscles strained as he jerked the wheel again, aiming up another street.

The Ungraessotti down this road were no longer interested in him. He saw pointing fingers and was close enough to see ashen, tense faces. The Ungraessotti had noticed the dirigible's pursuers. With a look over his shoulder he saw the full fleet of dirigibles, zeppelins and fighters sweep in over Azzara.

Anti-aircraft guns boomed. Tanks fired. The air before the advancing ships filled with explosions and shrapnel. The Octunggen flew on, through the fire and smoke. Several of their craft erupted, scattering in pieces to the roads and buildings below. Heedless, the rest came on.

Avery turned to face the front. His dirigible sank faster—faster.

The road shot up at him, littered with debris and broken cars, bodies strewn between broken pieces of buildings.

"We're going to hit!" he said. "Brace yourself!"

Everyone grabbed hold of gunwales and ropes. Avery held onto the wheel with both hands, mashed gears, shoved the dirigible up so they would hit level.

The road pitched up—

The impact knocked him off his feet. For a moment, he was weightless. Then his back struck the floor. Air exploded from his lungs. He slid, his back rasping. He bit his tongue and tasted blood in his mouth. The screams of Hildra and the curses of Janx filled his ears. The dirigible had hit the street and gone sliding.

Wood scraped loudly on asphalt. The friction shook Avery even through the hull of the gondola. Rumbling and juddering filled his body. The friction slowed the dirigible, and at last it struck something that squealed with metal. The impact flung Avery toward the bow. He hit something and cried out.

They had stopped. His head spun, and he spat blood. He tried to get his bearings. He felt strong hands beneath his arms. Janx pulled him to his feet and patted him on the back.

"You did good, Doc, but we gotta get movin'."

Avery coughed and nodded.

The others picked themselves up and dusted themselves off. As they climbed from the wreckage of the dirigible, Avery saw that they had struck the ruin of a truck. Up the street massed lines of soldiers and military vehicles. Soldiers rushed toward the downed dirigible, guns drawn.

Avery stumbled into the street, stepping over the corpse of an old woman. Her teeth, coated in dust, shone in a ghastly smile.

Janx shoved him toward an alley.

"C'mon, hurry!"

Staggering and disoriented, the band pressed between the high, cracked walls of the buildings.

The Ungraessotti were better organized than Avery had bargained for, however. One group must have radioed another, for before Avery and the others had gone fifty feet a score of soldiers burst from a side-alley. Avery, still muddle-headed, could only blink and sway as soldiers surrounded him. He knew he and the others must present an odd sight: bedraggled, covered in fading boils, obviously not Octunggen soldiers.

The band pressed tight against each other, back to back. They eyed the soldiers that surrounded them warily.

The troops' leader stepped forward, a stalwart-looking fellow of medium height. Several days' worth of beard grew on his not-unhandsome face, and where it grew out over his scars it was white. He stared at the group and questions flickered behind his eyes.

"Come with us," he said.

"I'm Captain Hunried," he said as he led them through alleys and down blasted streets. In the distance, Avery could still hear explosions. Fighters whizzed overhead, their machine guns rattling. There came a concussive bang as an anti-aircraft gun was destroyed.

The Ungraessotti soldiers surrounded Avery and the rest, herding them, but they did not point their guns directly at any of them, and Avery wasn't sure if the group had been taken prisoner or not. As he went, his mind cleared. He smelled grease and gun smoke and the rot of days-old bodies. He waded through heaps of debris, through burned-out cars, some with corpses still sitting at the wheels. Whatever had happened here had happened fast.

He asked Capt. Hunried about it, and the captain said, "We were hit by a time-bomb. You've heard of them? Well, it suspended us. *In time.* We just froze stiff, while the rest of the world moved on. Just for a few seconds, but it was enough. When we came out of it, the Octs were swarming everywhere and half the city was bombed to hell. We just barely managed to drive them back. One of their spies had disabled a processor, leaving us vulnerable. We got it running again, though, and we've held out this long. We stockpiled hot lard and other substances before the Octs arrived, but they're running low. Luckily they've mainly been hitting us with their regular troops; their weird shit must've been tied up elsewhere. But now the damned *Over-City* has arrived." He spoke the name with dread.

Capt. Hunried led them out of the narrow streets into open areas, and they crossed a great courtyard. Finely-made statutes of Ungraessotti heroes posed defiantly, those that still stood. Several had been reduced to blackened stumps or lay shattered across the stone tiles. All around loomed the impressive edifices of Ungraessotti buildings. A few of the pre-L'ohen structures remained, proud and gray, but by far the majority of the buildings bore the more elegant craftsmanship of L'oh. Avery saw graceful arches, weightless flying buttresses, airy domes, all the more impressive for being fashioned of granite and marble in the Ungraessotti way. Many bore black scorch marks and great rents, and some had collapsed entirely.

The captain ushered them toward a wall of tanks and soldiers and anti-aircraft guns, then through it. Soldiers eyed Avery and the others strangely. Many grouped around artillery cannons and anti-aircraft guns, or filed behind hastily-made walls and readied for combat in case of Octunggen land attack. Others smoked cigarettes, cleaned guns, and listened tensely to radios. Rows of dead and wounded sat directly on the ground, with frantic-looking doctors and nurses crouched over the living, tending to them with what meager supplies they'd managed to save. Avery could not resist feeling the urge to roll up his sleeves and help them, but Hunried led them on, deeper into the Ungraessotti encampment.

Finally the captain drew them toward a still-standing but non-functioning fountain, a grisly piece of art depicting, Avery knew, the beheading of Emperor Nuanis, the so-called Half-Lord. Water would have gushed from the place

Nuanis's head would have sat; the head itself was held up by the hair, in the grip of a victorious Emperor Mortel, the Half-Lord's brother-in-law and the rival for his sister's affections; it was a strange old story. In the statue, Mortel held his sword in the hand not holding the head, and Avery noted that the sculptor had even managed to depict blood coating the weapon. The statue, of course, had been commissioned by Mortel to celebrate the event and even long after his death no one had dared remove it.

Before the fountain a group of commanders stood over weather-beaten fold-up tables and studied maps and files. Some barked orders to junior commanders. Hunried, apparently a leader of some standing, dismissed most of his men and instructed Avery and the others to come with him.

The captain sat down upon the rim of the fountain and went about the motions of building and lighting a cigarette, then stared up at them. A few of his men had remained, and they stood as unobtrusively as possible, baring their guns but not aiming them in any particular direction. Avery was only partially reassured.

Hunried studied Avery and the rest, smoking silently. Finally he said, in Ungraessotti, which Avery spoke a smattering of, "You're not Octunggen, that much is obvious. And you had the whole fucking Octunggen fleet after you. Clearly you're no friend of theirs, which *should* make you a friend of ours." Fighters whizzed overhead, and Avery jumped. Hunried didn't bat an eye. "Who are you?"

Janx, Hildra and Avery looked at each other. Janx shrugged. Avery raised an eyebrow at Layanna. She seemed more pale and sickly than ever.

"We're a great enemy of Octung," Avery said, speaking in what he hoped was passable Ungraessotti. "That may sound melodramatic, but it's true. And we need your help."

Hunried blew a plume of smoke at him. "Speak on."

"Are the Tunnels of Ard still accessible?"

A wry smile twisted Hunried's face. "The Hallowed Halls? Yeah, I guess. Lot of it's been collapsed, but the Soul Door still stands—and will, long as the Palace does." His expression went flat. "Why?"

"We need access to them."

That seemed to surprise the captain. "You want to die?"

"No."

Hunried frowned. "The Halls are sacred."

"Nevertheless, they're our destination."

"Only the God-Emperor can give living men access to the caverns—that's why his fathers built the Palace over the entrance—and I can tell you right now—"

Janx stepped forward. Hunried's eyes widened slightly, taking in the whaler's massive dimensions.

"Then I guess we need to see the God-Emperor, don't we?" said Janx.

Hunried frowned. Behind him an anti-aircraft gun thundered. Overhead the bi-wing of a whizzing fighter caught flame. The plane spiraled out of the sky and smashed into an already-pocked building that lined the courtyard. The impact sent burning bricks and shattered glass in all directions. The band hunkered low. Flames roared and crackled all around.

Hunried continued to stare at them, thinking. Smoke curled up from his hand-rolled cigarette.

Finally, he said, "I'm just a captain. I don't have clearance to give you access to the God-Emperor. I'll need to get you an audience with the General."

While he orchestrated this, Avery and the others waited. In the distance the boom of anti-aircraft guns eventually faded, as did the rattle of machine guns and the roar of planes. The Octunggen had broken off their attack, but surely only for the moment. Avery held no doubt they would try again, and soon, especially now that the Over-City had arrived. Idly he wondered what had become of

Sheridan. Had she and the rays given up the hunt once they entered the warzone? He doubted it. He thought of her glistening naked by candlelight. He thought of the shotgun shell she had given him.

Hildra and Janx spoke some measure of Ungraessotti, as it was one of Ghenisa's closest neighbors, and so they were able to communicate when called upon. To Avery's relief, the Ungraessotti were able to provide him with medical equipment, and he saw to Hildra—a piece of shrapnel had sliced her arm—and Janx, who had several deep cuts from the crash. Another doctor treated Avery's wounds on his back and neck.

The sky darkened, and freezing winds tore through the streets, bustling with cement and asphalt dust. Avery alternately shivered and coughed. He was exhausted and simply wanted to sleep. His stitches itched. In the distance dogs howled, or perhaps wolves—these *were* the mountains—and bands of soldiers patrolled the streets. There were still people living here, hard as it was for Avery to believe. He saw them from afar, drifting like ghosts through the ruins, coming home from their jobs—*jobs*, in this insanity—or venturing to the meager markets. The nearest temple had been shelled, but worshippers had cleaned it out, done what repairs they could, and as Avery watched they filed into the building and began a service. Candles flickered in the broken, dust-streaked windows. He wondered if they were faithful Vericans worshipping the God-Emperor and praying to their ancestors in the Hallowed Halls.

Two hours after dark, an aid came and requested that the band accompany her to one of the command tents. General Rossit sat, tired and irritated, behind a fold-up desk in his mobile office. He seemed a hard, grim sort, bone-thin, almost bird-frail, but he held himself with dignity and authority. He did not ask his guests to sit. There was only one chair other than his, and by unspoken consensus they let Layanna occupy it.

The general's eyes fell on her. Avery had told them she did not know Ungraessotti, but it was obvious from the general's glance that they still had questions about her.

The wrinkles to one side of the General's mouth deepened. "You lot continue to demand to see the God-Emperor? Not just anyone is granted an audience with His Eminence." When no one spoke, he went on. "However ... because of the unusual nature of your arrival ... the obvious fact that Octung considers you an important threat, I am tempted to allow you a visit to the Palace." His voice lowered, and Avery heard a note of lament in it. "But, I warn you, you would rather deal with me. The God-Emperor is ... well, let us say ... eccentric. You will not find him easy to deal with."

Avery glanced to the others, then the general. "If you can grant us access to the Halls, we're very happy to deal with you."

The general shook his head wearily. "Only His Eminence can grant you that. The Halls are off-limits to the living. And for good reason."

"Then we'd better see him."

"And you won't say why?"

Avery sighed. "All we can tell you is we're on a vital mission to stop Octung. To end the war."

The general drummed his fingers on his desk. "That seems unlikely, but so be it. I'd rather not have you here as a distraction. The troops are very curious about you. I'm dispatching Captain Hunried to take you to Lord Haemlys himself, and I'm officially washing my hands of the lot of you."

Maqarl, capital of Ungraessot, was far from Azzara, and it was determined that they would set out for it at first light. That night the band was given a tent to sleep in. To the sound of wounded men crying out in the background and large military vehicles trundling by, Avery lay down on the ground, as there were no more cots available, and prepared for slumber.

"You sure this is the right thing?" Janx asked. The whaler lay on his back, fingers threaded behind his head, staring at the ceiling, which rippled in the wind. A lamp on low flame flickered, throwing leaping light onto the walls. "Goin' to see the Emperor?"

"We need access to those tunnels," Avery said. "To the Soul Door. It's the only way I can think of to reach Cuithril, whatever it really is. For our purposes, merely a waypoint on our road to Lusterqal."

"I don't like this," said Hildra. "Caves! At least you can see what's coming at you on the surface."

"Yeah," Janx said. "Bullets."

"But do we need to go all the way to Maqarl? Hunried said the Tunnels'd been bombed. That some'd collapsed. Might be there's a way open, a way easier than dealing with the damned God-Emperor."

Avery shook his head. "First of all, we're not going to be aimlessly wandering the Front exploring caves. Second, if we *did* find a cave that led to the Halls, and we were willing to travel for hundreds of miles in the darkness of the caverns, lost and going in circles ... they're not empty."

"What d'ya mean?" said Janx.

"I don't know the details, but there's ... things ... living down there. The only way for us to survive the Halls is to ride in the Emperor's dirigible."

"*Dirigible?*" said Hildra. "In a *cave?*"

"The Emperors all take sojourns into the Halls to commune with their fathers," Avery said, "and ultimately, according to legend, to dwell there. It's where they go to die, I suppose. At any rate, the Emperor will keep a dirigible at the Soul Door, in one of the main cavern halls. It's that dirigible we need, and that hall. There we can fly it above any ... things ... that live there."

Janx looked glum. "If you say so, Doc."

"Then it's settled. All that's standing between us and reaching Lusterqal through the caverns is the eccentricity of the God-Emperor."

In Octunggen, Layanna said to him, "It will not be that easy."

He tried to put it out of his mind and sleep, but instead he found himself fantasizing about Maqarl. Ungraessot was the last country left still ruled by a L'ohen Emperor; technically it was all that was left of L'oh now that Es'hem was gone. And he was about to visit its palace! He'd studied L'ohen history all his life, fascinated by the romance of the ancient empire, with its jade temples and crimson knights, and now he was going right to its heart. He was even going to meet an *emperor*.

The fantasy faded, and the nightmarish shape of Uthua loomed above him, mountainous and awful, pseudopods crashing down. A shiver coursed up his spine, and he prayed the Mnuthra would not find them.

He awoke with a gasp to the sound of bombs.

The ground shook. People screamed in the distance. The roar of great planes split the night. Anti-aircraft guns boomed, and somewhere sirens rang.

Avery crawled to his feet, trying to get his bearings. The others were stirring too, swearing and wide-eyed. Janx was already shrugging on his clothes.

A great explosion ripped through the night nearby. The ground jumped beneath Avery's feet and nearly sent him back to the ground.

The tent flaps burst in. There stood a breathless Captain Hunried, unshaven, shirtfront open. "Get going! We leave now, while it's still possible."

They stared at him. Avery felt his mind shifting gears, too slowly.

"You want your visit with His Eminence, right?" Hunried demanded. "Then get a fucking move on!"

Janx shoved a duffel bag into Avery's hands, and Hildra called to her monkey, trying to calm him. Layanna grimaced and stood. They readied themselves while the captain brought around a jeep, and they all piled in.

As Captain Hunried stomped on the gas, Avery's belly lurched, and he hung tightly to the back of the seat. Hunried wound his way through the chaos of the encampment, which was still dark, the eastern horizon just turning the ghostly gray-white of early dawn. Men and women hurried among tents and tanks like phantoms. A sharp chill cut the air.

Bombers lumbered overhead and pounded anti-aircraft guns on ground and rooftops. Buildings flamed and crumbled. The greatest concentration of bombs smashed around the largest of Azzara's functioning processors; once it was destroyed, the Octunggen could bring their otherworldly weapons to bear on the city in force. In the distance Avery heard the rattle of thousands of guns, and with a feeling of horror he realized the Octunggen were striking by land as well as air. They had used the night as cover to draw close enough to spring.

Captain Hunried drove the band through Azzara and out. As the jeep bounced down dim mountain roads, Avery watched the silhouette of the city flame and smoke on the horizon, and he thought of all the soldiers, all the citizens praying to their gods for deliverance, then looked to the others in the jeep, who were turned backward in their jouncing seats. They too stared at the fires, grim and silent. He knew they were all thinking the same thing he was, that the Octunggen attacked because of them, that the Azzarans were dying because of them. Of course, the Octunggen were going to strike at some point no matter what, it was just a matter of time, he knew that. *And yet ...*

Avery looked to Layanna and saw flame dancing in her eyes.

For nearly two weeks they traveled through the mountain roads of Ungraessot. They passed innumerable convoys headed toward the front lines, crossed over wide, sturdy bridges between mountain slopes and a few small, shaky ones. Several of the larger ones had been bombed, and Captain Hunried was forced to find alternate routes, some of them quite time-consuming. Once they crossed over on what the locals called a *high ferry*, which consisted of a platform suspended from a huge crane. The crane swung the platform from one mountain shoulder to another, over a steep, narrow gorge. Looking down into the mist that filled the gorge and seeing rocks poke through the cottony layer (and wondering if that was lichen or blood that covered them), Avery had never felt so ill. He would be monstrously glad to be out of the highlands. Unfortunately, Ungraessot was about half highlands, and the flat areas were all occupied by Octung.

The jeep passed not just military and supply convoys but ragged lines of refugees. Their homes and cities had been destroyed and now they wandered, homeless and hopeless. Avery saw endless campfires dotting the peaks at night between the pines. From time to time, planes flew overhead toward the front lines, and when they did Avery could hear refugees cheering raggedly to the side of the road. Ungraessot still had some fight left in her.

The jeep stopped among the little rag-tag settlements to purchase food and necessary items when available, though more often it was the refugees that begged aid from the occupants of the jeep. From the vagabonds Avery heard tales of conflict with local ngvandi, as well as stories of refugees banding together into companies of bandits, rapists and highway robbers. The people had become desperate, willing to do anything to survive, even if it meant preying on their own. Captain Hunried and the others wound their way through the mountains with caution after that, trying never to travel by night, when the bandits were at their worst. Then they would park and sleep. And every evening before he drifted off, Avery wondered where Sheridan was. And Uthua.

During the day they passed through and near Ungraessotti cities, and in them Avery saw gaunt, grim people, waiting only for the day when Octung arrived at their doors. Some of the cities were intact, some ruined, some claiming secession from Ungraessot and therefore neutrality in the war. One even boasted a banner that read *We worship the Collossum. All hail Octung!*

"Fools," Hunried spat. "That won't save them. It will only make it easier for the Octs. They can concentrate on subduing the cities that offer resistance and save the rest for later. These lot deserve what they get."

Despite his harsh words, he waxed on with obvious pride about the grandeur of his country. "One of the oldest nations in Urslin, you know," he said one day as they were nearing a tunnel. "Existed two thousand years before the coming of L'oh, and some say even before that."

"We're more curious about the Soul Door," Hildra said, surprising Avery, who hadn't thought she had an interest in such things.

Hunried nodded as if this made perfect sense. "Most people are. It's not every country that has a portal to the afterlife."

"That's why the God-Emperor guards it, eh?" This was Janx.

"His sacred duty," Hunried said. "And being God-Emperor, when it's his time to go through the Door, he won't do it merely in spirit but body as well. When he tires of the mortal plane and wants to join his fathers in the Hallowed Halls, he'll appoint one of his sons as heir and take the long journey through the dark."

"Why do they call him the God-Emperor?" Hildra said.

"He's descended from the gods," Hunried said, as if it were self-evident. "His Eminence is directly descended from the line of emperors. His branch of the line Ascended during the Fall. When L'oh was breaking up and Emperor Hurn died under mysterious circumstances, his two sons warred for power—you know the story. Lord Mycra and Lord Tallis. Civil war. No? Come now, everyone knows it."

Avery knew it quite well, of course, but he let Hunried speak on.

"Well, Lord Mycra insisted on worshipping the L'ohen gods," the captain said, "but Tallis had an epiphany. He was ruler of the Eastern Islands at the time and had learned their gods. The gods of the sea. Story is that they communed with him. Spoke with him. Entered him. *Changed* him. With their power, he was able to survive the war waged on him by the villainous Mycra, who was forced to flee to Es'hem, while Tallis took over lordship of Ungraessot, greatest L'ohen nation still standing after the Fall. And so his line have led us ever since."

Avery didn't comment on the obvious bias in the story. Hunried was only repeating what he'd been taught. But the mention of gods of the sea ...

He turned to Layanna, who sat beside him.

She raised her eyebrows. "Yes," she said. "We tried other countries before Octung."

He was stunned. The story of the Fall of L'oh was legend, myth, infused with every aspect of the cultures of Urslin, and it was one he had studied intently.

"That was thousands of years ago," he said.

She gave a slow nod. "We have been here some time."

"But the Atomic Sea became the way it is only a *thousand* years ago."

"No. It started long before that. It started small and slow, then spread rapidly later, once the process was well under way."

Suddenly the light dawned. "The Ilaunth Quarter ..." A once-infamous region of the sea where ships were said to sink, or disappear and then return years later, sometimes with crews turned into monsters that then preyed on other ships. A million tales were told of that quarter, though it had faded into legend long ago.

"Yes," she said. "It started there. It took ages for us to develop our processors, get them going at full capacity. Only then did the affected region spread to encompass the first sea—the *original* Atomic Sea, though they didn't call it that back then, of course; atomic power hadn't been dreamt of—and go on to affect the rest of them. Back then they called it the 'Foul Sea' or the 'Sea of Death' or the 'Doomsea', or what-have-you. But it was always one name, not multiple, and always 'sea', even when it spread to encompass one ocean after another. And the Change isn't done yet. There are still a few bodies of water left largely unaffected."

The jeep passed into the tunnel, and the darkness made Avery shiver.

That night they camped with a hungry-looking group of refugees. Huddling in their torn jackets, some shaking in the cold, they grouped around barrel fires and listened to a radio whose static-warped voices filled the night. Avery went hollow when he heard the news.

Azzara had fallen. Azzara, home of the Half-Lord, proud bearer of the Amber Ziggurat, had been wiped out by Octung. Its processors had been destroyed, and the

Octunggen had been able to turn the Deathlight on its inhabitants. Avery, who had seen the effects of the Deathlight firsthand, imagined Azzara's streets strewn with writhing, gasping figures clawing at their boil-covered skin as a strong red light shone from a mountaintop.

At the news, Captain Hunried grew silent, but Avery caught him drinking from a flask later on. When the flask ran dry, the captain cursed and flung it away.

Avery used nearly his last note to buy a pint of whiskey. Together, he and the captain stood around a barrel fire and swapped sips.

"I'm sorry," Avery said. "You must have lost some good friends."

Hunried's face was impassive, but his eyes had misted. His voice, when he spoke, was a rasp. "They're in a better place now."

"The Hallowed Halls?"

"Oblivion."

They both took a long sip after that. Winter wind howled around them, and it began to snow. Soft white flakes settled on the pines all around. Hunried glared up at the clouds and cursed.

"I hate winter," he said.

The next day they reached Maqarl, capital of Ungraessot.

Chapter 18

"What the hell?" said Hildra, leaning forward in her seat, and Dr. Francis Avery had to agree.

They'd passed several checkpoints and were midway through Maqarl. Far from the warzone, the city seemed to be thriving, though it was possible that impression was only the result of the teeming refugees choking the streets, alleys, and even camping on rooftops. Laundry lines strung up in the alleys fluttered in the wind. The refugees looked cold, emaciated from hunger, and miserable. The locals didn't look much better. Nevertheless, the shopkeepers tended their shops, factories belched smoke, and people dined, if not well, in streetside cafes. Despite these outward signs, the populace looked skinny, malnourished and haggard.

People packed the temples, doubtless praying for relief. Hordes of Vericans, the God-Emperor's faithful, flooded a great cathedral to the God-Emperor on a sort of hill. The lords of Ungraessot post-Fall had never required their subjects to worship them, but the Verican cathedral was the grandest temple of them all—and, it seemed, the most heavily attended.

Everywhere loomed the beautiful, graceful architecture of L'oh—soaring minarets, multi-colored tips gleaming, proud, faceted columns lining grand buildings, huge, arching domes that seemed to weigh nothing and must weigh nothing because they defied gravity, colored windows winking like jewels, granite arches and marble stairs bowed in the centers by time. And it had all been adjusted to suit Ungraessotti engineers and conditions. The buildings were sturdier, thicker than they would have been elsewhere, hardy to withstand mountain winds and sieges and sudden ngvandi attacks. Many were pressed flush against the side of mountain walls and the insides would extend into the rock itself, some connecting in secret passages cloaked in intrigue.

Avery, who had been fantasizing about this moment for weeks, stared around him in awe, unable to stop the grin that spread across his face. *I'm in L'oh!*

Great suspension bridges spanned hazy gaps between mountain slopes, and autos trundled from one to another; Maqarl occupied five full peaks, but the valleys between them were steep and deadly and too dark even for trees to grow. Avery and the others made their way from peak to peak toward the largest, tallest mountaintop, the center of the city, where the palace could be seen glinting from far away.

But none of this is what had caught Hildra's eyes, Avery knew. Perched forward in her rickety seat, she pointed at the lines of animals being herded through the streets. Avery saw goats, sheep, calves, land-based batkin, giant furred toads being dragged along—their fur matted and muddy, their rear legs hobbled to prevent them hopping away— camouflage crabs being prodded with long staffs though their pincers were tied off, ice frozen in their joints. All animals shambled or scuttled uphill, through the snow, toward the monumental palace that loomed above the city, staring down over its citizens and landmarks, gazing across the misty gulfs that plunged beyond the mountain, out over the other city-lets on their peaks, out over the razored horizon.

Hildra scowled at the lines of animals. "Where are they all fucking *going*?"

Captain Hunried appeared troubled, but he did not answer.

They passed through another barrage of checkpoints, the most stringent yet, and Captain Hunried's papers and seal, given to him by General Rossit, were analyzed critically and finally approved. Hunried steered the jeep up the road, past herds of bleating goats, calves and other creatures, so close Avery could smell their musk (the giant valley slugs smelled particularly rank) and made for the palace. Proud granite columns sporting ornamental bulges held up a lofty canopy, and a great oaken door with brass bands centered the immense façade.

Shepherds led their various flocks through a side entrance, and Avery frowned to see the stinking animals vanish into the palace.

His consternation was soon forgotten. Royal soldiers wearing the distinctive crimson of the royal family stopped the jeep, helped its occupants out, and one drove the jeep away. It vanished into a cave to the side of the palace, where Avery presumed a garage was located. The palace itself was set against the mountain, surely merging with it on the inside, and rocky bulwarks loomed to either side. Directly above Avery the gold-and-glass dome and the surrounding minarets glinted in the sun. This was it, Avery realized. *I'm about to enter a L'ohen palace.*

A military man approached, and he and Captain Hunried clapped hands. They talked briefly, Hunried waved farewell to Avery and the others, and the two walked away. Avery supposed he would never see the captain again.

A royal aide wearing the finery of his office stepped forward and introduced himself. "We've been expecting you. I'm Jynad Elnithin. If you would ..."

He gestured them toward the heavy, banded doors, and Avery walked through them eagerly. He couldn't stop smiling as he passed down beautifully ornate halls and columns. Curling white stairways vanished behind golden walls. Shimmering crystal chandeliers hung down from high, domed ceilings, some cut with skylights. Shafts of sunshine flooded the chambers, glittering on bejeweled balustrades and monuments that sprouted from the floor like roses.

A statue of some ancient empress, Avery thought it must be Lady Halana, stood in regal poise, her gown fluttering behind her as if caught by a wind. One of her arms was uplifted, as if to a lover—surely the infamous General Morgaster, if Avery's suspicion about her identity was correct. A circlet crowned her head. Another statue depicted a kneeling young man. An older, one-eyed man wearing the garb of a priest stood before him, placing a circlet on his head. The young man wept as he accepted it, though not in happiness, and Avery, remembering the story, did not wonder why.

Stories. Everywhere about him there were stories, legends. In murals on the ceilings, in frescos on the walls, depicted in stained-glass windows, whirling through the air around him.

Wherever Avery walked he heard his own footsteps echo on the same stone and marble that countless emperors had trod. It was amazing. He could almost feel them, feel the presence of all that history, all that nobility. He almost floated as he walked.

"L'oh," he whispered. "We're walking through L'oh ..."

Ahead of him he began to hear noise. Laughing, talking, the sounds of cutlery. It was the sound of a great many people and much activity. Could it really be the Throne Room? *Almost there!* Paul would have killed to be here.

To Avery's surprise, the hallway he was traveling along bisected a side-hall, and out of this hall poured the tides of goats and calves and sheep and batkin and more. Avery saw a huge black slug, large enough to ride on, its neck garlanded with flowers and its flanks dabbed in scented oils, be led docilely along, its slime trailing on a priceless mosaic. The animals seemed to be traveling in the same direction Avery's party was.

"What the *hell?*" said Hildra.

"It does seem odd," Avery admitted. "I'm sure the Emperor has a good reason for it."

Jynad, the royal aide, just looked tired. He led them on down the halls, side-by-side with the bleating, chirruping herds, and the noise ahead grew greater. Avery noted that the shepherds were glum and emaciated. Why did everyone look so starved? There were obviously plenty of herd animals.

At last Jynad led them to a high, grand archway, inlaid with golden bas-reliefs. A riot of sound flooded from the chamber beyond.

"This way," he said.

The Throne Room, Avery thought, almost reverent, and felt his face break out into an idiotic smile. He caught Layanna looking at him, eyebrows raised, but the smile remained.

Jynad led them through the archway.

Instantly, Avery's smile withered.

Dear gods ...

They were in a huge chamber, what had to be the Throne Room—yes, he saw it there, far in the distance, sitting empty on its dais, *the very throne of L'oh!*—but the room had become so much more. For one thing, it was *huge*—hundreds of yards in every direction. But that was just the start of it. Avery's eyes strained to take it all in. His mind reeled. He heard Janx and Hildra cursing and making sounds of amazement beside him.

First, there were the great, long tables. Countless courtiers occupied the tables, which were heaped with food.

Laughing and gorging themselves, the nobles ate, and ate. And drank. Servants ferried flagons and tankards of ale and wine back and forth, and as they scurried the liquids dripped on priceless rugs, furs and ancient marble. More than one of the nobles appeared to be completely naked, and some lounged in various states of undress.

Thus the feast merged seamlessly with the great orgy, or orgies. Swarms of sweaty limbs, flushed faces and writhing bodies tangled the thoroughfares between tables and sprawled across the thick furs that draped the floors. Avery started to see beautiful women being ground under sweaty men and for beautiful young men to be used by old women, and men too. Commoners, he thought, being coerced or paid to participate. Of course, there were many noble-on-noble couplings, judging by the elaborate hair and soft skin of the participants. Grunts and gasps from the sweaty mounds echoed off the far walls, and men slurping wine at the tables shouted colorful comments.

But even *this* wasn't all.

Avery stared at the walls, at the long, bloody walls. Dozens, perhaps hundreds of altars had been built flush against them. Avery saw shrines to classic L'ohen gods, the many Star-Lords, great Na'thuur, lord of the underworld, M'kanagath, the mountain king, Sylissa, his sister and lover, Kaan, their volcanic progeny, and more, many, many more. There were other altars, too, shrines to pre-L'ohen gods. Altars shaped like flowers, geese, oxen, grinning jackals, and forms more fantastic. Suvaret, the elephant with three faces. S'us, the Great Maw, depicted as simply a gaping mouth lined with fangs. The serene jade face of Rasallas limned in thorns. And others. Countless others.

And at each one of these altars a priest conducted a sacrificial ceremony—sometimes to a small, rudimentary following, sometimes by himself. Speaking loudly as if to compete with the priest next door, he would read from a book while helpers dragged the sacrificial beast—goat, swine, slug or other—forward, and he would with brusque, tired movements slit its throat, if throat it had, or spill its entrails, or crack its head-carapace, or dispatch it in whatever other manner the scriptures prescribed. Mounds of corpses, some of them quite large, heaped before the altars. Servants carved into them, slicing out the best cuts and carrying them into rooms beyond, apparently the kitchens. Other servants carried the results of the culinary labors out to the tables on silver platters, where burping, pawing nobles continued to gorge.

Avery stared. And stared. The smile faded from his face, replaced by something else. A sense of crawling shame welled up through him and he found himself shaking in rage.

"This is obscene!" he said. "What ... what ..." His disappointment and anger were so large he couldn't find words for them.

Layanna could. In shockingly good Ghenisan, she said to Jynad, "Your people starve and yet your lords waste food appealing to gods that don't answer."

Jynad did not seem to notice her accent, such were the distractions of the room. He turned an apologetic gaze on them. "Do not judge His Eminence too harshly. He is above mortal law." With a sigh, he added, "Come."

He led the group forward. They bustled through orgies and feasts. Avery had to step lively around naked limbs and torsos. Some of the participants wore masks, some dressed as animals. A beautiful woman gasped in pleasure as an unidentifiable (under its disguise as a bear) lover pleasured her with its tongue; she clutched at Avery's ankle in her orgasm and he had to pull himself loose. A fat man ate a dripping beef rib while pounding into the rear of a naked young man. Avery smelled a riot of smells—savory meat and spices, spilled beer, sweat and body odor, a woman's state of arousal, another's yeast infestation, a man's farts, belches, the reek of split intestines and death drifting over from the altars. Sloppy sounds of rutting, grunts, groans and laughter swirled around him. Glittering jewelry and flushed faces and bare breasts spun before his eyes. It was too much, too much. He couldn't breathe.

No no no, he thought. *This is all wrong.* The lords of L'oh should be locked in debate with the Senate, planning against the invasion of Octung, plotting to win back the cities that had declared independence, appealing to the refugees that had become a menace to innocent people wandering the mountains, putting them to better use ...

Jynad led the group to a certain huge, tangled orgy, perhaps the biggest and loudest of the room, though in truth it was hard to judge. Scores of people drank and fornicated in a sweaty sprawl. Hairy buttocks pumped, a bald head gleamed, a long, feminine leg kicked, and a woman's rolls of fat jounced while a perfect pair of breasts was fondled by a gravy-stained hand.

"Your Eminence," called the aide. "Your Eminence, you have visitors."

The grunting and straining continued.

Jynad sighed, turned to Avery and the others. "I'm afraid you'll have to wait."

"Our task is urgent," Avery said.

The aid nodded vaguely. "His Lordship does not know that."

They waited. And waited. At last there came a series of groans, and a section of the sweaty tangle bulged, throbbed. The moans grew louder, louder, then climaxed with a primal roar. The bulge subsided, and a few moments later it parted. A strange, stumbling form arose from the chaos. It burped, wiped its mouth, and wove over to the group, though it was not clear whether in response to Jynad's pleas or not.

Instantly, the aide bowed before it.

"My Lord," he said.

The figure burped.

Avery blinked.

The Emperor was a mutant.

Emperor Ga'as Haemlys IV was not wholly mutant like the ngvandi. He bore the tainted, infected look of a normal person come into contact with the Atomic Sea. He was a huge, fat, hairy man, naked save for his many rings and the gold chains that hung down over his chest hair, which was thick enough to weave a blanket from. His erection was beginning to fade, but not fast enough for Avery's liking. The Emperor's bushy, curly red-brown beard was slicked with either grease or a woman's secretions. His blood-shot eyes glared drunkenly. But it was his right arm that seized Avery's attention. It was the segmented, carapace-covered arm of a lobster, complete with a great snapping pincer on the end. Avery could see where the crustacean shoulder joined the man's body, the carapace folding over the skin. Old scars showed there, where shell rubbed against flesh.

How is this possible? Avery thought. He stared, trying to make sense of it. Hunried had said the gods of the sea had *changed* Lord Tallis. At the time, Avery had taken that to mean they had converted him to their worship, but, though that may have been part of it, Hunried had spoken much more literally. And Emperor Tallis had passed his change on to the next generation, and the next. No wonder they thought him a god-emperor. Back then there were no mutants. He was the first one, at least the first one Avery knew of. And it was obviously something no one outside the religion spoke of, at least not explicitly, otherwise Avery would have known to expect it.

Jynad cleared his throat, and Avery looked down to see him kneeling. Reluctantly, Avery followed suit, and so did the others.

The Emperor barely glanced at them as he lurched toward one of the feasting tables. Avery got a look at his hairy buttocks, meaty and flexing as he walked. A piece of grease stuck to the right one, tangled and glistening in the hairs, which were black, not the red-brown of his head and beard.

"My Lord," Jynad said, rising and scrambling after him. Avery and the others followed. "These are the visitors General Rossit asked us to welcome. Remember, he radioed ahead, before—Azzara—?"

The Emperor only half looked back, idly glancing them over. Even their odd, bedraggled state was not enough to win his attention. They reached one of the long tables, and nobles all around hailed their lord drunkenly and with good humor.

"And who will quench their Lord's thirst?" bellowed the Emperor.

Several grabbed flagons and shoved them at him. He burped once, grabbed the nearest one with his pincer and drank. As he drank, he broke wind loudly. Nobles around him laughed, and one listed sideways on his seat and farted, to join his lord in rude behavior. More laughter followed, the loudest of all by Haemlys when he lowered his flagon and wiped his mouth.

"Give that man a castle!" he thundered.

Whether he was serious or not Avery couldn't tell, but after that there followed a series of farts and burps, and the men and their lord laughed so heartily the Emperor had to sit down or fall over from mirth. Avery was less amused.

Gasping, his laughter subsiding, the Emperor turned his gaze back on Jynad, seeking another source of humor. "What'd you want again?" he said. "Sum'ing to do w' a radio?" There was laughter all around at the absurdity of this.

Avery felt nails dig into the flesh of his palm.

Jynad colored. "No, my lord. These are guests. Visitors from the Front. You recall, General Rossit—"

"Ah, now *there's* a man that knows his boots! He polishes 'em night and day, he does, but give him a whore and he don't know which end is up!" More laughter.

Jynad persisted with the patience of long suffering. "General Rossit said they were very important, you remember. Said they were great enemies of Octung and wanted to confer with you privately about some favor they wish to ask of you, something that could harm Octung."

"*Favor!*" the Emperor roared, laughing, his face red. "*I'll* give them a favor!"

He stood up drunkenly, with some help from his mates, then reached down with his human hand, grabbed hold of his member, which had more or less gone flaccid, and, after some fits and starts, began pissing at the ground at Jynad's feet. When Jynad jumped back—droplets splattering—the Emperor urinated wider, sprinkling the marble floor. Avery felt drops bounce off the marble and strike his legs. He and the rest leapt back, while the Emperor and his friends roared with drunken hilarity.

"How d'you like *that* favor?" the Emperor said.

Jynad sighed and turned to the others. In a half-whisper, he said, "I am most sorry."

Avery could find no words to say. He no longer felt angry, he felt numbed. *I need a drink.*

Janx looked ready to rip the Emperor apart with his bare hands. Hildra laid a restraining hand on his arm.

A man in the robes of a priest approached the Emperor and whispered in his ear. Haemlys nodded sagely. He finished pissing, wiggled his member to get out the last drops, then flung a wave to his mates as he lurched away from the table, the priest at his side. They wound their way through the revelry toward the dais that held the throne.

"Where are they going?" asked Hildra.

Janx smashed a fist into his palm. "To find someone to shit on next, I reckon."

"Let's try again," Avery told Jynad.

The aide, resigned, straightened himself and said, "Follow me."

He led the way through the orgies and feasting toward the throne. In the distance, animals bleated in fear and mewled in pain, competing with the sounds of orgasms, grunts, clattering silverware and laughter. Ahead, the God-Emperor reached the throne, passed around it, and vanished into a small, ornate entrance behind the royal seat, slipping through a curtain of coral-colored beads. Jynad led Avery and the others in the God-Emperor's tracks, and in moments they rounded the throne and, with only a brief hesitation, passed through the coral curtain.

"Be quiet as you enter," Jynad cautioned. "It's a holy place."

Lips sealed, Avery followed the aide through the rattling beads and into the chamber beyond. Janx and the others did likewise.

It was not a large chamber. It was rounded, domed, made of bricks that appeared to be a mottled blue-violet color. An altar stood in the center of the chamber, but the altar did not resemble the ones in the Throne Room. Instead, it appeared to be a tiered fountain. Crystal water tinkled from the top level, where the statue of a fish-man not unlike Muirblaag stood in a kingly pose, cape draped from broad shoulders, trident thrust high into the air.

"Lord Tallis," Jynad explained. "The first God-Emperor."

Water trickled from Tallis's mouth, down over his scaly hide, to fill the first basin, the highest, which took the shape of a seashell, as did they all. A waterfall splashed from this tier to the next, and the next after that. Every basin spread wider and deeper than the one before.

Avery could not repress a shudder as he beheld the fourth and lowest tier. The widest and deepest, perhaps thirty feet in diameter and four feet deep, it was completely choked in dead bodies. They were not human bodies, but ngvandi. The reek of old ngvandi corpses filled the tight chamber, redolent of rotting fish and seaweed. Some of the corpses were bloated, some had split, some were mainly bones with ragged streamers of flesh trailing from them. A few crabs and fish had been placed in the basin, and they pinched and nibbled at the corpses, but not fast enough to prevent the foul odor that plagued the room. Avery tasted bile in the back of his throat.

"What the hell?" said Hildra.

Hastily Jynad motioned her to silence, and she glared but obeyed.

Oblivious, Lord Haemlys knelt before the seashell basin of the lowest tier, praying silently. The priest knelt beside him, and they prayed together, in some language Avery did not know. It seemed to be eerily similar to that the ngvandi spoke, and the unnatural, susurrus noises complimented the tinkling of the water as it sloughed over the corpses, stirring their ink-like blood.

Avery had not noticed the small opening to the rear of the room, but now four soldiers stepped out of it bearing a thrashing ngvandi between them. He howled and screeched, but his tongue had been torn out, as had his eyes. He could not protest or even see what fate held in store for him. Just as well.

Haemlys and his priest rose while the soldiers manhandled the thrashing ngvandi into position over the basin right where the two had knelt.

"Is he going to do what I think he is?" Hildra asked.

Jynad glowered at her. Hildebrand huddled low on her back, making scared little mewling noises.

"Yeah," Janx said. "I think so, darlin'. Y' may wanna close those pretty eyes."

"Fuck you."

Avery wished there was some way to prevent what was about to happen, but he knew there was not.

The priest produced a curved dagger from his robes. After some more chanting, he jerked the ngvandi's head back with one hand and slit his throat with the other. Blue-black blood sprayed into the basin, and strong, fishy limbs twitched and jerked. The ngvandi made pathetic gagging noises, and Avery looked away. At last the creature died, and Avery breathed a sigh of relief that his pain was over. Without ceremony, the soldiers heaved the corpse into the waters, and the bodies already in it bobbed at the movement. A bit of bloody water splashed over the lip and spattered the floor.

"You may go," the priest told the soldiers.

They bowed and left. The priest eyed Avery and his group next, seemed to consider asking them to leave, but then noticed Jynad. Apparently the presence of the royal aide was enough to legitimize their presence, and the priest ignored them after that.

Haemlys approached the basin, bowed his head and allowed the priest to cup water in his hands and drizzle it over his forehead and face, baptizing him in the fetid, foul water. That done, the God-Emperor looked up, smiling drunkenly, serenely, as if blessed. Beaming, he stared up at the drooling statue of Lord Tallis.

"I feel you, Father of my Fathers," said Haemlys, slurring the words. "I feel you 'oursing through me. Teach me, Father. Show me the way." He waited, staring up at the statue, clearly expecting—hoping—for something. Nothing happened. Water tinkled. Corpses bobbed. The God-Emperor broke wind.

"Fuck!" Haemlys said at last. In anger, he rose to his feet, made a fist, and crashed it down onto the ngvandi he'd just had sacrificed. Bodies bobbed more violently, and more water splashed over. Crabs scuttled out of the way. "Fuck fuck *fuck*!" Furious, he turned red-rimmed eyes on the priest. "Fuck you too, you fucking char'atan! How man' of these mis'rable shits do we ha' to go through t' get a fuckin' res'onse? Huh? A hun'red? A thousan'? *Why won't he answer me*?" He stabbed a meaty finger at the statue.

The priest cowed before the wrath of his lord. "I-I don't know, Your Majesty. W-we're doing everything in our power. Following the ancient scriptures. Making sacrifices of those with otherworldly flesh, just like the slaves the Great Ones gave your Father of Fathers. I-I don't know why it's not working!"

Haemlys struck him in the face, sending him flying back to the floor. Chest heaving, lobster claw clacking, the naked God-Emperor stood over his priest and glared down at him. "You'd be'er figure it out, old man! Al'eady I've had to beg the *other* gods for advice! *An' even they won't answer*!" He snorted in bitter amusement. "I'm the laugh'in'stock of the country! I pray and sacrifice to every god, e'en those that aren't my own—*and nothing*!" He threw back his head and let loose an animal roar. In a rage, he kicked the priest, again and again.

Avery stepped forward to intervene, but Jynad, white with fear, jerked him back and shook his head violently.

"You'd better find out!" Haemlys thundered, giving the frail old man one last kick in the ribs. "Or mebbe the nex' one I sacri'ice 'll be you!"

Sobbing and begging for forgiveness, the priest picked himself up with care and scurried from the room, as fast as his withered legs would take him.

Glaring, fuming, hairy chest heaving, Lord Haemlys turned his attention to Jynad and his visitors. "You!" He marched over. His lobster claw clacked loudly. "What do *you* want?"

Jynad cowered back. "N-nothing, my lord! I only wanted to i-introduce you to some v-visitors. They're supposed to be g-great enemies of—"

Haemlys snorted. After screaming at and kicking his priest, his rage seemed to have drained from him, at least for the moment. He'd already lost interest in Jynad. With a burp, he reeled from the chapel. "Fuckin' gods," he muttered. "If they won' answer me, maybe the 'tunggen will." Still muttering, he tottered away.

"B-but my lord!" begged Jynad, hurrying after him—with some courage, Avery thought. "What shall we do with our guests?"

"F-find 'em a room!" laughed the God-Emperor. "Give 'em some wine and tell 'em to join th' par'y. The las' days're up'n us. Enjoy as much pussy and grub while y' can."

With that, he passed through the bead curtain, leaving Jynad behind.

The aide paused, staring at the curtain, as if wondering if he should try one more time. Then, with a sigh, one of many, he turned back to the guests. "I ... I'm sorry."

Janx grunted. "I should take that claw and shove it up his ass."

Jynad's eyes widened. "Don't even *say* such things."

Hildra laughed. "I'd like to see that."

Avery cleared his throat. "About those rooms ..."

Jynad swallowed, nodded. "It will be cozy, I'm afraid. Half the nobles in the land have taken refuge in the palace. Their homes have been razed, their people killed or put to flight. They're the lords of none now. All they can do is revel, leech off His Eminence and wait for the arrival of

Octung. So ... it's crowded. But when I heard that you were coming, I managed to set aside a room."

"*One* room?" Avery frowned.

"Whatever," Hildra said. "Let's just do it. I'm tired."

Avery released a breath. "Very well. Jynad, if you would show us the way ..."

The aid bowed and led the band out. Before he left, Avery turned to Layanna, who had been very silent through all of this. She eyed the corpse-filled basin strangely, and for a moment he wondered at the odd expression on her face, but then he realized what it was, and he felt cold.

She was hungry.

Chapter 19

"Well, this is the fuckin' pit," said Hildra. Smoking, she leaned back in an expensive chair and stared up at the crystal chandelier. The rooms were large and splendid, the doorways arched and inlaid with gold and turquoise. Jewels glimmered from candelabra, and antique mirrors hung from the walls, their glass warped but strangely beautiful. Priceless oil paintings adorned the spaces between, and pale-looking lords and ladies, some showing undeniable signs of mutation, stared out from eerie, inky landscapes. Alchemical lanterns filled the room with exotic smells, nutmeg and lavender and fresh leather. It was a sumptuous suite, with several handsome bedrooms that spilled out into this common living area. Gold and burgundy rugs rested on the floor.

"At least the booze is good," Janx said. He tipped back his fancy goblet and slurped some of the aged spicewine. "Hells, I'm tempted to join the fuckin' orgy."

"Don't you dare," Hildra said.

"Why not? What's an orgy for if not to orge?"

"I would be wary of contracting disease," Avery said, perusing the bookshelf, wineglass nearby.

"You gotta learn to live a little, Doc," Janx said.

Nodding absently, Avery selected a volume and thumbed through it. All in Ungraessotti, of course, but that was fine. He read it better than he spoke it. Unfortunately the volume recounted some lord's adventures, just the sort of thing he had enjoyed many times in the past, reveling in his fantasy of L'oh, but right now the last thing he wanted was to relive his boyhood dreams, or remember that he had once dreamed them in the first place. *I was such a fool.* He shoved the volume back and selected another. From time to time he glanced at Layanna, who reclined on one of the handsome divans, eyes closed but not sleeping. He downed frequent sips of his wine.

"Look, I'm just gonna say it," Hildra said. "That fat fuck was trying to worship the same shitwads the ngvandi were. Things like *her*." She indicated Layanna. "What'd she call 'em?"

"The R'loth," Avery said. "Otherwise known as the Collossum. Or, I suppose, it would be more accurate to say the Collossum are R'loth in human form."

"Yeah, them. Wonder why they didn't answer?"

"Isn't it obvious?"

"Guess not," Janx said, taking another slurp.

"They didn't use the stones," Avery said. "Don't you remember, at the ngvandi city, the ngvandi used stones quarried from the mines near the grottoes; that's what they'd set their slaves to doing. I can only assume that the power of the Mnuthra leeched through the stone. Suffused it. They used those blocks to make their monoliths with, their altars, where they made their sacrifices, and that provided a connection to the Mnuthra. They could actually sacrifice to and commune with the ones they worshipped through the monoliths. Somewhere during the history of the God-Emperors, though, the God-Emperors lost that knowledge. It occurs to me we could get into the good graces of His Eminence by telling him how to resolve the problem—only I wouldn't want to help him do so. Gods know what would happen if he actually *did* get in contact with the R'loth."

"It would work not, anyway," Layanna said. She had cracked her eyes and was looking at him mildly.

"And why not?" Avery asked.

"Even if quarried stones from ngvandi mines, he only able commune with Mnuthra. Serves them no he. Their masters he serves." A look of frustration crossed her face. *"I hate Ghenisan,"* she said in Octunggen. Then, more slowly and working the words out, she said in Ghenisan— obviously she had been practicing, if only internally—"He would have to quarry stones from the deep, near one of our cities, or use our machines to awaken the altar. Such is what my kind gave Tallis, that and sacrifices he could use to breed, to continually bathe the altar in extradimensional energies. But those machines must have been lost to history."

"So it *was* your lot." Janx watched her with interest. "I wondered about that when Hunried mentioned fish gods."

She stared up at the ceiling. "We tried to convert L'oh, but we were new to world. Misjudged things. Created civil war, brother against brother. Caused end of L'ohen Empire."

Janx and Hildra shared a look. A strange smile, half admiration and half dread, flickered across Hildra's scarred face. "*You* caused the Fall of L'oh."

Layanna met her stare. "Not me. My kind. But yes, we set events in motion that brought about Fall."

"Amazing."

"They've helped shape our world—for thousands of years, it seems," Avery said. "They caused the Atomic Sea, they caused the Fall of L'oh, they caused the current world war, and gods know what else." He rubbed his cheek. "Did it bother anyone else that our lord host was talking about how the Octunggen might listen to his pleas as he walked away?"

Janx's eyes narrowed. "Yeah. I heard that too."

"Think he'd really betray his own country?" asked Hildra.

"He'd do whatever it took to save his own neck."

The night continued, and fire crackled in the fireplace. Logs snapped, and sparks flared. Avery worked on one bottle of wine—Janx was right, it was superb—and started another. He couldn't get the image of the orgies and the sacrifices out of his mind. The flame burned lower and lower in the fireplace, and the members of the band began to retire. Janx and Hildra traipsed to the same room together, and someone in there turned on a gramophone to mask their noises—unsuccessfully.

Trying to ignore them, Avery repaired to his own bedchamber, leaving Layanna on her couch to meditate.

Just as he began to undress, he heard knocking on his doors and opened them to see her standing before him. For a mad moment he thought the example of Hildra and Janx had motivated her to do something similar—she had mentioned taking human lovers, after all—but an instant later he realized it was not lust in her eyes. It was hunger.

He cleared his throat. "May I help you?"

She nodded, seeming uncertain, perhaps nervous. She still looked sickly.

She approached him and laid a hand on his arm. Her touch was warm. "Doctor," she said. "I need your help."

"Yes ... ?"

She gathered her nerve. "The bodies in the chapel. I need them, their extra-planar energies. They will be weak now that they're dead, energies drained off, but there are enough bodies there that I can still derive a substantial meal from them, more than any eelfish."

"How so?"

"Sentience breaks barriers, creates extradimensional facets that don't exist in lesser creatures. Doctor, I can *heal*. But I need you to stand guard while I do. We must do it before dawn, when there will be renewed activity in the Throne Room."

"But—"

"There is no time. Come!"

She pulled him after her. Fumbling for words, he allowed himself to be tugged along.

"Layanna, are you sure this is the right thing—"

"It's the only thing."

They left the suite and ventured down a hallway. As they rounded a bend, a pair of drunken nobles stumbled past, one male, one female, both groping at each other as they went. They didn't seem to notice Avery and Layanna and they surely wouldn't have cared if they had.

"This way." Layanna led down a connecting hall to a grand stairwell, its white balustrade tipped in gold leaf.

"Beautiful," Avery said, as his eyes found the great chandelier. A thousand candles blazed inside, reflecting the crystal facets, making the gold-leaf glow.

"You should see the lanterns of the deep," she said.

"Tell me."

"Imagine lamps, each lit in a different sphere, each plane affecting the light and sound and smells and more in unique ways, the lamps bleeding through the dimensions, from several at a time, different in every one."

"It sounds amazing."

"It is. But my description is ... inadequate. Imagine vast beings, you would perceive them as formless, bending through the spheres even as the spheres bend them, some joining, some passing through each other, some separate, lamps bleeding, winking, a part of the beings and yet not part, all around you echoing the great songs of worship to the High Ones who dwell in their palace in Yat'il'sog ..."

"Who are *they*?"

A dark look crossed her face, but also a look of awe. "Powerful beings, as unfathomable to us as we are to you. Heralds of the Outer Lords ..."

He felt a chill and was relieved to find that that's all she seemed prepared to say on the matter.

"This way," she said.

They had reached the bottom of the stairs and she pulled him on.

"Speak Ghenisan," he reminded her. "I know it's late, but still ..."

She made a sound of frustration. Still in Octunggen, she said, "I sound like an idiot when I speak Ghenisan."

"But a loyal idiot, not an Octunggen spy."

"Very well. Is this with you right better?"

She tugged him into the Throne Room, though he could have found it on his own. Once more he marveled at its massive dimensions and opulence. The party had wound down in the late hours of the night, but there were still people drinking and copulating. Many rested on the furs on the floor, some with blankets thrown over them, some naked and uncovered. Others lay slumped in drunken stupors along the tables. Against the walls heaped countless animal corpses, their various bloods and ichors staining the altars before them. The stink when Avery traveled close to them was unimaginable. He'd smelled many corpses in his time, but never so many different kinds so close together symbolizing so much waste. How much would the starving masses packed into the city beyond pay to have access to this room? It was beyond obscene.

"Haemlys must be desperate to venture outside his own gods," Avery mused. "By sacrificing these animals, he's even suggesting that he doubts his own divinity. His connection to even greater deities. He's risking open revolt."

"Desperate—or mad."

"Yes." Avery had considered that as well. He looked about furtively as they passed through tables heaped with old food and hunched forms. Some snored loudly. Others shifted. A few still ate, drank and talked, though their voices were subdued. They paid no attention to Avery and Layanna. "You think it might be possible?" he asked.

"Honestly I little care. He can be mad. Just give us what we need. Only ..."

"Yes?"

"Only it seems shame that his people must suffer him. Yes."

That almost sounded human coming from her. Avery was encouraged. They passed the last line of feasting tables and made their way toward the throne, picking their way around sleeping or mindlessly rutting forms. Avery supposed the God-Emperor might still be out here somewhere, spent and huddled together with his fellows. More likely he was in his stately bedchambers on the top floor. Avery had heard it took up a third of that level.

They rounded the bend, and Avery heard Layanna's breathing increase in pace, almost as if in sensual excitement.

As they passed through the curtain of coral beads, she gasped. He came through right behind her, prepared to find someone lying in wait for them. Instead he found her staring in joy at all the rotting corpses. Their stink was foul, even worse than the ones outside because of the tight quarters, but she acted as though she sniffed an epicurean banquet. Almost girlishly, she hopped forward and leaned against the lowest basin. She eyed the corpses eagerly, as if trying to pick out the juiciest one. She fairly trembled in excitement.

Avery thought he actually heard her laugh as she tore off her clothes, exposing smooth white flesh, rounded buttocks, long shapely legs. She didn't seem to care whether Avery watched or not. He felt himself grow hot in embarrassment.

Then, to his immense disgust, she climbed up the lowest basin and leapt in. Bodies bobbed up and down, water sloshed over the side, and crabs scuttled away. Up to her waist, Layanna grabbed the nearest, freshest corpse, hauled it close to her, and then, with no further ado, bent over and began ripping at it with her teeth. She used her hands to stabilize it while her mouth gnawed, tore, and pulled a chunk free. She lifted her head and swallowed, then shivered in ecstasy. Avery shivered, too, but not in ecstasy. She bent over and began again. Sometimes she lifted her head to swallow, other times she simply gnawed on the corpses like a dog, like a wolf, swallowing pieces whole. She gorged and gorged. Avery turned away.

He took up station at the bead curtain. Sticking his face partway out, not far enough to be observed, he kept watch while Layanna feasted behind him. He tried not to hear the sounds, the rippings, the tearings, the sloshing of water, the crunch of bone, the creak of gristle, the growling noises she made as she ate, but it was no use. He tried not to imagine her naked, swimming in inky blood, gnawing on the inhuman dead one after the other, half-clotted blood spraying her face, neck and breasts, but he could not.

She gorged for what seemed like hours, and his legs grew tired from standing, his back sore from bending forward. For a time he leaned against the archway. For a time he sat. That position encouraged sleep, and he pushed himself back to his feet. The sounds of feeding became mere background noise, and he hardly noticed it.

Finally, however, he became aware that the noises had stopped.

He waited. Nothing.

Hardly daring to look, he turned around.

Layanna lay slumped against the second tier, surrounded by bodies and pieces of bodies bobbing idly in the water. She breathed tiredly, a sated look on her face. Inky blood spattered every bit of her, dripped from her hair, ran from the corners of her mouth, and yes, trickled over her breasts and slim belly. He tried not to look.

"Satisfied?" he asked her.

Half smiling, she met his gaze. "I feel ... better."

"Good. Then let's leave."

She stood. Inky water coursed over her, making her body seem to shimmer. She almost looked dyed in blue. Some of the fluid tangled in her pubic mound, dripped from it down her long legs. He forced his gaze away.

She stepped forward. Water sloshed. Inadvertently he looked back. She reached the lip of the fountain, poised there, and leapt nimbly off. Little droplets of water sprayed in all directions as she landed, and her breasts shook at the impact.

He felt the back of his neck grow warm.

She stalked toward him, a strange smile curling from one corner of her lips. As before, the smile was hungry. Something glittered in her eyes.

"I feel better," she repeated. "But no. I am not ... satisfied."

"Um ..."

She was very near. He could smell her now, the odor of the sea. Perhaps he had become used to it. It almost smelled good. Enticing.

She stopped before him. Her eyes stared into his, and they were even bluer than the rest of her. Her breasts rose and fell, rose and fell. When they rose, the nipples just slightly, just barely, touched the front of his shirt. After a few moments he could feel the wetness soak in.

"Ah ..."

She reached out a hand. Gently, authoritatively, she touched the side of his head and traced a strand of hair to behind his ear. "It has been years since I've known a lover," she said. "And you ... you have saved my life time and again." She said the words impatiently, as if she knew they were obligatory for him, but she was in an animalistic mood; he could see the fire in her eyes, feel it radiating off her. She was an unstoppable force, a being of sex, of sensuality. There was no point in denying her, no reason why he should. His head swam.

She stared into his eyes, and he felt something stoked deep inside him. Warmth spread outward.

She stepped even closer. Her breasts mashed up against his chest. They were warm, wet, full and firm.

"Are you sure ... ?"

She leaned her face in hungrily, as if to kiss him, but her lips just lightly grazed his. She ran her lips over his one way, then another, almost roughly. He could just about hear her growl, feel it through his bones.

The warmth he felt inside him spread lower. He realized he had been feeling a stiffening for some time. His member strained against his pants.

She rubbed one of her legs against his side, stroked his back with her free hand. She was everywhere, surrounding him, inviting him. He could taste her on his tongue. He realized he had not known a woman, not happily, since Mari, years ago.

Slowly, almost hypnotized, he reached up and ran a hand through Layanna's hair.

Her breathing quickened. He felt the hot puffs of air on his face.

His breathing quickened as well.

"We should move this to the suite ..." he started. "The bodies ..."

"They haven't affected *him*."

She caressed his crotch.

"No," he said. "Please. Shower first. Come." He took her hand and led her from the chapel. Ten minutes later, her fire undiminished, she stepped from the shower in their suite and joined him in his room. Her skin was hot from the water, and she had not bothered wrapping herself in a towel.

She reached down, helping him free of his zipper. He felt a belt snapping, and his pants fell around his ankles.

She leaned forward. Her lips touched his.

He responded.

The next day Avery awoke in his bedroom, afternoon sunlight streaming in from a window. He sat up with a start, wondering if it had all been a dream. He felt strange. Lighter somehow. Clearer. He glanced idly around. Layanna was not in bed beside him. Yet he saw the sheets in disarray and was reassured it was not a dream.

Gingerly, head reeling—he'd had too much to drink last night—he climbed from the sheets and began his morning rituals, including a vigorous washing. One of the joys of the suite was its opulent private lavatories. As he cleaned himself, he tried to remember last night. It was only a vague, mad blur of passion and physicality, her moaning into his mouth, him thrusting inside her, squeezing a breast, her raking nails down his back, gyrating against him. It had been the first time he'd finished inside a woman since his married life.

He dressed slowly, his head pounding. The Ungraessotti had provided new clothes for them all. He could not help smiling as he donned a set.

In the main room, Avery discovered Janx entertaining Hildra with a naughty sailor's ballad. When he was done, Hildra clapped and whistled. Janx bowed. He looked to Avery, and Avery wondered at the knowing light in his eyes.

"Have a good night, Doc?"

Avery tried to hold himself with dignity. "Rather, yes."

"I'll bet," Hildra said.

Some tea had been made, and Avery sat down and helped himself to a cup, grateful to have something to do.

"Mmm. Delicious."

"Yeah," Hildra agreed, looking around. "I could almost get used to this."

Janx had come to stand before one of the portraits of the old emperors. The man in the picture looked distinctly fishy, quite like Tallis, the emperor the fountain was built after—or like Muirblaag. Staring at it, Janx looked suddenly morose, and Avery didn't have to wonder why. As if there was any doubt, Janx suddenly rubbed his arm right over his newest tattoo. During the jeep-ride through the mountains, Janx and Hildra—and Avery, by his own volition—had tattooed themselves with the names of Muirblaag and Byron, having borrowed the inking equipment from a refugee. Avery hoped Muirblaag's name was the last tattoo he ever received.

Hildra squeezed Janx's shoulder. "It's all right," she said. "He's better off now."

Janx said nothing, but the lines around his mouth deepened and turned down.

"How'd you and Muirblaag meet?" Avery asked him, honestly curious, but also hoping that the recounting would put Janx in a better mood. Avery leaned back, feeling the heat of the flames in the fireplace behind him.

Hildra groaned. "Don't encourage him. Story changes every time."

Janx glared at her mildly. "The truth never changes."

"Does when you're tellin' it."

Janx grinned slowly, and Avery was heartened to see it.

"Mu and me, we met out at sea," Janx began. "This was back during my pirating days. Mu had lammed it from Hissig to get out on a debt he owed Boss Tarl. Made his way halfway across the water 'fore his ship got hit and he wound up in the slave pens of me old ship, the *Sara Ann*. Captain Pink Eye—an albino from the west—he liked to sell mutes to alchemists on Crimlaw. Well, me and ol' Pink

Eye, we never did get on, and things came to a head when 'e said I was cheatin' at cards."

"And you never did," said Hildra.

"I'm wounded at the merest suggestion. So, ol' Pink tries to put me in irons. I had enough mates, though, that I made a fight of it. Knocked me way down to the slave holds and told the mutes if they fought fer me I'd set 'em free. Never did truck with slaves or 'chemists, an' I'd had half a mind to do it earlier. Well, with them at my back, I made a stand of it. Pink got the drop on me, but Mu stuck him right in the neck with an old rusty shiv. I kicked him overboard, and a big ol' crab-fish scoops 'im up in its pincers and takes him down. Me and Mu fought side by side against the rest. Afterwards I made 'im first mate.

"'course, Pink Eye wasn't independent. The wee admiral of our fair privateerin' company was the one and only Red Sethyc, and he didn't 'preciate me takin' over for Pink Eye. This was especially 'cause I refused to take slaves, which were good money. He set his dogs on me, and me and the crew of the *Sara Ann* had to haul it but good. Mutiny after leaving Hakk-na. Mu was the only one that stuck by me in the end. They had the decency to give us a boat an' a ragtag suit. No food or water, though, an' only a day's supply of air in the tank."

Hildra cleared her throat. "Last time it was two days' supply."

"Quiet. I'm about to tell of the mad scientist's isle. Me and Mu, parched and hungry, wash up ashore on this fabulous island ..."

Someone knocked on the door, and all heads bent in that direction.

"Come in," Avery said.

Jynad peeked in. He looked pale, even fearful, and for some reason he seemed unable to look any of them in the eye. Avery leaned forward, suddenly experiencing a wave of foreboding.

"What?" he said. "What is it?"

Jynad swallowed. "Lord Haemlys—he's invited everyone to a feast."

"A *feast?*" Hildra said. "Isn't his whole life a feast?"

Jynad shook his head wretchedly. "You don't understand. He's given up on the intervention of the gods. He's decided to treat with Octung directly."

Avery and the others stared at him. None could find anything to say.

"The Octunggen delegation should arrive soon," Jynad said. "He's holding a formal dinner to receive them." In a low voice, he added, "He's not expecting many to attend, so he's inviting everyone. Please come at once."

As soon as he left, Layanna emerged from her bedroom, yawning, and said, "What did I miss?"

The Throne Room was empty of revelers and orgies. Only a small, grim gathering hunched around the largest, most central feasting table. To Avery's surprise he did not find Haemlys there. A score or so of the God-Emperor's cronies sat sipping ale and wine and looking miserable. Long faces stared at each other, then glanced hastily away.

Some glanced up at the approach of Avery and the others, but they said nothing as the newcomers sat down, even those that moved aside for them. Avery perched on a sturdy oak bench and rested his elbows on the table. Greasy plates heaped atop it with random joints of meat thrusting out. Bejeweled goblets had toppled and stained the beautifully-polished wood, and flies buzzed about, alighting on one plate, then another. Some of the nobles made halfhearted efforts to swat at them. Evidently there had been a minor feast before the main one. The vomitorium would be well used today.

"Excuse me," Avery said, "but where is Lord Haemlys?"

Hostility and pain flickered across their faces. It was the latter that intrigued him. Just when he didn't think anyone would answer, one woman—middle-aged, in the elaborate dress and headgear of a duchess of antiquity—said, "I rather think he's hiding his face."

"And with good reason," said a man across the table from her. His butcher's countenance belied his puffy sleeves and pantaloons. He gazed at Avery and the others, as if mildly curious at their general otherness.

Janx leaned forward. "Why's he done it?" His Ungraessotti was better than Avery's. "Why's he agreed to talk to the Octs?"

One foppish young man snorted in a rather un-lord-like fashion. His floppy green velvet hat slouched over the side of his head. "He's decided Ungraessot can't hold back Octung much longer, and if it tries it will only be destroyed," he said.

"Which it will," added the middle-aged woman that may or may not be a duchess. "But we would die with dignity."

Avery gazed around at the greater room, thinking of the debauchery that was starving the general populace. "Right," he said. "But to simply give up ..."

She nodded, the folds under her neck bunching. The white powder coating her face had begun to liquefy under the barrage of her sweat, and the resulting grease drizzled down her ample cheeks, her forehead and tangled in her carefully-trimmed eyebrows. "We can't believe he's decided to treat with them," she said.

"*Treat* with the bastards!" As if enraged all over again at the merest thought, the butcher-faced man slammed a fist onto the table. His goblet jumped.

Another woman leaned forward. Though young and attractive, one of her eyes was obviously made of glass. In low tones, she said, "You know it's the only way, Surdan. If the Octunggen keep coming, they'll obliterate us. They'll conquer Ungraessot like they've conquered everyone else, and what do you think will happen then? We'll be the first ones they kill. They'll execute us in bloody public spectacles to show the people their leaders are dead and they must look to Octung for control. They'll burn the temples and kill anyone who refuses to worship the Collossum—and that will only be the beginning. Then will come the purgings, the slave camps, the experiments ..."

Surdan glared at her. "And you think they won't do the same if we surrender?"

She started to say something, but evidently could not. Chagrined, she sat back.

The foppish gentleman, who sat beside her, patted her hand. "It's all right, Sis. I for one agree with you. Treating with the Octunggen likely won't save us, but it's our only hope. They do seem to honor their agreements."

"Until it becomes prudent for them to do otherwise," added the middle-aged woman.

"It will buy us time," insisted the fop.

"Time for what?" growled the butcher-faced man, Surdan.

The younger man gestured vaguely with his hands. "Time to organize ... regroup ... maybe fight back."

"You're a fool. They'll kill us all immediately."

The white-faced woman's voice was sharp. "Then what do you suggest?"

Surdan glowered at her, then slumped back, weary and disgusted. He ran a hand over his face. "Perhaps this way is best," he said. "This way at least the Octunggen may spare our people."

Janx grunted. "Yeah. You lot seem like a real people-first bunch."

The silence at the table was sudden and chilly.

Avery cleared his throat. "What my friend meant was, Where is Lord Haemlys? Is he actually treating with the Octunggen now?"

It was the white-faced woman that spoke. "No. He's preparing to meet the delegation here. They're traveling by aeroplane and should be here any minute."

Avery turned to the others of his group and said in Ghenisan, "This is the worst possible news. Not only for Ungraessot, but for us. The Octunggen delegation will completely distract Haemlys. We won't be able to speak with him at all."

"Oh, I don't know about that."

Avery spun to the new speaker, who stood directly behind him. It was, to his shock, Lord Haemlys himself. Dressed in his finest royal clothes, with a burgundy-and-purple cape depending from his broad shoulders, his beard carefully combed, his lobster claw adorned with burgundy ribbons and golden baubles, smelling of fine cologne, he looked a much different man than the one Avery had met last night. Though, by the way he blinked his eyes and scowled, it was clear he suffered some degree of hangover.

"You speak Ghenisan," Avery said.

"I speak a hundred languages."

Not bothering to argue with the obvious exaggeration, the nobles at the table greeted him loudly, but there was no true enthusiasm in their hellos, and he seemed to realize it. He pulled at his beard and frowned out over them.

"I know my decision isn't the popular one," he said. "I know you have your doubts, and with reason. Yet I cannot stand idly by while our country collapses."

"But you're a god!" said one.

He pursed his lips thoughtfully. "I am a messiah of greater gods, as have all those of my line been. But my greater gods, the gods of my fathers and the Father of My Fathers, have all abandoned me. Perhaps I am unworthy. I don't know. I will continue to make sacrifice to them, pray to them, but I cannot depend on them. Thus I must treat with devils."

There was some outcry at this, shouted arguments and curses, a few praises here and there. Avery was impressed by how Haemlys weathered it all, just standing there, regal and poised, especially after his display last night. At last he raised his true hand to placate those of the table. They calmed in fits and starts.

When he had their attention, he said, "It's the only way. Now—prepare yourselves. I've been told the delegation has arrived and is being taken here. I want my friends around me in my time of need. We will feast them and wine them, win them over with our hospitality. Any treating that shall be done shall be done with them drunk and fucked to within an inch of their lives."

There were some reluctant nods and smiles, but most of the guests simply looked grim. Avery turned to see his group looking much the same.

"He's mad," Janx said, speaking in a heated whisper.

"Actually, I think he's on to something," said Hildra.

"Octunggen will not be swayed by food and wine and sex," Layanna said.

"What will they be swayed by?" Avery asked.

"The promise of power. And I'm afraid that can only be had once the aristocracy is dead."

Avery swallowed, remembering the dark times of Ghenisa. "So you think they should fight."

She made an apologetic face. "Fighting would be futile. You cannot defeat Octung."

He felt desperate. "What then?"

"Surdan is right. The nobles must sacrifice themselves to protect their subjects, at least as much as they can."

"That ain't gonna happen," said Janx, hiking a thumb at the room at large, referring to the halted debauch.

The main doors opened with a bang. Everyone jumped. People in conversation ceased talking. Even the priests quit slaughtering their animals. Flanked by guards and led by royal aides, a procession of Octunggen filed into the room.

"Holy shit," said Hildra. "It's really happening."

"Octunggen don't waste time," Layanna said.

The delegation approached. The room's lanterns, braziers and chandeliers glinted off the silver trimmings on their crisp black uniforms, shining boots, peaked caps, and sharp lines. Everything about their appearance was designed to invoke fear, awe, respect. And from the way they snapped their boots on the marble to the way they swiveled their ice-cold gazes around the room, taking it all in, they knew precisely how to evoke the feelings they wanted. There were about a dozen Octunggen, Avery saw, most dark-haired and gray-eyed, the Octunggen ideal, and they cut a neat swath toward the God-Emperor.

Haemlys, flanked by four royal guards, waited for them at the foot of the table. Other guards at the edges of the room stiffened and drew closer.

As the Octunggen approached, Avery could almost feel the temperature of the table decrease. The nobles drew away, just a bit.

With a snap of boots, the Octunggen halted, all in unison, directly before the God-Emperor. The aide that had brought them—not Jynad, Avery saw, but another—bowed to his lord and introduced the lead Octunggen, a tall man with steely gray eyes and more pepper in his hair than salt. His face was hard, businesslike, as if he were merely conducting a professional transaction from a place of some advantage.

"General Varicanus," said the aide, "may I introduce you to his Great Eminence, the Lord of Ungraessot, Wielder of the Jade Scepter, Father of Horns, the Boar in the Woods——"

"Oh, he knows who I am already," Haemlys interrupted. He stepped forward and gave a curt nod, not quite a bow, to General Varicanus, who returned the gesture, adding a stomp of his boot.

As one, the Octunggen behind him stomped their boots, as well, a peal of thunder in the hall.

"Shall we begin?" the General said. His voice was crisp and clear, his accent only seeming to sharpen his words.

Haemlys nodded, with just a hint of fear in his face. He gestured to the table. "Please, I would like you to join me at supper. I've had my finest chefs prepare a grand feast, just for you, and I would like you to enjoy some genuine Ungraessotti hospitality."

General Varicanus visibly suppressed a frown. "If we must." Avery was impressed that he showed no fear of poison.

Disgustingly obsequious, Haemlys ushered the Octunggen to the table, and his fellow nobles moved down for them, squeezing up against each other and shooting each other cold, hard looks. They clearly didn't like this. Avery's own skin crawled to be near the members of the delegation.

Even worse was the realization that he occupied a seat on the outer edge of the group of nobles. He would have to sit *next to* one of the Octunggen.

Just as he realized this, he heard a strange, familiar voice beside his ear.

"Is this seat taken?"

He looked up at the black-uniformed Octunggen that stood there. Short auburn hair framed a slightly squared jaw, and that old scar still showed on the bridge of her nose.

Blue-gray eyes stared at him from over a slightly predatory smile.

"You," he choked.

Sheridan's smile widened.

Chapter 20

He felt cold all over as Sheridan sat down next to him. She moved smoothly, confidently, showing not the slightest discomfort. Indeed, she seemed amused, enjoying this. Her leg actually brushed up against his as she settled in. As if receiving an electric shock, he recoiled.

His mind spun, and he struggled for words, for comprehension. How was this possible? Sheridan should still be pursuing him on her ray, or perhaps she would have returned to some other duty by now, having given up on catching him and Layanna now that they had entered a foreign warzone.

Janx and Hildra found words.

"Holy fucking crap!" said Hildra. "It's her!"

Janx glared at his former captain, his jaws clenching, fists shaking on the table. "The gall!"

No one seemed to notice their exchange. The Octunggen were talking casually amongst themselves, the God-Emperor was making some jest to General Varicanus, who did not seem amused, and the Ungraessotti nobles were whispering darkly to each other.

Rage and frustration, confusion and fear all welled up in Avery, fighting for supremacy.

Sheridan only gazed at him sideways, pleased. "It's good to see you, too, Doctor."

At last one of his emotions won out. "It's not so good for me, Admiral," he snapped, then winced at the brittleness in his voice.

"At the moment I'm not acting as admiral," she said. "I am here as a special advisor to the General."

Janx reached for a fork. Its points glittered in the light of the candles that dripped and sagged on the table. "Retired from navy life, eh?"

She leaned back casually, to all appearances quite comfortable. "Perhaps not. We shall see. At the moment Ghenisa considers me missing, presumed taken captive. A sad fate that our rays were ambushed, our men taken prisoner."

"I bet you loved that," Hildra said. "You probably rolled out the welcome mat."

"At any rate, here you are." This came from Layanna.

Slowly, obviously relishing this, Sheridan turned her attention to the woman from the sea, satisfaction glimmering in her eyes. "*You*. At last. Let me say that it is an honor to break bread with one of the Revered."

"I wish I could say the same."

A rueful twist lifted one corner of Sheridan's mouth. "You led me a merry chase. I almost thought you'd escaped. Fortunately our psychics traced your progress to Maqarl, and our spies were able to confirm you were in the Palace."

Avery reached for a knife. "You have spies here?"

Sheridan eyed his knife. "We have spies everywhere. You of all people should know that."

He forced himself to relax his grip on the utensil. "So. You're still on the hunt."

"*On* the hunt? Oh no, my dear, I'm afraid the hunt has finished." Her gaze flicked once more to Layanna. "I have my quarry in my sights."

"That is not the same as catching it," Layanna said.

"We shall see."

The tension did not ebb as chefs wheeled silver-domed platters out and began to serve the opening round. This whole affair was a hasty, last-minute effort, Avery knew, without the pomp and ceremony it would have normally had—a necessary measure, he recognized—but those in charge did not skimp. Avery had never attended a royal feast before, despite being married to a noblewoman (however impoverished and in hiding), and he found himself in awe at the waste, at the extravagance, at the sumptuousness. Course followed course, from pâté to caviar to braised pork ribs to salad to grilled squid and rice to bowls full of batkin eyes (a delicacy) mixed with dates and nuts to ox tongue to haunch of goat stuffed with cloves to ... And all of it was served with the richest wine imaginable. His mind reeled. His palate staggered.

With Sheridan sitting right next to his elbow, occasionally brushing it, he drank and drank, but it was not enough.

Sheridan, by contrast, sipped her drinks daintily and tackled her meals with relish yet precision. He occasionally caught her dabbing at her mouth with a napkin, her eyes on Layanna, as if confusing meal and prey. Perhaps they were all one to her.

Layanna ate little. She sat there staring downward at times, or letting her gaze wander over the members of the table. Janx ate loudly, taking his anger out on his food, his murderous glare on Sheridan, while Hildra followed Avery's example and let the wine flow freely. She'd found an expensive pack of Ungraessotti cigarettes somewhere and smoked one after another. Hildebrand, having consumed some wine, lay drowsing on the table, occasionally hiccupping. She petted him distractedly.

Meanwhile the God-Emperor laughed nervously and told joke after joke, trying to win General Varicanus over. Yet if the General was warmed he did not show it. Nor did he seem interested in the prospect of an orgy or "private entertainment", an idea which Haemlys wasted no time in laying before him. The God-Emperor's companions did not help very much. A few offered some nuggets of conversation, but most seemed disoriented and uncomfortable. How could they even pretend to make polite conversation with Octunggen?

Finally Sheridan stood and left the table—accompanied by two Ungraessotti guards—presumably to find a washing room, but Avery, who did not want to grant her any human needs, decided she went to scout territory, or, who knows, find a baby to eat.

Hildra took the opportunity to lean forward and say, "Doc, let's get the fuck *outta* here."

Janx nodded, chewing his slug fillet into submission. "I can't take any more of this." Yet he didn't stop chewing.

Layanna looked weary. "We must go to our rooms and pack. We must leave immediately by whatever means necessary. We will have to find another avenue to the Hallowed Halls." She started to rise.

Avery reached out and laid a hand on her forearm. He still wasn't sure what they were supposed to feel for each other after last night, or what he wanted them to feel, and the gesture was self-conscious.

"Yes?" she said.

He let out a breath. "I have a plan."

The others looked at him.

"What?" asked Janx.

"Packing our bags and trying to leave will get us nowhere. I think this delegation is a ruse, and the Octunggen's true aim is to secure Layanna. If that's right, then an attack should come at any time in order to provide cover. Don't you see? There is no escape, not that way. Besides, we're *so close*." He looked at them, meeting each gaze sternly. "All we need is Haemlys to give us access to the Hallowed Halls."

"Yeah," said Hildra. "And?"

Avery was patient. "What's the one thing he wants above all else?"

Hildra frowned. "To get in touch with his stupid gods."

"Exactly. And what is it that we happen to have, sitting right here with us?"

After a beat, all eyes traveled to Layanna.

Avery smiled. "Okay, here's how it will go ..."

Afterwards, they consulted with Jynad. Thinking they merely wanted a tour, the aide showed him and the others to the Soul Door, which actually turned out to be double doors, purple and thirty feet high. The grand, ornate, heavily locked doors were said to be the portal to the afterlife, at least for those of the Verican faith. The God-Emperor opened the palace up to visitors on holy days, and citizens from the furthest reaches of Ungraessot made pilgrimages to see the portal. Thus viewing the Door itself was not off-limits—it was the door to the afterlife; little chance of keeping that from the people—though it was set in a quiet area of the sublevels, guarded by well-armed guards, and kept locked with a key only the God-Emperor had access to.

"Nice," said Hildra, staring up at the high, purple-lacquered doors. Their edges were bossed in solid gold, and the knobs gleamed of gold as well. "So—behind those is heaven, eh?"

"Not heaven," said Jynad. "We are not Haggaran. Our afterlife is very real."

"We know what we need to do," Avery said later, when they'd left the Soul Door and separated from Jynad. "Everyone know what their assignments are?" They nodded. "Layanna, are you up for it?"

"After last night, yes."

"Then we'll all meet back here at midnight."

Janx and Hildra departed to scavenge for supplies, while Avery returned to the suite and packed. Layanna set out to get in place. Thus Avery was all alone in the suite when knocking came from the door.

Hairs prickled down his spine. He stared at the door, a pair of socks raised halfway. *Please no*, he thought. *I don't have time for this.* Already Layanna would be wrapping things up, if Haemlys kept to his usual schedule, or what guests of the palace had assured them was usual.

The knocking came again, more forcefully.

With some misgiving, he quit his packing and opened it.

Sheridan looked just as crisp and sharp in her black uniform as she had earlier. Ungraessotti guards stood to either side of her, not willing to let an Octunggen roam the halls unattended. She seemed to ignore them completely.

Avery's stomach dropped. *Damn her.* Everything depended on speed, on secrecy.

"Sheridan," he said.

"May I ... ?" She gestured to his suite.

He glanced from her to the guards, mentally debating for a moment—did he really want to find out what she would do if he refused?—then sighed and said, "Come in."

He pulled the door back for her as she entered. She smelled of musk.

The royal guards started to follow her in, but she spun and held them back. "I can't go anywhere in here. I'm harmless. And the doctor and I need privacy."

"Is that acceptable, sir?" one of the guards asked Avery.

He didn't see that he had a choice. "We'll be fine," he said.

The guards took up positions to either side of the door. Reluctantly, he closed it and turned to Sheridan.

"What is this about?"

She had a strange look on her face. Stern but sort of ... sad. Saying nothing, she pushed past him and strolled deeper into the suite. "Have anything to drink?" she asked.

"Admiral, this is quite—"

"Ah! Here we go." She found an expensive bottle, then a glass from the rack, and poured herself a healthy dose. "I'm going to need this. So are you."

"Why are you here?"

She took a sip. "Mmm. Yes, I must say that's not bad."

"Admiral!"

"You're not being very sociable, Doctor, are you? I would be friendlier if I were you."

"Why?" His voice had an edge to it.

She set her glass down and handed him something. It looked like a photograph. "See for yourself. You ... you'll want to sit down."

With a sniff, he accepted the picture. "This had better be good."

Her eyes betrayed nothing except pity. "Oh, it is. It is."

Something about her voice made his hairs prickle again. His gaze traveled to the picture. It took him a moment to focus on it, to take it in, and when he did it seemed as if the world tilted sideways.

"*Ani*," he choked. It was a picture of his daughter.

Nameless emotion rose in him. Pain flowered in his chest, and something burned his eyes. All at once, strength left him, and he fell to his knees. His vision blurred as he stared at the photograph in his hand.

The little girl was undeniably his daughter, Anissa. What was more, it was not an old picture. *It was new.* He could tell from the faint discolorations on her cheeks and neck caused by the disease that had killed her. And it *had* killed her— brutally, terribly, slowly. In the picture, however, her eyes glittered with life, and there was even a small smile on her face as she stared into the camera's lens. Despite the smile and glitter, though, she looked somehow sad. Even afraid.

She stood before a gray wall and held up an issue of a newspaper that was dated only weeks ago. She looked very skinny. Very frail.

"How?" he heard himself asking, his voice raw, strained. "How is this possible?" He wrenched his gaze loose from the photo with an almost violent effort. He glared up at Sheridan, who stood blurrily before him. "*How?*"

Even through the blurriness, she appeared sorrowful. "You worked with the scientists," she said. "You must have heard rumors of what went on in the levels below. You must have even known some of the doctors that worked there—Wasnair, for example."

"Wasnair ..."

"Surely you heard about the resurrection project he was overseeing. The attempt to bring battlefield dead back to life to fight for Ghenisa? No? The project has been going on for years, and only lately have they begun to enjoy some success. When you helped Layanna escape and vanished, I decided some leverage might be useful, something to hold over you. So—I emptied your wife and daughter's grave."

Pain flooded through him. Rage. Shaking, he forced himself to his feet. "*What have you done?*"

Her face hardened, as did her voice. Somehow he sensed this was not done in anger but to mask her feelings. "The bodies were preserved alchemically," she said, "but the alchemical agent was very cheap. You must have been ... quite poor." This was not said meanly, but almost regretfully. "It would have only preserved them for a short while, a few decades maybe. And the amount injected in your wife was simply inadequate. She'd already faded. Your daughter, however ..."

"No ..." Shaking his head, he staggered forward.

She stepped back. "We've brought her back, Doctor. Look, I'm sorry to tell you this in such a manner. I understand loss like you cannot believe. I had a daughter that was taken from me, too." Her voice hitched, just barely, but she cleared her throat and plowed on: "I would give anything for the chance you have now. Listen to me, Francis." It was one of but a few times when she had ever called him by name. "Listen. *You can have her back.*" She stared at him, letting that sink in. "And it's really *her*. Not some brain-dead thing. Not some horror. It's *your daughter*. She's in the care of Dr. Wasnair at the moment. She was only the third lab subject for the process to work on. Sadly, she'll be the last. I tried to retrieve the plans for the process for use by Octung, but they were too cumbersome to remove and too detailed to copy, so I had them destroyed. A shame to destroy the secret to immortality, but I could not let Ghenisa have an edge in the war, could I?"

For a moment, reason returned to Avery, but he could feel that it was shifting and elusive and would shortly be gone. "She's ... in a lab? Where? Brunt? How is she? *Tell me how she is.*" This last part came out in a growl. He took a step forward, hands bunching and unbunching at his sides.

"She's fine, Francis." Her voice deliberately hardened as she added the hook: "They're taking good care of her, just as they would with any specimen during the observation period."

Something triggered in him. Something berserk. He stalked forward and grabbed up a lantern.

Sheridan held her ground. "Don't, Doctor. It only takes a word from me and the observation period ends. Then they start experimenting on her. In doing so, they might be able to recreate the process."

He howled, and the lantern rose in his hands.

"Or I can simply have her destroyed," Sheridan said.

He brought the lantern down.

She stepped out of the way. His elbows flared as it shattered into a thousand pieces on the floor. A small hard fist struck his belly, then a knee, and he found himself gasping on the floor, staring upwards. Sheridan seemed to revolve around him.

The guards outside started to force the door inward, he could hear it thumping in its frame.

"Just take me to Layanna, Doctor, and Ani will be yours again," Sheridan said. She offered him a hand. "My agents lost her somehow, the Collossum. Please. Your daughter and you can be happy together. Just take me to—"

The doors burst in. The guards stormed toward Sheridan, guns drawn. Barking orders at her, they surrounded her and aimed at her chest. "Back away! Back off!"

Warily, she stepped back from Avery, and the guards followed her.

Wheezing, Avery climbed to his feet. The world spun, and he felt sick at his stomach. *Ani. Can it really be?* His rage had somewhat drained away, replaced by exhaustion, replaced by the urgency to return to Layanna and the others. They would leave soon. It was already midnight.

In front of him the guards indicated for Sheridan to lie down and not move. Ignoring them, she said, "Well, Doctor, what will it be? Layanna or your daughter?"

He started to answer, then shook his head. His mind still wasn't clear enough to form a reply. He honestly didn't know himself in that moment what he wanted. He hefted his bags over his shoulder and lurched toward the door.

He heard the ring of metal behind him.

A gunshot shook the room, and Avery jumped. Somewhere a body thumped.

He spun to see Sheridan slitting the throat of one guard with a blade that she had produced from somewhere while the other guard flopped about on the ground, the artery of his gun-wrist slashed. Sheridan wrestled the gun away from the standing guard and shoved him back.

Avery moved at greater speed toward the door. Behind him he could imagine Sheridan wiping blood from her eyes. Then she would be up, aiming—

The blast took him by surprise, even though he had half-expected it.

He had just cleared the door when he felt something whiz by his ankle. A puff of carpet shot up into the air.

He ran. A second round and then a third followed, but he was already bounding down the hall.

Ani, he thought, still bewildered, his mind fuddled. *Sheridan's brought her back!*

He pushed the thought aside. He needed what wits he had left to flee.

He turned just in time to see Sheridan stagger from the room, raising her gun as she did. He ducked down a side-hall. The gun roared. Plaster from the opposite wall sprayed him. Coughing, he lurched away. *Guards*, he thought. *Guards will be coming. I only need to last a moment.*

Just then, he heard the sound of Octunggen bombers overhead.

It was an entire fleet from the sound of it. Just as Avery had suspected, the Octunggen had never meant to honor any negotiation. Sending the diplomatic team had only been a ruse designed to get a team in place to retrieve Layanna.

Just as he rounded another corner, the first bombs struck.

The ground pitched beneath his feet. Flung him against a wall. His head rang. Gasping, he pushed himself off, tasting blood on his tongue.

Screams echoed up the hall. Air-raid sirens wailed both outside and inside, blaring in his ears.

Another bomb struck. Another.

The floors shook. The walls ahead buckled, and a plume of plaster dust engulfed him. Coughing, he pressed on. Agonized screams came from a room nearby.

A gunshot behind him. He felt something sting his neck. He put a hand to it, drew away blood. Just a surface wound. It burned like fire.

Another gunshot roared. A man stumbling from his bombed room took the round in the face. Brains exploded out the back of his skull. He reeled backward, hit the wall and slid down it, leaving a trail of blood and brain matter.

Avery ducked down another hall.

Sheridan coughed behind him as she entered the cloud of plaster. "Stop running!"

"Go to hell!" he screamed over his shoulder as he reached a stairway and started down it.

He passed a window and beheld the city of Maqarl laid out below him. Fire and smoke roiled up from the buildings descending the slopes, bright pyres and thick black columns that blocked out the stars. The great bridges that spanned the misty gaps smoked; one had collapsed. Fires dotted the mountain peaks on the other side, and huge bombers drove through the pall of smoke that hung over the city. Guns on rocky summits boomed, spitting fire. One of the bombers' tails exploded, and the craft corkscrewed into the central mountain and erupted with a bright flash. Many bombs struck near the processing plants, the great buildings that protected Maqarl from Octung's otherworldly weapons. If the Octunggen destroyed them ...

The balustrade beside Avery exploded, pelting him with shrapnel. He ran down the stairs, taking them two at a time.

More bombs rocked the palace. People took to the halls, stumbling and confused. Some pushed through the press, looking for escape. Soldiers rushed amongst them, on the way outside to help their comrades. Avery knew then that there must be a ground assault, too. Paratroopers.

He plunged into the crowd, elbowing his way through the thick of it. Someone tried to punch him in the ribs. He punched back. He heard shouts and cursing behind him. Sheridan followed. He craned his head to see a glimpse of her here and there. Bloody-faced, she had torn off her Octunggen tunic and had shrugged on the shirt of the man whose brains she'd splattered. Blood had dripped on it, but at least it was not Octunggen, otherwise the crowd might have torn her apart.

Avery plowed his way down a certain hallway, reached a stairwell going down. He had memorized the route but was still uncertain in the confusion. No, this was right. He recognized the statue of a six-armed jade goddess at the base of the stairwell. He hooked right at the statue and made his way down a richly appointed hall lined by prized artifacts in glass cases. There were fewer people down here, as there were no apartments and no access to the outside.

Sheridan yelled behind him. Her gun cracked. Beautifully stained wood splintered by his hip. She was not trying to kill him, only incapacitate him. Of course, one was as good as the other.

"You're a fool!" she shouted as he threw himself down another hall. "It doesn't have to be like this! There's a section in the east wing, they won't bomb there. It's where the General and the others are. Waiting for us. Just help me bring Layanna to them."

A lie, he thought. The General and his men would be out hunting for Layanna, too. Obviously the bombing was a diversion to draw the guards away so that they could abduct her, to create general confusion to make it easier. But they had not counted on Layanna being through the Soul Door.

And yet ... Avery believed her. There would be a safe area in the palace. There would be a place where they could take Layanna and ready her for transportation. But as for him ...

"You'll kill me—as soon as—you have—her!" he panted.

"No," she said. "I won't." Gasping, she called, "You'll be—safe with us. And you'll have—your daughter."

He didn't reply.

A gunshot cracked behind him. Splinters of woods sprayed his arm.

Almost there. He heard her reloading behind him. She had stolen the guards' ammo. Clever.

He reached another stairway, darted down it. Stumbled. Righted himself. Bombs shook the palace above. Dust rained down. In the distance, people screamed.

"I mean it," she shouted behind him. "You can have Ani."

He turned down a hallway just as another bomb dropped. The ceiling caved in. He lunged forward, threw himself flat and slid, but too late. Debris buried him. The impact was so great it ruptured the floor beneath, and he fell into a crater. Plaster dust choked his lungs, and he coughed and wheezed, struggling up through the avalanche. Something hit his head. Glanced off his shoulder. Somewhere he heard Sheridan cursing.

At last the debris settled, and he found himself trapped among sections of flooring material. Frantically, he tore away a section of wood planking, then shoved away a stone. He labored for breath.

Fresh air. He smelled it somewhere ahead.

A blackened stone block shifted before him, and he came face to face with Sheridan. She was covered in soot, her cap lost, her hair in disarray, and blood oozed from a cut on her scalp. Her gun was nowhere in sight. She was just far enough away that he couldn't reach her.

They stared at each other in the dimness, which was only brightened by vague shafts of light cutting through debris above. Avery felt a nail pressing into his side and shifted his weight. For some reason he couldn't tear his gaze away from her. Had he ever really known her? Who was she, really?

"I wasn't lying, Francis," she said, and her voice was almost gentle. "We have your daughter, and we'll give her to you. You can believe anything about me you like, but believe that."

"No." He shook his head. His skull ached, and he wondered if he had a concussion.

She let out a long breath. "Where are you going, Francis? Why isn't Layanna in the Palace? Why are you down here ... ?" Realization entered her eyes. "It's the Soul Door, isn't't? You're going into the Halls!" She laughed, half madly. "Why? What could *possibly* be in there to interest you? Where are you going?"

"I can't tell you, you know that." He sniffed. Fresh air wafted in from his right ... He shifted sideways and shoved away the obstruction.

"Ani," she said, and he stopped. "If you're going into the Halls, I'll meet you there. There's a place, supposedly the jewel of the afterlife—Cuithril."

He stiffened.

Her eyes gleamed. "So that's it, is it? Well, don't worry. I can meet you there. No, don't say no. You know you want to. Have Layanna subdued for me, and I'll give you your daughter."

"You're insane." He began kicking the obstruction away.

"No. But I'm a mother, or I was, and I know what lengths I would've gone to to save my little girl. And it's for the best, it really is. Trust me. You're on the wrong side of this thing."

He kicked and kicked. Debris rained down on him, but he didn't care. His leg throbbed. "I'm not listening to you!"

The obstruction gave way.

"Cuithril!" she shouted. "I'll meet you there!"

He rolled down the mound of debris, dusted himself off, shook away his dizziness, and staggered down the hall. There was still time. There was still—

Shifting behind him. He spun to see Sheridan climbing out of the debris, wrenching her gun out of the mouth of a broken statue. Coughing even worse than he, she slid down the mound and picked herself up.

He fled.

A round punched out a hole in the doorway to one side of him.

"Gods *damn* you!" he shouted, feeling himself start to snap. His nerves were frayed to their breaking point. "Don't you *ever* give up?"

It occurred to him that, for such a marksman, she was aiming awfully badly—

He went cold. *She was herding him.*

Well, the hell with it. She'd guessed his destination anyway. There was nothing for it now. Hopefully the guards at the Soul Door would drive her back or kill her. His heart smashed against his ribs as he ran for it. At last he rounded a final bend and came in sight of the purple-lacquered Door, rearing like the façade of a temple.

The guards were gone.

Shit.

The doors were open.

Panting, he stumbled through them and down the wide marble stairway below. The formal pathway ended and became a rocky pinnacle overlooking a black stone valley. A sort of dock structure clung to the pinnacle. Avery descended another set of stairs, these wooden and creaking under him. Darkness surrounded him. Bats chittered somewhere, the sound echoing across vast distances. The plink of water, the stink of minerals. Caves. *The Hallowed Halls.* He had made it.

Lights ahead.

He picked his way down the scaffolding, toward the glimmering lights. He saw lantern-light stroking the gunwale of a gondola, saw the long, golden balloon adorned with the Royal Crest of Ungraessot, a mountain peak against a flaming sun, saw Janx and Layanna in the dirigible's stern while Hildra fiddled with the steering column. To the side, on the docks, Jynad issued final instructions.

Avery darted past him and bounded over the gunwale. The others stared at him, shocked.

"Your gun!" Avery pointed to the pistol strapped under Janx's arm. He hadn't even known Janx had a gun, but he had counted on it. The whaler would have armed himself as soon as possible. "Give it—now!"

Confused but quick, Janx unholstered his gun and tossed it.

Just as Avery heard boots rattle above, he spun and fired up into the darkness. He saw a shape framed in the doorway and emptied a round at it. He didn't think he struck it, but the shape moved. A flash of fire burst from it. Something thunked behind him.

Avery fired again. The shape above cursed in Octunggen and lunged backward through the door.

Eyes wide, Avery turned to the others. "No time! Let's go!" He tossed the pistol to Jynad. "Here, you'll need this." Jynad fumbled with the gun, holding it like a dead rat. Avery considered. "I advise you to duck and hide. In fact, maybe you should come with us."

Jynad straightened his back. "My place is here."

"Good luck." To the others, Avery said, "Cast off! Cast off!"

Frantically Janx untied ropes. Hildra tended to the gears. Sweat stinging his eyes, Avery helped Janx. The dirigible cast off from the docks and drifted out into the darkness of the caverns.

Something appeared in the doorway behind, seemingly a hundred miles away, and a dark shape slipped down the docks. Something flashed in its hand, and after a moment Avery heard the gun's report. He hoped Jynad was hiding securely. The gun cracked again, again, clearly aimed at the dirigible this time, but the airship was too far away.

The palace trembled above. Sheridan fired again, surely enraged at their escape, but Avery and the others slipped away into the darkness.

Janx laughed and raised a bottle. They had snagged several from the suite.

"I gotta hand it to ya, Doc, it went off just like you said."

Hildra wrestled the bottle from him and took a long swallow. "Ol' Haemlys took the bait—hook, line and stinker. Wish I'd been there to see it."

Attention turned to Layanna, who had been the only one present during the event itself except for the God-Emperor. Hell, she had *been* the event.

She gave a small smile and tipped a nod to Avery. As she did, her eyes made contact with his, and he felt something pass between them, but then she shifted her gaze too suddenly, and he was left wondering what it had been.

"It was a good plan," she allowed. "You're lucky, though. Almost I missed him, the son of fathers. I nearly came too late."

"Tell us," Hildra urged. She shoved the bottle into Layanna's hands, the greatest display of camaraderie she'd ever shown her.

Layanna stared at the bottle as if wondering what it was exactly. Then, with a shrug, she upended it, gulping loudly. Avery smiled to hear such human sounds. When Layanna lowered the bottle, she grimaced, wiped her mouth and blinked. With care, she leaned forward and passed Avery the bottle, avoiding his eyes as she did.

"Tell us," Janx called.

Perhaps feeling the effects of the drink, Layanna smiled and leaned back against the gunwale, stretching like a cat. The wood groaned around them, and the canvas of the balloon crackled above, over the hiss of flame and gas. To all sides came the faint echoes of the dirigible's noises bouncing off cavern walls. Occasionally something would croak or hoot or chitter out in all that blackness, and Avery was glad for the feeble lights.

"Well," Layanna said, "first I hid myself in the altar fountain, just as the doctor prescribed, and ate while I waited."

"That's disgusting," Hildra said.

The bottle was passed around. Something chirruped in the darkness. Something splashed. A subterranean river ran below.

"The God-Emperor came, drunk and raging," Layanna continued. "The Octunggen were using him, he knew it, could sense it. He had received another ngvandi prisoner, and he had his priest prepare it for sacrifice." With satisfaction evident in her voice, she said, "I accepted."

Janx guffawed. "Beautiful!"

Hildra leaned forward. "What then?"

Layanna accepted the bottle back—it had reached her again—and knocked back a long, healthy swig. After grimacing, she said, "Once he saw me in my other-form and knew what I was, he did what he'd been wanting for a long time. He begged me for aid against Octung. I told him, quite honestly, that to stop Octung he must assist the visitors that had arrived yesterday. He must give them access to the Underworld, to the Halls of the Royal Dead, let them travel through them toward Octung. His eyes blazed, and he wept. He said he would gift them his personal dirigible, his royal mode of transportation when he deigned to visit the deeps, to pay homage to his kin, and eventually to journey there. And thus we are here. All thanks to the doctor."

They made noises of appreciation to Avery, and he smiled deprecatingly. "It just came to me at the table today," he said, "when Haemlys said he would continue making sacrifices to his gods. I thought, 'I wonder what would happen if one *answered*?'"

"Nice thinking," Hildra said, then her smile turned sad. "You think it's still going on? The attack?"

Something croaked and splashed in the waters below. Avery wondered how often Haemlys had cruised these lightless paths. How often had he communed with his fathers and their fathers? Did any still truly wander down here as the legends claimed, living here after their allotted time as rulers had passed? The Ungraessotti believed the tales. None but the God-Emperor and his retainers would even venture down here, and over the years it had become taboo for anyone else to do so. This place was dangerous, it was said—for the fathers were hungry. Dangerous yet sacred.

At last Layanna said, "It was a large-scale attack, but it was behind enemy lines, so I don't think they could have taken the city. But they could have knocked out the processors and set it up for destruction later. Or they could have done enough damage to scare Haemlys into surrendering. But primarily the attack was a feint so Sheridan and the general could capture me."

She handed the bottle to Avery, who took the last swig and opened another. They passed the new bottle around, and a gloom fell over them as they sipped in silence. They had destroyed, possibly, two cities after entering Ungraessot, may have doomed the nation, and for what?

Janx broke the mood. "Oh, fuck it," he said. "We're alive and it's clear sailin' to Octung, more or less. We get there, we do our business, and get out. All's well, the world saved, and free pussy for all."

Hildra cleared her throat.

"And cock," he amended. "Now. I see a gramophone over there—the emperor knows how to travel in style—so let's have some music. And let's have some dancin'." With that, he reached his hands into a recess and pulled out the gramophone, along with several records. He scanned them, smiled and placed one on the turntable. The sounds of jazzy music filtered out.

Hildra laughed, and she and Janx climbed to their feet. Janx bowed to her and offered a hand. "Would ya?"

"Oh, deary me, lord sa, I'd love to."

First she reduced their speed and tied off the wheel so that the ship was traveling down a straight line, then she took his hand, laughing drunkenly, and they began to dance. They moved about the deck of the dirigible, now pressed against each other, now twirling, now jimmying and jiving. And all the while the dirigible moved through the darkness, and Avery imagined dark creatures watching them from the waters and mires below. But with the singing and dancing, the things that lived in the blackness seemed somehow muted and powerless.

Avery, surprising himself, hauled himself to his feet and looked down at Layanna.

He stretched out a hand. "Madam, would you care ...?"

She stared up at him as though he were mad. "You must be joking."

He shook his head, smiling a little. "No. I'm afraid I'm quite serious."

She started to protest. Then, very deliberately, she paused. She thought about it. The jazzy music played on, bright and gay in this dark place, and Janx and Hildra continued dancing. It was clear the merriment moved Layanna much as it did Avery. At last, looking surprised at herself, she reached out, grabbed Avery's hand and allowed him to pull her up.

Her body pressed up against him, and he felt awkward as he positioned himself against her. He felt her breath against his cheek. They were about the same height. *My mermaid,* he thought, wonderingly.

Slowly in the beginning, haltingly and uncomfortably, they danced. At times they bumped up against the gunwale, at times they nearly stumbled over something lying on the deck, but by degrees they got smoother, better. What was more, he felt good doing it. He felt warm. That hollow place inside him felt at least partially occupied for the first time in a long while.

At one point they backed against the steering column, and Layanna was pressed up against him. After some awkward fumbling, Avery led her back a few steps and they renegotiated where to position their hands.

Her face looked very pretty in the lantern light. Her lips were very full.

Impulsively, he kissed her.

It seemed to take her by surprise. For a moment, she resisted, but then she kissed back.

At last she pulled away. "No ... no." She placed her hands gently but firmly on his chest. Shaking her head, she walked away.

Part of him wanted to go after her, but instead he let her go. The gramophone played on, and Janx and Hildra danced.

Alone, Avery moved to the gunwale and watched the cavern walls scroll by, and suddenly, no longer distracted by dancing and music, he remembered Sheridan.

Ani.

He was shaking by the time he removed the picture over his heart, the photograph of Mari and Ani. His gaze moved to Ani, so happy, so beautiful. Then he took out the new picture, the one Sheridan had given him. Ani smiled back at him, scared and sad but alive. His eyes burned. His throat closed off.

Sheridan will meet me in Cuithril. There's still a chance. There's still a chance! All I have to do is damn the world.

Trembling, he returned the pictures to his pocket.

He crossed to the wheel and took it. Everything would be fine, he told himself. They would find their way through the caverns, through the legendary Cuithril, they would locate the Black Sect in Lusterqal, Layanna would build the Device, and the world would be saved.

But not for Ani.

Chapter 21

The dirigible was sinking. It only dipped slowly, so it was hard to notice at first. Finally, though, Avery realized the cavern ceiling was farther away than it should have been.

"I think we've got a problem," he announced.

The brief dance after their victorious getaway from the palace had ended, and Avery and the others quickly searched the dirigible, at last finding a small hole in one of the gas bags. A thin whisper leaked out.

"Shit," Hildra said. "That bitch shot our fuel."

"Lucky it didn't blow us up," Janx said. "Here, we can patch it."

He sounded confident, and sure enough it didn't take him long to seal it up. Yet the dirigible continued to sink—slowly, yet inexorably. Avery and the others tried to find another hole, but if there was one they couldn't locate it. Avery estimated that they had another hour before the dirigible touched down.

Worried, the group began looking over the gunwale in an effort to see what waited for them down there. The answer was not encouraging.

"Those things are really old kings?" Hildra said.

Below them ngvandi—or beings very much like ngvandi—moved through the stone tunnels, naked, some holding spears or crude clubs. On some of the spears severed heads were mounted.

If those are the kings, I'd hate to meet the subjects, Avery thought. He knew the mutants that lived down here were supposed to be the descendants of Ungraessotti god-emperors and the retainers they had taken with them into the dark; over hundreds of years there had developed a population of sorts. But the mutants Avery and the others saw were wild, degenerate specimens, worse than the ngvandi that roamed the Borghese.

"We may have to set down amongst them," Layanna said.

"Let's hope it doesn't come to that," Avery said. "Hopefully our fuel will last."

"Last till *when?*" Hildra said.

Avery sensed it before he saw it, the roar and susurrus of water. And even, from up here, the stink of brine. The others noticed it, too, and they all rushed to the bow.

The cavern they were passing through had opened out and become enormously tall and wide, almost so wide that it was like being outdoors. Below them the land terminated at a rocky shore extending left and right as far as they could see, and ahead stretched a vast black body of water.

"A sea," Avery muttered. "An underground sea."

Far above the water, what seemed like perhaps a mile, a shaft of sunlight lanced in through a thin crack in the cavern ceiling. The shaft beamed down past massive stalactites about which flittered dark shapes that might be giant batkin or slug-like flails, beamed down through air so black that the light only seemed to illuminate how dark it truly was, down onto the slowly surging sea below. White caps denoted waves, turgid, lazy waves that rolled back and forth, sometimes smashing with languid force against rearing stone towers that must be ancient stalagmites from before this area was flooded. Ghostly wisps of fog curled above the waves, coiled about the stalagmites and then pressed on, moving with mysterious purpose. A huge white shape breached the black water far out, let out a strange moan, then sounded.

Avery stared. The others made sounds of awe.

The ship sailed through the air over the water, below the huge stalactites that hung down like the fangs of gods. Avery felt their weight hovering over him, immense and deadly. The muddy nests of flails studded some of them, and the sticky, winged slug-things could occasionally be seen sweeping over the misty water or sucking slime off a jutting stalagmite.

The ship passed through drooping bulwarks of minerals, and Avery felt small and puny, aware of just how insignificant the ship was over such a sea. The waterway wound along a huge cavern, then hit another. Avery supposed a whole system of great caverns must enclose the sea.

"At least it's not the Atomic," he said, the wheel gripped tightly in his hands.

Janx grunted. "Ain't that the truth. Don't have to worry about gettin' hit by lightning. No environment suits. Shit, you could take a swim if ya wanted."

"Have at it," Hildra said.

Bubbles ripped the surface of the water, and Avery saw a huge steaming burst of air belch from the sea. The gas, methane possibly, drifted up and up to lodge against the ceiling overhead. He saw other bubbles, too, spaced out over the water. There could be whole clouds of trapped gas over the sea, slithering among the stalactites. Possibly volatile gas.

For a moment he feared that the dirigible's flame might ignite the vapor, but the flame was well enclosed. However, if someone lit a match ...

"No cigarettes," Avery warned, then, to Janx: "Or cigars."

Avery felt as if he was in some primordial time, perhaps back when the giant bugs known as Carathids lumbered across the land and filled the skies with their incessant buzzing; even the atmosphere felt different. And all the while the dirigible sank lower ... and lower ...

At last it skimmed above the water, and Avery recoiled at the thought of setting down. The dirigible *might* float, but—

"I hear something," Hildra said.

"What?" said Avery.

Her expression was puzzled. "I don't know. Just a general ... humming."

Frowning, Avery guided the ship through up-thrusting spires of rock while Hildra stood at the bow and used a pole to shove them off any stalagmites that drew too close. Avery could smell their mineral reek, the odor of copper and iron and ozone and stone. The air grew colder, and when the fog caressed his skin he found it oily and unpleasant.

Shortly he heard sounds. At first he perceived the sounds collectively as a sort of hum, a background noise, oddly familiar. Then, as they grew louder, he began to break the sounds down into their component parts. A clanging here, a squeal there ...

They came upon it with unexpected speed. It rose out of the mist like a mountain. Like a range of mountains. The mist seemed to roll away from the dirigible, clear from it for just a brief moment, and in that moment Avery felt his jaw drop open.

Ahead, beyond a rocky beach, huge towers rose high, strange and humped—and many. One after another, great spires hunched and thrust toward the cavern ceiling, some even seeming to merge with massive stalactites hanging down. A layer of mist—no, *cloud*—stirred against the ceiling between the giant stalactites, and to Avery's shock he saw what looked like precipitation falling onto the city below. Those towers were *buildings*. Lights blazed in a thousand windows—ten thousand. Bridges spanned the airy gaps between structures, and figures shuffled across the bridges bearing torches and lanterns which shone even over the mist-filled sea.

All at once the strange hum Avery had heard, and the clangs, and screeches, and the rest, all resolved itself into an unmistakable noise—the noise of a city.

"Gods below," said Janx.

"Cuithril," Layanna said.

"Are you certain?" Avery asked her.

"Yes." She paused, as if just sensing something. "I can feel it. Yes, yes there it is ..."

"What?" asked Hildra. "What do you feel?"

"A functioning altar."

Avery tried not to frown. He knew Layanna had been hoping for just such a find. Only through a so-called functioning altar could she transmit the plans for the Device. If she could do that, she would save their little crew the trouble of having to navigate through the Hallowed Halls and reach Lusterqal at the heart of Octung. But to find an altar here ... He didn't like it. He suspected this could only lead to trouble.

Layanna, however, looked optimistic. "We're here at last," she said.

"Just in time," Janx said, his eyes on a light blinking from the console. "We were about to have to start using this heap as a boat. Get ready to set down."

"The locals may not be friendly," Hildra said.

"At least they're civilized," Layanna said. "Unlike the ferals we've been seeing."

Avery lowered the dirigible toward the shore, not that it needed much lowering. Vast docks crawled along the beach of the metropolis, heaped and shambling. Small wooden towers blinked lights out over the harbor. Numerous boats plied the harbor's black waters, the activity clearing some of the mist. Hunched forms carried nets and poles. Fishermen. Avery realized he and the others must have passed over boats on the water without even realizing it.

Avery set them down on the rocky ground just past the docks, with a groan and a jar that nearly pitched him off his feet. He climbed out and shook his head.

The stench of fish was everywhere as fishermen hauled in their catches, some still squirming in their nets. The fishes' sides flashed and glinted by the light of torches mounted on regularly-spaced poles. Some were not normal fish but held interesting deformities, spines adorning fins, tongues growing out of gills. Avery didn't have time to study them, though. Janx, veteran of the wharfs of the world, shoved the way before them and barked for the others to follow at his heels.

The fishermen were mutants, of course. Infected. Or at least the progeny of infected people. Avery had noticed it without surprise, but now he saw specific details; a scar bisecting a set of pulsing gills, still glistening; a bulging red-shot eye, a fishy mouth whose slashed lip oozed pus; catfish-like whiskers.

"A city of mutants," Avery marveled.

The mutants eyed Avery and the others doubtfully. He knew his little band didn't look normal to them, or whatever passed for normal around here. However, there was enough variety among the mutants around him—indeed some looked more human than not—that he hoped their physical appearances would escape suspicion. Or perhaps it had been their method of arrival that drew the attention. There was a lot of activity along the docks, though, and dirigibles were apparently not unheard-of, for the people here only took passing notice before going back to their business.

A mutant emerged from the throng and stepped in their path. He was tall and broad, covered in scales, and when he opened his mouth he revealed jagged needle-like teeth. Coal-black eyes with no whites whatsoever glared at Janx in the lead.

"*Ti gunth ir ablun se cun gana?*" the creature barked, his hands tightening on the length of pipe he carried. Two thug-like specimens that seemed to be his mates hovered at his back, tense and ready with the rusty chains they carried at their sides. One boasted spikes and barbs, the other heavy blunt objects, oversized nuts and bolts.

"What the hell'd he say?" Hildra said.

Avery was trying to decipher that, as well. As best he could tell, the creature spoke some degraded and likely ancient form of Ungraessotti. Translating it to himself, he said, "I believe he wants us to state our business."

"*Suyen!*" ordered the creature with the black eyes. He was growing visibly agitated. "*Suven un grata!*"

Avery was mustering his Ungraessotti together for a reply when Janx spoke up.

"We're here on our own business," the whaler said. He spoke, clearly and levelly, in modern Ungraessotti.

"Where are you from?" the dock creature responded in the same tongue as before. His voice was thick and watery, his dialect strange, but after struggling with it Avery began to pick up his words. The creature evidently understood Janx just fine.

"Like I said, that's our business," the whaler said.

"I must report you."

"No. You don't." Janx clapped a huge hand on his shoulder, and the creature raised his pipe. Janx squeezed, just a little. "Not so fast. See, we're on your side."

"How's that? You're foreign, maybe hostile. From Castursab for all I know. Whatever you're about can't be approved by the Great One."

"What I'm here for is to make you rich, my good man." Janx gestured back the way they'd come, toward the dirigible. "See that? That's yours if you can answer one question the way I want it."

The fish-man studied the ship, and his eyes widened. "Is that ... a ship of a *God-Emperor*?"

"It is indeed. Now the question: what place is this?"

The man looked at him as if he were an idiot. "This is Cuithril."

Janx turned to Avery and the others and muttered, "Had to be sure. It's the waypoint Layanna saw, right?" To the mutant, he said, "The ship is yours."

The infected man cast a nervous look back at his thugs, perhaps wondering how much of a cut they would demand. At last he told Janx, "You've got a deal."

Janx grabbed his hand and pumped it, then, without giving the others time to object, he ushered them quickly past the docks.

"Nicely done," Hildra said.

"Bribery works on every dock I've ever been on."

Avery was hardly listening. "I'm not sure of the wisdom in abandoning our vehicle. We have a long way to go yet through the Hallowed Halls."

"That ship was trouble, Doc," Janx said.

"Too recognizable," Hildra agreed. "We need something less, well, kingly. Or emperor-ly."

"Then we should have at least gotten some money for it."

"*Then* it wouldn't have been a bribe," Janx said. "Don't worry, we'll steal something if we have to. Mebbe we can find some other way."

"We may not need to," Layanna said. "If I'm right, our journey might be over. All we have to do is locate the altar and the quest is fulfilled—at least your part in it. After that, it will be up to you."

"I like the sound of that," Hildra said.

Their feet found a road and took it. Reeking mutants flooded all about them, jostling and lurching, hooting and squelching. Avery had never been in so alien a place, never seen so many wild mutations. Generally he was used to seeing a certain mutant trend in an individual—a resemblance to a certain sort of fish, say—or squid, or crab, or what-have-you. Here he saw mutation stacked on mutation, a jellyfish creature with crab-like legs, a man with the hide of a stingray but the mouth of a barracuda and the eyes of a dolphin, a beautiful woman with the coloring of an angelfish but the lower limbs of an octopus.

"Amazing," Avery said.

They moved on, and towers rose to either side of them. Avery felt the coldness of their shadows, felt their immense weight looming over him, ready to fall, to crush him. And the towers themselves were amazing. Some looked like coral monoliths. Many had been hewn out of massive stalagmites hundreds of feet high. Doorways and spiraling stairs dotted their surfaces. They were grand, monolithic structures, their windows winking, their facades shaped into great, fishy faces or fantastic forms, with windows and doors for eyes and mouths. Huge bridges arched from one stalagmite spire to another. Other buildings had been cobbled together from immense stones, or erected from what looked like mud, or junkyard debris, or both, held together with wire and great rusty metal bands. Some listed and sagged. Ragged tenements clustered, rickety lean-to's flowering from the sides of tipping buildings, tacked-on structures winding hither and yon. Avery received the impression of beehives, of honeycombs. There were ghettos, even in the afterlife.

And more. Much more. Palaces and mansions crowned stalagmite mountains, which seemed to have been hollowed out. Greenish light flooded from yawning doorways that would have dwarfed most houses back home. Even more impressive, Avery saw what looked like beautiful manses depending from the ceiling what seemed a mile or more overhead, carved out of stalactites. Their downward-facing domes glinted with crystal facets, and Avery saw strange lights flashing in the buildings' interiors, bathing their domes in surreal illumination.

And all around him mutants thronged and called to each other. One brushed up against him, and he felt for his wallet. Still there. The heady reek of fish and sea creatures filled his nose.

Deep gorges spilled down into valleys, then plunged into terrifying abysses. Shadowy structures struggled up low ridges. Great hills bristled with monolithic towers. It truly was a vast cavern the city occupied, or perhaps caverns. Mist pattered on him from above, and looking up he saw vapor roiling against the ceiling—*clouds*. Would there be lightning, too?

Barking vendors displayed cuts of meat that at first looked appetizing. Then Avery saw fingers, toes, identifiable arms, trays full of human or human-like eyeballs ...

Starting, he saw a group of mutants in chains being whipped before an armored crew, whips and guns in hand. Some of the captives were children. One especially large taskmaster slashed his whip across the chained mutants' backs, and they groaned and pulled forward. Avery and the others had passed into a ravine, and Avery saw other groups of what must be slaves being herded in and out of dark caves.

"Cannibals and slave-owners," Hildra said. "It just gets better."

Avery noted the naked, scarred and ragged state of the captives and said, "The slaves seem to be the ones we've been calling ferals. I would bet that these so-called civilized mutants hunt and round up the feral ones for use as labor and ... whatever else." He didn't like to think on what that would be, but it wasn't hard to guess.

Shadowy figures stirred to either side of the little valley, and Avery felt queasy at the way their eyes glinted. More and more he became conscious of the great buildings looming above him. He continued seeing activity above, figures stirring on the levels and tiers and the bridges that spanned misty gaps from tower to tower. Lights and music and activity. Things that might be restaurants or bars. Apartment buildings. Hotels. Offices. And more and more he came to regard his fellow wanderers of the streets as rough-looking and dangerous.

"I think we're in the wrong place," he said.

Janx and Hildra had pressed close together. The big man looked tense, and Hildra had her hook half raised. Thugs with glowing alchemical tattoos had drawn near.

Layanna pointed to a ramp. "I suggest we go up."

Soon they realized that the city was a vertical one, and that much if not most of its commerce and activity took place high above the dark and deadly streets, with their slave pens and ghettos and diseased food and worse. Above, fresher-smelling food sent sweet smells to entice Avery's nose, and festive music poured out of cantinas bored into stalagmites or junkheap structures bound together by wire and luck. More healthy and reputable-looking mutants thronged about him, passing from tower to tower over wide bridges, gracefully moving about the great stalagmites via ramps and scaffolds and ropes and ladders. The further up Avery went, the darker and more dismal the winding ways below seemed.

Just as he was about to investigate a restaurant, curious as to whether they would accept the few coins he had left, the drumming began.

Deep, throbbing drum rolls erupted from somewhere in the heart of the city.

Avery jerked to a stop and snapped his head up. Janx and Hildra did likewise. Hildebrand shrieked. Layanna only frowned. Around them, the citizens of Cuithril paused in their actions, looking toward the source of the noise. It rolled on and on, *boom boom boom*, rhythmic and awful.

Then, as one, the people stopped what they were doing—and moved toward it. They picked their way in the direction of the drums.

Avery exchanged glances with the others.

Janx grinned nastily and waved a hand as though he were a waiter seating an honored guest.

"After you," he said.

"I'm really not sure we should be doing this," Avery said as they followed the throngs of mutants that crossed dizzy gulfs and scrambled around rusty spires, making for the center of the city. "I think our primary goal should be to find the temple."

"The drumming probably comes from the temple," Layanna said.

That was true, Avery realized, falling quiet as they made their way toward the sound. He held his breath as they crossed rickety bridges, and though he tried not to look down into the black gulfs, he couldn't help it. At the sight of dark canyons stretching away under his feet seemingly without limit—and perhaps they had none; there seemed to be a sort of chasm below—his stomach seized into a knot, and bile burned the back of his throat.

All around and in every direction mutants swarmed through the city, making toward the drumming, which still rolled, slow and rhythmic, summoning the denizens of this black place to some event Avery couldn't imagine and didn't want to. The entire city had simply dropped what they were doing to attend. Some citizens looked eager, some blank, some fearful.

Avery swallowed and forced himself on. The drumming surrounded him.

At last they reached it. He pressed into the backs of those who had already arrived and nearly received an elbow in the face. Confusion reigned as the city-dwellers spread out, above and below, straining toward the platforms' railings and ropes, trying to get a better view. Infants perched on fathers' shoulders, and those behind them threatened the fathers. Scuffles ensued. With Janx shoving a path clear, Avery, Hildra and Layanna made their way and eventually found a position a few levels up from the one they had started on, pressed up against a fraying rope that served as barrier between the creaking wood platform and the empty air beyond. Around them mutants pushed and cursed, and Avery had to struggle not to be thrown off.

Suddenly, a voice called loudly:

"CITIZENS AND TRAVELERS, WELCOME TO THE COURT OF THE GREAT LORD."

Avery saw the speaker, and his heart sped up. The robed man stood on a circular platform, an arena really, that crowned a huge stalagmite mountain, in what must be the very center of the city. The population of Cuithril had gathered on the terraces and platforms of the many spires all around, shoving and jostling on the tiered levels, staring out across the clearing around the black tooth to the strange arena-like platform that topped it, which must be fifty or sixty feet across. Torches burned along the arena's circumference, casting hellish light on the speaker. Avery frowned to see black robes and a cowl.

"PREPARE TO BEHOLD THE SPLENDOR OF HE WHO HAS COME TO DELIVER US!" spoke the robed man, surely a priest, into a bullhorn. His voice rang out metallically, echoing off the buildings and stalagmites so that the last word of each sentence was staggered. "ALL HAIL ... *THE GREAT LORD!*"

The crowd buzzed and shouted. Movement came from overhead.

A great, carved stalactite hung directly above the arena. Like some fantastic castle tipped upside down, its towers stretched down, their tips crystal globes glowing from lights within. On the lowest (tallest) and most central tower, the one that depended directly over the arena, there was activity. A terrace jutted from the crystal globe of the lowest level of the tower, the one nearest the arena. A tall figure draped in shadow emerged from the interior.

The murmuring of the crowd increased. "The Great One!" some whispered. "Hail him!" Calling out their love for the figure, some dropped to their knees and prayed. Others looked sullen and kept their silence.

The figure stepped forward, and the enthusiasm of the crowd increased tenfold. Thousands cried out their love, and the figure raised its arms as if to allow the crowd to bask in its presence. Cries and chants and fist-poundings echoed off the walls and mountains.

Avery felt his sweat turn cold.

After a moment, he turned to Janx. The whaler's eyes blazed.

Avery turned back.

The figure above, the Great Lord, had stepped from the shadow into the light. Torch-light fell over him now, glinting on his scales, on his crested head, on his huge, muscular chest crisscrossed with scars.

Muirblaag grinned and drank in the worship of the crowd.

Layanna let out a long breath and leaned against Avery.

"So *that's* how he did it," she said.

"What?" he said, still stunned. "What ... ?"

"Don't you see? *Uthua beat us here.*"

"Gods damn," Hildra said, though whether in response to Layanna or not Avery couldn't tell. She just seemed dazed.

Janx's glare speared the figure above as if he could do Muirblaag injury with only his eyes. *He just about could*, Avery thought. At last Janx said, through clenched teeth, "How?"

"It's not Muirblaag anymore," Layanna said. "It's Uthua, the Mnuthra I fought in the Borghese. He's old and powerful, though he'd let his human self fade. I sensed a change in him, but I didn't think ... I didn't know he could ..." She took a breath. "Somehow he was able to anchor his extra-planar self in your friend. To put it simply, he's possessed Muirblaag."

Janx's jaw muscles bunched.

Hildra squeezed his shoulder. To Layanna, she said, "So what's ... *Uthua* doing here?"

"Waiting for me. Our minds touched, and I believe he discovered our plan to pass this way. Indeed, I discovered this route from him, remember."

"Shit." Idly Hildra stroked her monkey, whose gaze was also fixed on Muirblaag. His eyes looked very round.

"Our search is over, anyway," Avery said, pointing to the palatial upside-down building Muirblaag—Uthua—apparently occupied. "That must be the temple. The altar will be in there."

"Yes," said Layanna.

"Oh, no," Hildra said. "You can't mean what I think you do."

The announcer called again. Shouting through the bullhorn, his voice echoing metallically off the walls, he said, "WE HAVE SPLENDID NEWS, CITIZENS OF CUITHRIL. MOMENTARILY WE EXPECT POWERFUL ALLIES TO ARRIVE AND PAY HOMAGE TO OUR MASTER. WHILE WE AWAIT

THEM, LET US HONOR HIM OURSELVES." He stepped aside, into a small lowered area of the arena fenced by spiked iron posts.

Before the gate had even latched, Uthua leapt down from the terrace of his temple onto the arena. He wore a cape, scarlet and embroidered with a gold pattern, and it fluttered behind him. He landed gracefully, the cape folding neatly about him, and the crowd shouted their adulations. He raised his arms and grinned, showing sharp teeth.

Almost as soon as he lowered his arms, trapdoors burst open in the arena floor, and lurching figures stormed out. These were the familiar mutants of the tunnels. The ferals. They seemed much the same as the citizens of the city, save for tribal tattoos and scars. They were armed with spears and swords, nets and maces. They blinked around them, their backs hunched, their teeth bared, until their gazes settled on Uthua.

They threw back their heads, howled in fury, and rushed him.

Uthua let them come. When they were almost upon him, he moved. With grace and power, he dodged a thrust spear, stepped around a slicing sword, caught a net and flung it back, ensnaring two mutants. The ones that were still loose stumbled, disoriented. Tried to regroup. He leapt, tearing at them with inhuman strength. He twisted the head off one, ripped the arms off another. His clawed talons disemboweled a third.

And, as the blood sprayed, he drank it up. Even as the bodies flopped at his feet, he knelt over them ... and fed.

Disgust filled Avery. He wasn't the only one, either. All around him, citizens of Cuithril looked dark and sullen. They glanced at Uthua, then away. Some wept. The majority, however, roared out their love and worship. Even as Uthua crouched among splintered bodies and ropes of intestine, tearing into them like some starved wolf, gulping down the still-warm remains of people he had slaughtered, blood spattering his face and chest, trickling over his fish-like lips, the crowd cheered. At last, gorged and covered in blood, Uthua rose to his feet, a bit unsteadily. Drunken.

More trapdoors opened. A new tide of mutants streamed out. These were not armed, and they did not appear to be ferals. By their clothes, their more sane demeanors and lack of tribal markings, Avery judged them to be citizens of the city—and by the looks of hate they cast at Uthua, he realized something else.

"Dissenters," he said. "This must be what he does with those that don't like his rule."

The quiet citizens of the city, those that didn't seem to appreciate the spectacle, turned even more ashen. Possibly the dissenters were their friends. If nothing else, they were their fellows in suffering.

The newcomers on the arena spread in a circle around Uthua. Some shook in fear. All looked pale and terrified. They knew they were going to their deaths. Nevertheless, they decided to make a go of it. Surprising Avery, they advanced on Uthua in a coordinated strike, howling as they came.

He didn't toy with them.

Newly gorged, he *changed*. A dark, gelatinous form erupted from within him, superimposed over him, and expanded, filling up half the arena, a great black mountain fringed in tentacles and bristling with ungainly limbs. Thrusting pseudopods reared up and crushed attacking mutants, and dark tendrils wrapped around others, stinging them and killing them. Their screams filled the air, along with the otherworldly sounds and smells of the Mnuthra. The very fabric of reality seemed to bend and rip to accommodate him. The air blurred, and shapes that should appear solid were not. Strange lights flashed from the being's interior.

And still the crowd cheered. Here at last was a god that did not need to be sacrificed *to*. He would take his own.

Not all seemed so enthusiastic, and Avery noticed one group nearby looking particularly furious. *They'll do.* Hoping this wasn't a mistake, he approached them.

"Excuse me, I don't mean to intrude. I'm not from here," he said, trying to express an awed sort of concern, "and I was wondering, well—how long has the Great Lord been here? I didn't know there *was* such a ruler in Cuithril, but ..." He gestured vaguely toward the arena.

"How long does a god need?" one young man said with a sneer.

Another said, more gently, "A couple of weeks."

They studied Avery, and he tried not to appear suspicious-looking—whatever that might look like here. *Keep your eyes steady.* In picture shows, shifty eyes generally denoted a traitor. On the other hand, Avery was counting on these men's dislike of Uthua to provide him with information, so he couldn't appear too naïve, either. He settled for a belligerent indifference.

"I don't know where you're from, buddy," one of the fellows said, "but you *must* have heard the Call."

"Yeah," said another. "Uthua's priests have been sent all over the Halls. Every city in the Underworld's been given the word."

"Oh. Yes," Avery said. "I've heard it, certainly. The Call." He considered. Looking around, he made sure no one else was in earshot, then said, "Listen, maybe you can help me. I'm trying to enter Uthua's temple." He saw their eyes fix on him and added hastily, "To, uh, pay him homage personally. I was sent from my town to greet him on behalf of our people and to pledge our loyalty to him. So ... how can I get in?" He made his voice sound incredulous, but with a hint of hope. "Are there ... *secret* ways? I'd like to avoid the mob. If you know what I mean."

"Not trying anything untoward, are you?" one youth said, then laughed bitterly. "Have at it. But the only way in is through those three bridges that connect to it."

Another youth said, "And the only ones who can cross them, other than the Lord, are his priests and sacrifices. The nobles have been sending him prisoners as ... gifts. To appease him. They ruled here before, and they're afraid he'll move against them to solidify his power."

"There's no resistance?" Avery said.

Anger flashed in their eyes, and he saw impotent frustration there. "How can you fight a god?" one snapped.

"We were raised to worship the Fathers and their gods," another said. "Now one has *come* to us. But it's not like the priests said it would be. You can't know, stranger, all the terrible things we've seen. And heard. The rituals, the rapes, the disappearances ... the screams from the Temple. They've built strange machines there—to awaken the altar, they say—"

"We shouldn't be talking about this in public," another said.

The first youth swore. Without a backward look, he and his mates slipped away. Layanna, Janx and Hildra approached Avery.

"What now?" Janx said.

Avery started to speak, but shouts interrupted him.

"There! There they are!"

The voice had come from a platform overhanging the one they were on. A half dozen robed priests occupied the edge.

The leader pointed a gnarled finger at Avery. *"Get them!"*

Instantly a space cleared around Avery and the others. The mutants nearby looked bewildered and frightened. A few, those who had been most vocal in their support of Uthua, stepped forward to obey the priests. One man raised a wrench that he'd been carrying in a utility belt, looking about him for support. Finding it, he closed in on Avery and the others at the head of a handful of zealots.

Janx grabbed Avery by the shoulder and propelled him on. "Go go go!" the whaler said. Avery moved, and the crowd parted. Some made halfhearted efforts to clutch at him, but either Janx or Hildra quickly put an end to such notions, and the zealots fell behind.

"This is ... bad," Layanna panted beside him. "With the temple—"

Uthua rose before them, eyes murderous, blocking off their path. How had he gotten around them so fast?

"Oh, fuck me," said Hildra.

Uthua did not smile or gloat. His all-black eyes, glistening like black pearls just ripped from an oyster, stared at Layanna with grim sobriety. "Welcome to Cuithril," he said.

Her lips thinned. She said nothing. Her eyes stared glassily at the thing that had once been Muirblaag, her back hunched and legs slightly bent, as if poised to flee or attack. Avery thought she looked like a rabbit in a trap.

Desperate, he glanced over his shoulder only to see Uthua's priests, some carrying unfamiliar weapons, some guns, closing in from behind, eclipsing the mob. With a leaden feeling of dread, Avery returned his attention to Uthua, his stomach becoming acidic. Spots flickered and streaked before his eyes. *This is it*, he thought. *We've lost. Gods damn it all, we've lost.*

The Mnuthra had eyes only for Layanna, and for a long moment the two Collossum just stared at each other; Avery could feel the tension thicken the air, turn it into a string and twang it, violently, a guitar cord about to break. The crowd murmured in thrilled gasps and whispers, wisely drawing back from the confrontation. Somewhere bats chattered, and water dripped from ancient stalactites. A vague wind stirred the air, rustling Layanna's hair.

Uthua's all-black eyes no longer looked warm, as they had when their former owner had possessed them. They looked cruel and cold and monstrous, and a malice so deep it was palpable played across the fish-man's features. And when Uthua spoke, he did not speak in Muirblaag's comradely tones, but in the voice of one who believed himself a god worth sacrificing countless lives to. How many had he killed over the years? Thousands? Millions? *Gods*, Avery thought, *it could be millions.*

"We've been looking for you for a long time, Layanna," Uthua said.

Layanna still said nothing. Perhaps fear had closed her throat.

"Surrender and it will go easier on you," Uthua went on. "Either way, I need those plans. And I need to know the location of the Black Sect."

"Then come and get them," she said, and, sure enough, Avery could hear the strain in her voice. *She knows she can't win.*

Uthua stepped forward.

Avery's stomach clenched and he felt the blood drain from his face. Trembling, he put himself between Uthua and Layanna.

"No," he said. *"No."* It was all he could say.

He felt Layanna's hands on his shoulders firmly but insistently pushing him away. He dug in his heels. He knew she could move him if she wanted, but he hoped she would honor him with the dignity of a brave last stand.

In his ear, she whispered, "This is my battle, Francis."

"Your battle is mine."

Uthua's other-self exploded outward, huge and gelatinous.

A dark tentacle seized Avery and lifted him up. Immediately fire filled him—venom. Alien, extradimensional venom. He screamed. He knew nothing else but pain. The rest of the world receded.

He felt himself hurled away. Breath exploded from his lungs as he struck the ground and slid. His groping hands slowed him before he could vanish over the side of the platform and into the abyss.

Gasping, he looked up, and light dazzled him.

Layanna had released her amoeba-self—the reason Uthua had freed himself of Avery so suddenly. Pink-limned pseudopods squirmed and roiled, tiny purplish fringes wriggling and straining like anemone. Long, clear jellyfish-like tentacles thrust and curled. Encased in her otherworldly self, Layanna lifted off the ground and floated.

The Mnuthra rushed her across the deck.

Layanna met him with a crash that Avery felt through his hands and the soles of his feet. Whitish tentacles lashed at dark, gelatinous material, and ripped away great chunks. Dark pseudopods rose high and slammed down on pink-purple flesh. Dark veins of ink-like substance ran from the points of impact through Layanna's other-self. Black veins spiderwebbed her amoeba sac, intersected red and orange organelles, and the organelles withered.

Layanna plunged her tentacles deep inside the Mnuthra. Avery could see the effort on her face as she spent her strength, stinging Uthua, filling him with venom, perhaps seeking out the material host, Muirblaag, so that she could destroy it.

Uthua surged around her. Avery had seen before that he was the greater, the more powerful of the two, and he had only gotten stronger. As he glommed forward, he began to devour her, to roll over and around her. She slowly disappeared inside him. Pain and fear showed in her face.

Breathing heavily, his shoulder aching where he'd struck the ground, Avery forced himself to his feet. He slipped around the huge bulk which rippled just inches before him, looking for a weapon, something long and sharp. Perhaps ...

Layanna was all but swallowed. He could only see her here and there, through momentary partings of Uthua's flesh. She seemed to have fallen unconscious and was floating downwards, eyes closed. Her jellyfish-white sac boiled away around her, devoured by the Mnuthra.

Janx, who'd been knocked to the floor, shook his head and staggered to his feet, pulling Hildra up with him. Avery joined them.

Before they could organize some sort of attack on Uthua, the Mnuthra's priests converged and surrounded them.

"Don't move," one said.

By then it was over, anyway. Uthua emerged from his other-self and stood over Layanna's unconscious form, his chest heaving, steam from her body rising around him. Avery's heart lurched at the sight of her lying still like that, open and vulnerable, and for a moment he thought his knees would give out. If Janx hadn't grabbed him just then, they probably would have.

"Take her to the Temple," Uthua told his priests. "To the place prepared for her. When she's given us what we need, I'll send for her to be returned here, and present her to the High One." Obeying, a group of the priests lifted her up and carried her away. Uthua's gaze fell on Avery, Janx and Hildra—lingering on Avery. "You," he said, after a thoughtful moment. "I remember ... yes, the trident." He gave a small smile, showing needle teeth wet with saliva.

Avery said nothing.

"I almost admire what you did," Uthua said, black eyes sparkling. "For one so low to reach so high. Just the same, it is an effrontery on a grand scale—should a gnat destroy a star?—and must be punished." To the priests, he said, "Put them with the other sac— "

He broke off suddenly, his gaze turning in the direction of the sea Avery and the others had flown over, as if he'd become aware of something the others could not sense

"Great One!" shouted the high priest a moment later. "The Octunggen are arriving!"

With an inhuman bound, Uthua leapt back into the arena--or Arena, Avery supposed, mentally affording it the honorific based on its central position and obvious importance in the city--and stood there expectantly. Muttering rose up from the packed masses, louder and louder. The high priest in the Arena weathered it for a few moments, then raised a finger and pointed. With his other hand, he placed the megaphone to his lips and said, "THEY COME!"

The audience shifted and looked. Avery squinted.

A dozen black dirigibles cut through the airspace of the city, swerving in and out of the drooping stalactites and upthrusting spires. A stylized bolt of lightning adorned the envelope of each one.

Unable to help it, Avery doubled over, trying to suck in breaths that refused to come.

Janx clapped him on the shoulder. "Clutch your knees and stick your head between 'em," he said.

Shortly the spots faded. But when Avery looked up the dirigibles had neared the Arena and drifted to a stop. The priest called out, "WELCOME OUR FRIENDS FROM OCTUNG, WHO COME TO HONOR THE GREAT UTHUA."

"I don't believe it," Hildra muttered. "I just don't believe it."

"Did they come through Ungraessot?" Janx wondered. "Or did they tear some hole in the ground?"

The dirigibles stopped at the edge of the Arena and threw down ropes. Priests tied them off and the dirigibles lowered. Ramps were thrown across, and Octunggen soldiers in crisp black uniforms disembarked. At their head was Admiral Jessryl Sheridan, late of the Ghenisan Navy. Her new Octunggen uniform clung to her as if she had been born to it, and her short auburn hair fell from her peaked black cap. *So*, Avery thought, *she's kept her appointment after all.*

Despite everything, a terrible hope rose in him.

There might still be a chance for Ani.

The Octunggen led infected captives, perhaps captured ngvandi, down from the dirigibles and paraded them around the Arena. Only then did the high priest direct his underlings to chain the captives to the ground, connecting the chains to bolts sticking out of the Arena floor. The high priest said, "OUR GUESTS BRING GIFTS FOR THE MASTER."

Some of the crowd applauded, some fell to their knees, but the majority made no move or sound. Many looked as ill as Avery felt.

Uthua waited.

Sheridan stepped away from the delegation of Octunggen and knelt before him. She spoke, but she was too far away for Avery to hear what she said, and the Mnuthra responded in kind. The exchange went on for several minutes, and at last Uthua nodded and stepped back. Sheridan returned to her group, then led the captives over. They appeared to have been drugged, as they stumbled when they walked.

Uthua accepted the offerings and nodded in an exaggerated show of gratitude to Sheridan. He turned his head and spoke to the high priest, who had been watching without expression.

The high priest informed the crowd, "THE GREAT MASTER HAS WONDROUS NEWS. ANOTHER GOD APPROACHES EVEN NOW. IT COMES FROM THE OVER-CITY, WHICH FLOATS ABOVE THE BATTLEFIELDS OF THE WORLD. COMMANDING IT IS NONE OTHER THAN A LORD OF THE COLLOSSUM, AN ELDER BEING THAT EVEN THE GREAT UTHUA PAYS HOMAGE TO. THIS ANCIENT AND WISE COLLOSSUM WILL ARRIVE IN THE FLESH TO DELIVER PUNISHMENT TO THE CAPTIVE AND REBELLIOUS GODDESS THE GREAT UTHUA HAS JUST CAPTURED. THIS WICKED GODDESS THREATENS THE VERY WEAVE OF THE COSMOS. OUR MASTER WILL EXTRACT CRITICAL INFORMATION FROM HER, AND THE ELDER SHALL JUDGE HER."

The priest went on, but Avery hardly heard him.

"An Elder," Avery said to Janx and Hildra. "Uthua must have told Sheridan about Layanna, and she called it in. Obviously Uthua's been planning for this."

"What was that he told his priests earlier?" Janx said. "'Take her to the place prepared for her'? I didn't like the sound of that."

Avery nodded. "If Uthua gets that information out of her, it will all be over."

"It might end sooner than that," Hildra said. "If that Elder gets here first. Look." She pointed to a group of nobles leading charges across one of the three equidistant bridges that connected to the Temple. Through the mists that swirled around the bridge, Avery saw priests at the Temple's doors accepting the offerings, one at a time, after searching them thoroughly—very thoroughly. Perhaps they feared the nobles would try to sneak a bomb through and attempt to reclaim their city. Shortly another group of nobles appeared, leading more captives toward the Temple. The captives' hands were all shackled.

"Trying to appease Uthua before it's too late," Avery said, understanding. "Before the Elder arrives."

"Soon that'll be us," Hildra said, her eyes on the lines of sacrifices. Hildebrand chittered nervously.

Janx leaned in close. "Now's the time," he whispered. "While they're distracted. We can escape. I think I see a way."

"No," Avery said. "We're exactly where we need to be."

Janx made a sound like a snort, or as near to one as he could contrive without a nose. "How do you figure that, Doc?"

"Only priests and sacrifices are allowed into Uthua's temple. We're not priests, so that leaves sacrifices." He paused, then leaned forward. "Do you still have your picks?"

"Never go anywhere without 'em," Janx said, patting a pocket.

"Good. Place them where you can reach them after they manacle our hands."

Janx frowned, studying a group of sacrifices being led across a bridge, then shook his head. "If they search us like they just searched that fella, they'd find a *mole* outta place. Not even my picks would make it through—an' they don't take up much space, believe me."

Avery's eyes fell on Hildebrand.

"Fine," he said. "Then here's what we'll do ..." Quickly he whispered to them, and they stared at him in horror.

"You're mad," Janx said.

"It's the only way."

Reluctantly, they did as he'd suggested, and none too soon. The priests that had taken Avery and the others captive suddenly shook themselves.

"The Great One wanted them placed with the sacrifices," the lead priest said. "Let us take them."

Chapter 22

The shackles bit into Avery's wrists. One of his hairs had been caught when the temple guards snapped it shut, and as more of them prodded him from behind it pinched and pulled. Gritting his teeth, he twisted the hand, and the hair pulled taut, then tore out by the root. Sharp pain came, then relief.

The guards prodded him, Janx and Hildra over a swaying wood-and-rope bridge toward the Temple. Almost directly below, Uthua held court over the Octunggen. Sheridan appeared relaxed and composed as several of her number played strange silver pipes for the amusement or veneration of the Mnuthra. The fish-man looked pleased, perched on an odd metal throne that resembled a trident. Other chairs had been carried up through the trapdoors, and several of the Octunggen delegation sat on them as they played their instruments. Sheridan remained standing. Soon, Avery could feel it, the Elder would arrive. The very air was pregnant with it.

Meanwhile nobles from the city herded droves of captives over the three equidistant bridges that led to the Temple. Uthua noticed, and he could be seen giving a single nod to each patriarch or matriarch that brought his priests sacrifices. They were safe from extermination, it seemed, at least for the moment.

Janx and Hildra cursed and grumbled behind Avery, Hildra loudest of all. The leader of the priests had hit and kicked Hildebrand, sending the monkey away from his mistress. The last Avery had seen of the animal he had been huddling on a nearby stalactite, chittering and hurling feces at the priests.

"Bastards!" Hildra said. "You'll regret this. I'll make sure of it!"

The priests ignored her.

The grand façade of the Temple drew nearer, and Avery marveled at the structure. It had been carved out of a massive stalactite, but one would never have known it, so skillfully was it done. Its architecture rivaled any Avery had ever seen, and he felt nauseous to see its towers plunging straight down, each shaped something like a narrow stalactite. Its great stained-glass windows were set within layers of molding, and crenellations and bas-reliefs and fish-finned gargoyles adorned every inch of it. The Temple seemed slightly purple, slightly gray, and Avery supposed it had been alchemically stained. In any case, the fantastic purplish towers stretched away below, half vanishing in the mist, half framing the Arena, where Uthua, Sheridan and the Octunggen could still be seen waiting. Avery pictured the vast Over-City pulling into position in the skies above, drawn by some homing beacon in the dirigibles.

As if the thought was a cue, suddenly there came a great rumble, a huge earthen roar, and all heads glanced in the direction of the sea. Avery saw a shaft of sunlight break through far away, and then he heard a huge splash that must have been tons of rock and earth falling into the water. Many of the citizens of Cuithril screamed, but most just drew away.

A huge dark shape lowered through the opening, dust swirling around it. Avery wanted to stop and stare, but after a moment the guards shoved him forward. Between shoves, Avery peeked.

It was a zeppelin, massive and unwieldy, almost ridiculous in the tight spaces it found itself in. Bloated and slow, but moving with eerie grace and majesty, the great airship sailed above the underground sea, threading through drooping stalactites, sometimes actually scraping off them with little explosions of dust. Relentless, indomitable, like an oversized worm wriggling through the earth, it plowed for the city.

Many of the citizens of Cuithril fell to their knees and prostrated themselves before it, and Avery didn't have to wonder why. *The Elder is aboard. Damn it all, it's the Elder.*

Below, Sheridan turned and watched it come in. Avery could only see the back of her head. Part of him thought, *Ani.* A pain burned in his chest. He tried to will it away, but it remained, and his head felt full of cotton.

As he and the others reached the Temple, the distracted priests accepted charge of them, while more priests searched them (these less distracted and annoyingly thorough), and began to lead them in.

Below, Uthua gazed at the approaching zeppelin, all his attention fixed on it. Sheridan said something, he nodded, and she called several of her troops over. Together they began to board a dirigible. There was some delay, however, as the priests were too preoccupied to cast them off, and it appeared that they might have to wait for the Elder to arrive.

Other priests led Avery, Janx and Hildra into the Temple, down high, cold halls of the same purple-gray as the exterior. Fantastic chandeliers hung from the ceilings, and their glittering light sparkled off walls which undulated like waves on the sea. Indeed, the whole place gave off an aquatic feel, and Avery half expected to hear the groaning of whale songs echo down the corridors. The light danced on the walls like the dapple of sunlight on the surface of the ocean.

If Avery was grateful for anything, it was that Uthua's priests here practiced much better hygiene than their counterparts in the ngvandi city. Not only did they smell better, but their robes were made of cloth, not human skin. For all that, they were equally as terrifying.

They led Avery, Janx and Hildra down twisting halls toward what sounded like ... yes, it *was* singing, but in no language Avery knew. The singing swelled in the direction the priests led, then swelled some more. At last the priests ushered them through a fantastic archway and into what Avery could only think of as the Altar Room.

"Holy shit," Hildra said.

It was a great, cavernous chamber, the walls far apart and arcing gradually upward, like cresting waves. The sound of rushing water filled the room, and to Avery's surprise four waterfalls, perhaps channeled from underground springs, gushed from high up on the walls to pour into bubbling basins. The basins overflowed into channels that ran to grottoes and streamlets, connected with the other basins, creating a sort of circular perimeter to the room, then curling inwards. Avery and the others were obliged to step over a bridge as they entered, then another. Bodies choked the riverways—mutants, hundreds of them, butchered and defiled, parts of them eaten away as if by acid, others torn apart as if in fits of madness. The salty stench of rot filled the chamber. In the center of it all stood a raised dais, mounted on a series of tiered daises, each smaller than the one supporting it. Sloping rampways led up to the altar—or Altar, Avery supposed—at the peak of the dais pyramid, black and glistening. Bodies littered it as well, heaped and scattered. Blood coated it, running in tacky streams from its sides. Around the Altar, priests knelt and sang.

But that was not the end of the spectacle. Wires ran from the Altar, strange crackling wires threading between singing priests to bulky, odd-looking machinery that surrounded the Altar in a rough circle. The machines looked like metal carapaces of prehistoric creatures, and some flickered with lights. Around them the air seemed to blur. Avery remembered that the god-emperors and their priests had forgotten how to properly use their altars, so it made sense that this one did not function as well as it should, though the priests of the Underworld appeared to know the old ways better than the ones above. Uthua seemed to be leading an effort to, through the machines, correct and augment the Altar, to enable it to commune with the priests' gods, just like the Father of their Fathers had once done. Just like the ngvandi had done in their nameless city. Some sort of energy radiated off the Altar, and Avery's hairs stood up along his arms and the back of his neck, and he could feel the electricity on his tongue and eyes, even his balls. But there was more to it than electricity. He felt as if the world had shifted subtly, as if perhaps a gateway had been opened. A gateway ... to *elsewhere*.

But what truly shocked him was Layanna. She overhung the Altar, encased in a glowing yellowish gel that filled a cell of some kind, what looked like thick glass with bands of brass holding it together, a type of aquarium prison that sprouted like a multi-faceted, upside-down blister from the ceiling. She floated in the midst of the gel, completely naked, her head thrown back, her mouth opened in a scream, though Avery could hear no sound. Pain filled her face, and her other-worldly self, or pieces of it, churned the liquid around her. Pinkish tentacles smashed against the glass. Flagella, pulsing with light, stabbed at the brass bands.

To no avail. She was securely locked in. Wires and hoses ran from her cell directly down to the great, sinister machines that ringed the Altar, and Avery had to wonder if she were connected to it somehow. That's what they had come for, for her to communicate through the Altar, but her prison apparently prevented her from having any liberty in the matter. It could commune with her, but she couldn't commune with it.

Hitching posts and rails stood throughout the room. They looked newly installed, the posts mounted in holes crudely bored through the rock. Hundreds of prisoners had been chained to these stations, all pressed tightly against each other. Some looked as if they had just arrived, and they were fully clothed and showed fewer signs of having been beaten. Those who had been here longer were a ragged lot, horror stamped on their faces and bodies.

Priests trickled throughout the room, tending to the machines and sacrifices. The ones herding Avery, Janx and Hildra led them over to a stretch of railing already occupied by teems of captives. The priests shoved and whipped those already there until a space opened, then snapped the manacles of Avery's hands around the rail, then Janx's, and finally Hildra's—both wrists, at least. The priests had had a tin can mounted over her hook and tied about her left wrist, rendering the hook harmless. They hadn't done anything about her tongue, though, and she cursed them soundly as they locked her to the rail.

The lead priest seemed immune to her threats. In a voice of disdain, he said, "I wouldn't be so haughty, girl. You lot aren't even blessed. You're practically worthless to the Master."

"If you mean infected, that's just fine by me," she said.

"You *will* have to partake of the holy flesh," the priest continued, which Avery took to mean the priests would have to cram their mouths with diseased food before they would make worthy sacrifices.

The cleric started to go, but Avery said, "What are you doing with her?" He indicated Layanna.

The priest paused, as if unsure whether to waste words on one such as Avery, but the opportunity to gush was evidently too great to pass up. "She's the key," he said. "*She* will win the war for us. It's almost done. We should have the information directly. We already have part of it. We've just succeeded in extracting the location of the Black Sect from her, and operatives in Octung are preparing a strike against them as we speak."

"Damn it," said Janx, half under his breath. "So fast ..."

"The Great Uthua designed the chamber," the priest said. "She's a powerful one, and she's fighting it, but she cannot last against His arts, and soon her secrets will be ours. First the Black Sect. Then we'll pull the plans to a certain machine from her, something she devised to hurt us, but which we can use for our own ends—we're so *close*. When we have it, we'll be invincible." He cleared his throat. "Well, Octung will be, and the Master is a god of Octung, so we are their allies now. The priesthood is now—and always has been, though we didn't know it—in service to the Collossum. She's connected directly to the Altar, so the plans will flow straight to them. At any moment! Just think! Lord Uthua will be exalted before the Elder, and praise shall shine down on us all!"

He turned on his heel and stalked away, the junior priests swept up in his wake. Avery shared a dark look with Janx and Hildra.

"This ain't good, Doc," Janx said.

"No," Avery said. "No, it's not."

He studied the press of captives all around him, nodding to the tall, thin man shoved up beside him, but the man didn't respond, just stared off into space, his eyes made blank by exhaustion and terror. He stank of stale sweat and grime. Looking around at the others, Avery saw gloomy, hollow faces everywhere, and he wondered if the captives were to be sacrificed to Uthua or the arriving Collossum, perhaps as some sort of welcoming gift.

"Now what?" said Hildra.

Avery flicked his gaze to Layanna. She still screamed and twisted in pain from some source Avery could not determine. Was it the gel itself? Perhaps the wires and hoses that connected to the cell?

"We rescue her," he said.

Janx rattled his chain. "Yeah, and how'm I supposed to do that?"

Avery met his gaze. "The plan will work." Then, suddenly worried, he glanced at Hildra. "It *will* work, won't it?"

"Sure," she said. "Sure, it'll work."

"It had better."

"You think I don't *know* that?"

They waited. Avery shifted uncomfortably, horribly aware of Layanna screaming and twisting in the center of the room. He wanted to go to her, wanted to help her, and he couldn't stand being confined. The captives to the side of him sagged and cursed. The frustration of being so impotent seemed to have broken some of them, but many of the newer ones shouted at the priests and shook their chains defiantly.

Suddenly, Janx stood straighter. His eyes moved to something over Avery's shoulder. Avery turned. He saw nothing amiss, except for the chaos of the room with its struggling captives, gushing pools, sparking machines, bustling priests ... but there! There, if he was expecting to see it, a small dark shape, scurrying from a rail filled with slaves, to a statue beside a gurgling streamlet, across the floor ...

Hildra whistled.

Hildebrand adjusted his course and made for her, going as cautiously and quickly as he could. Avery's heart leapt inside him to track the monkey's progress, from slave station to hissing machine, to swing along under a bridge, then to a low couch slicked with blood and with a bottle of wine sitting to its side, surely Uthua's absurdly casual lounge. At last Hildebrand scurried toward them—and leapt on Hildra's shoulder.

Never was Avery more glad to see anyone, man or animal.

"Finally you earn your keep, you mangy bastard," Janx said.

Hildra's face was tight and pale, and she used her eyes to direct Hildebrand to Janx's hands. Hildebrand scrambled across to Janx's shoulders, then down to his large hands. Into them he dropped a gleaming set of picks.

Looking as tense as Avery had ever seen him, Janx picked the locks—deftly, hurriedly. One snapped free, then another. Avery thought he might pass out from relief. Next Janx freed Hildra and Avery. Avery rubbed his wrists gratefully.

"I told you it would work," Hildra said, but she sounded almost as relieved as he did. Of course, she'd been the one to most verbally abuse Avery's plan to give the picks to Hildebrand. That way it wouldn't matter if they were searched or their hands bound; he could drop the picks right in.

"No sudden movements," Janx whispered to Avery and Hildra, as they rubbed circulation back into their wrists.

The captives to either side had witnessed their liberation, but they weren't about to risk unfolding events by drawing attention to them. A few did whisper desperately in Janx's direction, and he met their eyes and said, "Soon."

"All right," Avery said, eyeing the chamber. "How are we going to do this? Whatever we do, we have to hurry. Sheridan's coming. Remember, Uthua said he would send for Layanna, and Sheridan was boarding a dirigible as we entered the Temple. She must be coming to bring Layanna to the Arena—to the Elder—so that it can kill her publicly once they have the information they need."

"She hadn't left by the time we came in here," Hildra said. "She was held up by the Elder."

"Maybe we'll get lucky and she'll get bogged down in some sort of ceremony—but we can't count on it."

Janx let Hildebrand scamper to the ground, where Hildra scooped him up.

"Then let's be about it, already," the big man said.

"We need a plan," Avery said.

Janx grinned. "I've got one."

"But—wait—"

Janx moved away from the line of captives, bent over to avoid attention. Hildra went next, ripping off the can that hid her hook.

Avery watched them go, marveling at their boldness. Should he follow?

Janx tapped the shoulder of a passing priest, who spun about. Janx smashed him across the jaw with an enormous fist, and the priest lifted off the ground and flew backward. When he landed, Janx knelt over him, and as he grabbed a set of keys Avery realized why Janx had selected that particular priest. Janx flung the keys to the line of slaves, and a cheer went up.

"Go to it, lads!" Janx said.

Chaos broke out.

The room was large and hectic, but several priests saw what had happened and rushed toward the slaves that were freeing themselves. A couple held staffs that sparked on their ends, like ornate cattle prods. Others reached into their robes and pulled out guns. Several were of odd design and Avery wondered if the priesthood possessed extradimensional technology.

Janx dodged a strike from one priest's sparking lance, grabbed the weapon in both hands, tore it loose, and kicked the priest away. Another rushed up, and Janx stabbed the weapon at him. It struck the fellow in the chest, and he erupted into green flames—and began to dissolve. Janx hit a third priest in the belly with the butt of the lance on his backswing, then smacked the first one in the face with the shaft, sending him reeling into a pair of priests who'd just been raising their guns. Janx leapt for them.

Hildra tackled the feet of one of the priests, rolled out from under him and slashed him across the throat with her hook. Even as he flopped and floundered, spurting inky blood, she wrenched his gun free and shot another through the skull.

Avery, stunned by the *suddenness* of it all, looked for a way to help. Darting forward, he shoved the back of a priest coming up on Hildra from behind, unbalancing him and giving Hildra time to recognize the danger and kill the priest, opening up his guts with her hook. Avery scooped up the dagger dropped by the priest.

By this time a dozen of the slaves had freed themselves, and more were being loosed by the moment. They leapt on priests and wrestled away their weapons. Several were shot, stabbed or melted, but the survivors were not deterred.

Avery's gaze strayed to the Altar. To Layanna. He knew he wasn't much use in a fight, but there *was* something he could do. While the others were occupying the priests, he had to get her out of there.

Legs trembling, he wove through the chaos toward the Altar. He stepped around a priest fighting a former captive, dodged a hurtling body—he wasn't sure whose—and pressed forward. He kept his head down and his feet fast.

He stopped at the line of machines that ringed the Altar and studied them. They were bigger than he'd thought, huge and bulky. Bits and pieces hummed and sparked, and several seemed to vibrate. He could feel the throbbing in his feet. It all seemed unstable to him. Jury-rigged.

Various hoses and pipes snarled across the floor from the machines, then vanished upward into Layanna's cell, or aquarium, huge and banded in brass, filled with unearthly chemicals. Inside it, she twisted and screamed soundlessly. *I'm coming,* Avery thought. *Just hang on a little longer.*

He crouched over one of the hoses and began sawing on it with his stolen dagger. A priest saw him, broke off his attack on a freed woman and rushed over, reloading his pistol as he went. Avery sawed through the hose and lifted it just as the priest raised his gun. The yellowish fluid from the hose blasted the priest right in the face. He staggered back, clutching at his cheeks, which came away in slimy strips. Steam trailed up from his head, and his eyes ran like jelly from their sockets. He toppled backward and didn't move again, save to deflate.

Avery snatched up the pistol—delicately, making sure there was no fluid on it—and shoved it through his belt.

He dashed from hose to hose, sawing through them, sweating more with each one, and letting the fluid spew across the floor, where it steamed and hissed. It stank like rotting meat crossed with battery acid, and he had to resist the urge to retch. Sweat stung his eyes. Steaming rivers of the fluid ran across the floor, pooling and creating barriers for combatants to navigate around. Where he could Avery aimed the streams at groups of priests.

As the last hose was cut, he looked up to see a gratifying sight: Layanna lay pressed against a grime-streaked glass panel, stirring weakly in the now-emptied aquarium. She looked too weak to free herself.

Avery wished Janx or Hildra were at hand, but they were off fighting and rallying the former sacrifices against the priests. Avery saw bands of former captives pour from the Altar Room and spread violence through the rest of the Temple. Screams and howls echoed from down the halls.

Having no choice, Avery grabbed one of the hoses snaking from Layanna's cell and began hauling himself up, hand over hand. He grunted and strained. At times he thought he would simply fall off, but he began to make progress.

Closer, closer ...

The cable shook beneath him. He glanced down. A particularly large priest scaled the hose right under him, knife clamped between his razor-sharp teeth. His red-tinged gills pulsed angrily. His bulging eyes glared hate. He ascended, swift and sure.

Avery reached for his gun, but the priest's ascent shook the cable too violently, and Avery, with only one hand on the cable, the other going for the gun, nearly fell off. Hastily he grabbed on with both hands.

The priest closed the distance. Avery climbed. The Altar seemed very far below now. The priest was faster than he was, and gaining. Avery feared any moment now he would feel one of its red-tinged claws grab his foot.

Avery reached the aquarium, pulled himself up, fingers digging into the edges of a brass band, and fought for purchase with his toes. A clawed hand swiped at him, skidding off his shoe. The priest clawed again, and Avery kicked the hand away, nearly losing his balance on the thin ledge. The hand reached up one more time—

Avery shot the priest through the head. The man fell away, seeming to spin forever before he struck the floor. Gasping, Avery sagged back against the aquarium.

He blinked and got himself together. Desperate, he searched the side of the aquarium. It must have some means of entry.

There! A brass doorway with ornate hinges and a subtle knob. He scaled over to it, all the time telling himself not to look down. He reached the door, fired a round into the locking mechanism, and wrenched it open.

Gas billowed past his face, hot and foul-smelling, and he swung away from it. It continued to pour out, a great billowing cloud, and he could feel its heat, smell its briny, acidic stink. It took forever to empty. At last it stopped gusting out, and, sucking in a deep breath, he climbed into the aquarium. Heat enveloped him. Steam hissed around his shoes. *Touch nothing.*

Quickly, he scrambled over to Layanna. From here the aquarium looked like a huge multi-faceted insect eye staring down on the Altar and the chaos of the chamber, and Layanna lay at the apex of the eye. He shrugged off his jacket, wrapped it around her, and lifted her up. She was heavier than she looked, though, and he couldn't help a grunt. She stirred in his arms but did not speak or open her eyes. What had they done to her?

He waddled, half-climbed back to the door, then, very delicately, leaned out and grabbed a cable. With one arm securing Layanna to him, and her arms half-consciously around his neck, he swung out and down. Part of him felt like some hero in a picture show, and he almost smiled as he settled down to the ground, the maiden safe in his arms. Then he looked up and saw that several of Layanna's phantasmagorical tentacles had clung to the cable, helping him.

"You're awake," he said, staring down at her face. She looked flushed and fevered, and a strand of blond hair hid one brilliant blue eye. The other stared up at him, and a feeble smile trembled on her lips.

"Francis," she said.

At the word, something happened in his chest. He had the overwhelming urge to kiss her, but as he pressed his lips close to hers she put a hand against him and said, "Let me wash first."

The slimy gel still coated her. It had even soaked through the jacket he'd wrapped her in so that he could feel a burning on his fingertips.

He laid her down gently. Around them raged chaos, but for now, for this one moment, they had a sphere of calm.

"There's an Elder coming," he said.

"I can feel it." There was a rasp in her voice that might be fear.

"Is there any way to fight it?"

She smiled sadly. One of her hands rose to trace his jaw, but she stopped short. "No," she said. "I'm afraid this might be the end. All we can hope for is to send off the message before it arrives. Though ... there might be time for you, in the confusion—"

"I'm not leaving you."

A look of dread—even shame—crossed her face.

"What is it?" he asked.

"They ... got it. They got it out of me."

He couldn't breathe. "The plans for the Device?"

"No. The location of the Black Sect. They pulled it out of me, out of my mind. I had no way to resist. They're planning an attack even now. I must warn them. And ... give them the plans for the Device. I must ... get to the Altar."

"Of course. But you're so weak ..."

She grimaced—it might have been a smile of sorts—and struggled to her feet. The jacket fell to the floor, but she didn't seem to notice.

The sudden shuffle of footsteps made Avery look up. A group of priests had seen Layanna. As one, they rushed toward her.

"Layanna, I think—"

She pushed him to the floor and *changed*. Her amoeba-facet crossed over, superimposed over her, and spread to engulf a large area. Strange lights radiated out from her, illuminating the faces of the oncoming priests. They hesitated, but only for a moment, then charged in, their lances sparking. She seized several in stinging tentacles and squeezed. They screamed and writhed in her grip. Blood sprayed. Some stabbed her with their lances, lighting her up at the places of impact, and she screamed inside her sac, her phantasmagorical flesh withering and flaming where she was hit. Her tendrils shot out, grabbed up the offending priests, and squeezed. Dripping bone shards jutted from between her coils. Others she passed poison into, or electrocuted, or set afire. The worst fate was reserved for those she drew within her sac and began to feed from.

Avery made himself watch as their bodies dissolved and began to swirl among and through her organelles. As she absorbed them, she grew visibly stronger, her colors more vibrant, her sac larger. She floated in the midst of it all, serene, her hair billowing around her as if in an underwater current.

She met Avery's gaze once, nodded, then—her tentacles dragging her apparently weightless amoeba-body—climbed the dais toward the Altar. Surrounded by violence and with the Elder on the way, she plunged her tentacles down through the black slab and unleashed a stream of power. Avery felt the charge in the air. She straddled the Altar in her amoeba-self, but more than that, she had *plugged into* it. She would commune with her comrades in the Black Sect, transmit her knowledge to them, and her warning.

Avery felt a spring of hope well inside him, but he didn't let himself think about it. He shot another priest who trained some bulky, surely extradimensional weapon on Layanna. He had to protect her while she transmitted the plans. This was the most critical time of their whole plan. Everything depended on her getting off that message.

Avery shot another priest, then another. *Gods, what have I become?* he thought, even as he fired at the second one. *I'm a doctor, not a killer!* And yet he didn't stop firing for a moment.

All around him, former sacrifices tore into the clerics that had abused them with an almost mad glee, seeming to revel in the carnage. Janx and Hildra fought not far away, both covered in blood, much of it their own. They looked weary and grim, but they left a trail of bodies in their wake.

Suddenly, submachine gun fire split the air, organized and overbearing. Avery spun to see, coming from one of the two main entrances to the Altar Room, a phalanx of Octunggen troops.

Chapter 23

Damn it, Avery thought. *And we were so close.* Disappointment drove the breath from his lungs.

The Octunggen laid waste all about them, submachine guns spitting fire. Slaves and captives pitched over backward, blood jetting across stone floors already heaped with bodies. The Octunggen stormed in, a great black wedge, visors and shields glimmering with light, and all opposition crumpled in their path.

Sheridan strode at the phalanx's head, submachine gun clutched in firm hands. She fired, gun smoke coiling up, her square jaw clenched firmly. She shot one mutant down, then blew half of another's head off. With every shot she took she advanced further into the room. Her eyes speared Layanna, taking it all in, and Avery had no doubt she guessed what was going on, guessed how high the stakes were.

Avery picked his way down the steps of the tiered dais, stepping over and around bodies as he went. When he reached the floor, he put his back to one of the carapace-like machines, shielding himself from Sheridan's gaze. His heart beat like a drum. Screams echoed all around him.

Above, Layanna glowed, pulsating. She floated in her sac, eyes closed in concentration and surrounded by otherworldly lights, even as her tentacles stabbed down through the surface of the Altar and vanished from view. How much more time did she need?

Avery glanced around the edge of the machine, trying to get a glimpse of Sheridan. The Octunggen advanced, step by step. When their submachine guns ran out of bullets, the soldiers threw them down and withdrew pistols or shock-prods. With grim determination, they continued their march toward the Altar. Sheridan tossed down her own submachine gun—empty—and pulled out a pistol. It was the same one she had shot Layanna with, Avery saw, or one identical to it, overly long and odd-looking, certainly extradimensional.

No, Avery thought. *Please no, please no—*

Sheridan came within range. She wasted no time, but checked the slide, thumbed the safety off, and raised it to sight on Layanna—

Avery began to throw himself out from behind the machine and fire at her. He didn't expect to hit her, but he might distract her long enough for Layanna to send off her message. Of course, Sheridan would probably shoot him for the trouble. Before he could so much as take a bead on her, however, one of the freed men lunged at her, a man with suckers growing along his arms, and she had no choice but to dodge aside and strike him down, clubbing the butt of her pistol against the side of his head.

Other mutants swarmed all around. Now that the Octunggen's submachine guns had run dry, the men and women that would have been sacrificed to the Elder were emboldened to throw themselves on the soldiers with greater furor and numbers. Even Sheridan could not escape their attacks. Desperate close-quarters fighting broke out. The former captives attacked with gun and blade, fist and lance, and the orderly advance of the Octunggen became a writhing mob.

Avery stared at the chaos, unnerved and out of his element. He had to do something, before Sheridan could break away, and he had to do it now. He hurried forward, gun clutched in hand.

Janx stumbled past him, reeling backward. Three priests sliced at the big man with bladed weapons, and fresh blood trickled down his chest. He was armed only with a knife and barely fending them off. Trying not to think about it, Avery shot one in the back. As that one collapsed, the one next to him turned to look, and Janx sprang, stabbing him in the throat. The third lunged, and Janx hurled himself backward. Avery wanted to stay and help, but there was no time.

Not far away a priest pinned Hildra to the ground, one hand around her neck and the other grabbing her hook arm, preventing her from using it. She beat at his face, gouging long furrows in his cheek, and Hildebrand shrieked and bit at his skull, but the man was determined and little by little Hildra was losing strength. Avery wanted to shoot the man in the back, but he was afraid the bullet would pass through and hit Hildra. Instead he took careful aim and fired at the man's arm. His first shot missed, but his second clipped the man's elbow. The man yelled and released Hildra's hook arm. She plunged the hook into his gut, and his eyes went wide. As she unearthed herself from him, two more priests approached her, and Avery tried to fire at them, but the gun clicked empty. He threw it away.

He searched for Sheridan. The Octunggen were wresting back control, or some of it, from the mob. Guns fired, and sparks exploded from electric sticks. The freed captives did not give up.

Sheridan picked herself off the floor, wiped a stream of blood from her face, blew the hair out of her eyes, and raised her gun toward Layanna—

Avery knocked the pistol aside and punched her in the face. Her leg came up and smashed into his knee, almost breaking it. He stumbled back, his grip so firmly on the gun that he tore it loose from her gasp. One of her men tried to shoot Avery, but a freed captive cracked his head with a stolen helmet, then set upon him.

Sheridan's eyes took in Avery and widened. When her shock faded, she merely said, "So. You kept the appointment."

Ani. "Looks that way."

Sheridan stared at him with an expression he could find no warmth in, no trace of all their nights together. Had it all meant so little to her, or had she simply become adept at masking her true self?

"Except it's not you that has Layanna," she said, "it's the Mnuthra. I'm afraid that won't do your daughter any good."

He had been trying to reverse the gun in his grasp, fumbling as he did so, but just as he straightened it out Sheridan kicked it out of his hand. Before he could recover, she punched him in the throat, nearly crushing his larynx. Choking, he lashed out, striking her in the jaw. Her eyes blazed.

He tripped over a corpse and sprawled backward. Felt his teeth click. Tasted blood on his tongue. He rolled aside as Sheridan's boot came down at his head. He grabbed up the lance of a fallen priest. He didn't know how to activate the sparking tip, so he swung the shaft at Sheridan's legs. Swearing, she jumped back. Began scanning the ground for a weapon.

Avery climbed to his feet and thrust at her with the lance. Its tip was sharp, if nothing else. She glared at him and moved backward, out of range. She slipped in a pool of blood and nearly fell.

Behind her the Octunggen line was reduced to a shambles. It was an all-out brawl. Almost all the prisoners had been freed, and there were more of them than priests and Octunggen combined. Some of the soldiers still carried weapons with ammunition, and gunfire sounded periodically over the shouts and screams. Others had had their guns taken away by former prisoners, and more than one soldier flew backward riddled by gunfire.

Avery saw the fallen Octunggen pistol and launched himself at it as Sheridan recovered her footing. He slid across the floor, feeling something sticky smear his chest and throat, and grabbed the weapon triumphantly. He spun about to aim it at Sheridan just as she grabbed up another pistol and aimed it at him.

Still choking, his head spinning, he locked his gaze with hers. Hair fell before her eyes, and she downed quick, fast breaths. Her cheeks were red. Somewhere behind her something burned, but she didn't seem to notice. They stared at each other, guns pointed.

Gingerly, Avery picked himself off the ground and put himself between Sheridan and Layanna.

"It doesn't have to be like this," Sheridan said. "Remember Ani."

Avery's eyes stung, and he suddenly felt very heavy, very slow.

"Remember Ani," Sheridan repeated.

She stepped forward, and Avery stumbled back—toward the Altar.

"I ..." Avery opened and closed his mouth, but no words came out. He wanted to shoot Sheridan but knew that he could not. Their nights together might mean nothing to her, but they did to him.

His heel struck a body, and he carefully stepped over it, kept edging backward, as Sheridan pressed forward.

"You can have her back," Sheridan said. "You can have your Ani back. Just think about it. She would be safe, and loved, and you would be happy together. You would be a hero of the Lightning Crown, and we would put you up somewhere special. A mansion, perhaps, right in Lusterqal. All the little toys Ani could want. We have the best bakeries in Octung. Does she have a sweet tooth? She would love it. And, if you wanted, I would ... visit you occasionally. If you liked."

He stared at her, shaking his head. She almost sounded as if she would have liked it, to visit him, and he remembered their few happy times together, remembered feeling that warmth that almost was. More, though, he remembered Ani.

He remembered his little girl. He remembered taking long walks with her, sometimes with Mari, sometimes not, through the forests and mountains near Benical. Ani had loved nature and would listen avidly as Avery told her every animal's name and habits, and then she would promptly rename them. She said she wanted to be a biologist someday, wanted to work with nature. She had screamed like a baby the first time she fell off her bicycle, and seeing all the blood that wept from her knee had nearly given Avery a coronary. It didn't matter that he saw worse than that every day at work; *she was his daughter.* But after he put on the bandage, she climbed right back on and pedaled away, faster this time, and laughing. Somehow he had taken her pain into himself, and she no longer seemed to feel it. Later, when she had grown sick, he had tried the same trick, for her and her mother, but it hadn't worked any longer. Avery remembered cradling her in his arms as she faded, day by day, remembered staring into her eyes as they lost their luster, as she ... as ...

Suddenly he couldn't see Sheridan anymore. All he could see was one big blur. Everything was misty and runny. Through it all a Sheridan-shaped smear stepped forward, and he heard the awful words—the wonderful words—"*She lives*, Francis. You can have her back. Still. Even now. Even after all you've done. Just turn that gun around and *shoot the bitch*."

Avery blinked and wiped at his eyes. Slowly the world cleared. He felt like he couldn't get breath fast enough. He could hear his heartbeat behind his eardrums.

"Ani," he wheezed.

Sheridan nodded, almost sadly. "She's yours, Doctor. Only turn that gun around."

Avery felt as if he'd lost all strength. He wanted to sink to his knees and melt away, like the victims of the crustaceans back in Hissig. He didn't think he had the strength to hold the gun any longer. Didn't have the strength to make the decision. *Ani, how could he not choose Ani?*

The chaos of the rest of the room seemed very far away as Sheridan stepped forward again, and he stepped back. His heel struck the first step leading up to the Altar. Behind him hovered Layanna. Around him spread the ring of machines.

"Choose!" Sheridan said. "Your daughter or the bitch!"

Avery closed his eyes. The whole war had come down to this one moment. No one else could help him. It was all up to him. Time seemed to slow, even stop, and the screams nearby seemed miles away.

By the time he opened his eyes, he'd decided.

He swiveled his gun and fired. The round tore through the extradimensional machine Sheridan was standing near. Sparks exploded, and she threw her hands before her face and lunged aside. Avery fired again, and the machine erupted. He leapt backward, feeling the heat blister his face. He shot another of the machines, and another. Fires spread from carapace-like bulk to carapace-like bulk. The flames turned green and blue, white and crimson. Strange fires ringed the Altar.

Above, Layanna slumped across the black slab, and her otherworldly self drained away. Avery rushed up to her, afraid that his destroying the machines had interrupted her at her task, even afraid that he had hurt her. She looked weak and exhausted. Her other-self had burned away the last vestiges of the slime from the aquarium, and she embraced him with trembling arms. Her skin felt hot, and it was flushed and sweaty.

"It's done," she breathed. "It's done."

Her voice was so strained that he felt the words more than heard them, soft warm puffs in his ear. As soon as they registered, relief filled him, and he embraced her tightly.

"Wonderful!" he said.

The whole Temple shook, and Layanna screamed.

"He's here!" she said. "The Elder is here!"

The halls trembled to the movement of the Elder, and dust drifted down from the ceiling. Screams filtered in from the hallways, echoing up from below.

"We don't have long," Layanna said.

There was something else wrong, too. Around Avery, beneath him, through him, the dais throbbed. All the machines had been wired to the Altar, and with the machines in flames something had gone wrong. Avery felt the pressure seep up through his feet, felt it press against his eardrums, against his tongue.

"Something's off," he said, as he helped Layanna to her feet.

She stared around her, at the flaming machines. "You broke it. Broke the connection." She looked ill. "You made a fissure."

"Is that bad?"

The machines hummed and shook louder all about them. Sheridan must have realized it, too, as Avery saw her running to her remaining troops and shouting for them to follow her out. They fled the room, fighting as they went.

From below came a sound of great weight and movement. Avery could almost feel the Temple rock from side to side. Strange thoughts and sensations spun through his head, and he saw colors he had never seen before, and smelled scents—*scents*—that nearly drove reason from his head.

"The Elder's approaching," Layanna said.

Janx and Hildra rushed up, breathless and drenched in blood. Janx had a bloody lip and Hildra a black eye, along with numerous other contusions. "Let's get the fuck out of here!" said Janx, and Hildra added, "And he means now!" Hildebrand screeched from her shoulder.

Moving in the direction opposite the one Sheridan had taken, Avery led Layanna down the stairs of the dais and across the carnage-strewn chamber to the other entrance. As soon as they reached it, a great grinding noise filled the air, along with powerful emotions and fragrances. The few priests still in the Altar Room prostrated themselves before the far entrance. Strange lights bathed the walls beyond, spilling inside, some of them quite beautiful, drawing closer and closer, brighter and brighter, pulsing as if in time to some fantastic heart.

Avery, despite himself, hung back; he wanted to *see* the Elder. Just a glimpse ...

Layanna pulled him along, and Janx and Hildra jostled by on either side.

"No time to stop, Doc," Janx said.

With walls shaking all around them, and somewhere screams still echoing—though from whom it was hard to say—they ran. They reached one of the exits, and Avery felt the stir of wind on his face. He stepped outside onto the bridge—

Janx and Hildra pulled him back. Blinking, he stared. The bridge was in flames and falling toward the city below. Former captives on the opposite side screamed in triumph, perhaps thinking Avery and the others to be priests in pursuit.

"Idiots!" Hildra said. "They've trapped us."

"Maybe we can reach another bridge in time," Avery said. It was their only chance, and they continued through the halls.

They almost stumbled directly into the fray.

Masses of former captives wrestled with priests and Octunggen soldiers directly before an opening in the outer wall of the temple. There must have been three dozen combatants. A priest stumbled into Avery, blood running from his jaw, and Janx tossed him aside. A former captive with a jagged knife through the side of her throat nonetheless beat an Octunggen soldier into the floor, using a spent gun as a blunt instrument. It was a chaotic scene, and it only began to make sense when Avery saw that the opening was in fact the docking bay to a dirigible. They were fighting over who got to leave.

Despite the chaos, a group of Octunggen were trying to cast the dirigible off. The Temple shook ever more violently.

Janx and Hildra, navigating through the fight, stormed aboard. Avery and Layanna followed quickly behind. Layanna, still strong enough to exert her other-self to some degree, tore two Octunggen soldiers apart with her tentacles. Avery, marveling at himself, kicked one distracted trooper in the knee and knocked him to the ground, then went directly to the controls. Hildra, after dealing with another trooper, cast off.

Someone had reached the wheel ahead of Avery. Sweaty and ragged, Sheridan stood before the console.

"Not again," she said tiredly.

He looked about for help. Layanna in her amoeba-form was currently fending off three Octunggen who were trying to subdue her with spitting lances. Someone had struck Janx on the head and he was down, moving feebly, blood weeping from his shaven pate.

By then the dirigible was already leaving the dock, Hildra having unmoored it. She shouted for former captives to jump across, but none did and then it was too late. Avery felt the deck lurch as the ship moved away.

"You're outmatched," he told Sheridan. His knees bent as he readied himself to dodge an attack. "We have Layanna. Give up."

"*I'm* outmatched?" She grabbed up the radio mike and spoke into it in rapid-fire Octunggen.

Avery didn't know who she spoke to, but he rushed forward to knock the radio aside. She punched him hard in the gut and he doubled over, but not before grabbing the speaker and wrenching it from her hands. She struck him across the cheekbone.

"Damn you," she said, sounding as full of emotion as Avery had ever heard her. She reached for something at her belt—

Hildra tackled her from behind and carried her to the floor.

Avery stared at them fighting—punching and kicking and biting—and decided Hildra had a better chance at pacifying the admiral than he did. In the stern, Layanna's amoeba-form was dwindling as the Octunggen struck at her with their shock-sticks. Her whole self lit up with every blow, and he could see her wince through the sac and organelles. Her amoeba-self shrank with every strike. Shaking his head, Janx tried to climb to his feet.

Meanwhile the dirigible listed to one side, drifting toward a nearby upside-down palace. The shaking of the Temple behind them was growing louder. They didn't have much time. Seconds, if they were lucky.

Avery moved to the wheel. He mashed gears and levers, and the craft lurched, then shot away from the Temple. He could almost feel the pressure building behind him. Building ...

He shot the dirigible forward …

The Temple blew.

Whatever the Altar Room's machines had been, however they had ripped apart dimensions to facilitate communication between gods, they had been powerful things and did not take destruction lightly. The explosion was the greatest burst of power Avery had ever felt, imagined he would ever feel. He felt the vibration in his teeth, in his bones, in his soul. The flames fanned outward in brilliant colors, blazing vermillion, dazzling ruby, a wall of turquoise, all rushing outward to engulf him. He steered the dirigible forward, riding the shockwave just ahead of the main blast. The airship shook and shuddered around him. He glanced over his shoulder to see the blast rushing toward him.

Gradually, it fell behind. There came a tremendous groan and squeal, and the Temple, or the flaming remnants of it, collapsed onto the Arena. A tall dark figure, not Uthua but the high priest, jerked his head back to watch the great mass fall upon him, and then he was obliterated entirely by a thousand tons of rock and flame.

Behind him Avery heard sounds of fighting, but he ignored it as he steered the dirigible around one rearing tower, then a dripping stalactite palace. He glanced once more over his shoulder to make sure there would be no second explosion—and swore.

The Temple would not erupt again, thank the gods, but suddenly Avery realized who Sheridan had been calling on the radio, and the news was not good. Nine of the dirigibles that had accompanied this one to the Arena had cast off and were in pursuit.

Avery spun the wheel. A hulking junkheap tower just barely scraped by, missing the dirigible's envelope with inches to spare. Behind and around him the fight continued. Figures thrashed and rolled about on the floor and slammed up against the walls.

The nine dirigibles shot closer, narrowing the gap. Soon they would be within range. Avery aimed the ship around rearing towers and dripping stalactites, and soon he saw the lights of the city glinting on water ahead. The city must occupy an island or peninsula. Cuithril stretched on, tower after tower, and Avery wove his way through it, mindful of the need for urgency but also caution.

The nine dirigibles threaded their way through the spires and dripping palaces with greater skill—and speed. They closed the gap all too quickly.

Suddenly something slammed up against him and knocked him away from the wheel. It was a writhing Sheridan, locked in combat with Layanna this time, not Hildra, and Layanna was now too weak to bring her amoeba-self over. Sheridan punched and jabbed at her, and Layanna just barely fended off the attacks. The two women knocked Avery to the deck and rolled into the gunwale. He slammed into them, driving the breath from his lungs.

Sheridan elbowed him in the ribs. Gasping, he punched her in the lower back, aiming for a kidney. She moved. He missed.

Around them the last spires of the city slipped past. Below them stretched water, black and wide.

Behind the dirigibles advanced, all too swiftly.

Sheridan sliced Avery across the chest with the knife, then reversed her swing to take out his throat. He grabbed her wrist, forced it away. She kneed him in the groin. He twisted. With both hands on the handle, she drove the knife toward his heart, and he just barely grabbed her forearms in time. They wrestled on the gunwale, grunting and straining against each other. Slowly, the knife inched toward his chest. Closer. *Closer ...*

"Leave him alone," said Layanna.

Sheridan glanced sideways, just in time to receive the shaft of one of the Octunggen's stun-clubs in the face. Avery heard the smack of bone, and then the admiral pitched over the side.

Breathless, he stared over the gunwale, watching as Sheridan plummeted, finally striking the vast darkness of the sea. Then she was gone from sight. He sucked in a deep gulp of air and turned to Layanna. Too weak to thank her, he just nodded. Tiredly, she nodded back.

Hildra manned the wheel, swinging the dirigible in and out of the stalactites that threatened to smash them to splinters. Janx was stabbing the last Octunggen through the eye. That done, he hurled the corpse overboard.

Behind, the nine dirigibles closed the distance. Lights flashed on their decks, and Avery knew they were about to bring their otherworldly weapons to bear.

He noticed a certain smell. The air turned sour and thick, difficult to breathe.

"Down!" he said. "Take her down!"

Coughing, Hildra complied, and the dirigible quickly lowered, stalactites receding. So did the stench.

A familiar green light fell over the craft, and Avery gasped as pain filled him. A blister formed under the skin of his right forearm. He could feel another growing under his neck. He heard himself groan.

"Shit," growled Hildra, as a bubble burst on her hand. "Shitfuckshit!"

This was just the beginning, Avery knew. The Octunggen's otherworldly weapons would soon be the end of them.

He glanced up, saw the vague stir of vapor against the cavern ceiling, the vapor he and the others had just left. It was surely the same gas that had bubbled up from the sea on the other side of the city. The pack of dirigibles was just entering it.

"A gun!" he said. "I need a gun." *If I can make a spark ...*

"What for?" asked Janx.

"Just find one!" Avery screamed, searching the corpses all around him. All the guns were empty.

"Will this do?" Janx pressed a flare gun into Avery's hands.

Avery stared at it in wonder. "Yes," he said. "It will do just fine."

He raised the gun and pointed it at the cavern ceiling. He fired, and a bright red burst shot high into the darkness. It rose and rose, and the dirigibles plowed on, heedless.

The green light intensified, and other colors began to join it. Avery felt pain all over, and he sank to his knees in agony. Beside him Janx and Hildra did likewise. Layanna, unaffected, moved toward the wheel.

The flare hit the pocket of trapped gas.

The explosion ripped the darkness apart, engulfing the dirigibles.

Avery hunkered low, and heat washed over him. Debris rained down, peppering the black sea with sparks. He imagined Sheridan dragging herself out of the water on some dark shore and staring up at the fiery destruction, and he felt a wave of satisfaction.

Janx and Hildra whooped. Avery let out a breath and sagged against the gunwale. Layanna rested beside him.

The last lights of Cuithril faded behind them. There was no further pursuit.

They had made it. For a moment, Avery felt dizzy with relief. Then he thought of Ani, and something terrible came over him, a sort of gasping claustrophobia. The world contracted and spasmed around him. He had gone against Sheridan. If she still lived, then Avery had damned his own daughter.

"She'll be fine," Layanna said. Gently, she squeezed his shoulder.

"How did you know?"

"I heard what Sheridan said. Don't worry. If it's possible to help your daughter, we will."

He opened his mouth to say something, but no words came out, and he realized there was nothing to say. The dirigible soared on.

Janx stared sadly behind them, and Avery could guess what he was thinking.

Hildra squeezed his arm. "You think Mu made it?"

Gripping the gunwale, Janx said nothing for a long moment, then: "The awful thing is, Hilly—I don't even know if I want him to have."

"He lives," Layanna said. "If that is any comfort. Or at least his body does."

"You sure?" said Hildra. "That blast ..."

"Uthua wasn't on the platform when the Temple fell. I can *feel* him."

Janx's face tightened. "I'd rather him be dead, darlin', than that bastard *wearing* him." His voice almost cracked on the word.

Trying to cheer him, Hildra said, "Uthua can wait, damn it all. We did it! Can you believe it? We ended the war. *We saved the world.*"

"Amazing," Avery agreed. "It's still hard to take in."

Janx was silent for a moment longer, his eyes distant, but then he visibly shook off his grief. Dully, he said, "I wonder how long it'll take before the last shot's fired. A month? Two?"

"Six weeks," Avery said. "I give it six weeks."

Something glittered in Janx's eyes. It wasn't right up at the front, or overly bright, but it was there. "Is that ... a wager?"

Avery laughed, relieved. "I have just enough money to buy a cup of coffee, Janx."

"Wanna double it?"

Throughout all this Layanna had been strangely silent, so much so that it began to grow conspicuous. Suddenly wary, Avery turned to her, and so did the others. Layanna could not meet their eyes.

"It's over," Janx said. "Right, honey?"

"It is," Avery affirmed, then hesitated. "*Isn't* it?"

Layanna sucked in a breath and let it out. Slowly, she said, "No. It's not."

Wind rattled over the gunwale, and Avery shivered.

Layanna visibly gathered her resolve. "I *was* able to establish a connection with them, but I was too late to warn them," she said. "They were already being attacked as I transmitted the plans." Grief stamped her face, and her voice fluttered. "Several died."

"I'm sorry," Avery told her.

"All isn't lost," she said. "They believed they would be able to escape. To relocate. They've done it many times before, and they've been attacked more than once. But in the attack, a sound-bomb ... it poisoned them. *All* of them."

Avery felt a wave of foreboding. He sagged backwards, hoping he was wrong. For some reason, he couldn't speak.

Fortunately, Janx could: "And that means, what?"

A tear spilled down Layanna's cheek. "Dying—they're all dying."

"Dear gods," said Hildra. "After all this ..."

Avery felt as if he'd been punched in the gut. "But the Device ..."

"Yes," Layanna said. "I succeeded in passing the plans on to them, my colleagues in the Black Sect. They believe they'll have time to build it. It should be waiting for us. We did that much. We accomplished that much. It was worth it, all of it. Because of what we did today, the key to ending the war will be fashioned." She watched them steadily. "But, because of Uthua, I'm afraid it may be up to us to do the unlocking."

"*Waiting* for us," Janx said.

"Yes," Layanna nodded. "In Lusterqal. That's where they are, of course, the Black Sect. The Device will be there if my friends can remain free long enough to build it. But it's unlikely they'll have the strength or time to activate it. Only one of my kind can do it. Soon ... soon I'll be the only one left, at least with the will to see it done. The last of the Sect."

"Well, godsdamn," said Hildra.

Layanna met their eyes. "I doubt I'll be able to make the journey alone. You ... you've proven your usefulness time and again."

"Hell," said Hildra. "We can be *less* useful."

There was a long silence. Hildra steered the dirigible around a low-hanging stalactite, then another. Janx frowned, and Avery's head pounded. He wished he had a drink.

Avery searched Layanna's face, then the others'.

"We must see this through," he said.

"Lusterqal was our destination anyway," Janx muttered. "We got our hopes up with the altar an' all, but that didn't pan out so well."

"It did," Layanna insisted. "But it didn't end our journey as I'd hoped."

"Fine," snapped Hildra. "Fuck! We'll go to Lusterqal. Shit! The capital of fucking Octung! Fuckety fuck!" She breathed out. "Janx's right, though. It's where we were going anyway. But I want it on record that I said this blows."

"Duly noted," Avery said.

Hildra kicked the gunwale. "Well, shit. We're still fugitives in Ghenisa, and Ungraessot's out. Everywhere else is a battlefield. Hell, maybe the safest place to be is Octung." But Avery could tell she didn't really believe it. He didn't.

"It won't be easy," Layanna said. "I won't lie to you."

Hildra grunted. "No. You would *never* do that."

"I'm in, too," Janx said. "My friends died for this." He raised his eyebrows. "And you're still holding us to our oaths, I take it."

"I ... I am," Avery said. It was almost as if Janx had wanted him to say it.

"Then so be it," Janx said.

Hildra rubbed something around her neck. Avery had never noticed it before, but he saw it now, perhaps because of Hildra's preoccupation. It glimmered faintly of bronze, sharp and wicked and lethal. When Avery saw what it was, he nearly choked. *It was Nancy.* Hildra wore Janx's old harpoon-head around her neck. The significance of that could not have been small. And yet they *never* spoke of it. Avery's mind reeled.

"Alright," Hildra said. "Fuck it. To Octung we go."

Avery swallowed, shaking off his surprise. "Good," he said. "Then it's settled."

Layanna let out a deep sigh, and the dirigible sailed on into darkness.

Three weeks later Avery and the others ascended from the tunnels. They had passed under three countries, only coming up occasionally, and now were at the western edge of Lathralc. They stole up through the caverns, then the sewer, and out into the tangle of streets and alleys. They were in the city of Vunhydt, and the sun shown down on a fierce procession. Guns glittered and silver buttons caught the light as a military caravan trundled down the road, tank tires grinding loudly. Smoke belched up from the machines, and grim-faced Lathralcites watched the caravan pass from terraces over the street. They looked starved, gray and terrified. How many of them had been taken in the night, how many to the reeducation centers designed to perpetuate the faith of the Collossum? How many had simply disappeared?

Hildra, familiar with the city, as she had once led a thieving life here, so she said, led Avery, Janx and Layanna up to the rooftops, and in silence they passed over the Octunggen-occupied town. In some courtyards Octunggen soldiers dragged prisoners into the open and tied them to posts. Firing squads formed up. The sounds of rifles cracked over the tiled roofs. In other courtyards Octunggen loaded up civilians to be transferred to some undisclosed destination. Some would doubtlessly be brainwashed or tortured for information about dissidents.

"I don't understand," Avery said. "I thought Lathralc was a vassal state to Octung."

Layanna nodded. "Originally Octung pledged not to implement their harsher policies among their vassals, if only the countries would aid them in the war. Now, however, the war cannot be stopped, not by them."

"So they lied."

"They lied."

Silent and ashen, the group passed over the city, and then out of it, into the rugged, pine-covered hills beyond. The hills separated Lathralc from Octung along this stretch of the border.

For hours they labored up the slopes, threading their way through dense pines and once evading an Octunggen patrol, until at last they reached a peak. Sweating and flushed, Avery paused to take in the view. Before him stretched another city, its buildings huge and monolithic. Bombers rumbled overhead, heading in formation outward, toward distant targets. Smoke belched up from factory after factory. Searchlights lanced the sky.

Layanna swept her arms. "Welcome to Octung."

**THE END
OF VOLUME ONE**

Made in United States
Orlando, FL
07 April 2022

16595212R00241